An Unfinished Murder

JUDE DEVERAUX

An Unfinished Murder

mira

ISBN-13: 978-0-7783-0539-2

An Unfinished Murder

Mira
22 Adelaide St. West, 41st Floor
Toronto, Ontario M5H 4E3, Canada
BookClubbish.com

Printed in U.S.A.

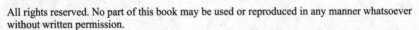

Also by Jude Deveraux

Medlar Mysteries

AN UNFINISHED MURDER
A WILLING MURDER
A JUSTIFIED MURDER
A FORGOTTEN MURDER

AS YOU WISH
MET HER MATCH
MEANT TO BE
MY HEART WILL FIND YOU

Providence Falls

CHANCE OF A LIFETIME
AN IMPOSSIBLE PROMISE
THIEF OF FATE

Look for Jude Deveraux's next novel
available soon from MIRA.

For additional books by Jude Deveraux,
visit her website, judedeveraux.com.

ONE

"I JUST HAD THE MOST EXTRAORDINARY CALL," Kate said as she looked at the two people in front of her. But they didn't express any interest.

Jack was sitting on one of the blue couches, his long legs stretched out, and looking at the screen on his laptop. Kate wasn't used to his new look, but he'd only been back a few days. He'd spent months in the wilds of Colorado, building and hunting, and it had changed his body. Now he was leaner, more agile, and as difficult as it was to believe, he was more muscular.

Besides the physical, he'd changed in other ways too. Last night he'd said… Her heart seemed to do a little jump at the memory of his words. They'd had years of friendship, of laughing together, working, figuring out problems, but last night, "friends" wasn't what he'd meant.

When Jack felt her staring at him, he started to turn his head, and Kate quickly looked at her aunt. Sara was on the other couch and bent over one of her notebooks, colored gel pens in hand and writing fast. Maybe it was the quiet of the lockdown they'd just been through, but lately she'd been writing more. Years ago, her aunt had retired from a long, successful career of writing romance novels as Sara Medlar. "The waitress genre of the publishing world," she said. "Everyone looks down on us but we take care of them all." She said that the abundant sales of romance novels made it possible to publish the "literary" works, meaning books that made little money but might possibly live forever. Kate didn't know what her aunt had been writing lately, but she was absorbed by it.

Annoyed by the way they were ignoring her, Kate said louder, "Truly extraordinary!"

Jack gave a bit of a nod and Sara lifted her chin about half an inch, but that was all.

"Old house," Kate whispered, knowing that those words would get the attention of both of them.

It took a moment, but Sara looked up at her niece. It took Jack longer. He was Sara's "honorary grandson," the actual grandson of the man Sara had long ago loved and lost.

The three of them lived in Sara's big house, each with a private area. But since Jack had returned just days ago, the three of them had not wanted to be apart.

"What old house?" Jack asked. He was a building contractor and specialized in restoring old places.

Kate was glad to finally have their attention. "That was Melissa, and she said some man gave me a listing." Melissa and Kate were Realtors. "He specifically asked for me and said he won't accept anyone else. I don't know the house, but Melissa said it's magnificent." She knew that since Jack and Sara had been born in the little town, they were sure to know of it. She took a breath to give drama to her announcement. "It's Lachlan House."

She waited for exclamations of surprise and delight, but

there were none. Jack looked back at his computer and Sara at her notebook.

"Turn it down," he said. "It's not a good investment."

"A white elephant," Sara said. "Nobody will want it."

"Are you kidding? Melissa said it's a million-dollar listing. Where is it? I assume it's here in Lachlan but—" She broke off because her phone dinged. Melissa had sent photos of the house and Kate paused to look at them.

As it sounded, the house was big. It was two stories, with a long one-story wing to the side. The center entrance was dramatic, with a huge door surrounded by white marble. Tall windows and a covered portico were upstairs. It was, without a doubt, a true mansion. An estate.

There was a page of stats. Eighty-two hundred square feet, six bedrooms, seven-and-a-half baths. There was also a two-bedroom guesthouse and a one-bedroom gardener's cottage and a three-car garage, all on three acres. The description ended with "No pool. Needs repair." Since the whole house was draped in Florida's floral attempt to reclaim the land, yes, it needed some work.

As Kate looked at the photos, it was as though her mind started drifting. She sat down on the arm of Sara's couch. "I wonder who wrote this description." She spoke so softly she could hardly be heard. "This makes the house sound cold and unfeeling. It doesn't even mention the ballroom. It's in the wing and it has glorious doors that open out to the fountain. And there's the Palm Room. It's a library." Her voice was rising. "And what about the bedrooms upstairs? And the rooms at the top? Why aren't they in the listing? Who cares if there's no swimming pool?" She was almost shouting. "And what about the basement? That's where all those bottles are. Dad said—"

The mention of her father brought her back to earth. She looked up, blinking.

Sara and Jack had swiveled about, feet on the floor, and were looking at her with interest and some shock.

Kate looked from one to the other. "What?!"

Sara gave a little smile—the kind you give to a person who is on the verge of going insane. "Nice house, is it?"

Kate turned to Jack. He looked like he was about to pour her some tequila and tell her everything was going to be all right. "Stop looking at me like that. It's a big old house. You know I love them. I must have seen this one somewhere."

"So when do you plan to visit it?" Sara's voice was full of patience.

Kate narrowed her eyes. "Why should I go at all? You two—in all your great wisdom—told me to not take the listing. I guess I'll turn it over to Melissa."

"Would she even know what a ballroom is?" Melissa was not Sara's favorite person. "What if we go see it together? How about right now?"

Kate was still smarting over the way they'd ignored her, and too, she was bothered by her own reaction to the photos.

When her niece was silent, Sara gave Jack a look to take over, then she picked up her phone and went to the kitchen. She called her brother, Randal, Kate's father. "I need you to meet with us. Now."

"Can't," he said. "I have a client in half an hour. She—"

"I don't need the details," Sara snapped. Randal was a personal trainer and it seemed that every woman over fifty who lived north of Miami booked him to go to her house. Just the two of them. "You must come."

"I can be there after this session, then I'll—"

"Kate was given the listing to sell Lachlan House. And

she seems to know the place. Of course that has to do with you, so—"

"I'll meet you there as soon as possible." He cut off the call.

Jack stepped into the kitchen. "What's this about?"

"I have no idea, but as soon as she said 'Dad,' I knew my brother was involved."

"So Kate saw the old house in the past and she remembers it. She's your relative and you remember houses more than people. Why does that bother you?"

"I don't know why, but I have a creepy feeling about this. Cal used to work there when we were in high school. He and James Lachlan—the man who built the house—were friends." Cal was Jack's late grandfather, the man Sara loved.

"That's probably why the listing is being given to Kate. For the connection. And if she went there with her dad, it all fits."

"I guess," Sara said.

"Get your camera and lots of batteries, and we'll go see this house. Last time I drove past it, it looked like gators had taken it over. It's probably bulldoze material."

When she didn't reply, he put his arm around her small shoulders. "Afraid of the memories?"

She nodded but said nothing.

"Come on," he coaxed in his deep voice. "Don't you have a new camera and some fancy new lenses?"

"I do," she said.

"Who's going to drive?" came Kate's voice from the entryway. She was ready to leave.

Sara and Jack broke apart, and she hurried to her suite of rooms to get her ever-ready camera bag. She made sure her new Sony a1 and the 20mm f1.8 GM lens were in there. She shoved in half a dozen batteries and ran to catch up with Jack and Kate, who were already in his truck. Like always, she sat on the end, with Kate in the middle. Of course, Jack drove.

★

Unusual for the trio, they rode in silence. Sara was aware of the tension between Jack and Kate—and she was pleased by it. Until a few days ago, he and Kate had acted like brother and sister. But when Jack returned from months away, bearded and smelling of wood smoke and sawdust, things had changed. Now Jack rarely looked at Kate, but she kept stealing glances at him.

It all made Sara smile. Her niece and Cal's grandson. She couldn't hope for any more in life.

"You're sure this is the right way?" Kate asked.

Jack didn't answer, so Sara did. "Lachlan House used to be on a few hundred acres. Mr. Lachlan had a citrus grove, but after he died, pieces of land were sold off. For this." She waved her hand to indicate the houses around them. They were nice, middle-class houses, obviously built at the same time, probably by the same builder.

They went around a curve in the road and there it was: Lachlan House.

Jack stopped the truck at the end of the long driveway and they looked at it. The wide brick house was covered in vines from the ground to the roof. Parts of it could barely be seen.

Sara remembered it in its glory in the 1960s, when she and Cal spent time there. He mowed while she pulled weeds in the flower beds. She wasn't paid for her work, but then she and Cal just wanted to be together.

"Looks better than I thought it would," Jack said. "I don't see any holes in the roof."

"It's the most beautiful house on earth," Kate said. "Let's go in!"

She was leaning so far forward that Jack looked behind her

to Sara and raised his eyebrows. They were both curious as to what Kate knew. And from when?

Jack rolled the truck down the drive as he leaned on the steering wheel and studied the house with a builder's eye. It was good that the windows were intact, not smashed by kids taking dares.

When the truck stopped, Sara got down quickly. She was afraid Kate might climb over her in eagerness to get to the house. While Sara got her camera equipment out, Jack followed Kate to the front door. "There's no lockbox," he said as he tried the big knob.

Kate pulled a handful of plants away from the brick wall. "I don't think these vines have done much damage, but then, the house is well constructed. Dad might know the year it was built." She'd exposed the brick facade enough to see a small lead ornament that had a hinge on top. Without a break in talking, Kate lifted it, pulled out a big key, and handed it to Jack. "Once these vines are removed, I think you'll see that the house is in good condition. There's always been a caretaker. I'll have to ask Melissa who called and asked for me."

Jack turned the key, opened the door, and Kate briskly stepped past him and went inside. Jack and Sara followed her.

"This is it!" Kate was twirling about in a circle, her arms outstretched. She was like a child at play.

They were in a two-story entrance before a beautiful curved staircase with an ornate iron railing. On the ground floor, doors led off in three directions. The house appeared to be furnished, but sparsely.

"That's the ballroom." Kate pointed left. "The living room is that way. Aunt Sara, there's an office off the living room, but come through here first." She started toward the far doors, but halted, frowning at a wall. "Where's the big cabinet? It was the best hiding spot. Greer and I used it." Kate kept going.

Jack and Sara looked at each other and mouthed *Greer*? Jack nodded to the shape that was outlined on the wall. It showed that something large had been there. They hurried after Kate.

"The big dining room is that way. They had dinner in there because the man wanted it, but we liked to eat in here." She went through a doorway to enter a pretty room with a half-round wall and tall windows. A round oak dining table and chairs filled the space.

Through the windows, they could see a tangle of weeds outside. "There's a fountain in that mess," Sara said.

"There is!" Kate replied happily. She was looking about the room. The two built-in cabinets in the corners were empty. "The dishes are missing!" She sounded angry. "They had pink flowers on them. The kitchen is this way." She ran out of the room.

Sara was staring out the window and Jack went to stand beside her. "Remind you of when you were here with Grand-dad?"

"Yes. There's a round pool and it was always filled with moss. Cal and I cleaned it out."

"This hasn't changed!" Kate called to them.

Jack took Sara's hand and kissed the back of it. "Come on and let's see what the kid is up to now."

Sara laughed. Kate did sound like she was about six years old. "I want to know who 'the man' is."

"I bet Randal will know," Jack said.

"I'm sure he does."

They walked through to the kitchen, then stood there with grimaces on their faces. Worn out linoleum was on the countertops, and half the cabinet doors were missing. The kitchen was an awful place. The only redeeming factor was the heavy oak table in the center.

Usually, Kate looked at houses with the eyes of a remodeler. How did she make it livable enough to sell? But she seemed to be seeing this kitchen as though it was a beauty with granite countertops and maple cabinets. She ran her hand down a deep, long cut in the tabletop. "I did that. Rachel said I could use a knife. I think she meant a fruit knife, but I..." Kate trailed off.

"Used a meat cleaver?" Sara asked.

"I did."

"Glad you still have your fingers," Jack said.

"That's just what Barbara said. And Uncle Roy said that if he'd been here, he would have tanned my hide. We can use the back stairs to go up." She didn't wait for a reply, just disappeared through a doorway.

"Uncle Roy?" Sara asked Jack.

He looked at her with wide eyes. The only Roy they knew was Jack's late father, Roy Wyatt.

They heard Kate's footsteps above them and hurried up to the second floor. She'd already opened several doors. "A lot of the furniture is gone." She sounded ready to do battle.

"If the land was sold, maybe the furniture had to go too," Sara said. "Who used all these bedrooms?"

"Barbara was in here, Lea here, the man in that one and the big bedroom was Billy's." Kate disappeared inside the last room.

Sara and Jack were staring in astonishment.

"How does she remember people?" Jack asked. "She couldn't have been too old when she was here."

Sara knew what he meant. When Kate was four, she was taken from Florida and spent the next twenty years living outside Chicago. "It had to be before she left here."

"I don't remember what happened when I was four. Do you?"

"Oh yes," Sara said. "And I've put every memory in my

books. Who is Billy? And 'the man'? Not to mention all the
other people. I've counted seven so far." Sara opened another
door to see a small bedroom with twin beds. "Kate!" she
called. "Where did you and your dad stay?"

Kate came back to the hall. "That's the one." She meant
the room Sara was looking into. "Now for my favorite room
on this floor."

As Jack and Sara followed her to the end of the hall, they
paused to look into the bedrooms. It was obvious that they
had once been beautifully decorated, but the furniture that
was still there was scuffed and rickety and very dusty. You
could write your name on the surfaces. The rooms were sad
copies of what they had once been.

"The bedroom she and Randal stayed in is a servant's
room," Sara said to Jack. "My guess is that when my brother
worked for Mrs. Meyers, he and Kate came here with her
for a visit."

"Sounds like there were a lot of people here."

"A good, old-fashioned Edwardian house party."

The dreamy way Sara said it made Jack shake his head. "Are
we living in one of your books?"

"We should be so lucky."

"Come on!" Kate called, and they went to her. She was
standing by the double doors of a beautiful room. The wallpaper was of huge jungle plants. There were shelves filled
with books, DVDs in cases, and neatly labeled VHS tapes.
The furniture was a desk and chair, a couch, and a big leather
recliner that faced a white screen.

"It's a movie room." Sara was turning around to look at it.

"It's a time capsule," Jack muttered, and not in a good way.
"It's a bit freaky for me."

Sara's attention was caught by the framed paintings on the
wall. They were street scenes of somewhere in South Amer-

ica. None of them were very big, but they were original oils. She went to one of them. "I may be wrong but I think these are Brazilian. In fact, I think most everything in this room was made in Brazil." Sara had done a lot of traveling in her long life.

"Anything valuable?" Jack asked.

"Possibly."

"I always thought the pictures were pretty." Kate sounded defensive. "Who wants to see the secret rooms?"

Sara and Jack looked at her in amazement. She did sound like a child.

"You know me," Sara said. "I love secrets."

"As long as they're not yours," Jack said, then hurried after Kate as she left the pretty room.

Sara stayed behind. As a true introvert, she recognized that the room was someone's sanctuary. It had been created as a haven, a place to get away from the outside world. She looked at the titles on the movies. Some were commercial hits, but Sara recognized a few titles for the obscure, cultlike movies that they were. She'd seen several of them.

Reluctantly, she went to the doorway. She very much wanted to stay there. "Who are you?" she whispered. "Who created this hideaway?" If land and furniture had been sold, probably for the need of money, why was this room left untouched, even to leaving valuable paintings on the walls?

As she gave one last look around, a curtain moved, yet there was no wind. Sara smiled. Ghosts? If so, they certainly didn't scare her. One thing about aging was that it made you feel closer to the spirit world.

She went back into the hall and called out, "Where are you two?"

What looked to be a wallpapered panel swung out to show Jack standing at the bottom of a flight of narrow stairs.

"Oooooh," she said. "Secret stairs. Secret rooms. I'm in love."

At the top of the stairs, Jack stopped by a closed door. It was painted white and in good condition. "Another untouched room?" Sara asked.

"You're going to like this one." With a flourish, he opened the door.

Inside was a children's playroom. It was big and dusty and there were some cobwebs, but they couldn't hide the beauty of the space. The hardwood floor had a large, handloomed rug that showed a Florida swamp. Alligators, flamingos, blue herons, and fish were peeping from under dense foliage.

There were toys everywhere, mostly wooden but a few metal trucks. To one side was a two-seater glider painted blue and white. One wall was all windows with a deep seat under it. The cushions matched the colors in the big rug. Shelves were filled with books and soft toys.

Kate was in front of the books. "I know all of these. Everyone read them to me. Barbara was the best. She could make any animal sound."

Jack picked up a metal truck and looked at Sara.

She was studying the room with an historian's eye. "My guess is that it was made in the nineteen twenties, and it doesn't seem to have been changed since then. It's yet another time capsule."

"Whose was it?" He was speaking to Kate but she didn't seem to hear him.

"Two boys," Sara said. "There's two of everything and no dolls anywhere. I think the duplications were someone trying to stop brotherly wars."

Jack looked at the truck in his hand and his eyes filled with sadness. His half brother, Evan, had been killed in a crash. In *Jack's* truck. He put the toy down.

"Kate, do you know whose room this was?" Sara asked.

She came out of her reverie and looked around. "Maybe Mr. Lachlan's son? Dad might know."

"Might know what?"

As often happened, Randal Medlar had arrived and no one heard him. He was a man for whom the term "silver fox" was created. He was in his sixties, very handsome, and built like the gym instructor he was. Women, young and old, stopped and stared at him.

"Took you long enough," Sara said. She was *not* in awe of her brother.

"I was all the way over by the Galleria." He looked around the room. "This certainly brings back memories."

"Want to share them?" Sara asked.

"Kate and I came here with Mrs. Meyers. That was an exhausting week! Every woman here thought I was her personal butler. I was running from dawn to midnight."

"So you left your young child alone and she played with a meat cleaver?" Sara said.

Randal wasn't bothered by his older sister's criticism. "Trying to control Kate was like holding on to a greased eel. Besides, she was adored by every one of the guests." He looked at his daughter with fondness and she smiled back. "So Billy is putting the place up for sale?"

"Who is Billy?" Jack asked.

"I guess you'd call him the caretaker. His older brothers gave him this place to look after. He said it was to keep him out of their hair. He was a wonderful conversationalist. He—"

"Who is 'the man' Kate mentioned?" Jack asked.

"That would be—"

"Look!" Kate said. "There's Reid's toolbox and—" She gasped. "It's my dog!" She bent down to pick up a little wooden dachshund on wheels, but the string disappeared under a door and couldn't be pulled out. She tried the knob. It turned but the door didn't open. "It's stuck." She looked at Jack, eyes asking for help. "It's a door to a closet with some old clothes in it."

He went to her and examined the narrow door. "Somebody's put caulking around it and sealed the door shut. That's odd."

Kate was still bent over the toy dog.

"We could cut the string."

"Jack!" Sara sounded disbelieving.

He gave her a smile to let her know he was kidding. On the floor to his left was the wooden toolbox. "I'll rescue the critter in seconds. Stand back." His tone was exaggerated, teasing.

There was a chisel in the toolbox, pitted from years of lack of use, but serviceable, and a ball-peen hammer. It took him a few minutes, but he went around the whole door and chipped away the old caulking.

Still teasing, he looked at Kate. "Ready for the big reveal?" Like a game show host, he turned the knob and pulled the door open in front of him. "It's all yours."

When the other three didn't move, he looked from one face to another. They were staring at the inside of the closet. Color was draining from their faces. Jack saw Kate's face grow pale, and he stepped forward. "Are you okay?"

She stood up straight. "No, I'm not," she whispered.

Jack still had his back to the closet and he looked at Randal, who nodded toward what Jack had just exposed. He turned toward it.

Inside was a skeleton. It had on the remnants of a tuxedo and was being held upright by hooks over the suspenders.

The skull had a full head of thick, black hair. The arms hung down, the skinless hands exposed below sleeves that were tattered. The shirt still had an onyx cuff link. The shredded trousers showed one bony knee, then led down to leather shoes that were still tied.

Kate was the first to speak. "Maybe he was hiding and no one found him."

"And didn't miss him?" Sara asked. "But maybe they thought he'd left so they didn't look for him."

"Yes!" Kate agreed. "This room was kept locked. Rachel used to open it for me."

"She would." Randal sounded sarcastic. He looked at Jack. "I believe that's a wallet by his shoe."

Jack went to the toolbox, picked up an old-fashioned folding rule, and opened it to full extension. He flipped the wallet without touching the skeleton, then picked it up and looked at the ID. He turned to Randal and said, "Derek Oliver."

Sara glared at her brother. "Oliver!" She knew her brother had once worked for a Mrs. Oliver—and things had gone missing. "So he was there at your party?"

Randal gave a brief nod.

"I should have known this was about *you*," Sara said. "It's all about those blasted jewels you stole, isn't it?"

Randal was unperturbed by his sister's anger. He'd had many years of dealing with it. "As I've told you, I didn't steal any jewels. I gave what I did find, which was a pittance of what I'd seen, to the others. The only piece I had, I gave to my daughter."

Sara didn't give up. "If there are jewels involved, it has to do with you."

"I didn't do this!" Randal was getting louder. "I was too busy taking care of the women to deal with what Derek said he was going to do to me."

Sara gasped. "He was *threatening* you?"

"He did make a few rather colorful suggestions as to what

he'd do to me if I didn't give him what had been stolen from his stepmother. He said—"

Jack cut him off. "No one noticed that this man disappeared during the house party?"

"It was over twenty years ago," Randal said. "I don't remember where Derek Oliver was every minute of every day." As always, he hadn't quite answered the question.

Kate said, "Lea told me he went home. She was so happy! She and I blew up balloons together."

They turned to look at her.

"The word of a four-year-old is more reliable than yours," Sara said to her brother.

Randal smiled at his daughter. "Everything is better with Kate."

"I hate to interrupt this little family lovefest," Jack said, "but we need to tell someone about this."

At that, their faces fell. The Broward County sheriff's office already called their little town Murder City—and any other names they could come up with. What excuse would the Medlar-Wyatt gang give this time? That they were trying to release a toy dog and a skeleton appeared?

They were standing in silence, dreading what was coming, when they heard a creaking sound. They turned toward the skeleton. In extreme slow motion, the bony creature began to fall forward, pulling against the rotting suspenders.

The four of them held their breaths.

The old suspenders didn't snap, just gave way, and the skeleton slowly fell out of the closet. It hit the floor in an explosion of shattering clothes, with bones grotesquely scattering.

The pile of human remains on the floor was such a macabre sight that they didn't move. Kate and Sara stood close together.

Then, to their shock, with a clunking sound, the skull came off and rolled across the wooden floor. They watched it in fascinated horror. When it came to a toy box decorated with clown pictures, it stopped.

Sara started to take a step forward, but then halted. The show wasn't over yet.

The skull teetered to the side, and the hair, a toupee, came off and fell into a ratty pile. With the weight of the hair gone, the skull tipped backward. Then, like a broken glass ball, the barren bones fell into two pieces. The jaw didn't move, but the top, above the eye sockets, fell back. The skull opened like it was hinged, exposing rough saw marks all around. As the skull fell back, out spilled sparkling jewels. A couple of bracelets, a few earrings, and one ring with a very large green stone tumbled out.

Hypnotized, no one moved, just stared.

A ray of sun came through the grimy windows and hit the emerald ring. It seemed to wink at them as though to say, "Glad to meet you."

Sara, who was experienced in imagining how things were done, knew that someone had sawed open the skull, removed the brain, filled the cavity with jewelry, then… What? Glued it all back together? "I think I'll sit down," she said.

"Me too." Kate and her aunt sat close together on the nearby window seat.

"Are those jewels from…?" Sara asked her brother.

"Yes," he said. "I recognize those pieces. They were owned by Mrs. Oliver. It's not all of them, but some."

Jack hadn't stopped staring at the skull. "What's that?" He was pointing to a fuzzy bit of fabric that appeared to have eyes.

Randal looked at it in astonishment. "I think that's what's left of Kate's hedgehog." He turned to her. "Remember it? When you lost it, you were crying so hard. Lea was rocking you." He looked at his sister.

"It's the one I gave her?" Sara asked softly.

Randal nodded.

Jack spoke up. "I think the jewels were inside it. Could it have fit in a brain cavity?"

"I don't know from personal experience," Randal said quickly, "but I think so."

"So someone put jewels in Kate's stuffed animal, then…" Jack said.

"Then shoved it into Derek Oliver's skull," Randal said.

"After sawing it in half." Jack glanced at the toolbox.

"And after removing the brain," Sara added. "It, uh, took up space so it had to go." She was swallowing hard.

The men were standing in front of the women on the window seat. No one wanted to look back at what was on the floor.

"Who's going to call Sheriff Flynn?" Kate asked.

"Jack," Sara said. "He's the alpha male. He should do it."

"In normal circumstances," Randal said, "I'd resent that, but in this case I don't even want to be a beta male. D minus is my speed."

"Speaking of alpha," Jack said, "who is Uncle Roy?"

"Your father," Randal said.

"He was here?"

"Yes." Randal's tone told that he was tired of defending his friend. "Often. Your father wasn't always in a tavern starting fights."

"My mother wouldn't agree with that. She divorced him because—"

"Hey!" Sara said. "Let's stay on track. Who is going to call Sheriff Flynn?"

They were silent for a moment, then all heads turned toward Kate.

"Why me?" she asked in a whine.

"Because he adores you," Randal said. Sara and Jack nodded in agreement.

Kate sighed. "Okay, but who is going to tell Billy that we found a skeleton in his house? And that he is a suspect for murder?"

"We don't know when this happened," Randal said. He'd had a lifetime of false accusations—and some not false.

Sara paid no attention to him. "I think it's safe to assume that Derek Oliver was murdered during that house party, which means that everyone who was there is a suspect." She looked at Jack. "Even if he or she is no longer alive." She meant his father.

Randal spoke up. "Once Flynn gets here, we can leave and go see Billy. He's bound to know something about this. Bodies can't just be stuck in a closet and left there undetected. They tend to...well..."

"Right," Sara said. "They decay."

"Last I heard, he was in the Shadow Palms nursing home," Randal said. "It's not far away."

"You're saying we're to leave Sheriff Flynn alone with the body?" Sara asked. That sounded nicer than saying "the bones of Derek Oliver."

The two men turned to glance at the skeleton, then back at Sara. "You want to take some photos?" Randal said.

"You mean before Broward shows up, takes everything away, and tells us it never existed?"

"That was on my mind, yes," Randal said.

Sara's camera bag was by the door. "I have two cameras with me and you guys have phones. Let's cover every inch of this room, then send the pictures through to the cloud. They won't be able to tell us that we made it all up."

"Sounds like a good plan," Jack said. "What cameras do you have?"

Two

SHERIFF DARYL FLYNN WASN'T HAPPY TO BE TOLD
there was another dead body in his town. He said he hadn't
yet recovered from the woman who had been shot, stabbed,
and poisoned.

At Lachlan House, he stood about four feet away from the
split skull with the jewels scattered about. The clasp of one
of the bracelets had caught on a tooth. If he let himself think
about what he was seeing, he might throw up. Randal had
told him of some long-ago house party, but he didn't com-
prehend much. "Uh…" He couldn't think of what to say.
He straightened his shoulders. Thanks to his association with
Randal, he was in better physical condition now. His stomach
was flatter and he moved more quickly. But the good didn't
override the Medlar-Wyatt propensity for complicating his
life. "I have to call Broward." He sounded as if he were saying he had to amputate one of his limbs.

"Maybe they'll…" Even Sara couldn't think of a creative
possibility. As the sheriff pulled out his cell phone, they braced

themselves for the big shot Detective Cotilla to come on the line. Flynn put it on Speaker. He didn't want to be alone.

"They found a body." Flynn didn't explain who "they" were.

"Skeleton," Sara said.

"I recognize that voice," Cotilla said. "Who is the dead person?"

"Derek Oliver," Flynn said. "It's possible he was murdered in 1997."

"Ninety-seven? So there's no blood?"

"Just bones, but the skull has been… Well, it's… It's bad." Flynn couldn't finish.

There was a pause, then Cotilla said, "You sure you didn't find some animal?"

Flynn's voice rose. "It's wearing a tuxedo!"

"That sounds cute. Maybe—"

Sara put out her hand to take the phone and Flynn gladly gave it to her. "You want us to call you when we find out what kind of animal it is? And we'll make sure this scene is well photographed?"

"You can do that? In spite of the fact that so many of the photos you've turned over to me in the past were blurry?"

"I'll try," she said in fake innocence.

"That sounds good. We are drastically understaffed here, and some old case might find itself buried under more recent problems. You understand me?"

"Perfectly," she said.

"Good! Just let me know when you have it all figured out and send me a pretty report. We do so enjoy the way you write and illustrate those."

"We will do that," Sara said.

"I gotta go. I have a meeting with DeSantis."

Sara smiled at that. "Lucky you. We'll take care of everything."

"See that you do."

They clicked off, Sara handed the phone back to Daryl and turned to the others. "It looks like we have a case to solve."

"I'm going back to the office," Daryl said. "If you need anything…" He trailed off, not sure what to say. "Just get me to retirement," he mumbled, then went down the stairs.

"Wait!" Randal called out to him. "You need to stay here while we go visit Billy."

They could hear the sheriff's groan all the way up the stairs.

★

Once Randal had persuaded Sheriff Flynn that he had to stay there, the four of them went outside. Randal had called ahead and was told that Billy Pendergast would love to see them. Randal's sedate sedan was parked beside Jack's truck. It was battered from years of heavy use.

"Shall we have lunch?" Randal asked as he looked from Jack to Kate, then back again. They were standing close beside each other, but their faces were turned away. It was an odd position.

"Too much adrenaline in me to eat," Sara said. "Let's go see this Billy person. How's his mind? Will he remember you?"

Since his sister was an advocate for Old Doesn't Mean Stupid, he looked at her in surprise. "I've been rather busy for the last twenty-plus years so I have no idea."

Sara ignored his feel-sorry-for-me tone. "I'll ride with you. I have some questions you might be able to answer."

Randal was even more surprised. The others were an unbreakable trio. One time he'd said in sarcasm, "Are you three *ever* apart? Meals? Showers? Sleeping?" Sara had given him a look of disgust, and the others ignored him.

But now Sara wanted to ride with her brother? What was going on?

Randal told Jack where the home was, and he and Kate got into his truck. Even to Randal, it seemed odd that Sara's spot was empty. When he was in the car with his sister, he said, "What do you want to ask me?"

"Nothing."

"Then why are you with *me*?" He was leading the way toward Broward Boulevard.

"You haven't noticed anything unusual with the kids?"

"Jack looks different. Colorado changed him. I was going to tell him he looked good, but a skull rolling across the floor distracted me."

"I want to give him and Kate time alone."

"Oh," he said. "You think…?"

"I hope they will at last get together."

When he stopped at a light, they smiled at each other. One thing they agreed on was that they deeply and truly wanted Jack and Kate to get "together." As in rings and champagne and a lavish ceremony.

Randal glanced in the mirror at Jack's truck behind them.

"How are they doing?" she asked.

"Sitting far apart and not saying a word."

"Not good," Sara said.

"This is your job," he said. "Romance is how you've made your living. You need to put them together in a way that they have no choice but to actually speak to each other."

Sara smiled. "I do love pretend-to-be-married romances. Second only to mail order brides. I'll see what I can do. Now, about Billy. What do you know?"

"I think he hated Derek Oliver as much as the rest of us did."

"So Billy murdered the man and shoved his body in a closet?"

"Maybe." Randal pulled into a parking lot. "This is it. You can ask him everything. He dearly loves to talk."

"Maybe he can give Jack and Kate lessons," she mumbled as she got out.

★

If there is one thing Florida knows, it's how to take care of aging people. Some retirement communities were whole villages. There were beautiful, manicured landscapes with residents walking about in tennis outfits. Swimming pools were full of residents and instructors. The houses were well-kept. The doctors were busy dealing with the rampant STDs.

The outside of the Shadow Palms building was very pretty, but once they were inside, they could see that it wasn't what they'd thought. It appeared to be more of a hospice, a place to die rather than to live. The woman who greeted them was nice.

"Billy doesn't get many visitors," she said. "I'm sure he'll be glad to see you."

"He's cognizant?" Randal asked.

"Oh yes. Billy's mind works well. It's his body that isn't behaving." Her cheerfulness was a good contrast to the solemn feeling that ran through the place.

She led them down a long hall where they passed pretty rooms with private baths. At the end, they went through double doors and the space changed. Vinyl tiles replaced carpet and the walls were plain. The rooms were smaller and had shared baths.

Sara glanced back at Kate and Jack and they nodded in understanding. They were now in the cheap part.

The woman leading them seemed to understand what they were thinking. "All our residents get the same medical attention, but we do cut charges on the decor." She opened a door to show a man sitting in a wheelchair. It didn't take a doctor's certificate to see that the thin man didn't have much longer to live. His skin hung off him and it didn't look like he could walk—but his blue eyes were bright and excited.

"Randal!" he said. "You're as handsome as ever." Surprisingly, his voice was strong. He looked at the four solemn faces, then stopped at Kate. "Dear little Kate. You have grown into a beautiful young woman. But then, you were the cutest child with your red-gold locks and green eyes. And you were insatiably curious. Do you remember any of the week you spent at my house?"

Kate moved forward and took his old, frail hands in hers. "It seems that I remember a great deal of it. I know you used to read books to me and tell me stories. You said the house was haunted. There was a lord?"

Billy was smiling deeply. "A laird. It was a story I made up. The Lonely Laird. It was great dinner table entertainment. The candles were lit and it was raining outside."

"And there was a fire in the big fireplace. I remember it well."

He gave a dry laugh. "You should have been in bed that late."

"And miss any of your glorious stories? Never!"

There were tears in Billy's old eyes. "Oh! I have missed this. Please sit down. I'd offer you food and drink but…" He waved his hand to indicate the barren room, all gray steel and rough white sheets on the bed.

Jack placed four metal chairs in a half circle around him.

"So!" Billy said when they were seated. "Can I assume you found Derek?"

Randal was the first to recover from shock. "We did. So you do know about him?"

Billy again smiled at Kate. "I knew that if I gave you the listing, you'd find him right away. You so loved the old nursery. Is it intact? Just the way it was when you were there?"

"Exactly the same," she said. "My toy dog's string was caught under the closet door. It was sealed shut but Jack got it loose."

For the first time, Billy really looked at Jack. "My goodness. You are even more handsome than your father." He turned to Randal. "Remember how dashing Roy was on his big motorcycle? I thought Barbara was going to pass out from lust."

"Barbara?" Sara asked.

Billy turned to her. "You're the famous author."

"Not famous, but I have written a few novels."

As often happened, Billy immediately proposed a plot idea. "You should write about James Lachlan. Now there's a *real* story. Utterly true. All in one horrible year, 1944, his nephew was executed for murder, his son ran away forever, and his wife plowed her car into a tree. It was believed to be a suicide."

Sara was used to this. *I'll tell you a story, you write it, then we'll split the money.* She'd heard it many times. "I see," she said. "The Lonely Laird. He never married again? Spent the rest of his life grieving alone in his movie room?"

Billy blinked at her. "Yes. How did you know? Who told you? Did—?"

Impatiently, Randal spoke up. "Derek Oliver was murdered and hidden in a closet and you knew about it?"

"Of course I did. I put him in there. After I glued him back together, so to speak."

The four of them leaned back to stare at him.

"No, no," Billy said, "I didn't kill him, if that's what you are thinking. I just found him lying there. Empty-headed, as it were. Quite disrespectful."

For a few moments they just stared at him, trying to understand what he was saying.

"My hedgehog?" Kate asked.

"Sorry," Billy said. "I know you loved it but it had been used to fill the gap. I guess it was the right size. I couldn't very well pull it out and return it to you. It wasn't, uh, clean."

They worked to keep their composure. Obviously, Billy didn't know about what was inside the little stuffed animal.

Randal seemed to recover the quickest. "You're saying you found Derek Oliver on the floor, his head sawed open, and inside it was a child's stuffed animal?"

"Yes," Billy said. "I don't like to remember the details."

"Start at the beginning," Randal said.

"If I must," Billy said. "We'd had a lovely lunch because odious Derek wasn't there. No one even asked about him. When we finished, it was raining so I went upstairs to check the windows." He glanced at Kate. "You do so love fresh air."

"Still do," she murmured.

"There he was on the floor. Dead, and obviously murdered. Honestly, I wasn't surprised. The method was a bit much, but the fact of it was that it was understandable."

"Who did it?" Sara asked.

"I assume one of my guests did. However, it was quite thoughtless to leave the body lying on the nursery floor." His voice was rising. "It was without concern for other people. What if little Kate had seen it? Randal was run ragged by all of us, so Kate had free rein of the house. I still don't know how she found the old playroom."

"Greer," Kate said.

Billy looked sad. "Oh yes. That poor girl. So unattractive and so awkward. Did you know that she was hit by a train a few years later? Her brother Reid was devastated."

Jack spoke for the first time. "It was his toolbox."

"Yes, it was." Billy was looking at Jack in appraisal. "Your voice is the same as your father's. I'm sure you'd give Barbara palpitations." He looked at Sara. "Is that word still used?"

"It is in my books. Your plotting needs some work. I'm getting confused. We really want to know about the murder."

"That's because you didn't know Derek Oliver." Billy gave a dry sound that seemed to be a laugh. Kate got up, poured him a glass of water, and handed it to him. He drank deeply, then looked at Randal. "Have you ever met a man more un-likable than Derek Oliver?"

Randal considered for a moment. "No. I don't believe I have. More violent, yes. But not a less likable human being, no."

"I guess I should explain some things," Billy said. "I was sent to Lachlan House by my late father and my two very-much-alive brothers as a punishment. They're all lawyers with the family firm and I was supposed to join them."

"How tedious," Randal said.

"Yes, it was. When I didn't pass the bar exam, they gave me another job in the firm." He looked at them. "Accounting."

Randal and Sara drew in their breaths.

"A man needs to *live*, doesn't he? There was all that money coming in." Billy shrugged. "I didn't think they'd mind if I borrowed a small bit. Not many zeros. But they did!" He sounded offended.

"So they sent you here?" Randal asked.

"No." Billy's old face showed horror. "They got me a job in construction in New York City. For one whole year."

As old as Billy was, it was easy to see that he wasn't made for building anything.

"Then they sent you here," Sara said. "After you learned your lesson."

Billy nodded. "They were the executors of the Lachlan

estate and they needed a live-in caretaker. I was to look after the place and see that it didn't fall into ruin. I was given just enough money to buy food and bits of clothing. They really were stingy."

Randal was piecing it all together. "You supplemented your income with parties."

"I did," Billy said proudly. "The big, gracious house, my abilities as raconteur… It was perfect. People paid well for the experience."

"Are you saying that it was Derek Oliver's party?" Sara asked.

"Of course. He paid for everything and he made the guest list."

"So they were *his* friends?" Sara asked.

"Heavens no!" Billy said. "He had no friends. He invited people and they *had* to come." No one was understanding. Billy said, "Darlings, he was blackmailing them all. Each and every one of them. But then, no one on earth would spend a week with Derek Oliver if he weren't threatening them."

Sara's eyes were wide. "Blackmailing them for what?"

"I don't know, but it was something bad for each of them."

"Except Lea," Randal said.

"Her most of all." Billy looked at them. "Lea was Derek's wife, but we all knew he was trying to find a replacement for her. The money she brought to the marriage had run out, so he wanted to get rid of her." He looked at Randal. "But I imagine you know all about what was going on in that marriage."

Randal made no reply.

Jack spoke. "You found him dead, his brain extracted and a toy inside, so you glued his skull back together, then you put him in the closet and sealed the door."

"I did," Billy said. "I put his toupee on too. It was ugly, but

I knew he hated being bald. After I, uh, reassembled him, I pulled him into the closet. That wasn't easy! The coat hooks were low for the children, so I latched him to them, closed the door, then sealed it. I'd learned how to caulk in my year of construction." Even so many years later, he shivered at the memory. "Besides, I felt some responsibility for it all as I was the one who sent Reid up there to repair a window. I was worried about little Kate being safe."

"What about the mess?" Sara asked. "It must have been some."

"It was surprisingly clean." When Billy paused, the others looked at each other, then back at him to tell more.

"Afterward, I opened all the windows," Billy said. "They were screened so I thought it would be safe from birds and things. Then I locked the whole floor up. I told Reid that Roy had borrowed his toolbox, and I told Kate that a monster was up there." He looked at her. "Sorry for the lie."

"Under the circumstances, I think that was acceptable."

"After that, the rest of us went on about our business." He smiled. "We had such a good time!"

"You kept partying even after a guest went missing?" Sara asked.

"Actually, we started partying after he was gone. Lea said it wasn't the first time he'd run off and left everything behind for her to take care of, so his absence caused no concern. And with Derek not there making all of us miserable, we quite enjoyed ourselves. There was ample food and drink and music. Barbara and Roy danced all night." He looked at Jack. "Can you sing like Roy did?"

"I didn't know my father could sing," Jack said.

"Yes," Kate said, "Jack has a beautiful voice. He sings with bands, and sometimes he sings for just Sara and me. He can do opera and country and rock and roll. His voice can bring tears

to an audience or put them in the throes of ecstasy. He—"
They were all staring at her and her face turned the color of
her hair. "Yes, he can sing."

Billy looked at Randal in question and he nodded.

Sara wanted to put them back on the subject. "But you
knew Oliver hadn't willingly left the party."

Billy's lips tightened. "What I actually knew was that that
horrible man had changed my life forever. Because of him, I
knew I wouldn't be able to give any more parties. I couldn't
when there was a, you know, upstairs. Someone was bound
to notice."

"Don't you mean that the *murderer* changed your life?"
Sara asked.

"You can look at it like that, but if Derek Oliver hadn't
been such a despicable person, no one would have felt com-
pelled to remove him from the earth. I'm sure that the life of
every person there was improved by his death. The murderer
was the brave one, and the others should thank him—or her."

"What an awful epitaph," Sara said.

For a moment, they were silent. It was Jack who spoke first.
"If we invite them all back, will they come?"

"I assume that whoever killed him will return," Billy said.
"He or she must want to know what happened to the body."
He gave a little smile. "That person must have been surprised
when he or she went to the nursery and found it empty. It
must have been like some Broadway play."

No one laughed.

"You didn't see who went back to the nursery?" Sara asked.

"Heavens no! Why would I want to know which of my
guests sawed—" He paused. "It really was awful. Anyway,
as for their returning here after all this time, I guess it depends on if they still need to keep the secrets Derek Oliver
had on them."

"It must have been big secrets if they murdered him to shut him up," Sara said.

"Ewww," Billy said. "What a marvelous idea. They *all* killed him. That makes sense." His face changed. "But why did they leave the body for *me* to take care of? That was so rude of him—or her! After they left, I had to move to the other side of the house because it was quite, uh…"

"Fragrant?" Kate said.

Billy nodded. "It certainly wasn't perfume. There were moments when I thought about telling someone, but I was afraid that old sheriff, Captain Edison, would think that *I* did it."

"He was as corrupt as they come," Randal said bitterly.

Sara asked, "Who were the guests and how do we contact them?"

Billy looked at Randal. "You know Barbara."

"I've been out of commission for a while." His voice dripped sarcasm. "We haven't kept in touch."

Billy looked surprised. "You must have been living on another planet to not know who she is."

"You're close to correct," Randal said.

"Oh!" Billy said sharply. "That's right. I forgot that you were…" He didn't finish his sentence. "She's Barbara Adair."

"The movie star?" Kate asked.

"Back then, she'd just had a few roles, but she did indeed go on to achieve fame."

"Who else?" Sara asked.

"Let's see. There was Mrs. Meyers and her granddaughter, Rachel. That girl was a bit of a rebel, but now she's probably in Greenwich, Connecticut, living on some estate with her hedge fund husband. She had that air about her. I once heard Mrs. Meyers say something about some jewels. Do you know anything about that?"

"No, nothing," Randal said quickly.

"Who is Reid?" Jack asked.

"The handyman. He was very young, and I think he had some distant family connection to Mr. Lachlan. Not sure."

"And Oliver's wife, Lea?" Sara asked.

"That poor woman," Billy said. "We all felt so sorry for her."

The door opened and a nurse stood there. "I see that your visitors are still here." Her tone made it clear that it was time for them to leave. She closed the door behind her.

The four of them stood up, but then Randal paused. "What's your gut feeling about who and why?"

"Well…" he said, dragging it out. "My brothers would say I'm insane, but I think it has something to do with the inheritance."

"You mean the jewels you mentioned?" Sara asked.

"I know nothing about them. I'm talking about the Lachlan estate. There's not much of it now, but in '97 it was worth a lot of money. Not to mention prestige. To someone like Derek Oliver, the estate reeked of old world wealth. I always thought he was trying to get the money from the others so he could buy the place. But of course that was impossible."

"Why?" Sara asked. "Your brothers wouldn't sell it?"

"Good heavens! My brothers would sell me if they could get a penny. They couldn't sell it because of James Lachlan's will." Billy knew he had their full attention and he loved it. "In 1962, a man won a Nobel Prize for discovering DNA. That fascinated Mr. Lachlan. You see, he believed his son, who had run away, was alive and well somewhere. Mr. Lachlan just had to find him. He willed the house to his eldest descendant—if he could be found. But there's a time limit, and it's at the end of this month. Exactly forty years after his death."

"How hard has your family law firm looked for the inheritor?" Sara asked.

Billy smiled. "They asked me to do it."

Randal shook his head. "And if you found him, he'd take over the house and you'd be homeless."

"Exactly." Billy was making it clear that he hadn't looked at all.

Kate, always a Realtor, said, "This means you put the house up for sale prematurely."

"I wanted to give *you* a chance at it instead of some snob from Sotheby's," Billy retorted. "And besides, the attic needed to be cleaned out."

"Right," Kate said. "Skeletons tend to hinder sales."

Billy smiled. "Not if there's a buyer who wants to turn it into a haunted bed-and-breakfast, and there is one. He loved my Lonely Laird story so much that he wants to expand on it. He wants me to write it down." He glanced at Sara to let her know she was missing a great opportunity, then turned back to Kate. "Would you like to have his card? I think he's a cash buyer."

Kate looked sick at the thought of what would be done to that beautiful house. "Maybe later," she said.

They said their goodbyes, promised to come again, and left.

As they walked out, Sara said to Randal, "Do me a favor and get him transferred to the best room in this place. Would you?"

"It will be my pleasure."

In the parking lot, they stood by the vehicles, everyone looking at Sara.

She started to make a snide comment about involuntarily being made the boss, but she didn't. She looked at Kate. "You two go to Publix and get food. We'll meet back at the house and decide what we're going to do." She turned to her brother. "Let's go."

When they were in his car, Randal said, "You're planning to do this, aren't you? You want to recreate the house party."

"Maybe," Sara said.

"You could leave it alone. As Billy said, Derek Oliver was a despicable man. Maybe he deserved what he got."

"I take it you're concerned about who the killer might be. Exactly how much did you like his wife?"

Randal didn't hesitate. "The most of anyone since Kate's mother. If my life hadn't been cut off, there might have been something between us. Her husband really was planning to divorce her."

"You were married at the time."

"Not happily." A muscle worked in his jaw.

"Pull in here." Sara was pointing at a long row of stores. The shopping in South Florida was excellent. Anything you wanted was at your fingertips.

She put her hand on the door. "Call Billy's place and get a count of residents and employees. Billy is going to throw a party for them. There'll be food and flowers, and later Jack can arrange some music. And I'm going to order him a phone so we can stay in contact with him at all times."

He smiled at his sister. "He'll like that very much."

"I think he's an unappreciated person," she said. "Tell me when you get the number of people we'll be feeding. I'll be in the flower shop, then you and I can go choose food."

"I like it," Randal said as he picked up his phone.

THREE

KATE WAS IN THE TRUCK AND SITTING AS FAR AWAY from Jack as she could get—and they weren't speaking. The truth was that she was in a state of shock from what he'd said last night. A skull toddling across the floor had been a momentary distraction, but there were some things in life that could *never* be overridden.

Last night, Jack had talked of...well, a child. After he said it, he went to his room and they hadn't spoken of it since. This morning he'd been his usual self. Well, maybe a little quieter, but nothing odd. Certainly nothing to hint at what he'd said.

The lockdown had changed things for all of them. Early in 2020, Gil, Jack's friend and foreman, said he wanted time with his twelve-year-old son, Quinn, so he'd bought some land in the Rocky Mountains. He said he was taking months off so he and Quinn could build a cabin and do some hunting and fishing. Jack wanted to help them get started, so the three of them cleaned out storage units of building materials, loaded two pickups and two trailers, and headed to the mountains.

Right after they arrived, the lockdown began. Jack called Kate and Sara to say that he wanted to stay until the country opened back up. The women were glad for him to have a few weeks of male-only time. When the separation continued, they kept in touch as best they could, considering there was no cell service at the cabin. Sara sent long letters, trying to get laughter out of what was going on at home with Kate and her new circumstances of dueling mothers. Sara dubbed it "The Parent War," with Kate being the center of a lot of seriously unpleasant emotion.

Jack wasn't fooled by Sara's attempt to sugarcoat it all. He knew what Kate was being put through. But he didn't dwell on it as that would have made Kate feel worse. Instead, Jack replied with photos of Gil and Quinn and him fishing, hiking, laughing.

The women could see that he was happy. "You did this," Sara said to Kate. "You changed his life. It's good to see him smile."

They were nice words, but Kate frowned. She missed Jack tremendously.

It was months before he returned—and when he did, he was different. For one thing, he'd changed physically. "A Colorado winter takes off the fat," he said to Sara.

To Kate, he didn't say anything. He just looked at her.

She'd seen photos of him and had laughed with Aunt Sara that Jack and Gil weren't shaving. But Kate was unprepared for the impact this new Jack had on her. His beard was down to his collarbone and there were strands of gray in his hair. It wasn't a perfectly shaped, city-man beard, but scraggly. *Like a Viking*, she thought. The gray seemed to say that he was now older, wiser, more experienced. More importantly, it seemed to say that now he knew what he wanted in life.

Between the beard and his new leanness, she had that ancient female reaction of her legs turning to butter. If they'd been alone, she wasn't sure she could have stayed upright.

But they hadn't been alone—and it took effort to recover herself while the others talked. Usually, she and Jack tossed words back and forth like little daggers, but this time she could think of nothing. Finally, trying to sound sophisticated, she said, "Good heavens, Jack, you could braid that beard."

He didn't reply, just turned away. But minutes later, when he bent close in front of her to pick up his bag, he said, "You can braid it for me."

Kate drew in her breath so hard she fell against the couch. Jack headed down the hall to his room. He didn't look back.

She thought she'd seen every aspect of him. She'd seen his temper, she'd held him when he'd cried in grief, and she'd experienced the fierce, selfless way he protected the people he loved. But she hadn't seen this man who spoke of her braiding his beard. And oh how she wanted to do it!

It had taken the loud closing of Jack's bedroom door to bring her out of her trance. She shook her head to clear it.

To her embarrassment, her aunt Sara was watching her—and smiling in such a knowing way that Kate's whole body turned red.

"I think I'll see if B&H has any ring lights," Sara said in a voice of fake innocence. "Jack could do that TikTok challenge. You know, where he's shirtless and holds the circle light above his head? He'd be half naked, with his muscles showing their deep, dark shadows. I bet he'd get a million followers on the first day." Sara narrowed her eyes as if in warning. "Lots of women will want him."

Kate tried to speak, to make a who-cares? retort, but it wouldn't come out.

Aunt Sara turned away, went to her room, and shut the door.

All that happened on the day Jack returned. The next day he was clean-shaven and he avoided looking directly at her.

Then there was last night. Sara went to bed early so she and

Jack were alone in the family room. In the past, he would have pulled her feet onto his lap, like she was his sister. But he didn't.

"Are you okay?" she asked. "Is something bothering you?"

He took his time answering. "Sometimes you see something that you want. I mean, really want. With all your soul."

"Like a piece of jewelry?" she asked, teasing, trying to get it back to normal between them.

He didn't smile. "Like a life. Gil and his son. What they have, what they share. I realized that bond was everything." He took a breath. "I'm tired of living in one room. I want my own house. I want my own...child."

The hair on Kate's neck stood up, but she said, "Are you planning to adopt?"

"I thought maybe I'd try to make one."

Her heart seemed to put itself on hold. "Like building a house? With a hammer and nails?"

Once again, he gave her "that look."

"How about with a hydraulic nail gun on full power?"

His meaning was so clear that Kate couldn't think of anything to say.

He didn't say any more but got up and went to the single room where he lived in Sara's house.

When Kate was alone, she found that she couldn't move. She was frozen in place, her eyes wide, her mind feeling like a centrifuge. What had just happened? Was Jack saying what she thought he was?

She didn't go to sleep until the wee hours, then was awakened by her phone screeching loudly. It was Melissa from the office calling. *What now?* she thought. They were out of coffee? There was a palmetto bug on the floor? Alligator in the bathroom and Melissa wanted Kate to get it out?

But what Melissa said was that some man was putting the Lachlan House up for sale, and he was demanding that Kate get the listing. Melissa's tone suggested that she considered that unfair. "It's probably because you're so famous." That was meant as a jab.

Kate was used to Melissa so she wasn't bothered. "Lachlan House? That name sounds familiar but I'm not sure why."

"It's the name of this town. Remember?"

As always, Kate ignored her coworker's nastiness. "Maybe I should go see the lister."

"No. He wants you to go to the house today." She rattled off some stats of the house, including words like "magnificent" and "million dollars."

"Why—?" Kate began, but stopped. She knew it was no use asking Melissa what was going on. "Okay. Send me photos. I'll get dressed and go see the place. Is there a lockbox on the door?"

"I don't know. It's not *my* listing. But then, I'm never considered in any of this. For years I've had to worry if some killer was going to mistake me for you and kill me, but that doesn't mean anyone tells me anything. I just have to endure all of it and—"

Kate hung up. There wasn't a word she hadn't heard Melissa say. One time she'd glared at Kate and said, "Why haven't I been considered as a suspect in your murders?" She sounded like a murderer was a celebrity. Later, when Kate told Sara, her aunt said, "Melissa is a victim-type, not a murderer." Jack and Kate had agreed.

*

Since that call, Kate thought about how everything had turned upside down. It looked like they were yet again setting out to solve an old murder. They'd done it before, working together, depending on each other—but now things were different. True, her father was with them, but that added, not subtracted.

But the estrangement she felt with Jack was so uncomfortable she didn't know how she was going to function. Not even a skeleton in a closet was taking her mind off the problem.

There was a Publix every mile or so. To Floridians, the stores were a way of life, not just for groceries.

Jack pulled into a parking lot. He turned off the engine but didn't look at her. "Seafood? Salads? What should we get?"

Kate was silent for a moment. "I can't do this. What you said last night was too much."

"Right." His voice was hard and cold. He opened the door and started to get out.

"No!" she half shouted. She knew he was taking what she'd said the wrong way. *Stubborn pride*, Sara called it. *It runs in the Wyatt blood.* Kate glared at Jack. "Do not leave this truck."

He closed the door and looked straight ahead.

She took a breath. "I've had days of your innuendos, your hints, and the new way you look at me. I want you to tell me what's going on."

"I…"

She knew he was struggling with pride. "It's me," she said. "You can tell me anything." She was quiet and listened.

He started again. "I'm trying to get up the courage to ask you what Sara would call *the* question. I greatly fear rejection." Turning, he gave her a look that had no armor on it. He was putting all his feelings out for her to accept—or to destroy.

Kate felt happiness flow through her like lava down a mountain. Until that moment she'd had no idea how much she wanted this. Months without Jack had left an emptiness in her that she hadn't been able to fill. "Are you talking about sharing a house?"

He nodded, not sure if she was agreeing. "Children?"

His eyes began to sparkle. "Yes."

"You and me? Home? Family? Everything?"

She saw that the sparkle in his eyes was tears. She knew Jack had had a hard life and he'd never thought normal things would come to him.

Kate smiled until her skin seemed to crack. "Well..." she said slowly "...if you did ask me that question, I'd have to say *yes*." She saw him swallow and he blinked several times. She sat still, thinking he'd kiss her, but he didn't.

"Scallops," he said. "Sara loves them. I think I'll get some steaks too. What do you want?"

Kate quit smiling. "What do you think I want?"

Jack didn't say anything, just got out of the truck, shut the door, then went around to her side, opened her door, held out his hand, and waited for her to take it. He looked at her hand for a moment, then into her eyes. "I love you." He let out his breath. "I've never said that to anyone who isn't a relative. I love you, Kate Medlar. With all my heart and soul, I love you. And I will forever."

"And I love you," she said. "I didn't know how much until you weren't near me every day."

He nodded, as though the deal had been sealed. But he still didn't kiss her, just held on to her hand tightly, and they walked into the grocery store together.

When they were choosing avocados, Kate suggested that they tell no one about the changes between them. "Not yet."

Jack agreed. He said he didn't look forward to all the "speculation about the future."

Kate knew what he was really saying. How did they tell Sara that the inevitable was going to happen? Kate and Jack were going to move into their own home. Sara would be left alone in her huge house where they'd all lived together in such harmony.

In spite of the problems facing them, it was two very happy people who bought way too much food.

FOUR

WHEN JACK AND KATE WALKED INTO THE HOUSE, laden with grocery bags, they were quite cheerful as they greeted Sara and Randal. Kate told a cute story about buying the big prawns, and Jack remarked on the four salads they'd bought.

They were so easygoing and pleasant that the older duo stared at them, their faces wearing identical looks of concentration. They were trying to figure out what was going on.

Glad they'd kept their private business to themselves, Jack and Kate went into the kitchen to put things away.

Randal looked at his sister, his eyebrows raised in question.

"Fridge," was all Sara said.

Randal gave a quick nod and followed the two young people, then got four crystal flutes out of a cabinet, removed the bottle of champagne from the refrigerator, and opened it.

By the time he was pouring, Jack and Kate had stopped moving and were looking at them in shock. "How did you know?" Jack asked.

Randal and Sara smiled as they handed out full glasses. "How could we not know?" she said.

"To the future," Randal said. "Wherever it may lead."

"I want at least three of them," Sara said under her breath to Kate. She didn't have to explain what she meant. Three kids.

"I think it's too early to—" Kate began, but everyone drank to the toast and she didn't finish.

When their glasses were empty, Randal refilled them—and they fell into what had become a well-practiced routine. They gathered food and took it outside to the grill on the big patio. By silent agreement, the older two did not bombard the younger ones with questions about when and where and how. That would come later.

It was when the table was filled with food that Sara said, "We have decisions to make."

"Yes, we do," Kate said. "Do you think we could hire Lachlan House for the ceremony? I didn't show you the ballroom but it would be wonderful for…"

Jack took her hand in his. Sara and Randal were looking at her.

"Oh," Kate said. "You mean murder. The skeleton. Blackmail. Sorry. For a moment, I forgot about that."

"Understandable." Sara smiled fondly. "But yes, I'll get Lachlan House for you."

Kate was too embarrassed to say anything more.

"What my sister is asking," Randal said, "is if we take on this case, should we try to recreate the party?"

"Actually," Sara said, "that's not my concern. We can make all the preparations we want, but how do we get them to show up? Do we contact people who were at the party and tell them the truth of why we're inviting them?"

When no one spoke, Sara imitated holding a phone to her ear. "Remember that party you went to in Lachlan, Florida, back in 1997?" She paused. "Yes, that's the one. At Billy Pendergast's big house." Pause. "Oh, I'm glad you had fun. Anyway, we found a skeleton of one of the guests sealed up in a closet. He'd been murdered." Pause. "Yes, we're sure it was murder. Someone had sawed his skull in half." Pause. "It is indeed dreadful. So, we'd like for you to come back to the house and let us figure out if *you* were the one who killed him. No, it won't take long—unless you're the murderer, then it'll take the rest of your life. Ha ha. Can we put you down for the fourteenth?"

Sara's enactment was so spot-on that they just stared at her.

Randal spoke first, his voice low. "We definitely should give this serious consideration. The murder was twenty-five years ago, and Derek Oliver was a vile man, a criminal. Do we *want* to find out who did the world a favor and stopped him? As we know, we could tell Broward and they'll remove the bones, then we can forget about it."

"You're afraid his wife, your girlfriend, did it," Sara said.

Randal tightened his lips. "In other circumstances, that might be true, but this wasn't an ordinary crime of passion. He pushed someone to the brink, yes, but it took mental illness to saw the skull apart, and..."

"Scoop out the brain," Sara said. "It's attached. Wonder what tool he used?"

No one had an answer to her question.

"Maybe it was two people," Jack said. "One killed him with drugs or maybe shot him. He could have died of a heart attack. We don't know for sure what happened. Then someone sawed the top of his head off."

"We do know that Billy hid the body," Sara added.

"And don't forget that Kate's toy had been stuffed inside," Jack said.

"What we don't know," Randal said, "is who sewed the jewels inside the toy."

"Or who removed the contents of the skull," Sara said.

Randal said, "I bet the killer was away, disposing of the contents when Billy found the body."

"What a shock to find the body gone." Sara grimaced. "Wonder if the killer ever knew the truth."

No one replied.

"We need to decide if we want to pursue this," Randal said. "If we do, someone's life is going to be ruined."

They were silent for a moment because Randal knew all about having a life that was destroyed.

"It's what Billy told us," Jack said. "If they show up, it will be because they still have something they don't want found out. Some secret that they want to remain hidden."

Sara nodded in agreement. "A secret so big that he or she killed to keep it from being discovered. Forever."

"Forever hasn't lasted," Randal said. "Do we want to force that secret being told? That could put everyone at risk. Someone killed to keep it hidden. It could be dangerous." He glanced at his precious daughter. "To us."

Kate spoke for the first time since her embarrassing moment. "Something no one is mentioning is the will. I'm curious about the descendant of James Lachlan. Who actually owns that house? I can't sell it until we know the owner." She leaned forward. "I'd like it better if those lawyers don't get the house. The land has been sold off and most of the contents of the house are gone. I think those lawyers have benefited enough!" They knew Kate hated seeing the house desecrated. She looked at her aunt. "Did you ever meet James Lachlan?"

"I did. He was a tall man, with a magnificent head of gray hair, and he had a heavy Scottish accent. He liked Cal a lot. I think..." She took a breath as she thought of the man she'd loved. "I think maybe he saw the bruises on Cal. His father was a bastard of a man! Cal and I didn't know the story, but if Mr. Lachlan had lost both his son and his nephew, maybe he was redirecting some of what he'd missed onto Cal." Her head came up. "I just remembered that one time I saw him at one of Cal's football games."

"So he didn't isolate himself," Kate said. "He didn't hide out in his movie room and grieve for years."

"I guess he could have done both," Sara said.

Jack looked from one woman to the other. "Okay, got it. Whatever we decide to do about the murder, Sara is going to do the research to find the true owner of the house."

She was smiling. "That appeals to me. So you three are going to solve the murder? All by yourselves?"

"We'll struggle along." Randal wore a bored look.

"So it's decided that we're going to do this?" Kate asked. "Even knowing that we could find out that an American Treasure like Barbara Adair is a murderer? What was she like?" She was looking at her father.

"She—"

"He had eyes only for Derek Oliver's wife," Sara interrupted.

Randal straightened his shoulders in defense. "Mrs. Meyers and her wayward granddaughter were in the guesthouse. I was running back and forth, day and night. I didn't have time to do anything else. I—"

Jack cut in. "We didn't see a lot of the house and missed the outbuildings altogether. What are they like? In good condition or falling apart?"

"When I saw the guesthouse," Randal said, "it was beautiful. There was a trellis to the second floor. Rachel used to climb out the upstairs window at night, sneak into the house, and steal wine from the cellar. Mrs. Meyers laughed about it. She said she was just like her when she was Rachel's age."

"And the smaller building?" Jack asked.

Randal shrugged. "That's the cottage. I never went in it. Reid and his sister stayed in there. They were workers, like me."

"It's two stories." Sara had a faraway look in her eyes. "There's a bedroom and bath upstairs. It's a loft and open at the end. On the ground floor, in the back, away from where people can see it, is a two story, fifteenth-century stained glass window. It came from a French cathedral that was destroyed in WWII. The morning sun comes through the glass and makes colors on the slate floor. It is indescribably beautiful."

They were all staring at her.

Jack said softly, "I guess you and Granddad personally looked after that place."

"Oh yes," Sara said in a throaty voice that made it unmistakable as to what the teenagers did in the pretty little house. "We most certainly did."

They laughed together, with Sara being the loudest.

"So we *are* going to take on this case?" Jack asked and looked from one to the other.

"I guess it's up to the guests," Sara said. "We can invite them and see what they say. They could tell us to get lost."

"Do we tell them the party is because we found a body? We'd make Sara's phone call a reality." Jack wasn't being serious.

Randal said, "Let's say we're giving a party for Billy. A celebration of his life and we'd like for them to come. It's a reunion of sorts."

Sara snorted. "BVU. Blackmail Victims United."

"If they do accept," Jack said, "then we'll know they have a reason." He glanced at Randal. "It might be to renew old acquaintances or..." He looked at Sara.

"To find out what we know about a dead man."

"One that was rudely left out in the open so poor Billy had to take care of it," Randal said in sarcasm.

"And what happened to the brain?" Sara asked.

"Yuck," Kate said.

"Yes, yuck," Sara said, "but we're all thinking about it. Was it buried? Taken away as a trophy? Is it in a jar somewhere? What?"

Again, no one had an answer.

"So what's our final decision?" Jack asked.

For a moment they were silent, then they looked at each other. Each one gave a nod of agreement.

"How do we start?" Jack asked. "Anyone have Barbara Adair's private number?"

"Not her, but I might be able to contact Lea Oliver," Randal said.

Sara gave her brother a raised eyebrow look. "Has she had her missing husband declared dead so she can remarry?"

Randal was reluctant to answer, but did. "I don't know. I know that at first she stayed with her husband's family in the house they owned together." He raised his hand. "But I know nothing else. After a while, I quit keeping track of her."

"That's one person," Jack said. "What about the others?"

"Billy said that Greer passed away," Kate said sadly. "I remember her. She was odd, but I liked her a lot. She was my friend."

"Odd enough to murder someone?" Sara asked.

"No," Randal said quickly. "She was quite young, a teenager, and she lived with her grandmother. It was her first job out in the world. She wasn't pretty and now that I think about it, she might have been autistic. Derek bullied her."

"The more I hear about that man," Sara said, "the more I dislike him."

Randal nodded in agreement. "Maybe Billy knows where the family lived. Someone might know how to contact Reid."

"What about Rachel?" Kate asked. "Should we just search all of Connecticut, as Billy suggested."

"Billy's lawyer brothers might know," Sara said. "When I talk to them, I'll ask."

"You want to get permission to do this?" Kate asked.

"No," Sara said. "I plan to hit them up for money."

They looked at her in surprise.

"That place is a mess," Sara said. "We can't invite people to return when we don't even know if the toilets are working. And what about sheets, and dishes, and all the furniture we're going to need?"

"They won't pay for that," Randal said.

Sara gave a little smile. "They will if I tell them that if they don't pay for it, I'll make sure the house is held up in court as a murder scene. It'll be years before they can sell it. And as Kate pointed out, was it legal for them to sell off pieces of land? And to denude the house of its contents? I bet there were some antiques in there. I'll point out that if they pay, they'll get the murder solved quietly and discreetly. And if Jack and his crew repair it at rock-bottom prices, maybe no one will mention what's missing. It's a win-win for them."

Jack was the first to laugh. "I feel sorry for them. I hope they don't argue too long so you don't have to raise the price."

"My thoughts exactly," Sara said.

"Dora!" Kate said. "She has cleaning friends who have retired. I bet they'd like a special job."

For a moment they all thought of the big house in Southwest Ranches, where Dora lived. It was inhabited by people they'd met while solving crimes. Ava was back in Chicago with her brothers, while Everett and Arthur were in Arizona researching their next murder mystery. Only Dora and Lenny were there now.

"What about Lenny?" Sara asked. "He could use a job."

"He'd scare people," Jack said. Lenny had a deep scar across the side of his head from a gunshot he'd survived. It had been remarked more than once that Lenny could play the villain in a horror movie.

"Did you know that he can cook?" Randal was a champion of people who were down-and-out. "Billy had caterers but I had to make midnight sandwiches and scramble eggs at 5:00 a.m. Lenny could do that."

"That leaves us with The Lady herself," Jack said. "Miss Adair."

"My L.A. agent can contact her," Sara said. "I can't imagine that she'll come."

They turned to Randal as though to ask him if she would.

"Don't look at me. She was a nobody back then. Married to a big deal producer, who she left at home."

"Didn't she fool around with Roy?" Sara was being sarcastic after Billy's many mentions of the fact.

"I believe there were a few motorcycle rides—and before you judge, her husband was much older than she was. And don't forget that *all* of these guests were being blackmailed by Derek Oliver."

Sara frowned. "If Miss Adair was being blackmailed for having an affair, it doesn't make sense that she'd have another one while hanging around her blackmailer."

"Could have been a two-for-one deal," Jack said. "With my father, who knows?"

It was getting late and they were beginning to clean up. "What about the house?" Kate asked. "Dora cleans it, but then what? There's hardly any furniture left. Even the dishes are gone."

"I thought about that." Sara looked at Jack. "You need to make a sketch of the rooms with measurements, then Kate will go to Baer's Furniture, spend a day with Rico, and choose everything." She turned to Kate. "Rico is brilliant and he'll help with all of it, including artwork and accessories. And it just happens that this week Baer's is having a 50 percent off sale on everything in the store. It's perfect." She picked up a bowl of salad and headed to the kitchen.

"Wait!" Kate ran after her aunt. "I don't know how to do that! We should get Ivy to do it."

"She's on a job in St. Petersburg," Jack said. Ivy was his half sister and an interior designer.

"I told you," Sara said, "Rico will help you. He has impeccable taste and knows everything about furniture. Baer's has modern pieces and items from all over the world. And you'll have Jack's plan so you have the sizes. You won't have any problems." She went on to the kitchen.

"I don't know how to do this," Kate whispered.

"You'll do fine," Randal said and followed his sister.

"Buy sturdy beds." Jack smiled as he carried dishes to the kitchen.

FIVE

SARA SUPPRESSED A YAWN. SHE'D BEEN UP SINCE four and she'd accomplished a lot. Sometimes she forgot what her life was like when she was writing full-time. She used to have fourteen-hour workdays, and it wasn't unusual for her to continue through the weekend. It was only later, when she started traveling, that her long days were broken up.

But last night and this morning had been full of things she wanted to accomplish. The feeling that she'd done it all gave her a sense of satisfaction that she hadn't felt in a long time.

The smell of bacon made her put her laptop aside and get dressed. She had a lot to tell the others.

The first thing she saw, intuited really, was that Jack and Kate had not consummated their relationship. There was still that brother-sister feeling between them. How very much she wanted that to end!

Randal, beautifully dressed, came in from the guesthouse and told them he'd cleared his calendar. He didn't fool his sister. She could feel his excitement under his cool exterior. It was easy to guess that he was looking forward to seeing Lea Oliver again. But at the same time, she could feel his trepidation. Older, years full of life, et cetera. There had been many changes.

When Sara got to the kitchen counter, they looked at her expectantly.

"I saw your light on at four," Jack said. "What have you found out?"

"Why were you wandering around the house?" Her meaning was clear. *Why weren't you in bed with Kate and too "busy" to see lights under my door?*

Jack knew what she meant and smiled as though to say it was none of her business. He handed her a plate of bacon and eggs and an almond flour muffin.

Sara ate quickly, then stepped back to look at the others. "I did the first part." She took a drink of her caffeinated water. "I called Billy and got the private number of his eldest brother and called him. I point-blank asked him about the cheap way he's treated his youngest brother and about clearing out Lachlan House over the years. Of course, nothing was admitted, but the expense of housing Billy in the best suite of rooms has been taken on by his family. And—" she paused, smiling "—we now have a carte blanche expense account for repairing and refurnishing." She looked at Kate. "Rico will meet you at the store at eight, before it opens, and you may buy whatever you want. Make Lachlan House beautiful."

"But I don't know how to do that," Kate said yet again.

Still, no one believed her.

"Who's coming?" Jack asked.

Sara looked at her brother and he nodded. "It looks like Lea Oliver will be there for sure. I hope you don't mind, but I gave us a date. Everyone is to arrive eight days before the expiration date stated in James Lachlan's will. The party is to

last four days, which means that we'll have four days afterward to… I don't know what we'll need to do. Anyway, this
gives us an entire eleven days before their arrival to clean,
repair, and furnish the house."

"Eleven days?" Jack sounded ready to laugh at the absurdity. "Plumbing? Electrical? The kitchen needs to be gutted.
I can't—"

Sara waved her hand. "Of course you can do it."

Randal was leaning back on his stool. "And what, may I
ask, Sergeant Major, am I to do?"

Sara ignored his snide tone. "You're to help Kate. I suggest
you get Jack's room measurements, then you and Billy go online and visit Rugs.com. What they have is in stock and they
can ship it fast. If not, you can drive to South Carolina and
pick up the rugs you two choose." She looked at the three of
them. "Any questions?"

"Who else is coming?" Jack asked.

"No other acceptances yet, but the invitations have been
sent out. My L.A. agent said it would be no problem to get
a message to Barbara Adair. Billy's brothers know Rachel's
family. He also told me that the grandmother of Reid is still
alive, so he'll contact her. I'll let you know when I hear from
them." She looked at Jack. "I need two strong men and a big
truck. Not a pickup. Bigger. I'm going to empty those storage units."

"At last," Jack said. He oversaw a lot of Sara's accounting, so
he knew she'd been paying rental fees for years. "How about
Gil and Juan meet you there in thirty minutes?"

"Perfect," Sara said. "Any more questions? Everyone knows
what they're to do?"

"How's Sheriff Flynn?" Kate asked. "He's alone in the
house."

Randal spoke up. "I called his wife, Evie, and she showed

up with wine and burgers. The top floor is locked, and Daryl said he has no plan to tell her what's up there. When I talked to him, he was feeling no pain."

"Good job," Sara said. "Jack, will you give me a ride to the storage units? Kate, take my car. Baer's doesn't deliver lamps and my back seat folds down. It holds more." With a wide grin, she started to her room. "I never did take photos of the house. I'm going to do a magnificent before-and-after spread."

When they were alone, Jack, Kate, and Randal looked at each other.

"I feel like I just survived a tsunami," Kate said.

"My sister is—" Randal began, but when they heard Sara's door click, they scurried apart. They had been given work to do.

Six

BARBARA ADAIR

BARBARA'S AGENT SENT HER A HAND-DELIVERED letter. One of the perks of her success was that she didn't have to answer calls or texts or emails. "If they want me, they know where I live," she would say. "And if they don't know where I live, then..." She always dramatically left the end of that sentence unfinished.

"Sell it, baby," her husband, Harry, used to say. "Remind them of who they believe you are." He'd died years before, but she still missed him.

She took the envelope into the kitchen. As always, her son was eating. At his age, calories just added muscle. Barbara knew that if she so much as nibbled a tortilla chip the weight would show up in her next film.

"What is it?" he asked, his mouth full.

"Another invitation, I guess," she said. She knew people didn't care if she showed up or not, just that the internet said she was there. She slit the heavy vellum open. Her agent believed in elegance. "I'm invited to go to—" When she saw the name "Lachlan," she felt dizzy. Only years of training made her able to stay upright. What had they found out? If that odious man, Derek Oliver, could discover the truth, others could too. It was so long ago that maybe now it wouldn't matter. But she knew that wasn't true. Old scandals were the love of the tabloids—and of that awful thing called "social media."

She put the invitation back into the envelope, acting as though it meant nothing to her, then put it in the roll out trash bin. Her hands were shaking.

"Someone else trying to use you as a stepping stone?" her son asked.

"How clever you are!" she said enthusiastically. "You always see through to the truth. I, uh… I have to make some calls. Are you going out today?"

"I thought I'd go see Phil and the guys. You'll be okay alone?"

"Perfectly. Take the Porsche."

"Thanks." He smiled at her fondly.

The minute she left the room, he got the envelope out of the trash. He hadn't been fooled by her act. Since he was a child, he'd been able to tell the actress from his "real" mother. He and his dad used to laugh about it. Sometimes they'd chant, "Real! Real! Real!" and she would drop the facade the cameras so adored. He and his dad loved the woman whose hair tended to fly about, who had circles under her eyes, and liked to tear off her nails. Her favorite outfit was a gray sweat suit with paint stains.

When he read the invitation, his heart seemed to stop. Lachlan? He knew what that meant.

He memorized the date, then carefully put the envelope back in the trash, exactly in the way he'd found it. His mother had an excellent memory for detail. She often corrected the set dresser when things were out of place from where they'd been the day before. She might see that her invitation wasn't exactly where she'd tossed it. Or, more likely, she'd return to put it in the garbage disposal.

Minutes later, she did just that, but by then her son was

bent over his phone and seemingly oblivious to all that was around him. He ignored the sound of the disposal.

That night when she said that she had to go see a site location and that she'd be gone for a few days, he didn't so much as look up from his video controller. "Sure. See you when you get back."

As soon as she left the room, he booked a plane ticket. One way, just in case. Like his father had been, he was a great believer in things happening for a reason.

RACHEL MEYERS TOLLMAN

The housekeeper handed Rachel a FedEx envelope, saying she'd had to sign for it to acknowledge receipt.

Rachel murmured thanks and the woman left, closing the door behind her. Rachel was in her office, her sanctuary in the big house. She'd inherited the eighteenth-century desk from her dear grandmother. "A life well lived," she used to say. "It's all you can hope for."

Rachel pulled the tab to open the envelope, and when she saw the name on the letter, she sat down hard. Lachlan House. That conjured up memories that she'd long ago buried. She did *not* want to bring them back to life.

For a moment, the memories overtook her. *What we did together,* she thought. *The two of us, both of us so very angry.*

She'd thought that what they'd done was forgotten—or at least undiscovered. But here it was. They wanted her to return to… To do what? Confess?

She closed her eyes for a moment. What was that animal? Was it a weasel? No. Something English. A hedgehog. Had it been found? Was that why Rachel was being invited to return?

It belonged to little Kate. What a child she was! Always

sticking her nose into everything. She'd be grown now. What did she know? What did she see? Did she remember any of it?

Rachel dropped the letter on the pretty desk. She knew she had to go. She had to at last bear the consequences of what she'd done. What *they* had done.

Her cell phone buzzed. It was an unknown number. In normal circumstances, she wouldn't answer it, but maybe it was the arrival of the letter that made her feel that she must answer. She didn't know it, but it was a call that would change her life.

"Hello? Yes, speaking." She leaned back against her chair and listened to the voice from the past.

REID GRAHAM III

Alish sent her grandson a text. For all of her great age, she liked technology.

Come home! Roy's son and those Medlars are recreating that week. You must be there!

When the text came through, Reid was in a meeting. His company's officers were staring at him in silence, waiting for his next orders. Reid liked to stay in control, a trait he'd inherited from his grandmother.

When his cell played the tune of that little Scottish ballad, he halted. His grandmother wasn't texting to ask how his day was going.

Reid turned his back on them and read what she'd sent.

The blood drained from his face, and he had to put his hand on the back of his big leather chair to steady himself. It wouldn't do to pass out in front of his staff.

From great self-control—which he'd had to teach himself—he stayed upright and turned to them. "I have to go away for a few days. My grandmother…" He didn't finish, but they nodded in understanding. They all knew he had a ninety-four-year-old grandmother. They'd never met her, but from the little they knew, they assumed she was a sweet little old lady who'd grown up in a quaint village in Scotland. Probably wore plaid everything and ate bannocks. *If they only knew*, Reid thought.

He turned to his VP and gave a curt nod. The man would take over while the boss was away.

Swiftly, Reid left the building. As he expected, his assistant had called ahead and the valet had his Maserati ready, the engine running, and Reid drove out of the city. It would take him about three hours to get to sleepy little Lachlan. Or maybe not so sleepy. In the last few years his grandmother had sent him info about murders in Lachlan—and how they'd been solved. "Roy's son is part of it," she'd written. "And so is Kate. Her famous aunt is back in town and they work together."

As he crossed the long, beautiful bridge, his hands tightened on the leather-wrapped steering wheel. Little Kate. She'd be about twenty-six now. She was a cute child so she might have grown up to be a beauty.

He got on I-75, headed down toward Naples and Alligator Alley, and thought, *Lord help us, but what does Kate remember? And the others? Have they found out anything about the past? About Greer? What she knew? What she* did?

LEA OLIVER

A ghost from the past, Lea Oliver thought when she received the invitation via email. At the sight of the name, Lachlan

House, a wave of beautiful memories went through her. Randal and Kate and her. She'd seen the three of them as the perfect family, something she'd always dreamed of. Other little girls imagined their weddings, but Lea had always thought of a home and children and a husband who made her laugh. Randal had certainly done that! He said he'd given up hope of finding love again, that he'd thought it was out of his reach forever.

The wonderful, glorious week in that big, beautiful house had made her think it could happen. Lea's husband wanted a divorce, and Randal couldn't abide his wife. He said separation would be difficult, but he could do it. He just needed time.

After a night of lovemaking under the palms, they'd parted with kisses, full of the joy they foresaw ahead of them. She trusted him to take care of his wife, so really, the only obstacle was Derek. She knew that if he were removed, all their problems would be solved.

But in spite of the path being cleared, she didn't get together with Randal and Kate.

In fact, she hadn't heard from him since they parted twenty-five years ago. Unfortunately, she'd been told what happened to him. How Mrs. Meyers had cried! She said that after Randal was taken away, little Kate had been catatonic for days. When she came back to life, the child seemed to have forgotten her father completely. After the hurried trial, Kate's mother—an extremely unpleasant woman—had taken dear little Kate away to cold, snowy Chicago. All Lea's attempts to contact them had failed.

For a while, Lea hoped Randal would reach out to her, but he didn't. And she hadn't had the courage to contact him.

Gradually, life had taken over. Derek had two unmarried cousins who were destitute. He'd conned them into "investing" with him. That meant living rich to impress people. As always, he lost everything.

When Lea had a business idea, they gladly helped out. Without Derek hovering over them, the women flourished.

Lea looked at the invitation and considered what to do. She had no doubt that this had something to do with Derek— which meant that it was bad. Maybe even very bad. But did the good of seeing Randal and Kate outweigh the risk?

Smiling, she sent the single word "Yes" to the email she'd received. Then she tried to decide what to pack, but nothing was good enough. In the end, she went shopping. Randal deserved to see her looking her best.

SEVEN

IT WAS NEARLY 5:00 P.M. WHEN RACHEL REACHED Lachlan. She'd almost forgotten how beautiful Florida was and how good the warm air smelled. She was glad she'd driven down from Connecticut, so she had her own car. She'd managed the long trip in three days. She was tired now and knew the best thing would be to go to a hotel in Fort Lauderdale and settle in for the night. She wasn't scheduled to arrive until tomorrow.

But when she saw the sign for Lachlan, she took the exit. She told herself she'd just drive by and look at the exterior of the house, then she'd leave.

The steering wheel seemed to turn on its own and before she knew it, she was pulling into the driveway of Lachlan House. Her first thought was what a shame that so many houses had been built nearby. The first time she'd been there, the big house had been surrounded by land and trees that still bore citrus fruit.

She couldn't keep herself from stopping the car and getting out. There were no lights on that she could see, so maybe the house was empty. It was probably prepared for when people arrived tomorrow.

The house looked good. The brick appeared to have been recently power washed and the woodwork had been freshly painted. She was glad to see the beautiful old house being cared for. She'd worried that lazy Billy had allowed it to go to ruin.

She stretched a bit, then started to get back into her car, but she hesitated. What was the back of the house like? And how was the big guesthouse? And what about the cute little cottage?

She took a moment to decide, then she walked around the side of the house to the back. Cautiously, she looked up at the house. If any lights were on, she'd leave. She didn't want to bother anyone with her early arrival. The house was dark.

Not far away, she could see the guesthouse. It too looked like it had been freshly scrubbed and painted. Through the trees, she could see the little cottage and it didn't look as though it had been touched in years. Vines covered it and the paint was peeling.

Rachel turned away, and to her surprise, she found herself heading toward the very back of the property. Was the mausoleum still there, or had Billy sold it off to buy yet another pair of Tod's loafers?

She was relieved to see that the mausoleum of James Lachlan and his wife was there, set under big trees and surrounded by bushes. It hadn't been cleaned, so green moss was on the two steps and up the sides. It was a plain stone structure. No angels weeping, no poetic sentiments carved into the stone. Beside the heavy double doors was a plaque, giving the names and dates of James Lachlan and his wife, Mary. He was born in 1895, died 1981, while she was born in 1899 and died in 1944.

Her death date brought back memories. Billy used to darken

the room, light some candles, and tell them the story of James Lachlan's horrible year of 1944. She had an idea that a lot of it was made up, but it was great drama. It ended with liqueurs and everyone trying to guess what happened to Mr. Lachlan's son. The consensus was that he'd joined the army and was lost.

"Did you know them?"

Rachel didn't jump at the voice. She'd figured someone might see her car. Turning, she saw a tall young man, blond, and pleasant looking. About fourteen or fifteen, in the awkward stage between boy and man. He wasn't the kind of boy that would make the hearts of teenage girls do somersaults. *Too bad*, she thought, as this young man was what girls needed. "No, I didn't know them." She was working not to smile at his assumption that she was old enough to know someone born in 1895. But at forty-one, she sometimes felt that old. "They were long before my time. I like the quiet here. Who are you?"

"Quinn Underhill," he answered. "My dad and Jack redid the house."

She thought for a moment. "Jack Wyatt? Roy's son? He was just a kid when I was here. He was a very pretty boy."

"Dad says he's too pretty for his own good."

She smiled. "So was Roy. He was good at fixing things."

Quinn nodded. "Dad and Jack are partners now. They renamed the company Lachlan Construction. Better than Wyatt-Underhill."

"Too much like a Hobbit?"

His eyes brightened. "That's just what she said."

"Your mother?"

"No. Sara said that. My mother died last year."

"I'm sorry," she said, and meant it.

"It's okay. I didn't know her. Dad says I'm the product of a one-night stand." He said it as though he might have to defend himself.

Rachel looked him up and down. "I'd say it was a pretty good night for your father."

He laughed at that. When it started to sprinkle, he ducked his head. "Come inside and I'll show you the house."

She couldn't imagine that the boy was there alone. "I don't want to wake anyone. I'm a day early. I'll go to a hotel, but tonight I couldn't resist looking at the place."

"It's just Dad here, and he could sleep through a storm. We'll be quiet."

His persuasion, coupled with her desire to see the place, won. The soft Florida rain was beginning to come down harder. They ran together and he went to a door at the back of the house and opened it.

They were in the kitchen. It was a room that Billy had cared nothing about. Barbara had said it was so decrepit it was a health hazard. "Billy!" she'd yelled one day. "Next hurricane, open the kitchen door and let it sweep this away." He'd just laughed.

But now it was modern and beautiful. "Wow," was all Rachel could say.

Quinn puffed up his chest a bit. "Dad got the cabinets from a house he remodeled. The woman didn't like maple and wanted black. He said he'd have them painted but she wanted all new."

Rachel and Quinn exchanged looks of agreement on the absurdity of that. "But it worked out. I like the cabinets. And you kept the table." She ran her hand over the gash in it. "I remember when Kate did that. I thought Lea was going to call the sheriff." She looked at Quinn. "Is Kate still around? She'd be grown up now."

"Yeah, she is. Dad said she and Jack are sort of engaged."

"Sort of?"

Quinn shrugged. He had no idea what that meant.

He started to lead her through the house, but she knew it so well that she went first. The smell of paint was strong, and all the furniture had that look of brand-new, never been sat on. Besides the new things, there was art from around the world. A huge toad made of jade, Chinese embroideries, divine rugs everywhere.

"This is beautiful," she said. "I always hated the old furniture. I think James Lachlan thought it was what rich people had."

"He was rich."

"But not born into it. There's a difference," Rachel said.

They went through every room on the ground floor. The little library had been stocked with books on history, and the office had a big oak desk. Before Quinn showed her how to open the door leading down to the cellar, she did it. She wanted to test her memory of the house.

It was an hour before they finished. They couldn't go upstairs, not with Quinn's father up there, but Rachel didn't want to leave. She was a believer in houses feeling the spirit of their owners. When Billy was in charge, it had been a place to show off. Now it felt like a home.

She looked at Quinn. "I make a mean grilled cheese sandwich. Would you like one?"

He was a teenage boy. Of course he was hungry. With a grin, he nodded at her and they went back to the kitchen.

She was happy to see that the big new stainless steel refrigerator was fully stocked. As she put six slices of bread on the flat grill, a wicked thought came to her. This might be her only chance to see something that had intrigued her for years. "When I was here," she said slowly, "Billy kept one room upstairs closed off. No one was allowed to enter it." That wasn't quite true; only *she* had been excluded from it.

Quinn looked blank.

"It was Mr. Lachlan's private den and it wasn't to be touched."

"Oh," Quinn said. She'd poured hot tomato soup into a tall mug and he drank it in one gulp. "That's the movie room. Jack told us hands off. Dora cleaned it but it's the same. I like the wallpaper."

"Oh?" She pulled popcorn out of the microwave. "I bet it's pretty." She put the sandwiches, popcorn, more soup, and glasses of ginger ale on a big tray. When Quinn reached for a sandwich, she pulled the tray back a bit. "I wonder what the movies are."

"Old VHS. Nothing new."

Rachel sighed. "I bet no one today knows how to work a VHS machine."

"I do," Quinn said, and again reached for a sandwich. But this time when she held it back, he understood. "We can take this upstairs and watch an old movie."

"What a great idea." Rachel smiled sweetly at him.

He carried the tray and she followed him, pleased with herself for arranging to see the "secret room." Billy had been such a jerk about it, saying she was too young to go in there. She might destroy something.

The old-fashioned room was better than she'd imagined. No wonder James Lachlan had retreated to it. There was a big couch, and Quinn set the tray on the leather ottoman before digging in. As she looked over the movies in their thick plastic cases, she came to one that had a cover that was nearly worn through. She pulled it out. *Only Once* was the title. When she saw that it came out in 1946, a mere two years after what Billy dramatically called "James Lachlan's Year of Death," she wanted to see it.

Quinn was busy eating, so Rachel popped the tape into the machine and turned out the room lights. It was a black-

and-white movie starring Taylor Caswell. "Never heard of him," she said, and Quinn looked at her as though to say he'd never heard of a movie not in color.

When the young actor came onto the screen, Rachel did a double take. "He looks like Roy."

"Looks like Jack," Quinn said sleepily.

"I guess when you get down to it, all TDH look alike." He was starting to nod off and didn't ask what TDH was. "Tall, dark, and handsome," she murmured, and settled back to watch.

It was about a seriously deranged young man who enticed plain-faced women to fall in love with him, stole what they had, then murdered them. The movie made it seem that the women thought death was part of their ecstasy. They didn't fight him. It didn't make any sense, but due to the charisma and skills of the actor, it was believable. Rachel looked the movie up on her phone. "A cult classic," it said. "Still selling today and watched in theaters all over the world, especially in midnight showings. Viewers tend to wear costumes of the victims."

"Never heard of it," Rachel said, but Quinn was asleep and didn't hear her.

She was halfway through the movie when a ghost appeared. At least it seemed so. A very large man, shirtless, with pale skin gleaming, and wearing only low-riding sweatpants, came into the room and stared down at her. She blinked up at him. "Are you real?" she asked. He was quite, quite muscular. Her eyes were wide.

"All of me is very real," he said in a voice of liquid honey. When he stepped near Rachel, she didn't move away. Bending, he slung tall, lanky Quinn over one broad shoulder and carried him out of the room.

Rachel sat still, not sure what she should do. Leave? She

wasn't supposed to have arrived yet, so she should go. But she didn't want to. Before she could decide what to do, the man returned. He'd pulled on a sweatshirt touting the Kansas City Chiefs, and he took Quinn's place on the couch. He picked up a handful of popcorn.

"So what's this movie about?"

She leaned back. "See that man? He kills women, but before he does, he makes them very happy."

"Through sex or by doing the housework for them?"

She laughed. "It's the 1940s. Women did the housework in heels and pearls. This guy did it with great sex."

"Cool," he said. "Does he get caught?"

"I hope not," she said, and they laughed together, then watched the rest of the movie.

★

The next morning, Gil, dressed all in denim, was in the kitchen early. Coffee was perking when Sara came through the front door and went to the back. He smiled as she was holding a can of caffeinated water. Since Sara didn't drink coffee, she had only recently discovered caffeine. Gil and Jack tried to outdo each other in finding her the strongest, no calorie drinks that put pizzaz in her step.

"Today's the day," Sara said. "They'll start arriving about ten."

"One of them came last night."

"Who?" she asked.

Before Gil could answer, Quinn came to the door. "Where is she?"

"Still asleep, I guess," Gil answered.

"I looked, and she's gone." He sounded angry. "I'll find

her." Quinn hurried out of the room and they heard the front door slam.

Sara blinked a few times. "Did a teenage girl show up?"

"No. It's Rachel Meyers—or whatever her name is now. I assume she took her husband's name. I was asleep when she arrived, so Quinn played host."

"Your silent son, who hardly talks to anyone, was the host?"

"Yes. He took her on a tour of the house, and they made grilled cheese sandwiches and soup and popcorn. Then they went upstairs and watched some old black-and-white movie together. Quinn fell asleep and I had to carry him to bed."

"Then what?" Sara asked.

"Nothing."

Sara looked at him. "You blush worse than Jack does. Even the top of your head has gone red. What happened after Quinn went to bed?"

"Nothing. Really. She and I watched the rest of the movie together, and we ate popcorn. She fell asleep and I carried her to bed."

"My, my, my," Sara said. "You certainly had a busy evening. And now Quinn wants to see her again. What about you?"

Gil didn't smile. "As I said, she's married. Taken. Not available."

"So where is she? And don't pretend you don't know."

"Out by the mausoleum."

"That place needs trimming. Cleaning. It's going to take hours of work."

Gil cracked a small smile. "My thoughts exactly." He set his half-full coffee cup in the sink and practically ran out of the room.

Eight

LEA ARRIVED ON THE APPOINTED DAY AT 10:00 A.M. sharp. Sara told her brother he was to greet her, but Randal ran away like a frightened two-year-old. Sara called out, "You have to face her soon."

"I will," he called back, then disappeared among the trees. She hoped he wasn't going to the cottage. She'd made sure it was locked, but her brother could open any door.

Sara started toward the front, but Kate came running down the stairs at an Olympic speed, passed her aunt without seeing her, and flung open the heavy front door.

Sara watched from the windows. Lea Oliver was a pretty woman, dark blond hair, a trim figure, and a nice smile. She wasn't one to send men into fits of lust. She was what people used to refer to as "wife material." It was an old-fashioned term that was frowned on in modern times, but it certainly fit this woman.

She and Kate stared at each other for a few minutes, saying nothing, then they fell into each other's arms. They were reuniting friends who didn't let a little thing like time hinder them.

When Sara turned away from the window, she was smiling all the way down to her bone marrow. She was a true believer in love being multiplied, not divided. She loved Kate so much that she was glad to see other people who felt the same way.

Sara went back to the library, where she was organizing the books she'd had in storage. It was great to see them again. She sent a text to Jack to ask him to please come over on his motorcycle at 1:00 p.m. She had a special errand for him. She felt a bit wicked for doing it, but that's when Barbara Adair was to arrive. Jack on his father's Harley might refresh her memories.

At eleven thirty, Sara realized that she hadn't heard from Kate. Shouldn't she be introducing her friend to everyone?

When Sara got to the kitchen, Lenny was there. She was used to his appearance but his scarred face was still startling. He was making a platter of Florida fruits, with pineapple and papaya at the center.

He looked at her as though to ask what she needed.

"Have you seen Kate?"

"She's with the new woman in the movie room." Lenny had an uncanny ability to know what was going on and where.

Sara frowned. "You think she's okay?"

Lenny took a plate from a cabinet, filled it with the fruit, and held it out. He always used as few words as possible.

"Good idea," Sara said. "Take some up to them and see what's going on." She stood below as he went up to the second floor.

Lenny gave a quick knock on the Palm Room, then opened the door. Kate's tear-filled voice said, "She's so young and now I have two half brothers."

He closed the door and went back down to Sara. "Someone needs to see to Kate." His voice was stern, brooking no argument. They all knew he liked Kate very much.

Frowning, Sara went upstairs and quietly opened the door. Kate was saying, "They took my daddy away. He was my entire world. I had no one else."

Sara closed the door and went back down. When she saw her brother, she told him to go to the Palm Room. Now. She didn't allow him to hesitate.

Sara and Lenny stayed below and looked up, waiting for Randal to give them a report.

As the others had done, he quietly opened the door. Kate was saying to Lea, "And Jack hasn't said *anything* since then! I'm glad he's so respectful, but a girl wants more! You know what I mean?"

"Oh yes, I do!" Lea replied. "A *lot* more."

Randal closed the door and hurried down the stairs.

The three of them found Jack and sent him up to check on Kate.

"She needs you," Sara said.

"And you three aren't enough for her?" Obviously not pleased, he went upstairs and opened the door. He heard Kate say, "All those years and all her fits of depression, and *she* did it! I was *not* the cause!" He closed the door.

Jack went back down the stairs and looked at them.

"Well?" Sara asked.

"I think this is what you women call 'a good cry,'" he said, then mumbled, "But not good for me." He quickly left the house.

"She has a lot to cry about." Lenny gave Sara and Randal a look of reproach before going back to the kitchen.

Randal put his hands in his pocket and said, "Lea is great, isn't she?" He left the house whistling.

★

Barbara was driving the rental car from the airport toward Lachlan House. She hadn't been this nervous since her first show on Broadway. Harry had arranged that for her. As often happened, all she had to do was say she'd always dreamed of that, and *voilà!* she was offered the starring role. That she did it without pay and Harry's company was in charge of the publicity had helped. She'd had to endure a little backstabbing from the other players, but not too bad.

Her hands on the steering wheel were shaking. When she'd first thought about how to appear in Lachlan, she'd imagined arriving in a limo. She'd have twenty pieces of matching luggage, and she'd do the full star treatment. Dazzle them. She'd let Roy's son, Jack, kiss her hand.

But in the end, she couldn't do it. She wanted them to *like* her. She decided she'd play Susan from *Sunday Morning,* one of her top grossing movies. She packed a corn-fed wardrobe. Should she put her hair in braids?

It was her son who made her realize how ridiculous she was being.

"Mom," he said. "Are you going to arrive singing 'Surrey with the Fringe on Top'?"

Children could be brutal. In the end, she packed her own clothes in a couple of Harry's beat-up old suitcases—and twelve pounds of makeup in a separate case. A woman had to look good, didn't she?

She flew first class, wearing the necessary heavy sunglasses and a designer jacket. She spent the night in downtown Fort Lauderdale, right on Broward, and the next morning, she took her time getting ready to go.

So now butterflies were doing leaps in her stomach—which

wasn't nearly as flat as she'd like it to be. She thought of their reason for restaging that party.

Exactly what did they know? Billy had been so afraid of his father and brothers that at first he'd kept the Palm Room locked tight. Fortunately, that hadn't slowed her down in getting inside it. All she'd had to do was bat her lashes at gorgeous Roy Wyatt and she was in.

Roy, she thought. *Roy, Roy, Roy.*

His son, cute little Jack, would be grown up by now. She'd only seen him once. He was ten or eleven and he'd looked at his father with angry, resentful eyes. She'd tried to talk to him, but he wanted nothing to do with her.

"Leave him alone," Roy said. "He likes his new dad better than me." There was pain in his voice.

Maybe it was the pain she felt coming from Roy that made her first notice him. Or maybe it was his deep, rich, male voice. Or his beautiful face and his big, muscular body. More likely, it was the pure, undiluted maleness that surrounded him. It was a strong contrast to her life at home!

At a stoplight, she closed her eyes in memory. She'd only spent a week near Roy, but it had been everything to her.

The driver in the car behind her tapped the horn. She waved an apology and continued driving. *What do they know?* she wondered. *Of course it had to do with that bastard, Derek Oliver. He'd found out the truth. Had these people also figured it out?*

Please, she thought, *don't let them know what happened. Please.*

She slowly pulled into the wide concrete driveway of Lachlan House. There were a couple of cars there, one a cute red-roofed MINI Cooper. Beside it was a pickup truck so battered it looked like it had been used to haul angry bears.

Roy drove a truck just like that, she thought as she got out of the car. As she looked up at the house, her mind filled with memories. She and Roy'd had to sneak about, but after Derek Oliver was gone, they'd had nothing but joy.

She was so deep in her thoughts that she didn't hear the rumble of the motorcycle until it was almost in front of her. And when she did hear it, she froze. Every sense, her eyes, ears, and even her skin, put themselves on hold. Coming toward her was Roy's Harley. She'd recognize it anywhere.

And sitting on it was a man who had a broad-shouldered, long-legged body that was exactly like Roy's. He stopped a few feet from her and took off his black helmet.

"Hello," he said.

It was Roy's body, Roy's face, Roy's voice.

Barbara Adair fainted.

★

Sara saw Jack carrying the inert movie star into the living room. Kate, her eyes red but face smiling, hurried down the stairs, with Lea close behind her. *Great*, Sara thought, *Kate seems to have acquired yet another mother.* She hoped three was the limit.

At the sight of Barbara Adair, everyone came out of wherever they were and gravitated toward her. *What was she like in life?* they seemed to ask.

But Sara went the other way, sliding into the shadows, deeply glad that everyone was busy elsewhere. There was nothing an introvert liked better than disappearing. "They" were occupied so she could slip away, unseen, with no one asking where she was.

When she got outside, she had a feeling of freedom. For days she'd wanted to go to the little cottage that was on the edge of the property. She didn't want to just look at it but to sink down into the memories it held. So far, she hadn't had time to risk an escape for fear someone would find her and ask, "What do you want to do with...?"

Endless questions were an introvert's nightmare.

So now, maybe a big deal movie star would keep everyone busy for at least an hour. Sara hoped the woman was a drama queen, asking them to fetch and carry for her. That might give Sara two whole hours of peace.

She had to push her way through the tough stems of plants. A couple of iguanas sauntered away. They were about four feet long and glistening colorfully in the bits of sun that came through the tall palms.

When she got to the front door, she had to stop to calm herself. She hadn't been here since she'd been with Cal. Even though it was long ago, she could still feel all those emotions.

He'd had a key made for her, and he'd hidden it rather cleverly in a metal box he'd made in his father's car shop. She hoped it was still there. As she bent to retrieve it, she heard a noise and saw a movement. Someone was there!

"Damn, damn, triple damn," she said under her breath, while thinking that she should go get Lenny or Jack to deal with the trespasser.

"Oh!" said a male voice.

She stood up to see a man, probably forties. He was dark and good-looking. *It's funny how you more easily forgive beautiful people*, she thought. She smiled at him.

"I'm sorry I startled you. I shouldn't be here," he said. "I just wanted to see the place again. Are you Miss Medlar?"

"Sara," she said. "Are you Reid?"

"Yes." He smiled at her. Nice teeth. "I'll go and leave you alone. You must want to see the place. Cal used to say—" With a hand wave, he took a step back. "I'll see you later."

"Wait," she said. "You knew Cal?"

"Yes, I did. Not well, but he came here to help Roy with

the maintenance work. Roy had, uh, well...other things to do, so Cal did the yard work for him." Reid looked up at the cottage. "Cal said this was a..." He frowned in memory. "What was it he said? Oh right. He said this building was 'a precious place.'"

Sara nodded in agreement, unable to say anything.

"You probably know that my sister and I stayed in here during the week of the house party."

"Yes." His words reminded her that she needed to get back to the business of why they were there. She cocked her head to one side. "Was Derek Oliver blackmailing you too?"

He seemed shocked at her bluntness but he recovered quickly. "Blackmail? Is that what he was doing to them? I guessed it was something nefarious. It certainly wasn't friend-ship." He smiled. "But alas, I had nothing he could have wanted. He hired me to take care of the house and do any-thing that was needed. To tell the truth, I was quite young and pretty worthless, but Billy told Mr. Oliver that I was part of the tradition of the house so I had to be hired." He gave a sheepish grin. "Actually, Cal covered for both Roy and me."

They stood there for a moment, listening to the breeze and the iguanas slowly moving about. "I can go get the key if you'd like to go inside."

Sara bent, pulled up a slab of slate, removed a key from a metal box, and held it up. "I have one."

"So that's how Cal got in." He took a step back. "I'll leave you then." His eyes twinkled. "And I won't tell anyone where you are."

That he understood made her smile. Part of her wanted to ask him to stay, but the bigger part wanted to see the cottage by herself. "They're inside the house. Barbara Adair arrived minutes ago."

"I've seen many of her movies. When I knew her, I never

guessed she'd became famous. All she seemed to want was—"
He broke off.

"Roy?"

He grinned. "You have been doing your homework. After
Mr. Oliver left, she said her life had changed. We all thought
she and Roy would stay together, but…" He shrugged. "Sorry,
I'm gossiping. It's going to be interesting to see everyone."
He took another step back. "Not to be nosy, but has Rachel
arrived?"

"She has." Sara looked at him. "Do you mind staying in
the guesthouse?"

"I would love that. It gives me privacy." He waved his hand
to indicate the cottage. "I'd like to make up for the work I
didn't do before. I'll go buy a weed whacker and you can tell
me how you want this place landscaped. Or—" he paused
"—I could just do it the way Cal did it."

"Yes," she said. "The way Cal wanted it done."

"I'll see you soon." He turned away and went through the
shrubs toward the house.

Sara watched him go. The key was tight in her hand and
when she looked at the door, she changed her mind. *Not yet*,
she thought. She didn't want to see the inside now—and
maybe she didn't want to do it alone. She'd like Kate to be
with her. Sara feared that the memories of what did and what
didn't happen might overwhelm her. *Age did that*, she thought.
Memories of long ago were stronger than what happened in
the last years.

She put the key back in the box, replaced the stone, and
made her way to the back of the cottage. A tall fence had
been put up, but it was hidden by hibiscus bushes. No wonder there were iguanas. They loved to eat the pretty flowers.

She went as far from the back as possible so she could
see the stained glass window. Mr. Lachlan had it installed.

It didn't fit the style of the cottage and it was way too big, but still, it was glorious. When she turned toward it, Sara was glad to see that it was intact. It was of a knight on a horse and a pretty young woman in a window. The two people were looking at each other. Even in the old glass, they looked like they were in love.

The thought made her remember that Mr. Lachlan said, "Reminds me of you two." Then he'd walked away. The way he said it made her and Cal laugh, which of course sent them into spirals of lust. They made love on the prickly grass, the newly installed window to one side, palm trees on the other.

The memory brought such deep tears to Sara's eyes that she ran from the place. Ran all the way back to the house, then inside to the kitchen. She slammed the door behind her.

★

Lenny was in the kitchen and the afternoon light through the window exaggerated the scars on his face. Sara couldn't help blinking a few times. His looks were still disconcerting. "Is her royal highness okay?" she asked.

"Her audience seems to think so."

Sara chuckled. Lenny had the ability to sum up people quickly. Over the last years, everyone had asked him about his life, where he'd grown up, that kind of thing. But he never told anyone anything. Sara liked that about him. "I guess they're all with her."

Lenny nodded. "Even the new one. He likes Rachel."

Sara frowned. He meant Reid. "So do Gil and Quinn. I hope she isn't one of those conquer-'em-then-dump-'em types." She looked at her watch. "The caterers should be here soon. You planning to help or disappear?"

Lenny gave a small smile. "Like you do?"

Sara laughed. "Touché." Days before, Lenny had found an apartment over the garage and had claimed it as his own. He never said so, but she had an idea that he was fed up with living in the big house in Southwest Ranches. He got stuck with too many people to look after.

Sara left the kitchen, went through the house to the living room, then stopped in the doorway. As Lenny had said, the great and wondrous Barbara Adair was sitting on the sofa and everyone else was seated around her. She may as well have been on a stage.

Kate glanced up and saw her aunt.

Sara didn't want to join in the mini play so she held up four fingers, then opened her hands to represent a book. Kate nodded—4:00 p.m. in the library. She'd tell Jack and Randal.

Minutes later, the four of them were in the library.

"An AUL meeting?" Jack asked as he sat down, stretching out his long legs in a relaxed way.

Sara raised an eyebrow at him. "So you're the celebrity's golden boy." It wasn't a question.

Jack grinned but didn't reply.

Sara remained standing. "Yes. AUL." She was the one to coin the term. *Agreed Upon Lies.* They were going to consult about what they would tell the others. Truth or lies didn't matter. They had a goal to achieve.

Kate's eyes were less swollen and most of the red was gone, but there were still hints of the long, deep cry she'd had. "Lea is very nice. We had such a good chat."

The others turned to look at her, eyebrows raised. Pouring out her very soul was a "chat?"

Kate kept her eyes straight ahead and ignored them.

"Well, uh, okay." Sara looked at Jack. "What do you really think of her?" They knew who she meant. "Has she conquered you?"

Jack gave a male scoff. "Far from it. She passed out because I look like my father. He has a lot to answer for."

"She wouldn't let us call a doctor." There was a strong hint of fangirl in Kate's voice.

Sara managed not to roll her eyes. She'd had forty-plus years of being around so-called celebrities. They didn't impress her. She looked at her brother and didn't have to say what she wanted from him.

"Lea is fine," he said softly. His eyes locked with his sister's and she knew what he meant. There was still feeling between them.

"What about Rachel?" Jack asked. "Anyone talk to her?"

"Gil and Quinn seem to have fallen in love with her," Sara said.

The others looked at her in disbelief.

"What can I say?" Sara said. "Love at first sight happens even outside my books. I met Reid. Charming young man. So!" She looked from one to the other. "All in all, they are the most likable bunch of people I've ever met." Her voice was full of disgust. "If I were stranded on a deserted island, I'd want them with me. They are interesting and nice. Am I right?"

They looked at one another and nodded.

"But one of them is a murderer," Jack said.

"Sawed a man's head." Kate shrugged. "A real psycho."

"I think we need to find the motive," Randal said. "Everyone can be driven to murder if the cause is strong enough. We just need to figure out what it was."

"In four days." Sara sat down, her eyes saying that was an impossible task.

"Ask them," Jack said.

Randal smiled. "Which one of you delightful people killed Derek Oliver?"

"And replaced his brain with *my* hedgehog?" Kate was indignant.

"That I gave you." Sara was smiling. "Was it really your favorite toy?"

Kate looked at her father.

"Her very favorite. She never put it down. She—"

Jack stood up. "I hear cars. The caterers must be arriving. We need to agree on what lies we're going to tell."

Sara sighed. "We're going to have to tell them that we found the body. We don't have time to drag this out."

"And we'll see what they say," Jack said in agreement.

"Right," Kate said. "And we'll watch their reactions. We can—"

There was a knock on the door. Of course the caterers had questions. Where were the spoons?

When Kate saw her aunt look toward the window as though she was planning to climb through it, Kate opened the door. She followed the staff to the kitchen.

The three left behind looked at each other. The show was about to begin.

★

Dinner was lovely. Sara had ordered Wedgwood china, a service for twelve in the India pattern. The yellow design made a cheerful table. The food was a Florida feast of seafood, with lots of pineapple and coconut. Randal had chosen the wine. It had been a long time since he'd been taught the niceties of upper-class living by Derek Oliver's stepmother, but he remembered them.

Randal and Kate sat at opposite heads of the table and they were easy hosts. Father and daughter were alike in their ability to make people feel at ease. Randal made them laugh with a story of his time at Lachlan House with Mrs. Meyers and how he had to fetch hats and bags and reading glasses. Kate told of playing near the fountain. Everyone expressed astonishment that she remembered anything from that week, since she was so young.

They spoke of how good the house looked. "It's all cosmetic," Jack said modestly. "I didn't change the structure at all."

Barbara asked if anyone would mind if she explored the Palm Room. Rachel told of seeing an old black-and-white movie in there the night before.

"Did you?" Barbara asked.

Only Randal noticed that when she reached for her wineglass, she almost tipped the glass over.

Lea said she was glad to see everyone had prospered in life and was doing so well. Rachel was mostly quiet. She seemed to be studying everyone.

Reid was the only one who appeared to be uncomfortable. When he said that he'd never sat at the big table before, there was an awkward silence. He'd been an employee, not a guest. But then he turned to Jack and said, "And Roy wasn't allowed inside the house either."

"Not in this room anyway," Barbara said in a suggestive way.

Her meaning was so clear that they laughed and the tension was broken.

"We welcome you now," Lea said to Reid, and they raised their glasses to him.

Sara and Jack were sitting side by side. Neither of them were relaxed around strangers. They needed to get to know people first.

When Barbara started retelling Billy's Lonely Laird story, Sara turned to Jack and said softly, "What's bothering you?"

"Nothing." His words were terse.

"Ah. You were told what my brother overheard Kate saying."

Only a slight movement of his chin said yes. "What if I make a mess of it?"

She knew he wasn't talking about murder or the tableful of guests. As always, his major concern in life was Kate. "All the heroes in my books have ultimate confidence—until they fall in love. Then they're scared out of their minds."

"Great. Now I'm someone you made up."

She knew he meant that in a derogatory way, but she didn't take it as such. "You mean you're like my heroes? The kind of man women dream of? Hope for? That they spend their lives searching for?"

He gave a half smile.

"Did you buy her a ring?"

"Years ago. I carry it with me always."

Sara grinned at that. "Then take Kate and the ring and a bottle of champagne to the cottage. Let that place do its magic." She put her hand on his forearm. "Don't leave it too long."

Barbara's voice grew louder. Obviously, she didn't like having her storytelling ignored. Again, Sara repressed the urge to roll her eyes. She knew a bit about storytelling.

★

After dinner, they went to the pretty living room. Contrary to Kate's protests, she had decorated it beautifully. There was much less color than in Sara's house. Like most people of Kate's generation, she had a love of white rooms. Sara, who had researched the meaning of color for one of her books, said it was "opening your mind to all ideas." Kate liked that.

The white upholstered furniture was interspersed with cushions and ornaments that Sara had kept in storage for years. A large bronze sculpture of a Kayan woman, rings around her neck, was in a corner on a pedestal. A tiny art spotlight shone down on her.

"I do so like this room," Barbara said as she sat down. "It's so much better than the way Billy had it."

"That was from James Lachlan," Lea said. "Billy had no choice. It wasn't his taste either."

"But yet, it was all sold," Reid said. His eyes rarely left Rachel, but so far, no one had seen her look at him.

"I miss the big cabinet in the hallway," Rachel said. "Greer used to hide in it." For the first time, she glanced at Reid, then away again.

Sadness settled on Reid's face. "Sorry," he said. "I still miss my little sister."

"I understand missing someone. It lasts forever," Barbara said. "Greer was an unusual girl. She was…" She couldn't seem to finish.

"Awkward and strange?" Rachel said.

Reid frowned. "She couldn't help it. She was isolated by our grandmother. She wasn't used to people."

Sara was standing by the fireplace and waiting for them to settle. She didn't want the job of being moderator, but no one else was stepping forward to do it. But then, the others were too involved with the guests to be fully detached. "Excuse me," she said loudly and they all turned to her. "We know who is deceased, but one of the guests is missing."

"Billy," Barbara said. "How is he?"

Sara glared at her. The actress knew who Sara meant.

"Oh yes. The other one," Barbara said. "I'm sure we all assumed that this party had to do with Derek Oliver. We just didn't want to face it." She looked at Lea. "What happened between you two when he finally got home?"

"He never showed up." Lea's tone told that she wasn't unhappy about that.

When everyone looked at Sara, she took a breath for courage. "Recently, through a series of events, we found Derek Oliver's body. He has been dead for years, probably from the time of the house party."

The Medlar group was watching the others and they all seemed to be astonished into silence.

Barbara recovered first. "Was he buried somewhere?" she asked. "On the property?"

"Hidden, not buried," Sara said.

When the guests opened their mouths to speak, Sara held up her hand. "I don't want to give any more details, but we'd like to hear what you remember about his disappearance."

"And why you came here the first time," Jack added.

No one spoke.

"We know that Derek invited all of you," Sara said. "It was his party and we don't think you came here because you liked the man."

"Oh!" Rachel said. "Are you thinking of foul play?"

"Derek was…?" Lea asked.

"I believe she's speaking of murder," Reid said.

For a moment, everyone was silent.

"I think I'm beginning to understand," Barbara said. "This is one of those Murder Weekends where you try to solve some crime."

"Only this one appears to be real." Reid leaned forward. "Do you have any suspects?"

Sara didn't speak, just looked from one to the other.

"Us," Rachel said. "You believe one of us murdered the man. Maybe—"

Lea spoke up. "In that case, I think I have to be your lead suspect. I despised my husband from the day after our wedding." Everyone looked at her in silence. "I guess I should explain. When Derek and I married, I was quite young and I'd always been sheltered. And my father was rich."

"You were a perfect target for a man like Derek Oliver," Randal said in bitterness.

Lea smiled sweetly at him. "Yes, I was. After the marriage, Derek rapidly went through the money my father gave me. My husband had the belief that if anything good was going to happen to him, it would be because people thought he was so rich that he didn't care about anything. Only his theory never worked. Anyway, just before we came here, he told me he was divorcing me. I believe he had someone else lined up."

"I don't mean to be disbelieving," Kate said, "but wasn't he old then? Was he very attractive?"

"Not physically," Lea said, "but he could be persuasive. I believe it's called 'love bombing.' I had no doubt that he could get another woman. And if he did, I knew his family's lawyers would leave me penniless, destitute. However, if Derek died, I wouldn't have to deal with divorce. I'd get to keep the nice big house he'd bought with my father's money, and what was in the bank."

"How did it work out for you when he was missing?" Sara asked.

Lea smiled warmly. "Splendidly. I had the house and two of Derek's cousins moved in with me. We were all quite happy without him. Actually, I don't believe he ever had a friend."

While they were silently staring at Lea, thinking about what she'd said, Barbara spoke up. "That's not a motive for murder! It certainly isn't as good as the one I have."

Everyone turned to look at her in interest.

"I assume that everything said here is to be kept private. It won't appear in some tabloid? Or online?"

"Absolutely," Sara said firmly.

"I too had an older husband," Barbara said. "However, he and I had a marriage of understanding. In modern slang, I was his beard." She paused to let people digest her meaning. "I made my husband look like what he wanted the world to think he was."

"And what did you get out of it?" Sara asked seriously.

"My choice of any of the roles in any of the movies that his studio produced. I didn't have to pay my dues with horror movies or be accosted by a lecherous director. My dear husband, Harry Adair, gave me protection and love and kindness." She looked at each one of them. "And Derek Oliver was about to take all of that away. You see, he had done extensive research and he knew the truth about my husband and me. And well, perhaps there was a bit of lack of discretion with some young men and hush money had been exchanged." She waved her hand in dismissal. "The point is, if all that were published, as that odious man threatened to do, it would probably have destroyed my husband."

"And your career that was just getting started," Sara said. "People would start wondering if your bit of success was based on merit or on covering up your husband's peccadillos. Everyone knows that publicity can be slanted in different ways."

With a raised eyebrow, Barbara looked at Sara in a haughty way that they'd all seen her do on-screen—just before she sent someone to their execution. "Writers! They can be such a bother at times, can't they?"

Sara looked affronted, but when the others nodded in agreement, she said, "Hey!"

"As I was saying," Barbara continued, "I was sent here by my husband to negotiate a price with Derek. My husband's entire career could depend on keeping Derek Oliver silent. Killing him would have solved all our problems. In fact, his disappearance did solve the problem."

While the others thought about this, Lea spoke. "I think my reason for murder is as good as yours. Mine affected me personally. You might have benefited if your husband was charged and taken away to jail. In your world, publicity only helps." She said it with no emotion, just as fact.

"Hollywood didn't already know the truth?" Sara asked.

"Of course they did," Barbara said, "but the public didn't. They do so love to keep their illusions."

"I still think my motive was the strongest," Lea said indignantly. "I could have—"

Sara cut her off as she looked at Rachel. "What about you? Did you have a motive for killing Derek Oliver?"

"The jewelry, maybe?"

Everyone looked at her with great interest.

"I don't know the full details, only the basics," Rachel said. "What I do know is that a lot of jewelry was given to my grandmother by her good friend, Mrs. Oliver."

"Derek's stepmother," Randal said softly.

"Yes, she was," Rachel said. "And Derek Oliver wanted those jewels. He seemed to think they were his by right. Does that make sense?"

The Medlar-Wyatt four nodded.

"Weren't you sent here as a punishment?" Barbara asked.

Rachel smiled, showing her perfect teeth. *Rich girl teeth*, they all seemed to be thinking. "Yes. Too many boys and not enough study. My mother sent me to her dreaded mother-in-law. It was the worst thing she could come up with."

"And were you straightened out?" Sara asked.

"Not in the least." Rachel gave a grin that was infectious.

"What about the jewelry?" Lea asked.

"I'm not sure, but I believe Grans came here to give it to him."

"*Give* it to him?" Lea asked in disbelief. "Why?"

"I don't know," Rachel said.

Randal spoke up. "I think I can answer that. As you said, Derek Oliver truly believed the pieces belonged to him. He thought they were like riches passed down through a royal family—him being the royalty. But Mrs. Meyers had them. I know she wasn't well, so she probably feared that Oliver would harass and threaten her family after she was gone."

"That sounds like her," Rachel said. "All I know for sure is that the morning Mr. Oliver didn't come to breakfast, I asked where he was. Grans said, 'I assume he got what he wanted so he ran away.'"

"That was it?" Kate asked. "You didn't ask what she meant?"

"I was still sulking over being punished and besides, I didn't care what the old people were doing. But I did know that if he got the jewels, I wouldn't."

They sat in silence for a moment, thinking about three motives for murder.

They turned to Reid. "I was working. Although, to be honest, I was looking forward to the man leaving. He was quite nasty to my little sister."

"He was," they agreed.

Minutes later, Sara suppressed a yawn, and the group finally broke up. Randal disappeared like he was in a magician's act.

Jack and Kate walked Sara to her room. She had insisted on staying in the Palm Room. They knew it was because she wanted to go through James Lachlan's documents. Whether they had anything to do with the current murder didn't matter to her. She loved research and finding out things. "Learning is what keeps your brain working," she said.

At last, Jack and Kate were alone, standing together in the

wide hallway. All the bedroom doors were closed and it was quiet in the house.

"We're down here," Jack said. During the insanely hectic days of renovating and refurbishing the house, he and Kate had had no time alone. Jack often collapsed in the wee hours on a recently delivered mattress, the plastic still on it. He slept until his men arrived at 7:00 a.m. the next day.

But now that was over and as part of the reenactment of the week, he and Kate were to share a room.

He opened the door for her—and they both halted. Twin beds had been in the room, just as they were when Kate and her father had stayed there. But now there was one bed with crisp white sheets and a pretty comforter.

Kate turned away. "I'll find a couch somewhere."

Jack didn't move until she'd taken three steps. Then it was as though he came alive, turning back into the old Jack. "No you won't." He took her hand. "Come with me."

Kate smiled. *This* was the Jack she knew. She worked to keep up with his long, quick strides. When she tripped on the stairs, he stopped and bent down in front of her. She put her hand on his shoulder while he removed first one of her high heels then the other. Standing, he tossed them onto a chair, then took her hand. Barefoot, she went with him, and his pace quickened.

He led them through the kitchen, then outside. She knew where they were going. Sara's beloved cottage was at the end of the path.

"Do you have the key?" she asked.

It was dark, but there was enough light to see his expression. Implying that there was a lock he couldn't open was insulting. When they reached the round topped door, he turned the knob and it opened.

Inside, the ground floor was one room, with a little kitchen in the corner. There was a marble-topped table and some cushions on the floor and a couch pushed against the wall. On the table was a bottle of champagne in a bucket of ice and two flutes.

"You planned this," she said.

"A bit," he said as he opened the champagne and poured. "To us." He raised his glass, then downed the drink.

Kate did the same thing. Jack refilled her glass and she walked to the big stained glass window that dominated the whole end of the cottage. "What did you think of them?"

"I agree with Sara. They're all so sweet they make my teeth hurt."

Kate finished her second glass and Jack refilled it. When she took a step, she wobbled a bit.

"That's going to your head. You didn't eat much tonight."

"Neither did you. Are you worried about something?" She fluttered her lashes at him.

"Yes. I'm worried about *you*."

"Me?" She was flirting with him. "How could you worry about me after all we've been through?"

His face turned serious. "Kate?" he asked softly.

"Yes?" Her lashes fluttered so hard and fast the wind almost knocked over the bottle of wine.

Jack reached into his trouser pocket, withdrew what was unmistakably a ring, then went onto one knee. "Kate Medlar, will you—?" He didn't finish because Kate jerked her chin up and stared over his head. Her eyes widened.

Jack knew the look. He instantly stood up and looked at what she was seeing.

Through a small window on the far wall, they could see the window at the apex of the big house. There was a light moving about. It had to be from a flashlight.

"Is it…?" Kate asked.

"The attic," Jack said. "Yes. The locked and secured attic."

"Where the body was."

Jack started to put the ring back in his pocket.

"That's mine!" Kate said fiercely and held out her hand.

With his eyes on the light, he absently handed it to her.

"Wow," she said, looking at it. "This is a knockout. I—"

"I have to go," he said as he hurried to the door. "I'll see you later and we'll finish this."

She was beside him instantly. "I'm going with you."

"No, you're not. You're barefoot and half-drunk."

In reply, Kate held out her hands, left one flat, right one holding the ring.

With a smile, Jack slipped the ring on her finger. Of course it fit perfectly. He opened the door. "Try to keep up."

"That won't be easy now that I'm hauling around three great big shiny rocks."

With a smile that showed he was pleased that she liked the ring, Jack took off down the path. Kate followed him, her skirt hiked up around her hips, her legs bare. She gave a few quiet "ouches" but she kept running. Florida sawgrass isn't for sissies.

Jack silently went in the back door, then up the old stairs Kate had used as a child. When they got to the nursery, the door was locked, just as they had left it. He had a key and opened it. He flipped on the light switch and all looked normal and tidy. Kate limped into the room.

"We missed them." Jack's tone showed his annoyance. They'd taken too long to get there. "I guess they were just looking at things."

"Ha!" Kate sat down on the window seat. "This place has been searched. Everything is out of order from where I put it."

Jack sat down beside her. "You're sure?"

"Absolutely. Dora cleaned, then I put it all back. See those pillows? I didn't leave them like that. And look at the books. They're out of order. And—" She stopped talking because Jack was looking at her in a way he'd never done before. It was like something out of a movie, with desire in his eyes. His eyes were hot and dark and full of fire.

They were alone in the big room.

She could feel her mind and body saying, *Yes, yes, yes.*

Jack pulled her into his arms and kissed her.

Years of pent-up desire, plus a long celibacy, guided them. Clothes came off in seconds, and they fell back against the newly upholstered seat.

At long last they made love. It was short and quick. They had too much passion to postpone anything.

The second time lasted a lot longer, leaving them both satiated—at least for the moment.

At 2:00 a.m., they slipped downstairs and raided the big refrigerator, carrying food and drink back up the stairs. They spread it out on the Lachlan boys' rug that showed the flora and fauna of Florida.

The only light was from a small lamp of a merry-go-round and Kate kept holding up her hand to watch her ring sparkle.

"You didn't answer my question," he said.

She knew exactly what question he meant. "You didn't finish asking me."

"Kate, my beautiful, the best friend I ever had, will you marry me?"

Her eyes glistened. "Friend? Better than Gil?"

He leaned forward. "Better than everyone."

"Oh my! Yes, I'll marry you."

When he leaned forward to kiss her, ever-practical Kate said, "Will you move into my apartment?"

He knew she meant the one in Sara's house. "No. I thought about…" He waved his hand to indicate the room they were in.

"Here? *This* house?"

"You said you like it. It's too big for us now but..." He shrugged. "Little feet and all that."

Kate felt blood rush to her face. She took a breath. "And Aunt Sara?"

"Cal's house," he said, then his eyes seemed to change color. In the next minute they were making love on top of the alligator pond.

★

After the group broke up, Randal took his time before going to his room that connected to Lea's. It had been Derek's and he wondered if it had been used by anyone since that week. Billy couldn't very well have parties when there was a rotting corpse upstairs.

The crudeness of his thoughts showed how apprehensive he was about this night. He didn't know how to play it. The women he trained, who worked to put their toned bodies in positions of invitation, were easy to deal with. Easy to say no to. But the instant he saw Lea, he'd known that his feelings for her were the same. His only other love had been Kate's mother.

On the way to his room, he looked out a window and saw movement. When he realized it was Jack and Kate, her barefoot, and him holding her hand and leading her toward the cottage, he smiled deeply. At last! Sara was going to be pleased. If he'd ever met two people who belonged together, it was his daughter and Roy's son.

When they were out of sight, he went into his bedroom. Standing still, he listened. It was something he'd had a lifetime of practice doing. There were times when his ability to be utterly still and listen with all his senses had saved his life.

He could hear Lea moving about. Was she waiting for him? Should he go to her or stay where he was?

He gathered his courage and gave a knock on the door. She softly said, "Come in," and he opened the door. It took him a moment before he could speak. She had on a long nightgown of peach-colored silk. It clung to her. He could see that she'd kept herself in excellent shape.

"Kate is wonderful," she said. "She told me some of what has happened to her in the last years. And to you."

He gave a smile that didn't let on that they had heard the depth of Kate's confession.

For a moment they said nothing. The air was full of the awkwardness of why they were there. Her husband's murder.

"What you must think of me," Lea whispered. "I was with you for most of that week. And with Kate. And…"

"You could have murdered him in front of me and I wouldn't have cared."

She smiled at that, but then her face turned serious. "You never contacted me."

He took a step forward. "And say, 'Wait for me?' I couldn't take away your hope of someday having love and family. For what? For *me*? I don't have that belief in my own worth."

She took a step toward him. "But I did. I believed in you."

They looked at each other in silence for a moment.

"It couldn't have been easy for you," he said. "You were left alone. When you went home…?" He didn't finish.

"No, it wasn't easy," she answered. "But I didn't have time to think. A month went by and Derek still hadn't shown up, but his two cousins did. My hideous husband had bankrupted them. The poor dears were living by selling things they had before he emptied their bank accounts. And there I was with that big house and a few grand in the bank. I thought I'd get a job, so I let them move in with me. Little did I know how heavily mortgaged the house was. Another six months and we'd all be on the street."

"What did you do?"

She smiled in memory. "It started out in a silly way. Months before, I'd broken a strap on my sandal and I put it back together with some cloth I had. Derek was embarrassed by it, but a woman said she liked it so I made some more. I sold three pair to a local shoe shop. Forty-eight hours later, they had all sold and I was asked to make some more so..." She shrugged.

"So you went into the sandal business?" He made it sound cute.

"We did. His cousins and I set up a little factory in the master bedroom. It was Derek's and we wanted to cleanse it. We worked night and day. It was hard, but we enjoyed it. We called ourselves the Braidy Sisters."

Randal lost his expression of cute. "Braidy? As in those shoes that even we heard about?"

"Yes. I started Braidys, but we sold it four years ago."

Randal's eyes were wide. "For millions?" he whispered.

She nodded.

He sat down on a chair, looking like he had just lost a battle. "This can't happen. My sister will think I'm after your money."

"Does it matter what she thinks?"

"She'd never believe it, but it always has. Very, very much."

Lea frowned. "But you liked me back when I was facing a nasty divorce and poverty."

He smiled. "And you were willing to live on my salary as a butler."

"I rather liked the thought of you and me and Kate living with Mrs. Meyers. I adored her. It would have been lovely."

Randal didn't look happy. "But now things are different.

You are rich in your own right. And contrary to popular belief, I have nothing."

Lea nodded in seeming agreement with him, but then she
moved to stand in front of him. "I understand how you feel.
Everyone will say that you're after my money." With serious
eyes, she slipped off a strap of her gown. "Which part of my
money do you like best?" She showed her bare shoulder. "This
million?" She exposed her other shoulder. "Or this million?"

Randal sat in stunned silence for a moment, then his eyes
turned dark. "I like *all* the millions you have. Every penny
of them." They fell on the bed together.

★

It was hours later when they lay in the bed, their bodies
entwined, half-asleep, that Lea brought up the word *blackmail*.

"I knew he was up to something besides trying to get Mrs.
Meyers' rich granddaughter to marry him."

That ugly idea woke Randal up. "Rachel? She was a teenager then. And she's quite pretty. Derek was a toad."

Lea didn't disagree. "What did he have on the people? Besides Barbara, that is."

Randal hesitated. He knew Sara wouldn't like it if he revealed anything. "That's what we hoped you'd know."

"Sorry," she said. "He never confided in me about anything. But when we were here, I used to hear him moving
things about." She nodded toward the door to his bedroom.

Randal put his hands behind his head. "If he was blackmailing people, he must have had some proof of whatever
he had on them. He couldn't just say 'I know what you did.
Give me money not to tell.' He had to have visible proof."

"I wonder where he kept it."

He turned toward her. "That's a question I should ask you. Did you look in your house?"

"Not specifically for blackmail paraphernalia, but I can tell you that there is no box of papers that incriminated anyone."

"You're sure? It's been over twenty years." He raised on his elbow. "Do you have the same house?"

"Yes. It's an old place so Derek would look like he'd always been rich. It was cheap because it was in such bad shape. I remodeled it. There were termites in the walls and bees in the chimney. It was major work. If there was a hidden safe or secret cabinet, we would have found it."

He sat up. "When you left here, what did you do with his clothes? Were they in his room?"

"Yes. I packed them, but that was normal. I always packed and unpacked for him."

"Surely he had documents in his room. He needed something to threaten people with."

"That's true. Derek was a believer in paperwork. I never thought of it before, but he probably did have documents hidden somewhere. Knowing him, he'd love flaunting them in a person's face."

"So where are they?"

"A bank? But I never received a bill for a safe-deposit box."

They looked at each other, then Lea spoke. "Could they be hidden in this house that has never been remodeled? Not structurally, anyway."

His eyes lit up. "The house that is exactly the same as it was when Derek was here?" He looked at the door to his bedroom. "I think I'll look for a bit. You go to sleep."

Lea rolled out of the other side of the bed and put her arm through a robe that matched the nightgown that was now on the floor. "I'm going to help."

Randal was never one to turn down help. "Just do me a

favor, will you? Don't show me any more of your millions or I'll stop searching and…"

"I promise. For an hour or so, anyway."

Smiling, they went into Randal's bedroom and in between kisses, they searched.

NINE

SARA WAS DREAMING.

Right away, she recognized the dream as one of her Gifts from Above. Or maybe this one was a gift from Lachlan House and its spirits. In her long writing career, this had happened only three times. She knew she was dreaming, and that what she was seeing and hearing was a compilation of her hundreds of thoughts and observations. All of it was converging to make itself into that greatest of blessings: a story.

Smiling at her good fortune, she looked about with intensity. She was trying to memorize everything she saw so that when she woke up, she could write it all down.

She was hovering, not a real person, but just an observing entity. She knew from experience that no one could see or hear her. It was a rural area, with trees and grass and a rough, unpaved road. *Oh goody*, she thought. *An historical*. She looked down the road, hoping to see men in armor. She could stand to write her twelfth medieval novel.

A woman came into view. She was walking along the far

edge of the road, as if she didn't want to be seen. Her head was turned, but Sara could see that she was young, maybe even a teenager. She had on a long pinafore over a flowered dress that had puffy sleeves. Sara noticed a couple of palm trees. *Rats!* she thought. It looked like the story wasn't set in England and wasn't a medieval. By the clothes, it seemed to be the 1940s. Sara did *not* want to write something set in WWII.

When the girl turned her head, Sara gasped. *Uh-oh.* This wasn't a heroine so beautiful that she made a duke fall in love with her. This girl's looks were...well, unfortunate. She had a big nose, teeth so protruding that they distorted her lower jaw, and there were half a dozen large brown moles on her face. She wasn't thin.

A good gym and a year with a couple of surgeons would help, Sara thought.

The girl was carrying a basket of pears, and she was walking slowly. She kept glancing over her shoulder.

Abruptly, the girl halted, then smiled in a way that made her chest rise and fall. Sara thought that if she were describing this in a book, she'd say the girl "smiled down to her very soul."

Only love can do that, she thought. The girl was in love with whomever she was seeing.

Sure enough, a young man came strolling down the road. He was tall, early twenties, and good-looking. Not hero-gorgeous, but nice. When he turned, she saw a red birthmark on the side of his neck. It went up to his ear lobe and was very noticeable. In a romance novel, it would be called a "port-wine stain."

He had on a blue cotton shirt, those loose 1940s trousers, and very clean brown and white oxfords. His clothes were simple but of good quality. From the look of the two of them, he was much richer than she was.

Ah, Sara thought. *The plot thickens.* The impoverished girl would be in a car accident, and he'd pay for her reconstructive surgery. She'd emerge as beautiful. She did have nice eyes. They'd marry and…

Plotting had to wait. Sara put her attention back on what she was seeing.

The young man—certainly not a boy—smiled when he saw the girl. Sara feared the girl was going to melt. When she spoke to him, there was no sound. He replied, and again Sara heard nothing.

She cursed. Who wanted a soundless dream?! But that's what she was getting.

The girl handed him a pear, he took a bite, and they walked side by side along the road. He wasn't like her in skulking along the edge, but he walked down the center. He did all the talking—not a word of which Sara could hear.

The girl laughed a couple of times. But then, from the way her eyes were dripping with love that was close to worship, she would have laughed no matter what he did.

There was a patch of little blue flowers beside the road and when he threw the pear core away, he bent and plucked one.

Both Sara and the girl held their breaths. Would he give her the flower? Was he a hero who could see past looks and into a soul? Would he love her in spite of those teeth? Those moles?

Before the questions could be answered, the sound of a horse on the road made them stop and turn. The happiness on their faces disappeared. For all the expression they wore, they could have put on masks.

A young man on a beautiful horse came into sight. He had on clothes that cried *Rich!* The son of the lord of the manor? He wasn't haughty or arrogant, just self-assured in that way that being born into money gave a person.

From his higher-up position, he looked down at the girl

and seemed to be genuinely confused. It was as though he wanted to say, "Why are you with *her*?" When he said something that Sara couldn't hear, the first man stepped in front of the girl in a protective way.

This idea came from seeing the nursery for two boys, Sara thought.

She'd been so dazzled by the man's elegant clothes and the beautiful horse that she had only glanced at his face. When she took a closer look, she was startled. The two young men looked very much alike. Except for the big birthmark on the first man, they would be hard to tell apart.

Sara smiled. *Oh yeah, I can plot from this.* Of course the two men had the same father. But one was a legitimate son and the other a bastard. The marked man—yes, that was a good nickname—was torn between the rich world of a father who didn't acknowledge him, and the poor world of the girl with the pears. There'd be lots of jealousy and many dramatic scenes. And of course many false accusations. Since she was always looking for a way to make a story different, she thought, *What if, for once, the rich guy was good and the poor one evil?*

She watched as the man on the horse extended his hand down, meaning for the other man—his half brother?—to climb on the horse behind him. In what was obviously a practiced movement, the first man easily and swiftly got on behind him.

This reinforced her idea that the boys of the nursery had been raised as brothers.

The two young men looked down at the girl, then the rich one tossed her a coin. She made no effort to catch it and it landed in her basket. She didn't look at it, and for a second there was a flash of pure hatred in her eyes. The man saw it too and he seemed startled by it, seeming to not understand her animosity. He turned away, leaned forward, and patted his horse's neck.

Behind him, the marked man leaned down and held out the flower to the girl. As she reached up and took it, the love returned to her eyes.

In the next second, the horse took off and the girl jumped back to keep from being hit by the hooves.

The girl stood in the dust that rose up and watched until they were out of sight. She tucked the flower into her blouse, against her breast, and, smiling, started walking.

Sara woke up.

She looked at the clock—2:00 a.m. Good! She'd slept long enough. There was no time better for writing than when the surrounding world was asleep, their loud thoughts not echoing in an introverted empath's mind.

Ever since she had written her first novel, Sara kept a notebook and pens on her bedside table. She turned on the light and began to write down what she'd seen. Physical descriptions, gestures, plus all that Sara had felt, she put into her notes. Her dream was enough for her to start plotting a new book. She'd been retired from writing for years, but obviously, she'd been thinking of plots and that had made all this come out. Maybe this dream was an omen, letting her know that she should start writing again.

It was 6:00 a.m. when she put her notebook down. She'd written pages. It was just beginning to be daylight and she thought she'd walk about the estate. Maybe more ideas would come to her. She needed character names and more of the plot. Did the marked man get together with the girl? Or did he marry someone else and the girl killed them both?

No! she thought. For the last years, she'd been involved in too many murders. She needed to go back to thinking about romance.

But how did she make a heroine out of a girl who looked like the one in her dream?

A challenge! Sara thought. This book would be a challenge to write. She just needed to figure out how to do it.

She got dressed, put on light makeup, picked up her notebook, three pens, and left the Palm Room. She was glad to see that all the bedroom doors were closed. An introvert's happy place. She tiptoed down the stairs and went outside.

She began walking toward the cottage. *Cal's house*, is how she thought of it. They were just kids but they'd loved each other without reservation. But then they'd shared a lifetime of abuse: his father; her mother. Cal's mother, a beautiful woman, had endured all her husband dished out so she could protect her son. But she died young.

Sara shook her head to clear it. Now wasn't the time to think of the bad of her life. Or of a skeleton found in a closet. She needed to remember the story the dream had hinted at and expand on it. Who were the people? She had to pin down a setting. Since there were palm trees, maybe it was meant to be in Florida. She should reread Marjorie Kinnan Rawlings's *Cross Creek* and watch the movie again to put the Florida of that time in her mind.

She needed to—

Her thoughts came to an abrupt halt when she saw Jack and Kate walking through the wet grass. He had on jeans and a T-shirt, while Kate had on a silk blouse, carrying her briefcase. It looked like she had a house to show and was going to work. They weren't far away but they were so absorbed in each other, they saw nothing or no one else.

Sara watched them, eyes wide.

Finally, she thought. She closed her eyes and tipped her head back in silent prayer. Thank all that was holy, Jack and Kate had *done it!* At last they'd given in to what every other person who saw them knew: Jack and Kate were deeply in love. On his part, it had been from the first, but Kate had taken longer. She had enough pride that she wouldn't give herself to a man who was notorious for being a playboy with a bad temper. Kate didn't want a bad boy. She wanted a good *man*. When Jack returned from his isolation in the wilds of Colorado, they could see that he'd changed.

Jack kissed Kate goodbye and she headed to the front of the house. Jack followed the path toward the cottage and was soon out of sight.

On impulse, Sara looked toward the window of the room where her brother was staying. He'd want to know this about his daughter. But the window was dark. A movement caught her eye. The next window had a light on and standing there was her brother. He gave a salute to his sister, letting her know that he'd seen Jack and Kate and he was very pleased.

When Randal closed the curtain, Sara realized that he was in Lea's room.

"Well, well, well," she said as she began walking again. What an extraordinary night it had been. Jack and Kate together at last, and it looked like Randal was with Lea. Plus, Sara had had one of her Magic Dreams. The other times they'd happened, those books had been top sellers. She remembered them well. There'd been the ghostly encounter at the monument. It was so powerful that she'd fallen to her knees. Later, the plot came to her in one big lump. She'd spent days in isolation as she wrote a hundred pages of dialogue.

Then there'd been the single sentence she read in a guidebook. A man wrongly executed in Elizabethan times. That night, she'd dreamed about him.

Sara stopped walking. Ghosts. All the dreams had spirits in common. Did last night's dream have ghosts? Or was it sent by them?

She looked up to see a young man, his back to her, mowing the tall grass along the back fence. His mower was quite old, with no electricity or liquid fuel. It was silent. It's what would have been used when the house was built.

I bet Randal arranged that, she thought. *Or maybe Billy.* But where did they find someone who knew how to use such an old-fashioned machine?

The man stopped mowing and ran a big blue bandanna over his sweaty face. Pushing the mower was hard work. When he glanced at the house, he halted, cloth over half his face.

Sara could only see his eyes, but they widened in shock. She looked toward the house. In the window was Barbara Adair, fully made up and wearing a pretty flowered top. He was probably shocked to see the famous actress.

Barbara leaned forward and squinted, as though trying to see something. She reached down, picked up a pair of glasses, and looked again.

Sara turned in the direction of Barbara's gaze. It was where the young man had been, but now he was gone. She frowned. Barbara wasn't one of those women who pursued young men, was she? How embarrassing! But then Sara saw the old-fashioned lawn mower, something that you'd see in a museum, and thought maybe Barbara was staring at that. She truly hoped that's what interested Barbara.

Sara wanted to sit down with her notebooks and get busy. It had come to her that the name of the girl in her dream should be Alice. She felt that the first young man's name started with a G. First letters of names were oh so important. Hero names had to start strong: R, M, S, T were best. Women had more variety. G was in the second tier of hero names but she could work with it. As for the guy on the horse, he needed a rich man's name: Nigel or Clive would do. Personality and background were told in one word.

There was a stone bench nearly hidden by a tall, overgrown hedge, and Sara hurried toward it. She could almost disappear there and no one would bother her. *Don't these people sleep?* she wondered. Usually, she was the only one up at this hour, but today everyone seemed to be awake.

She slid back on the bench, letting the branches nearly engulf her, and opened her notebook. *Florida with Alice and G,* she wrote. *How did they meet?* Sara knew she had to deal with the girl's looks. They lived next door to each other? A long-term association would make him see past her face. *Ah!* Sara thought. What if she has a smashing body? Exaggerated hour glass? She could—

The sound of a woman's voice interrupted her thoughts. Sara scooted back into the hedge, trying to hide.

"I'm sorry I woke you," the voice said, sounding urgent. "But it's important."

The frown left Sara's face. Gossip and overheard conversations were good writing fodder. The woman was on the other side of the hedge so Sara quickly leaned into it, spit out a couple of leaves, and listened.

"There are things you didn't tell me," she said, then paused. *It's Rachel,* Sara thought.

"I don't know how I can do this. I thought I could, but you—" Pause. "All right, but you have to tell me *all* of it. You know this involves *murder!*" Pause. "Where are you? I think—" Rachel stopped talking for a moment, then said, "She hung up on me!"

Who is she talking to? Sara wondered. She set her notebook aside, then parted the branches with her hands. She got scratched, but what did a little blood and pain matter? She looked through the hole she was holding open.

Rachel was alone, holding her phone, so she'd made the declaration to herself. Obviously angry, she jammed her phone in her pocket and started to walk away. She'd only gone a few feet when Reid came to her.

"Is nobody sleeping?" Sara muttered.

The two of them were too far away for Sara to be able to hear what they were saying. *What's with the audio today?* Sara thought. The dream and now this. Maybe I'll title my book *A Silent Romance*, or *Quiet Love*.

Reid was leaning toward Rachel in a way that suggested intimacy.

Sara was surprised. She'd seen no evidence that they even knew each other. And what about Rachel with Gil and Quinn? Was that an act?

Reid reached out and put a strand of Rachel's hair behind her ear. It was a universal show of lovers.

But are they still lovers? Sara wondered.

The answer came in the next second when Rachel gave Reid a hard slap across his face.

Sara's eyes widened. If they used to be lovers, it didn't appear that Rachel wanted to continue it.

She saw the anger that filled Reid's face and for a moment Sara thought he might hit her back. She prepared to yell, scream, whatever it took to stop that.

But Reid just turned on his heel and walked away.

Rachel stood there, her hands made into fists, then she took her phone out of her pocket and angrily finger-punched the screen. She listened but there appeared to be no answer. The second time she punched, she left a voice message. From the look on her face, her message was of fiery anger.

Eyes still wide, Sara moved back, letting the hole in the branches close as they scraped her neck and hands. She turned, then gave a startled gasp. Reid was standing there looking at her.

He was wearing such a look of shock and confusion that Sara felt sorry for him. She picked up her notebook, meaning that he was welcome to sit beside her.

They sat in silence for a few moments, then Reid's phone buzzed and he looked at it, read the text, tapped twice, then turned the phone off and held it. "That was from my grandmother. She texts me when she wakes up."

"Every day?"

"Yes. I reply with… Well, hearts." He held up his phone and showed Sara a long line of hearts. He clicked the phone off and tightly held it.

Sara was quiet as she waited for him to speak.

"You saw?" he asked.

She was embarrassed about snooping so she just nodded.

"I came here because I wanted to see Rachel again. When Billy called Grans and asked about me, I said I'd come and help out."

"But it was really all about Rachel."

"Yes. I've fantasized about her. You see, that week when she was slipping out of the guesthouse, it was because we were lovers. We were so young and it was our first real…" He gave a shrug. "I wanted to see her again. I wondered if she'd feel the same way about me." He paused. "In these many years, I've been married, and divorced. I also had a long-term girlfriend, but we broke up. But through it all, I've never loved anyone as much as I loved Rachel. Last night she looked at me as though she was glad to see me. It was quick, but it was enough. I thought…" He stopped.

"Maybe it was just old memories and she was saying goodbye."

He gave her a sharp look. "You sound like you know something that I don't. Is there someone else?"

Sara wasn't about to mention Gil. "Doesn't Rachel have a husband?"

"Did have. I did a search and found out that they divorced three years ago."

"Really? Was he a rich guy in Connecticut?"

"You looked her up too!"

"No. It's just something someone said."

"You think she doesn't want a poor guy like me?"

Sara smiled at him. "Why do I think you're not poor? Hmm. Lots of garden work and no sight of a car."

He smiled. "You are perceptive. What gave me away?"

"It's the way you walk and move. You have great confidence in who and what you are."

He laughed. "You sound like my grandmother."

Sara groaned. "I'd rather have a 'You remind me of my former girlfriend.' So what broke you and Rachel apart?"

"Back then, I *was* broke. And besides, I have my grandmother. Grans would have objected." His voice rose and he imitated a Scottish accent. 'She's above you, boy. She's a spoiled, horse-riding rich girl. You're the help.' And if that wasn't enough, Grans would have made Rachel's life hell. She's always wanted me to marry a woman who can carry wood and handwash clothes in a river."

"That's not easy to find in this day and age."

"It's impossible. And I wouldn't want her anyway. In any case, back then, during that infamous party, Rachel and I hid from everyone, even my sister, Greer."

"She'd be jealous?"

"Worse. She would have told Grans. They were tight. Look at this." He started to unbutton his shirt, then halted. "Do you mind?"

"You're asking a romance writer if she objects to a young man revealing his chest?"

Reid laughed as he continued unbuttoning his shirt. "Okay, for that you get an upgrade. You're like the aunt I never had."

"Skipped a generation in a minute. I'm winning."

Smiling, he slipped his shirt down his shoulder to show a tattoo of two Rs back-to-back. "Rachel and Reid," Sara said.

He rebuttoned his shirt. "I've lied to every female in my life about what that means. I get the most sympathy when I say it has to do with my old grandmother."

"And sympathetic women give sex. An adult aphrodisiac."

He cocked an eyebrow at her. "You have any of your books that I can read?"

Sara smiled, then turned serious. "So, all these years, you've lived in a fantasy about Rachel."

"You mean I've wasted my life. Maybe it was a love that didn't actually exist. I know she married a tall blond guy who came from money. She didn't want the boy who pulled weeds."

"I did," Sara said. "I wanted Cal, but he married a woman half as smart and half as pretty as me. It sure did crush my ego. But the truth is, that deep pain is what made me start writing. I needed a release. And a happy ending."

"It's horrifying how your life can change in a moment."

"Yes it is," Sara said softly.

They were quiet, sitting side by side and looking across the mowed lawn. In the distance they heard a loud burst of sound, familiar in South Florida as the streets were always being re-paired. The swamp was trying to reclaim its land.

In the next second, they heard a man shout, "Look out!" Then came a crash from the direction of the cottage.

"Jack!" Sara said. In an instant, she was running.

Reid, younger and with longer legs, ran ahead of her. Be-fore she got through the massive growth, he shouted, "He's all right."

Even with this reassurance, Sara didn't slow down. Jack was sitting on the ground and beside him was a pile of bricks, both loose and in mortared clumps. One of the chimneys had fallen to the ground. It was easy to see how close he'd come to being hit by the falling debris.

Jack seemed dazed and he was rubbing his head. Sara went to her knees and began pushing his hair back to examine him.

"I'm not hurt," he said.

Reid was standing in front of them and he was looking up at the roof. "I'm going up to see…" He didn't finish, just went into the little house. Sara knew that in the loft was an overhead door that allowed entry to the roof.

She sat down beside Jack. Her whole body was shaking in fear of what could have happened. Falling bricks could be lethal.

He put his arm around her small shoulders and drew her head to his chest. "It was Evan," he whispered.

Evan was Jack's half brother, who'd died years before. Sara'd had too many ghostly encounters in her life to be shocked by his words.

Seemingly out of nowhere, Lenny's scarred face appeared. He looked at Jack, at the fallen chimney, then at the roof. In an instant, he disappeared.

"Tell me what happened," Sara said softly.

"I got a text from Kate saying to meet her by the cottage. I assumed her showing was canceled. I saw one of her cards on the ground and bent to pick it up. Then I heard a shout."

"Someone yelled, 'Look out,'" Sara said.

"Yes. I turned to look and there was Evan. I froze. I couldn't move. He was…"

Sara squeezed his hand. Jack had never recovered from his brother's death.

"When I didn't move, he ran at me," Jack said. "Just like when we were kids, and I dodged him as I used to do. Then… Then…"

"Then the chimney came down."

Jack nodded, his eyes filling with tears. "Evan promised. When he was six, I ran after a dog that was chasing him. It bit me." Jack lifted up the leg of his jeans to show a scar. "Evan was very upset. He was afraid I was going to die and he said he'd save me back. He just did."

Sara held his hand, her head on his shoulder. When she looked up, she wasn't surprised to see her brother. He had on a bathrobe over blue boxers. That he hadn't take time to fully dress showed how upset he was. He'd heard it all.

Barbara Adair came through the trees. She was beautifully made up and had on a gorgeous silk kimono.

"What the hell?" It was Gil, and he was studying the bricks on the ground. He picked up one that looked like it had been burned on one side.

In silence, Lenny slipped around the side of the house and touched Gil's arm. The two men hurried away together.

Everyone was looking down at Jack and Sara, their expressions asking questions.

Jack recovered first. "Wrong place, wrong time," he said almost cheerfully as he disentangled himself from Sara. He stood up and offered his hand to her. "The cottage is in worse shape than I thought, and a chimney came down. My men and I will do a thorough inspection today and make some repairs. Until then, everyone needs to stay away."

"I agree," Randal said, then offered his arm to Barbara. "May I escort you back to the house? And may I say that you look as beautiful as the dawn?" They were soon out of sight.

Gil came back around the house, his face serious.

"What did it?" Jack asked.

"Old house!" Sara said loudly. "It was an accident. Right?"

Gil grimaced, not sure he should tell.

"Go on," Jack said. He was leaning against the wall. For all his bravado, it had been a harrowing experience.

Gil looked at Sara. "We did inspect this place. It was in good shape. Both the chimneys were solid. But..." He looked at Jack for permission to tell what he knew and was given a nod. "Someone removed some bricks at the base, then set a charge on it."

When Sara's knees weakened, Jack held her upright. "It was deliberate? Someone tried to hurt Jack?"

"Lenny and I think so," Gil said. "And that guy Reid agreed with us. Somebody wants to stop this investigation."

"I can understand that, but why Jack?" Sara's voice was rising. "I'm the ringleader. It should be me who is removed. I—"

Jack put his arm around her and kissed the top of her head. "If any one of us was taken out, the others would stop. I guess I was just the easiest one to remove." He stepped away from the wall, taking Sara with him. "I have a feeling Kate will be back soon, so let's have breakfast and talk about this."

"Let's all go home and stop sticking our noses into murder," Sara said.

"Too late to stop now," Jack said. "We know that one of our guests is a killer. I doubt if he or she will stop trying to silence us just because we chicken out before the exposé."

"Even if you did quit, the murderer would want to remove all three of you, just to be sure," Gil said.

"Thanks for that," Jack said.

"Anytime," Gil replied. "Think we should repair the chimney or leave it?"

"Leave it," Jack and Sara said in unison.

They heard a car door slam hard.

Jack groaned. "It's Kate and she's going to be mad."

"I agree with her," Sara said.

Together, they walked back to the house, bracing themselves to deal with the anger and fear from Kate.

TEN

IT WAS AN HOUR BEFORE THE MEDLAR-WYATT group sat down to breakfast. Lenny had filled the sideboard in the dining room for the others, but Randal and Jack made breakfast and set it up in the small morning room. They wanted privacy so they could talk. They knew that if any of the guests started wandering around the house, Lenny would stop them. What they said wouldn't be overheard.

Kate asked them to tell her everything that had happened, especially the part where Jack received a text from her. He showed it to her. It was short, saying that she would meet him at the cottage right away.

"I'd just seen you off," he said.

"I didn't send it," Kate said. "And I didn't leave one of my cards stuck in the grass. I went to meet the client but no one was there. I came straight back."

"And you had your phone with you every minute?" Randal asked.

"Of course!" She opened her handbag. "It's always—" She broke off.

"What is it?" Sara asked.

"I keep my phone in this pocket, but now it's in the middle." She took it out. There was no text sent that morning from her to Jack.

The four of them looked at one another across the round table. The text sent to Jack said it was from Kate.

"It's someone who knows how to really work a phone," Randal said.

"That's every person in the US under thirty," Jack said.

"Eight-year-olds could do it," Sara said gloomily.

"How? When?" Kate asked.

"Did you have your phone with you at dinner?" Sara asked.

"No. It was upstairs."

They knew that last night, no one was within sight at every moment. Bathroom breaks, moving about the rooms—anyone could have sneaked upstairs.

Randal waited a moment, then said, "I have news."

"You're in love with Lea and you'll probably marry her," Sara said without interest.

"If my know-it-all sister will hold back on her condemnation of me for even three minutes, I have *real* news."

"Sara?" Jack raised an eyebrow.

"I'll try," she said, and they turned to her brother.

"Last night Lea and I did some searching." He looked at Sara, daring her to make a smart aleck quip.

She made a zippered motion across her mouth.

"Anyway, Lea and I thought that if Derek Oliver was blackmailing people, he needed tangible proof. Documents for sure. Photos. Since he never left this house during the party, where was it?"

"Stored somewhere safe," Sara said, and they all looked at her. "Sorry. Go on with your story."

"We found it." Randal waited for that to sink in.

"Dad!" Kate said. "So help me if you don't stop putting on a drama play and just tell us, I'll—" She looked to Sara to finish that.

"Move your bed to the cottage," Sara said. "Now spill it!"

"According to the papers Lea and I found, the owner of this house, of this entire estate, is Reid Graham."

There was shocked silence.

"How?" Sara asked.

"His grandmother was married to the nephew of James Lachlan. His wife's sister's son was her husband. The papers didn't have a lot of detail, but the nephew died before their son—Reid's father—was born."

"The oldest living relative is what the will says," Jack said. "Since James's son has never been traced, it might hold up in court."

Kate was looking at her father. "What else did you find?"

"This is sad," Randal said. "There was a real estate contract for one point three million dollars for this place. It was never signed."

"It's not worth that now," Kate said.

"True, but at the time of the party it was. There was a buyer for the house and land and all those citrus trees," Randal said.

"Irony." Sara shook her head. "Poor Reid. No one knew, but he was in love with Rachel. He couldn't marry her because he was broke."

"And she was expected to marry money," Kate said.

"But if Reid had known this, he could have provided for his sister and grandmother," Jack said. "Back then, that was a truckload of money."

"Well!" Sara said. "It makes for a change to find a reason

that Derek Oliver should have stayed alive. If he had, Reid, who was chopping logs and cutting grass, could have sat at the head of the big table."

"Instead," Kate said, "he was sleeping in the stable. Metaphorically speaking, that is."

"Poor guy," Randal said.

"Do we tell him?" Jack asked

"We must. By the end of the month he can take claim," Sara said. "I'm so glad that this place won't go to Billy's greedy brothers."

"Who denuded it," Reid said.

"Reid will pay lower taxes since the house is now worth less," Kate said. When they looked at her, she shrugged. "It's my job to think of these things."

It was Sara, the storyteller, who thought of something else. "Oh no! I just remembered. The Lonely Laird. Billy's story."

No one replied.

"Billy said that in 1944, James's nephew was executed for murder. Is Reid the grandson of the executed man? Do you think that would make any difference to the inheritance?"

"What kind of murder was he charged with?" Randal asked. "One that was carefully planned or a you-insulted-my-mother then one unlucky punch?" Considering Randal's background, it made sense that he'd know about this.

"In this case," Jack said, "I can't see that it would matter how a man died. Reid Graham is related to James Lachlan and that's all that counts."

"By marriage," Sara said. "There's no blood shared, but it may be close enough of a relation for a judge to turn the property over to him."

"I hope so." Kate looked at her aunt. "Maybe you could do some research, then write a report making the nephew look innocent. Unjustly accused, that sort of thing. We could tell

a judge that giving Reid the property is righting a wrong."
Kate didn't look at Jack. They had spoken of what they wanted
with the house. This would certainly change things.

"His grandmother is still alive," Sara said. "I guess we
could ask her."

Randal gave a snort. "That should go over well. 'Was your
late husband a really bad man or was it all a miscarriage of
justice?' Guess which door she'll choose?"

"Especially when it could mean her grandson would inherit the property or not," Jack said.

In unison, they looked at Sara. "I know, get back to researching."

Kate nodded to the notebook on the table. "Is that what
you've been doing?"

Sara picked it up and flipped the pages to show a lot of
handwriting in many colors of ink. "I had a dream about a
book plot and I made notes." She put the book down. "How
are we going to deal with what happened this morning?" She
looked at Jack. "We don't want them all packing up and leaving in fear that an active murderer is among us."

Jack clamped his teeth together. He knew what was necessary. "We'll have to keep the lie that it was an accident. It
was my inability to see that a chimney was missing bricks and
about to fall down."

They could see that his pride was going to be hurt.

"That leaves us with the question of whether or not we
should tell Reid of his possible inheritance," Randal said.

"I'll do it!" Sara said.

Randal groaned. "So you can grill him within an inch of
his life about his ancestor?"

Sara smiled. "You know me too well. I will—"

She cut off because the two couples, Kate and Jack, Randal and Lea, were giving quick glances at each other. Like all

lovers, they thought no one saw them. But Sara not only saw but felt the vibrations from them. They wanted to be alone! "Anything else?" She could feel them holding their breath. Would she be like that annoying colleague who said, "I know everyone wants to go to lunch, but I have one more question."

But she didn't detain them. She waved her hand and the four of them vanished with the speed of cartoon characters. She expected to see white smoke behind them.

Passion that cannot be denied—as it was euphemistically called in her novels—was great on paper. In real life, for those not involved, it was a major nuisance.

She sat there for a moment, looking at the table that needed to be cleared, and was glad she didn't have to do it. Lenny had found others to help. *He's probably the one who hired the kid with the silent mower*, she thought.

When she went upstairs, she avoided looking at the two closed bedroom doors, then went inside the Palm Room. She didn't know what was "wrong" with her recently, but she seemed to be all feeling. It had started when she returned to this place where she and Cal had spent so much time.

What was causing this hypersensitivity? Why were all those memories flooding back into her mind? Was that what caused the dream that was still vivid in her thoughts? The people in it were so clear she could pick them out of a crowd.

She went to the window in the far wall and looked out. No wonder James Lachlan liked this room. She could see both ends of the garden area around the house. The guesthouse and cottage were to her right. To her left was a tropical jungle that needed cutting. It would be a good place to put a swimming pool. The only building out of sight was the garage. *Which is probably why Lenny chose it*, she thought.

A movement caught her eye and she turned to see the cottage. Gil was on the roof. He was removing a rope that he'd lassoed around the second chimney, the one that hadn't come down. It wouldn't surprise her if he'd attached the rope to his truck and tested if he could pull it down.

Had someone really targeted Jack? she thought. Was it to get him off the case? Or was there another reason?

Gil was wrapping the rope over his bent arm in that way men did so easily, when he suddenly halted and stared across the property.

Sara followed his eyes. Almost hidden under the trees were two people. It was Rachel and Reid—and they were kissing.

"Wow!" Sara said under her breath. "She slaps him before breakfast and kisses him afterward." Great for book heroines, but not so good in real life.

Sara looked back at Gil. He'd seen the two of them. He turned away and began circling the rope around his arm with force, like it was a noose. *That poor man,* she thought. He'd not had much luck with women in his life.

When the couple moved out of sight, Sara looked at Gil. Even at this distance, his expression was glum, as though he'd expected this.

In the next minute, she saw Barbara walking along the back fence. The way she was turning about, her head high, it looked as though she was searching for someone. Or something.

"Looking for a big fat emerald ring?" Sara murmured.

Barbara went out of sight behind the guesthouse.

The awful sound of a weed whacker made Sara look at the cottage. As he'd promised, Reid was clearing that area. *He left Rachel so soon?* she wondered. Were they back to slapping? Or still kissing?

Sara was torn between being glad for Reid and sad for Gil.

To her surprise, Rachel came out of the house. *Already?*

She was carrying an old-fashioned curved basket for gathering flowers. She had on a white dress that looked sweet and prim.

Sara shook her head in disbelief at how two-faced she was.

From the side, Quinn came running and stopped beside her. He was as tall as she was, and Sara had never seen the boy smile so big. She pulled a fat sandwich in plastic wrap from the basket and handed it to him.

She certainly knows the way to a teen boy's heart, Sara thought.

Still smiling, the boy went back toward the cottage. Rachel looked up at the roof, saw Gil, and raised her hand in a wave. But Gil turned away.

Sara saw the surprised look on Rachel's face. Actually, she looked hurt—and perplexed.

You were just kissing another man and you can't figure out what Gil is upset about? Sara rolled her eyes.

When there was a quick knock on the door, she gladly turned away. She was disgusted!

A large white envelope was being slid under the door. She picked it up. It was nice stationery, with a heavy vellum envelope. She withdrew the notecard. *William Pendergast* was printed in light blue at the top.

I hope you like the gift I've sent you. I knew who bought it, but he hasn't been able to sell it. Beauty is in the eye, I guess. Anyway, I'm sure Kate will like it—and it might remind her of a few things. Thank you for all you've done for me and I wish you the best of luck.
With my eternal gratitude,
Billy
P.S. Sorry, but you paid for this.

Nearly overwhelmed with curiosity, Sara hurried downstairs.

★

Abruptly, Kate sat up in the bed. She was nude, but she pulled the sheet over her body. She wasn't yet to that stage of lovers where nudity was commonplace.

Jack, half-asleep, murmured, "What is it?"

"We didn't tell Aunt Sara about the nursery."

"She's seen it."

"No! That someone was searching it."

"Maybe," Jack said. "It could have been Dora when she cleaned."

As Kate got out of bed and pulled on a robe, she made a hissing sound through her clenched teeth. "Is this what happens when I succumb to your baser urges? You start doubting my perception?"

Jack opened his eyes halfway. "I've always doubted you and *you* seduced *me*."

"I did not! I—" She tossed a pillow at him. "Get up and let's go."

"Up? Again? So soon?"

She ignored his innuendo. "Stay here. I'll tell everyone I wore you out." She stopped and listened. "Is that a truck?" She went to the front window and saw a moving van pulling out. "All the furniture I bought arrived. What's been delivered?"

Jack yawned, piled up pillows, and put his hands behind his head as he watched Kate get dressed. "Sara," he said. "If it's something weird and unexpected, it's Sara."

Kate nodded in agreement as she slipped her feet into shoes. She had on leggings and a tunic. After what happened in the early morning, she wanted to be mobile. "Wonder what it is."

"You two are the curiosity demons." Jack threw back the covers and got out of bed. He was not in the least shy at being nude. "Want to go see what she's up to?" He pulled on his usual jeans and T-shirt. After a vigorous bout of kissing, they left the room.

Kate was the first to reach the bottom of the stairs and she halted, staring in wonder. Her father was already there and he was smiling.

Before them was a huge wooden cabinet with double doors and intricately cut trellising at the top and bottom. In the middle was a solid panel with a round top. Billy had given the movers a sketch to show where the cabinet was to be placed. It was at the hub of the ground floor. From there the three doorways to the major rooms could be seen, plus the lower half of the grand staircase. The morning room and the kitchen were to the right. To get anywhere on that floor, a person had to go past the big cabinet.

"It's mashrabiya," Sara said, showing her extensive travels. "It's Arabic and quite beautiful."

"It's where you used to hide," Randal said to his daughter, then turned to his sister. "Billy told me it used to be full of silver serving pieces, but by the time of the party it was empty."

"Sold by the so-called caretakers," Sara said bitterly.

Randal shrugged. "My daughter used to hide in there and watch people." He pointed to the two lower, trellised panels. "Adults didn't notice the little eyes down so close to the floor, so she saw everything." His tone was affection personified.

Kate had a dreamy look on her face. "Billy gave us chocolate," she said softly. "We hid in there and watched it all. She said it was better than any movie."

"Who was with you?" Sara asked softly.

"Greer."

Sara opened the doors. Her gesture was obvious that Kate was to get inside. "I'll be Greer."

Smiling, Kate got in. It wasn't as easy a fit as when she was four. Sara, who was quite small and agile, got in with her.

Kate pulled on an old ribbon that had been stapled to the back of a door and closed it. She reached for the second door but her father's hand came in holding a box of chocolates he'd retrieved from the pantry. She took it and he shut the door.

Sara opened the box and held it out for Kate to take a piece.

It wasn't easy, but Kate, chocolate in hand, scrunched down to look through the lower panels. "We could see their feet and we laughed about their shoes."

Sara got down beside her. "Who do you see?" she whispered.

Kate closed her eyes for a moment. "Him! He was always chasing Greer."

"Why?" Sara's tone told of her suspicions.

"He didn't like her." Kate sat up. Outside the cabinet, the others were silent. As Kate began to talk from memory, Randal put his phone on Record.

★

"Shhh, he's coming," Greer said as she closed the door and held out the box of chocolates Billy had given her. "Don't let him find me."

They both knew who "he" was.

In the next second, they saw his shoes: shiny, polished, and silent. "Where is that ugly girl?" he said loudly. As always, he was angry. Trailing from his arm were half a dozen shirts he wanted ironed. "She is the most worthless creature alive. Billy!" he shouted. "Where is she?" When there was no reply, he growled. "I'll have to get that wife of mine to do it!" He stomped away.

Greer let out a sigh of relief, leaned back against the side of the cabinet, and stuck three pieces of chocolate in her mouth.

"You're not ugly." Kate searched for the coconut piece, the one she liked best.

Greer gave a chocolaty smile. "Only to you."

"Reid likes you."

Greer smiled broader. "But he's my brother. He has to. I'd like to kill that man," she added conversationally.

Kate nodded in four-year-old wisdom. "Nobody likes him."

"He's mean to Reid and all of them. He—" They heard voices so they went back down to peer through the beautiful trellising.

"It's Uncle Roy," Kate whispered when she saw the heavy black boots.

"Come on," Roy said, then Barbara's pretty shoes came into view. Greer had told her that Barbara was rich and Roy wasn't, so that was a problem.

"What if he tells?" Barbara asked as the two pair of shoes came close together. "Harry will be ruined. How did he even find out?"

"I don't know. Billy said that he nearly lived in that old room so maybe he read about it. Anyway, your husband will be forgiven."

"For murder?! Of a two-bit nobody actor? Harry was only eighteen. A child."

"Let's get out of here before someone hears us. There are too many people in this house!"

"Afraid your wife will see us?"

Roy gave a chuckle. "That's better. Jealousy is easier to deal with than fear. Let's go before Dad finds me and I get stuck cutting grass all day."

"Or making love to your wife."

As they left, Roy's laugh echoed down the hall.

Greer and Kate sat upright. "Uncle Roy likes her."

"But she likes her husband's money better," Greer said with heavy fatality. "I have to get back to work. Reid won't be happy with me if I miss too much. And all this candy is going to make me even fatter." She put her hand up to the door but drew back when she heard voices.

"It's Daddy!" Kate started to open the door.

"No," Greer whispered. "He's not alone."

They snuggled back down and saw Randal's nice shoes and Lea's broken sandal that she'd repaired with a piece of fabric like her dress. The shoes were very close together.

"Someone will see us," Lea said.

"Nobody knows about us."

At that, Greer and Kate put their hands over their mouths to stifle giggles. Everybody knew her father and Lea liked each other—and Kate was very happy about that.

Randal said, "Let's keep our secret between us."

"They'd be surprised, wouldn't they?"

"Your husband would be for sure," Randal said.

Lea snorted. "If he cared, maybe I wouldn't be here. Have you told your wife yet?"

Randal sucked in his breath in a way that sounded almost fearful. "I'll have to hide Kate before I tell her or she'll take my daughter somewhere. I'd never see her again."

"She wouldn't actually do that, would she?"

"You can't imagine what Ava is capable of. Someone's coming! Let's go."

Greer and Kate ate two pieces of chocolate each before the next couple appeared.

It was Cal with his gray hair and his muscular body. Kate didn't know him well, but he was nice. She liked his voice. He was with a boy she'd never seen before. He had lots of black hair.

"Come on, let's get you something to eat, then you can help me repair the window frames."

The boy said, "I think—" He stopped. Because he was shorter than the adults, he saw the two pair of eyes staring out of the bottom of the cabinet. He didn't give them away. Instead, he stepped in front, concealing them. "Yeah, I'm starving." He walked away and Cal followed him.

The girls sat up.

"Who is that boy?" Kate asked.

"Cal's grandson. He's Roy's son, but he doesn't like his dad."

"But Uncle Roy is so nice."

Greer shrugged. She didn't understand either. She opened the door, but again they heard footsteps. She didn't get the door fully closed before the person came into their view. Rachel ran past them, something clutched tightly in her hand.

"She has my hedgehog!" Kate tumbled over Greer as she got out of the cabinet. Greer held little Kate to keep her from running after Rachel.

"Let me go! That's mine."

"I know." Greer held on tight to Kate. "You can't start a fight with her. She'll win."

"But it's mine!" Kate was tearing up. "Aunt Sara gave it to me. She went away and Dad said—"

Greer hugged the child. "I'm sure you're right, but Rachel is… My brother would say she's 'an absolute bitch.'"

With wide eyes, Kate pulled back to look at her. "A what?"

"It's not a nice thing to say, so forget it. Tonight I'll sneak into her room and get your toy back."

"Can you do that?"

"Sure. One advantage of being ugly is that nobody wants to look at me. Wherever I go, they ignore me. Now come on and I'll sneak you up to the old nursery. You can play there while I iron that hideous old man's shirts."

With a sniff, Kate wiped her eyes. "Maybe I could go play with Cal's grandson."

Greer laughed. "You're too young for that. Come on before we get caught spying. I don't want to give them a reason to send me home."

"You want to stay here with your brother."

"Yes I do." Greer took Kate's hand, checked that no one was in the kitchen, then they ran through. Greer grabbed half a dozen pieces of fruit and, giggling, they ran up the back stairs.

*

When they were out of the cabinet, Sara turned to her niece, who was looking a bit dazed. "My guess is that these encounters happened separately, not one after another."

"I think you're right, but they all seem to run together in my mind."

Jack put his arm around Kate's shoulders. "How did you remember all that? You were a kid."

"She's my relative," Sara said quickly, then smiled at Kate. "You remembered me then." They knew that Kate had grown up without any memory of her aunt or even her father.

Kate looked sad. "But I forgot everyone later."

"PTSD causes great trauma," Sara said.

They were quiet for a moment, then they heard voices. "An AUL meeting in the library," Sara said quickly. "We need to discuss everything, but give me fifteen minutes." She was busily tapping away at texts on her phone.

A few minutes later, they were assembled in the little library off the living room. It was full of books Sara had collected over the years. There was lots of medieval history and specialty books on wagons and weapons, plus underwear— which was written about extensively in romance novels.

"Well," Randal said, "it appears that we've made a big discovery." They looked at Sara, but she was interested in her phone. They waited.

Finally, Sara looked up. "Yes. We heard that when Harry Adair was eighteen years old, he murdered a man. Or I guess I should say 'a two-bit actor.' That seems to be Hollywood speak for a person of no value. Somehow, Derek Oliver found out about it by using what's in the Palm Room. At least that's what I think is meant by 'the old room.' Did I miss anything?" At their silence, she looked back at her phone.

"That's it?" Randal said. "Shouldn't we arrest her?" He was being snide because he was annoyed by his sister's lack of interest in this new discovery.

"Hang on," Sara said, "I'm sending you the texts I just exchanged with Billy."

They took out their phones and read.

Sara: Was Derek Oliver in this house before the party?

Billy: Yes. About three months earlier. He was trying to get my brothers to invest in one of his schemes. They told Derek that first he had to perform a task for them. They wanted him to go to Lachlan and check on me. He came here, but of course my brothers gave him nothing.

Sara: That sounds like them. What did he do?

Billy: Derek and I couldn't abide each other. He spent the week in the Palm Room watching old movies.

Sara: Any of them of interest to him?

Billy: Maybe. One night he came to dinner smiling. I didn't know he could do that. He said he'd seen something that was going to change his life.

Sara: Did he say what it was?

Billy: With him, it had to mean money but he didn't say so. Was the cabinet any help to you?

Sara: More than you can imagine. Thank you so very much.

Billy: The pleasure was mine. What you have done for me has given me the most fun I've had in years. To be needed is a gift.

★

"So," Randal said to his sister. "You just have to go to that room and find out what it was that ol' Oliver discovered."

"Have you seen that room?" Sara snapped. "There are shelves full of movies and whole cases of books. And I'm to read and watch it all in three days?"

Unperturbed at his sister's anger, Randal smiled. "I have the utmost confidence in you."

Jack spoke up. "So what happens if we do find out who Harry killed? They're both dead now."

"Harry was alive back then, so it makes sense," Sara said. "But why is she here *now*?"

"Maybe she wants to protect her husband's reputation,"

Kate said. "You know how the media loves to tear people apart. Look at Cary Grant. Rock Hudson."

"I'm not sure anyone would care about a deceased movie producer," Sara said.

"Barbara would," Randal said. "If that's the reason she's here now, that is."

Jack said, "She and my father really seemed to like each other." It was so unusual for him to speak of his father in a tone that wasn't angry that they looked at him.

"If Roy had divorced his awful wife," Sara said, "and married an elegant woman like Barbara, it would have changed many lives. Especially yours."

"You could have had a singing career," Randal said.

"Or been a movie star," Sara added, teasing him.

Jack gave a snort of derision.

"Do you remember seeing Greer and me in the cabinet?" Kate asked.

"I remember Grandad teaching me about window frames." His eyes sparkled. "Did you really want to 'play' with me?" The air between them seemed to sizzle.

"Stop it!" Sara said. "You two can't disappear again. Not yet. We have work to do and little time to do it. We have to find a killer. We have lots of motive, but who did the deed? Which one of these lovely people is actually a psychopathic killer?"

"Barbara's motive for murder was strong." Randal looked at Jack. "Barbara Adair appears to be a sweetie but she's a very ambitious woman. She married a gay man because he could help her career. She gave up on love in order to keep her rich life—and Roy knew that."

"Do you think my dad committed a murder for her?" Jack sounded calm, but the look on his face was the beginning of the infamous Wyatt rage.

"I doubt it," Randal said in a dismissive tone, then turned to his sister. "As I said, you need to research and find out about Harry and what happened when he was eighteen."

Sara didn't react to her little brother's orders. "In other circumstances, I would love doing that, but Rachel puzzles me. I'd like to find out what's going on with her."

Jack was calming down. "So you can use her as a character in a new book? The one you've been writing about in that notebook you never put down?"

"I both love and hate that someone knows me so well," Sara said. "But honestly, I don't have time to dig into the entire life of some old movie producer. I'd be watching movies until—" Her eyes widened.

"What is it?" Kate asked.

"Billy and his army of bored old people. They spend their days watching reruns of *Bonanza* and drooling over Little Joe." Only Randal knew what she meant. She waved her hand. "If Kate can remember what happened when she was four, Billy can probably remember more about what happened both times Oliver was here."

"Like the fact that he didn't tell us that the man had been here months before the party?" Jack asked.

"Exactly. I wish I knew a tech guy to run all this. We'll need a couple of VHS machines to be hooked up. I wonder if the young man with the antique mower could do it. He obviously knows about old-timey machines."

Everyone gave her blank looks.

Sara glared at them. "Six a.m.? Silent mowing? You didn't see him?"

They were still blank.

"I'll ask Lenny. He'll know."

Jack and Kate started to get up, but Randal sat there. "You think Rachel is the murderer, don't you?"

Sara tried to suppress a smile, but the corners of her mouth turned up. "She is acting very oddly—and don't forget that she had the hedgehog. Did she raid the nursery to get it? Why?"

"Oh!" Kate said. "I forgot to tell you that someone searched the nursery. They tried to put things back, but they were re-arranged."

"Did you try to find out what they were looking for?" Sara asked.

"Well… We, I mean Jack and I… We were…" Kate stumbled.

"Occupied." Jack was grinning broadly. "That's a nice rug on the floor."

Randal, studiously ignoring the two young people, said to his sister, "You were speaking of Rachel."

Jack and Kate were silent, waiting for her to explain.

"She is breaking Gil's heart, and I don't like it. I'm very interested in what she did back then and what she's up to now. Someone else can deal with Harry getting angry and killing someone long ago. Besides, I don't think Barbara did it."

"I do," Randal said softly. "I think she had a strong motive to kill. She was facing the end of her career before it even began. She married a gay man to get what she wanted. That's powerful ambition. And Derek Oliver was going to take it all away."

"Do you think she got my father to saw the man's head open?" There was warning in Jack's voice.

"I don't know!" Randal snapped. "Love and money can make a person crazy." If anyone knew about that, he did.

"I vote for Reid," Kate said. "He's so good and sweet and nice that I want to run away from him."

"He owns this place," Randal said. "But the papers were hidden. If he'd been told back then, surely he wouldn't have murdered the man who knew. But I don't think Reid was told. He certainly doesn't seem to know it now."

"Maybe," Kate said. "But you guys haven't worked in real estate as I have. People do awful things in a fight over property."

"Surely, if he'd known, he would have claimed the place after Oliver disappeared," Randal said.

"Unless Reid was the murderer," Kate said.

Sara spoke up. "I'm with Kate. He's yours. Find out all you can."

In unison, they looked at Jack. It was his turn to choose a killer.

"Lea," he said softly and looked at Randal. "It's usually the spouse."

Sara turned to her brother. "Did you saw his head open for her?"

Randal was serious. "I coveted the jewels and was tempted. But murder? I can't even deal with live lobsters."

They all nodded. What he'd said was true.

"Shall we divide and interrogate?" Sara asked. "Each to their own suspect?"

Jack looked at Kate. "I'll take Reid and you get Lea."

She smiled. "I love your jealousy. Do you think it will last forever?"

"No," Sara said. "It lasts only about four years. Kate can't take Lea. She's too close to her. We'll meet back here at four and tell all. Are we agreed?"

Again, they nodded. They'd made a pact.

As they started to leave the room, Randal said, "Might I suggest that we issue luncheon invitations to our suspects? With wine. It will help break the ice as we ask about a murder."

"Says the man who gets the movie star," Jack said.

"I'll trade you," Randal shot back.

They all knew Randal would like to have every meal with Lea, but that would leave Jack with Barbara—who tended to faint at the sight of him. "Thanks, but no." Jack smiled. "Does Lea like roses? White or red wine?"

Randal didn't take the jealousy bait. "Champagne and pink peonies."

"Hate to interrupt this male bonding," Sara said, "but we should ask each one who he or she thinks is the killer. That might give us some insight. And text me *immediately* with anything important that you find out."

"Good ideas," Jack said.

"I'm going to change clothes," Kate said.

"I'll help," Jack said, smiling broadly.

They started to walk out, but Sara caught Kate's arm. "I saw Reid kissing Rachel."

"I thought that now she and Gil were…"

"Me too. I think maybe she's playing both men at the same time."

"Yuck!" Kate said. "Not fair to either of them."

Sara shrugged. "To each his own, I guess. Go on. Jack is waiting for you."

"Yes, he is," Kate said, smiling happily. She left the room quickly.

When she was alone, Sara sent a text to Billy:

Sara: I want you and your resident cohorts to help us solve this murder.

Billy: I thought you'd never ask.

Sara: We don't know much, but it may be connected to a murder that probably happened in Hollywood. I think in the early 1940s. An 18-year-old man killed a so-called nobody actor. The killer's name was Harry Adair, but he may have used another name at the time of the murder. I have no idea of the victim's name. Whatever and whoever did it, Derek Oliver found out about it from the docs and videos in the Palm Room.

Billy: And you want me—us—to find out the same thing that Derek did?

Sara: Exactly!

Billy: Old as it is, I think my brain can match his.

Sara sent an emoji of a laughing face: You and me both.

Billy: Send it all. It'll be a party.

In the kitchen, she told Lenny that documents and videos needed to be pulled out of the Palm Room. He said that Dora and her friends could go through things and box them. Sara started to ask if she could do that. After all, she was sometimes called "Daffy Dora." But Lenny's look stopped her. "Anything 1940 to 1946," she mumbled.

"It will be done."

She paused at the doorway. "I want a gift sent to Billy. Does anyone know where to get one of those tall red popcorn machines? And a giant bag of corn and lots of butter?"

Lenny's nod was his answer. If he didn't know, he'd find out. And with all of that to do, he'd be too busy for kitchen duty. She didn't want to overtax him.

Sara left the room. She needed to figure out how she was going to play her interview with Rachel—a woman she had

come to seriously dislike. "I think you have the personality of a killer," would not be the way to start a conversation.

Sara then did something she truly hated: she made a telephone call. Emails and texts were fine with her, but talking
on a phone was something she avoided. She called Bessie at
the Mitford Tea Room and asked if she would please, just this
once, deliver a lunch to Lachlan House. She could even send
food that had carbs in it.

"That's drastic," Bessie said, then sucked in her breath.
"You have another murder, don't you?" When Sara was silent,
Bessie laughed. "I knew it! I'll be there in twenty minutes.
And don't worry. I won't say a word. But later, I'm going to
tell everyone that I knew about it beforehand."

"I'll thank you in my book," Sara said and clicked off. So
far, so good. Now she needed to find Rachel and arrange
to meet in the nursery—which Sara guessed she'd probably
searched. Looking for a hedgehog full of jewels?

With her teeth clenched, she went searching. Gil or Reid?
Which man was Rachel going to focus on? Or both at the
same time? "Over my dead body," Sara mumbled. After she
met with Rachel, she was going to warn Gil.

ELEVEN

"I'D LIKE TO INVITE YOU TO LUNCH," RANDAL SAID
to Barbara. As he could have predicted, she hesitated. A person with her fame had to be cautious. "White wine, salad
and pasta, with fruit drenched in Grand Marnier? None of
my sister's low-carb, no-booze diet."

She was softening.

"Bring a swimsuit. It's at my sister's house, and I'll cook."

"You sold me. When do we leave?"

"Now."

"I do love a decisive man. Five minutes."

She was as good as her word, and about eight minutes later,
she was at the foot of the stairs. The only thing she carried
was a handbag. "I assume she has towels."

He raised an eyebrow that her suit was small enough to fit
into the little package. "Shall we go?"

They went in Sara's car, small and intimate.

At Sara's big house, he opened the door for her. Inside,

she looked around approvingly. "California in Florida." She meant it as a compliment.

"Bite your tongue! Certainly let no Floridian hear you say that."

She laughed and he directed her to Sara's bathroom to change. As for Randal, he had trunks on under his clothes.

In minutes, she returned in her white swimsuit. It was a one-piece retro design that showed off her flat stomach and her beautiful legs.

Randal gave her an appreciative look.

She smiled demurely. "I have a personal trainer."

"He's done a very good job."

"Thank you," she said, looking at him. "I think your clients must do well."

He gave a nod of thanks. With their mutual compliments exchanged, they went to Sara's big pool. For thirty minutes, they swam and showed off and enjoyed themselves.

When they left the pool, they went inside. Barbara put on one of Sara's robes and sat down on a stool at the kitchen counter. Randal, in shorts and T-shirt—designer, of course—began making their lunch. He was the one to start the conversation. "I have the oddest feeling that you want to ask me a question." He braced himself for *the* question: *What happened to you after the house party?*

"I'd like to know about Jack," she said.

Randal's eyes widened.

"Not like that!" she said quickly. "He's Roy's son. I want to know how he turned out. I know what I've seen, but what's the truth?"

Randal was relieved. "Jack isn't like Roy. I was told that he was headed that way, but he had to start behaving himself when he was given massive responsibility at a young age. And thanks to Sara, and now Kate, he's a very good young man."

"I loved Roy, but he was dangerous. Being with him was like playing with a stick of dynamite. Exciting but not what you want all the time."

Randal put the pasta in the pot of boiling water. "And your job was exciting enough."

"Yes!" She paused. "I went to Roy's funeral. In secret, of course. I was quite dramatic, all in black, with a veil covering my face. Pure Victorian. I didn't fool his wife. She spit on me. Through my veil."

"Did she know who you were? I mean your name."

"No."

Randal took a breath. He needed to get to the point. "Kate remembered hearing you say that Harry killed a man."

Her shock couldn't be concealed. It took a moment for her to compose herself. "So my big secret is revealed."

"I assume that's what Derek Oliver was using for blackmail."

"Yes, but I didn't know anything about that. Harry didn't have the courage to tell me the truth before I got here."

"You told us that you arrived here thinking you were to do battle for justice."

"Exactly. I didn't lie when I told that."

"You just left out the bloody part," he said. "Like to tell me now?"

She took a breath. "When Harry was eighteen years old, he got drunk, had an argument, and a young man died."

"A would-be, nobody actor."

She laughed. "Little Kate did hear me. What an amazing memory."

"Who was he?"

"I have no idea." She put up her hand. "There's no use asking me a lot of questions because I don't know. All Harry told me about the trip was that I was to negotiate a deal and settle on a price. It was to keep it out of the press about his sexual orientation. When I got here, Derek Oliver told me about the murder. I was livid and I called my husband. But Harry wouldn't tell me the details, and I assure you that I asked him. At the top of my lungs."

"Oliver would keep quiet for money?"

"That's what he said. Do you think he would have?"

"No."

"Me neither," Barbara said softly.

They didn't say any more, as she had just verified her motive for murder. If Derek Oliver hadn't died, their lives might have been ruined.

It was when they sat down to eat that Randal asked, "What's the connection between your husband and James Lachlan?"

"Is there one? I know we met at his house, but I thought it was for convenience."

He didn't know if she was telling the truth or not. "There must be a connection. We're pretty sure that Derek found out what Harry did from information that's in the Palm Room."

Barbara didn't reply.

"They're all dead now," Randal said. "Harry, the murder victim, and Oliver the blackmailer. There's no more danger, so why did you come here *now*? It makes no sense—unless you're the murderer. Did you kill him?"

Barbara gave a bit of a smile. "No, I didn't. I really believed what Billy told us, that Derek had urgent business and left suddenly."

"His wife must have known that wasn't true."

She gave him a look he'd seen her do on the screen. The recipients always backed down. "You would know more about that than I would."

Randal just smiled—and waited. He knew she was trying to redirect the conversation to keep from answering his question.

She gave a sigh that sounded like defeat. "It's going to come out so I might as well tell." She put her shoulders back as though for courage. "Roy and I had a child, a boy. He knows about Roy's family and he wants to meet his brother. I came here because I wanted to find out what Jack was like. When I first saw him and he looked so much like Roy…" She shrugged. They'd all seen her faint.

Randal tried to conceal his shock. "You said he wants to meet Jack?"

"Troy idolizes him, even though he's never met him."

Randal couldn't stop the widening of his eyes. "Troy?"

"Roy with a *T*."

"Did you tell Roy about his son?"

"No, never," she said quickly. "It's hard to believe, but at the end of that week, I was pretty sure I was pregnant. I had tingling, nausea, et cetera. I was out of my mind with fear. I'd met Roy's wife. She was so awful! I asked him why he'd married her. He said, 'I'm an honorable man. I marry every woman I knock up.' He meant it as a joke, but I knew he was telling the truth. I knew that if I told him I thought I was pregnant he'd move heaven and earth for us to be together. But I also knew what a life with him would be like."

"And you didn't want that."

"Of course not. My life with Harry was so very comfortable."

"Ah yes, Harry. Everything depended on him. You must have worried that he would throw you out when you told him."

"I was deathly afraid. Shaking with it." Barbara smiled. "But my darling husband was pleased. In fact, he'd talked to someone—probably Billy—and he knew all about my affair with Roy. He'd even asked for a description of him. Harry said, 'Our child will be beautiful.'"

"And is he?"

"Quite beautiful. Not dark like Jack, but then, I'm blonde. Troy is lighter than his father."

"Do you have any photos of him?"

"One or two." She was being sarcastic. She went to her handbag and pulled out a small leather case that held several photos and handed it to him. "I'm going to…" She waved her hand to mean the bathroom.

He looked at the photos, all of them of a young man who looked like a softer, less angry Roy.

Randal picked up his phone. I don't mean to distress you, he texted to Heather, Jack's mother, but do you have any photos of Evan?

In minutes, a picture came through. Jack had his arm around a young man with light hair and eyes and they were laughing. Evan and Troy looked very much alike.

When Randal heard Barbara approaching, he quickly put away his phone. It wasn't his place to tell her that her son was there and that he'd probably saved Jack's life. Randal wanted to get back to the main subject. "What proof did Derek have that your husband had killed someone? What did he have to back up his threats?"

"I don't know. It was a long time ago, and I was angry at Harry for not telling me the whole story, and there was Roy and…it was all too much for me to remember the details."

Randal gave her a hard look. He didn't believe her. After all, she'd been on Broadway in Shakespeare's plays, with all those lines to memorize. He raised an eyebrow. "Afraid you'll incriminate him?"

She squinted her eyes at him. "All right. Derek Oliver said, 'Tell your husband that I have the script and the film.'"

Randal's shock showed. "You think Harry wrote about the murder?"

"You mean the accidental death?" she said haughtily.

He wasn't intimidated by her look. "I mean a story about who Harry killed, and how he got away with it." Randal put up his hand. "You don't need to answer that. My sister says the writer's creed is, 'Never let an emotion or an experience escape your pen.' Maybe Harry believed that too. What were—?"

She cut him off. "Don't ask me which and what or when. I've made it my business to not know any of that. I told you! When I left this house, I was pretty sure I was pregnant and I had to face my husband with evidence of my infidelity. Everyone was going to know it wasn't his child. Discretion was important to Harry. When he welcomed me home, I wasn't about to ask him what happened when he was a kid. We never spoke of it. Not ever!"

Randal wanted to change the subject—something Sara said he was good at. "So who do *you* think killed Derek?"

Barbara looked startled, but pleased at being asked. "Of course I've thought about that, and Lea and I've had a good chin-wag about it."

It was Randal's turn to be startled. Lea hadn't mentioned that!

"There's Reid," Barbara said. "I hardly saw him. He worked outside. Carried in the coal buckets, in a way of speaking. I can't imagine he had much of a reason to murder Derek. Besides, he just doesn't seem like the type."

The man who owned the place, Randal thought. "Rachel? What was she like?"

"She was eighteen and a spoiled brat. The worst of her kind. She was sulking and angry. She let everyone know that she didn't want to be there. I could see her killing if someone annoyed her enough."

Randal raised his eyebrows at that condemnation. "And Lea?" He was a bit afraid of what he'd hear.

"Downtrodden. It was like she'd lost hope for life. But then you and Kate made her light up. As for murder, anyone who had such low self-esteem that she'd marry a jerk like Derek Oliver isn't one to plot a murder. On the other hand, she must have been repressing a lot of rage. It could have come out."

Randal was quiet for a moment. "I guess we better get back."

Barbara didn't move. "You missed someone."

"Billy? Mrs. Meyers?" He wasn't serious.

"The girl, Greer. She was so awkward and odd. She was sixteen but she seemed much younger. Billy told us she'd been homeschooled, and that she'd been nearly kept a prisoner by her grandmother. Working for us was her first real job. Reid looked after her. She adored her big brother. Hmmm. Maybe Reid got sick of the way his sister was being treated. He was good with a hammer."

"Kate said the girl thought she wasn't pretty."

"She was not." Barbara shook her head. "He was a real bastard to that poor girl. Her teeth, her face, her weight. He never let up on her."

"Did no one defend her?"

"We all did. Well, maybe not Rachel, but Lea and I did. The truth was that none of us wanted to anger him." She paused. "I did a terrible thing. I was to play a character who was strange and made everyone feel uncomfortable. I mimicked poor Greer. I even used that fight—" She looked at him in surprise.

"What did you remember?"

"Greer and Rachel had a blistering fight."

"About what?"

"Rachel was shouting that Greer stole something. 'I know you did it.'"

"Do you know what she stole?"

"No, I don't."

"Could it have been a toy? A stuffed animal?"

She gasped. "Yes! I think it was. Lea and I thought it was ridiculous."

Unless the toy was filled with jewels, Randal thought. His phone buzzed.

"Please take it," Barbara said. "Maybe your sister has solved the case. I'll meet you outside." She left the house.

Randal looked at the text from Billy.

In 1995, Barbara Adair played a neurosurgeon on a TV medical series for eight episodes. In an interview, she said she'd had to learn how to saw the top of a skull off. She added that she found the whole process fascinating and that she got quite good at it.

When Randal caught his breath from that bit of information, he texted Billy:

Harry Adair wrote a script and may have made a movie about the actor who was killed. No date on it. Don't think it was a blockbuster.

He sent a text to his sister:

It looks like Greer had motive and was capable. Barbara had motive and the know-how for all of it.

He included copies of the two texts he and Billy had ex-changed.

Randal shut his phone off. He hadn't told about Troy. He'd save that information for when he was with them. He wanted to see Jack's face when he was told that he had a brother.

Smiling at the thought, he went outside to meet Barbara.

TWELVE

KATE WAS NERVOUS ABOUT ASKING REID TO LUNCH. He seemed like a nice guy, but as all women know, some men misinterpret any invitation from a woman. She'd just be careful that they went to a public place. Or maybe they should stay there at Lachlan House. She could make it into a picnic. Outside where Lenny could see them.

She found him on his way back from the cottage. He'd been working on the landscape and had just emerged, showered and in fresh clothes. With great effort, she controlled her nervousness and asked him to have lunch with her.

He smiled. "Thank you, but I can't go. Maybe tomorrow." He turned away.

Kate was annoyed with herself for being ego-hurt. She was quite a bit younger than he was, and well, she was attractive. It took her a moment to get herself under control, then she hurried after him. "I can't tomorrow. Today is the only day I can go."

He frowned but then his face cleared. "You've been assigned to ask me questions, haven't you?"

She could feel her face turn red. She would never make a spy! She gave a curt nod.

"How about later? This afternoon about four? We can have tea."

All Kate could think about was telling the others that she'd failed. "Couldn't you change your appointment?"

"I'm having lunch with my grandmother. It would upset her if I canceled. I hardly see her anymore."

Kate had to bite her tongue to keep from saying, *The woman whose husband was executed?* "I'd love to meet her," she managed to say.

Reid hesitated, but then smiled. "She might like that. Can you be ready quickly?"

Kate opened her arms to say she was ready now. "I'll meet you in the front."

He turned away to go around the house, while Kate went inside to get her handbag. She paused by Lenny to say, "I'm going with Reid to see his grandmother." She'd learned to let people know where she was going to be. Lenny nodded. She saw no one else as she went through to the front.

Reid was standing by a rental car, a Toyota. He didn't open her door and she was glad. She didn't want this to seem like a date.

"I hope you like haggis and Guinness," he said as he pulled out of the driveway. He smiled at the look on her face. "Just kidding. I got her a cook to come in, but it'll still probably be soup and a sandwich."

"She lives alone?"

"That's what she wants. I've tried to get her to go to one of those places with other people her age, but she won't do it. The house I got her—" He broke off. "I mean, her house is nice, and she's happy there."

"What do you do?"

"The most boring job in the world. I sell insurance. Or at least the men who work for me do." He paused. "Sorry. I guess I'm blowing my own horn."

"I think you should be proud of your accomplishments. What about your parents?"

He instantly looked sad. "They were killed in a multicar pileup just after I graduated from high school. What about you? I've met your father but not your mother."

Kate's supply of mothers was too complicated to go into. "She's around. Tell me about your grandmother."

His face softened. "She hasn't had an easy life. She was widowed early, then her only child, my father, was killed in that car crash."

"And Greer?" Kate was watching him intently.

He took a deep breath. "That was the worst blow. Grans was so afraid of losing anyone else that she kept Greer at home with her. She felt she'd be safe there, but she wasn't. My grandmother has lost everyone."

"Except you."

He shook his head. "It's not easy being someone's 'Only.' I'm her only surviving relative."

"But you take care of her."

"I do my best, but I live in St. Pete. I'm going to try to stay here more often. This trip has made me see how frail she is."

He pulled into the driveway of a very pretty house. Light brown Florida stucco with palm trees and shrubs. Everything was perfectly trimmed. As a Realtor, Kate knew the house was worth about three hundred grand. Not cheap.

Reid didn't open the door but turned to Kate. "My grandmother is quite old and her mind isn't always stable. In the last few years she's reverted to what she knew when she was a girl. Sometimes she still thinks she's living in that remote Scottish village."

Kate wasn't sure how to reply to that. "It sounds charming."

"Yes and no. For some reason, she recently decided she has Second Sight. Do you know what that is?"

"Premonitions? Able to read minds?"

"Whatever she is or not depends on the day. I just hope she doesn't decide she's a tight rope walker and climb on the roof." He gave a weak smile. "Sure you can handle this?"

Kate gave a little snort. "Are you kidding? Someday I'll tell you about the woman who raised me. I can handle anything."

He was pleased by that. "Then let the adventure begin."

Kate followed him into the house, and his grandmother was standing there waiting for them. Kate's first impression of her was how mobile she was. She didn't shuffle, didn't use a cane. She was short and stout, but not fat. Her face was lined, but not badly. Kate doubted if she had ever been a pretty woman. Her teeth were all capped—or were dentures—and her nose was large. There were several big moles on her face.

That she reminded her of Greer, made Kate instantly like her. Her eyes were bright and alert as she listened to Reid explain who Kate was. He left out everything about the murder and the investigation. Instead, he said she and her family were guests of Billy. He made it sound like a party.

When Kate shook her hand, she was pleased to find it was quite strong. "Thank you for having me, Mrs. Graham."

"Call me Alish." She pronounced it with a long *A*.

"Alish," Kate said, and would have liked to sit with her and talk about her life. She must have seen a lot. But Reid told them lunch was ready.

The dining area was to one side of the living room, so they had a view of it all.

Reid must have called ahead as there were three place settings, and as he'd predicted, they had soup and a sandwich. There was no sign of a cook. Reid did all the talking. He was fairly entertaining as he told his grandmother about Lachlan House and how it looked now. He raved about what the Medlar-Wyatt team had done to it. "They did it very fast and Kate decorated it all."

Part of her was glad to hear that he liked the house so much. It wouldn't be long before he found out that it was his. Another part was sad as she remembered Jack's idea of living there.

As Reid went on, Kate looked about the house. All the furniture was old, but not antiques. If a movie script called for a "grandmother's house" this would be it. There were a few knickknacks, mostly Scottish, but not many. No plastic Eiffel Tower, nothing from a trip to the Grand Canyon. In fact, there wasn't anything personal anywhere. As Reid kept talking, Kate realized that there were no photos. On the walls were scenic pictures, the kind you see for sale in a frame shop.

When Reid paused in talking, Kate turned back to him. He and his grandmother were staring at her. She wasn't sure what to say. "Thank you. It was my first decorating experience. I wanted them to get Jack's sister to do it, but she was on a job, so…" She trailed off and the silence was awkward.

They left the table, the dirty dishes staying where they were, and went into the living room.

"Reid, dear," Alish said in her Scottish accent, "I think someone was trying to break into my bedroom. Would you please look at the windows?"

He hesitated, then turned and gave a rolled eye look at Kate, telling her his grandmother was prone to imagining things.

When he was out of sight, Alish opened a little wooden box on the coffee table and took out something round and silver. There was a spark of green as she took Kate's hand and pressed it into her palm. "Take this, and it will make you dream of your true love."

"I've already found him." Kate was smiling.

"Yes, you have. I can feel that your heart is full now, but it hasn't always been."

From down the hall, Reid shouted, "Which window?"

"The one by the yellow cabinet," Alish yelled back.

Kate's eyes widened at the strength of her voice.

"That's in the guest bedroom!" He sounded annoyed.

"Yes, it is." Alish's eyes were twinkling with mischief. She was holding her hand curled around Kate's that held the disk. "Then give it to the storyteller. Her mind is open to all. It is never full. Put it under her pillow and it will help her listen."

"That's Aunt Sara all right. You should visit us. Or all of us can come here. We'd love to—"

Alish dropped Kate's hand and stepped back. Her eyes lost their twinkle. "No! Do not do that. I could not—" At the sound of Reid's footsteps, she dropped her shoulders and looked down. Kate thought that if Aunt Sara was there she would have called it Old Woman Pose.

Reid came into the room and looked from one woman to the other. "You two all right?"

"Great," Kate said. "Your grandmother is going to show me how to do tatting."

"What?" he asked.

"Lace making," Alish said. "The storyteller likes it."

"Story—? Oh," he said. "Sara. She and I have become friends. Perhaps you can meet her. But now you look tired. Should I help you to your room?"

"Yes, please." She gave a glance at Kate, then turned back to Reid, and they left, with her leaning heavily on his arm.

Kate wanted to look at what was in her hand, but she didn't want Reid to see it. She wasn't sure why. She grabbed her handbag and dropped it into the inside pocket.

Minutes later, she and Reid left the house. As they drove away, Kate was silent. She wasn't sure what she'd seen or felt.

She wished Sara or Jack or her father had been with her and heard it all.

She assumed he was going back to Lachlan House but instead, he pulled into the parking lot of a small group of stores.

"There's a coffee shop here. Mind if we sit and talk? Or do you need to get back?"

"I have time." She wanted to know what he had to say.

The shop had outside tables to take advantage of South Florida's divine weather. Kate ordered a matcha latte and Reid had a tall black coffee. He wouldn't allow her to pay for theirs or even her own.

As soon as they sat down, he said, "I want to apologize for today. Grans put on her 'timid old lady' act. In spite of her age, she is the least timid person on the planet. The truth is that right now she's very angry at me."

"About where she lives?"

"Yes! You're perceptive."

"I just imagine telling Aunt Sara that she should move into an old folks' home. Bombs would go off."

"So you do understand. Last night she and I had another big argument. I want her to live with me but she refuses. She says I have to move my entire business and all my employees here. Can you imagine how much that would cost?"

"Give me some numbers and in twenty minutes I can give you a spreadsheet."

He laughed. "It's too much! But Grans won't bend. She refuses to leave Lachlan. I don't know how to solve this. We were going to talk about it more today, but…"

"I invited myself," Kate said.

"You were a welcome break in the tension. Sorry I talked so much, but if I'd let Grans say anything, she would have had no qualms about bringing up our personal problems in front of you."

Kate was sipping her drink. "Why won't she leave?"

"Ah," he said. "That. The grave of my grandfather is here. She says she owes him and that someone must remember him and be with him forever—or as long as she lives, that is."

"True love," Kate said.

"I guess."

Kate didn't know how to ask what she wanted to. Aunt Sara would have blurted it out. "You said your grandmother was widowed early."

He gave her a look so intense that Kate turned away.

"You know how he died, don't you?"

"Billy did mention the Lonely Laird story." She didn't add that they knew of Reid's connection to James Lachlan.

Reid took his time answering. "I guess it was bound to come out. Grans and I don't talk about it." He took a breath. "Yes, my grandfather, Reid Graham, the first of that name, was hanged for murder."

She wanted to know more but how did she ask without being invasive? "Premeditated?"

He gave a half smile. "I don't think any of us Grahams are that clever. My father, the second Reid, managed to get through law school and pass the bar, but he didn't win many cases." He paused. "All I really know is what Grans told me. It's purely one-sided and I have no idea if it's true or not."

"I'd like to hear any version."

"Of course my grandfather was innocent."

"I wouldn't have thought otherwise."

"Okay," he said. "There was a bar fight and a man was killed. Same old story."

Kate tried to keep the look of surprise off her face. A bar fight? A man killed? Was it the same murder she'd overheard Barbara speak of years ago? It didn't make sense that it could be the same one, but still… "You wouldn't by chance know who was killed, would you?"

"Tom Skellit. Grans told me the name. According to her, he was a drunken lout, and he deserved to be killed."

"Hanging for an accidental death seems harsh. Wouldn't it have been manslaughter?"

"That is the part Grans is most angry about. She said it was all James Lachlan's fault."

"How?"

"He wasn't in the US when it happened. He was in Russia selling oranges and got caught there by snow. The judge in the case was one of the families who'd come over from Scotland. I guess you know about them."

"Not at all."

"There were eight families who arrived here, all of them broke, but only James went on to become wealthy. The most wise thing my family ever did was to hitch themselves to him from the very beginning. We were always comfortable. Not rich, but good. Mr. Lachlan took care of his people. Even today it seems to be a tradition that I cut his lawn."

"But I guess the judge went his own way."

"Yes. As soon as they arrived in the US, James offered him a partnership. But the man laughed at him and said his fruit trees were ridiculous."

"I can see where this is going," Kate said. "The judge did not succeed in any endeavor."

"That's right. He failed at every business he tried, except being made a local judge. People said his bitterness was legendary. He'd give ten years for stealing a bunch of bananas."

"And death for a barroom brawl."

"Yes, he did. He sentenced my grandfather to be hanged. Even the begging of his pregnant wife wouldn't change his mind. Grans was determined to delay it until Mr. Lachlan returned, but the judge was more determined to carry out the sentence before he got back."

"And the judge won."

"He did."

"What an ugly story," Kate said. "I'm beginning to understand why your grandmother won't leave here." She was starting to see that Reid and Alish deserved Lachlan House. "James's son disappeared."

"Yes. Aran, that was his name, ran away. He and my grandfather were raised together. Aran couldn't take his cousin's death. No one knows what happened to him. Probably joined the war. Maybe he's in one of the tombs of an unknown soldier. I guess we'll never know."

"So you're Reid Graham the third."

"I am. Pretentious as it is."

They sat in silence for a moment, then he said, "We better get back. Jack may think I've kidnapped you. If he's like his father, he'll punch a man in the face before he asks questions."

Kate felt defensive, but said, "Jack would wait for the answer, and if he doesn't like it, then he'd hit you."

Again, Reid laughed. It was a nice sound.

She gathered her courage. "You probably want to get back to Rachel."

His shock showed on his face. He was a good-looking man. If his eyes were a bit different and his nose narrower, he might be handsome. "You people don't miss anything, do you? Did Sara tell you that I was in love with her?"

Kate didn't answer that. "Are you still?"

"Maybe," he said as he got up. "I hope to find out. Are you ready?"

Kate didn't move. "Who do you think killed Derek Oliver?"

He sat back down. "The million-dollar question. I'm sure you've been told that I wasn't in the house much, but I did go in to check on my little sister."

"So you saw things."

"Enough to know that everyone hated the man."

She took a breath. "Including your sister. I remember that much."

His eyes widened. "You *remember*? You were four years old."

Kate wished she hadn't said that. "Only vague images. I remember that I liked Greer."

He grimaced. "You and I were the only ones. They made fun of her. Not when I was around, but twice I found her crying."

Kate frowned. "I can't imagine that Roy or Barbara or Lea would hurt her."

"I don't think they did it intentionally, but she was excluded from things. People went silent when she showed up."

"I thought she was fun!" Kate again felt that she was four years old. Greer was her friend.

Reid smiled in a reassuring way. "She adored you. She talked nonstop about you to Grans. Greer used to say she wanted to get married and have a dozen children just like you. We never told her that was impossible."

"Why was it?" Kate asked quickly.

"I'm sorry. I don't mean to upset you. I loved my sister very much but her mind wasn't…wasn't the highest functioning. That's why Grans and I—" He abruptly stopped.

"Why you what?"

"Protected her as much as possible." He took a while before speaking. "You have to understand that Derek Oliver was a very nasty man. He believed that putting a person down made him rise higher. I don't know how Oliver was killed, but my sister was a big girl. Strong. Grans and I are afraid that she…" He didn't finish.

"Like what happened in the barroom brawl?" Kate asked softly. "He drove her too far and she snapped? Hit him with something?"

Reid gave a shrug of not knowing. "Grans and I really and

truly hope that you find out who committed the murder. She and I want to be *sure* it wasn't our dear Greer. As for the others, I have no idea. They probably all had a reason to get rid of him. Their lives seem to have gone well without him. Maybe that's a coincidence, or maybe the good happened because he was no longer around. I don't know."

He reached across the table to put his hand over hers. "Please. Grans and I beg you to find out who killed Derek Oliver. We want Greer's name cleared."

"We will do our best." Kate pulled her hand away and looked at her watch. It was almost four. "I need to get back."

"Of course," he said as she stood up. He put their empty cups in the trash. "Whatever happens, thank you for bringing all this to the light."

Kate just nodded. Her mind was full of a hundred thoughts and facts.

When they got back to Lachlan House, Kate texted Billy:

James Lachlan's nephew, Reid Graham, was hanged for murder in a barroom brawl. Don't know the year but his wife Alish was pregnant with Reid II, a lawyer in town. Lachlan's son was named Aran.

She sent a second text to Sara:

Young Greer seems to be a possibility. Reid's granny sent you a gift. I got Billy and co looking at the execution. See you at four.

Like her father, she included the texts she'd exchanged with Billy.

THIRTEEN

JACK WASN'T SURE IF HE'D EVER HAD A MORE UN-comfortable task. From seeing Lea and Randal together, it was quite possible that she might someday be his mother-in-law. It wouldn't be good to start out by asking her if she was a murderer. Of course she'd say no, then he'd have to figure out if she was a liar. Either way, it was bad.

He knew that the guests had figured out that each person had been assigned an interrogator. Jack overheard Barbara say, "We don't get to choose who grills us? Will we be put into a barren little room and told we can't smoke?" Lea answered, "I could stand an afternoon with Randal." Barbara said, "Jack is mine."

With a red face, Jack hurried away. He didn't want to hear any more. So now he'd postponed the interview long enough and he had to face Lea. He had no idea how to begin.

She was sitting in the living room, wearing black pants and a white blouse, her handbag beside her. She looked like she was ready to go somewhere.

"Hi." Even to himself, he sounded cautious.

"Hello," she answered.

"Could I take you to lunch? Whatever you want to eat, we have it in South Florida. How about Cuban?"

"You know what I'd like?" She didn't wait for his answer. "I want to know everything about Randal. He won't talk about himself much, but I want to know."

Jack was pleased at that idea. Telling about Randal was preferable to asking about murder. He'd just segue into what needed to be asked. "I can understand that. He's been through some pretty awful stuff."

"Will you tell me about it?"

"How about we have lunch, then I take you to see the house where he and Sara grew up?"

She looked delighted at that idea. "How about picking up some greasy fried takeout, and we eat it at the house?"

Jack's eyes sparkled. "I see why Randal is in love with you. KFC?"

"Love it!" she said.

"I'm afraid I don't have a car here. Mind riding in my beat-up truck?"

"Are you kidding? For years I drove nothing else. I had a manufacturing company to run, and I had to pick up supplies and deliver crates to be shipped and—" She waved her hand. "All of it. Being a boss is no easy job."

"No, it's not. Tell me about your business." They got into his truck and as she talked of constructing sandals, Jack thought of saws and skulls being cut open. It looked like she had the know-how, along with the strong motive of getting rid of her abusive husband.

At the KFC window, he ordered two three-piece boxes, original recipe. He liked a woman who wasn't afraid of fried chicken. He smiled when he remembered that when he first met Sara when he was a teenager, he took her out for huge, greasy burgers.

"Tell me about the houses," Lea said.

"Built for soldiers returning from World War Two. Plain, sturdy, small."

"And Cal was Sara's next-door neighbor?"

"Yes," he said, but then elaborated. "They were each other's saviors. Cal's father was a bastard, and his stepmother couldn't have cared less."

"And Sara?"

"Her situation was just as bad. Her mother loved Randal but couldn't stand Sara." When Lea gave a laugh, he looked at her in surprise.

"Randal can make anyone like him. It's a talent, like music or art. He was so nice to my husband, he even made him smile a few times. But then Randal passed me in the hall and said, 'I hate your husband.' It made me laugh hard."

"Sara isn't like that."

"No, she's not. I can see that she is totally honest. If she dislikes you, you know it."

As Jack stopped on the driveway of the Medlar house, he looked at Lea. He was glad she seemed to really know Randal. She wasn't fooled by his elegant manners.

She seemed to understand and they exchanged smiles before turning away to look at the house. "It looks good."

"Thank you. We had plans for a major reno, but we haven't had the heart to do it. I've done a lot of repairs since I bought the house. It's stable and clean, but it hasn't really been changed. I was in Colorado for months, and Sara said they put in some furniture. I haven't seen what they did. You ready?"

She nodded, and they took their food boxes and drinks inside. It was cozy and very much like stepping back in time.

Very 1950s decor, even to the flowered wallpaper around the front window.

"Looks like Kate and Sara did more than they said." Jack shook his head. "I have a feeling I'm never going to be allowed to renovate this place."

"I'll bet you Randal had a hand in this."

"Probably so."

They put their food on the skinny-legged coffee table, then Jack followed her around the house. The kitchen had retro appliances and new laminate countertops. No granite allowed. The bathroom was turquoise tile with white fixtures.

"Perfect," Lea said as they went back to the living room and sat down to eat. "I want to hear about Randal."

As succinctly as he could, Jack told her about Randal's life. The story wasn't pretty. Jack elaborated on how Randal had been favored by his mother. "It's not good for a child to be told he's right in whatever he does. That hurts him."

Lea looked at Jack. "Or for a child to always be told he's bad."

He knew she was referring to Roy's relentless belittling of him. He turned away but was glad for her understanding.

Jack spent the most time telling of what happened after Kate was born. When he told who betrayed Randal and why, Lea stared at him in disbelief.

"When Kate was here, she and her father were inseparable. I've never seen a parent and child love each other more. That they were separated—" Lea turned away to blink back tears.

"Yeah," Jack said. "The poor kid was so traumatized she blocked out all memory of him, and of Sara."

"Ah, yes, Sara. How are you attached to her?"

He told how Sara had more or less rescued him, his mother, and his sister when Jack's stepdad died unexpectedly. Sara gave Jack the money to start his construction business, and later, she showed him the world outside Florida. "Come on," he said. "Let me show you where Cal and Sara met from the time they were children."

They closed their empty boxes and went outside. Next door was the Wyatt house, where Cal had grown up. Jack showed her the path covered in old hubcaps. It had almost been buried over the years but Jack had restored it. He explained that Cal's father ran an auto repair shop. "When a car fell on the old man and crippled him, Cal gave up college and stayed in Lachlan to run the shop and support his father and his step-mother."

"Who were horrible to him," Lea said.

"Right."

Jack led them to the end of the path. There was a crumbling concrete floor. "Used to have a wooden frame with vines over it."

"A love nest."

"Probably." He nodded toward a wooden bench. "This is new." They sat down.

They were silent for a while, then Lea smiled. "Cal was a darling. That week we were at Lachlan House, he did all the work Roy was paid to do. Did you know that Cal and James Lachlan were great friends?"

"Sara said something about that, but I didn't think it was a 'great' friendship."

"Oh yes! One day I made lemonade and brownies and took them out to Cal. He'd been on the roof doing something and he was sweaty. He apologized but..." She grinned. "Lord! But he was a good-looking man. No offense, but he was even better than you and Roy."

Jack was far from offended. "The Magnificent Three. That's what he and his two buddies were called in high school."

"I can believe it. Cal and I sat in the shade and talked. He told me about how much he missed James. He said he'd been like a real father to him. Cal said that when he was little he and his mother visited Lachlan House often. She cooked for him. Poor man. I can understand. James was a childless widower for many years."

"I knew Grandad worked here, but I didn't know they were actual friends," Jack said in wonder.

"James used to play catch with Cal. And football. Not American but soccer. Cal said his mother showed them how to kick the ball around. She was quite good at it."

"Renata?" Jack was astonished.

"If that's your great-grandmother's name, yes. She was from Argentina, I think."

"Brazil," Jack said. "She died long before I was born. I know Grandad always missed her. She was the buffer between him and his father. What else did he say?"

"That's all. Cal saw Roy doing nothing and went after him." She gave Jack a sharp look. "How did you and Cal turn out so good and Roy was so...?" She waved her hand, unable to think of the words.

"Mothers," he said. "Cal had Renata and I had my mom, Heather. Roy's mother was a woman named Donna. She is not a nice person."

"Is that a big understatement?"

"Oh yeah."

"She's still alive?"

"Yes, but I don't see her. She liked her son and no one else on earth."

"Not her beautiful husband, Cal?"

"Especially not him."

"Then why in the world did he—?"

Jack looked at her.

"Oh. Preggers."

"Yes."

"I don't mean to be nosy but why didn't Cal and Sara marry?"

"No one knows, and Sara won't tell. If you ask her, she turns into a statue. Immobile and soundless. She just plain freezes. Sometimes I wonder how different everything would have been if Sara had married him. For one thing, she would have been my grandmother."

"Too bad she isn't," Lea said. "If she were a blood relative, she might have helped you in your business, educated you, and encouraged you in your pursuit of a woman like Kate. It is certainly bad that she's not your *real* grandmother."

Jack laughed, then leaned over and kissed Lea's cheek. "Thanks." He paused, then said, "Would you like to see the inside of Granddad's house?"

"I think you and I should talk about why we came here."

"I told you about Randal."

She gave him a look that said he knew what she was talking about. "I didn't kill my husband and I don't know who did. None of you have even hinted at *how* he was killed, but we don't think it was a firearm. Someone would have heard it. As for opportunity, all of us were all over the house. We would have seen a stranger, so it had to be one of us."

"No guesses?"

"That's hard to say. Everyone disliked him so very much. He was rude, sarcastic, and loved to put people down."

"Yet you married him."

"I can assure you that before the wedding, he was the kindest, most thoughtful person in the world. But I do understand why he was murdered."

"It's a matter of who."

"What if you never found out? What if you just left it alone?"

"As Sara has said, 'No matter how vile a person is, you can't kill them.'" He looked at her. "Is there something you haven't told me?"

She didn't speak for a moment as she seemed to be pondering something. Leaning back, she dug into her trouser pocket, withdrew a ring, and handed it to him.

It was obviously old, with an intricate yellow gold band and three reddish-brown stones.

"I found it. It's not really valuable, and I never saw Mrs. Meyers wear it. Maybe it was sentimental."

"Are you saying that this had something to do with the murder?"

"I have no idea," Lea said. "As you know, Randal and I had to sneak around to see each other, so one night I was hiding in a doorway. It was a full moon and quite bright. I saw Rachel running across the lawn. She had a paper bag in her hand and she dropped it. The lawn had been watered and I guess the paper broke. She went to her knees and I could hear her cursing as she searched for whatever had been in the bag. It took her what seemed like an eternity to find all the items."

"And you were in a hurry to get to Randal."

"Yes. I was afraid he'd leave. He does love punctuality. Anyway, Rachel gathered whatever she'd found in the grass and rolled it into her top. I still don't know how she did that because that girl wore practically nothing. Barbara used to make jokes about her shaving. Oh! Sorry. Just girl talk."

"And this ring was left behind?"

"Yes. The next morning I thought about what I'd seen. It was just barely daylight and I heard Derek in his room. As always, I wanted to avoid seeing him, so I went outside. I looked in the grass about where Rachel had been and I saw the ring."

He waited for her to say more but she was silent. "You didn't give it to Mrs. Meyers?"

"It was a dilemma. Should I give it to her or to Rachel—who I was pretty sure had stolen it? But I'd seen that she had a whole bag of things. If I gave the ring to Mrs. Meyers, she might check what else was missing. Then I'd get Rachel in trouble. And if I gave it to Rachel, she'd know I knew her secret, and I'd make an enemy. And trust me on this, you do *not* want Rachel for an enemy! In the end, I did nothing. It was cowardly of me, but at the time, I had other things on my mind."

Jack was looking at the ring. "When Rachel dropped all the stuff, you didn't see anything green, did you?"

Lea's eyes widened. "Like that big emerald ring Mrs. Meyers owned? I only saw it once at dinner. It's so big that it has a name and a history. She told us. It belonged to some Indian prince hundreds of years ago. She said her husband gave it to her on their twentieth anniversary. We were all quiet because she looked like she was going to cry. She held her hand to her heart and whispered, 'I will miss it.'" Lea looked at Jack. "Was Derek going to take it from her?"

"We don't know, but maybe."

Her head came up. "If Rachel hid it somewhere, then her grandmother couldn't give it to him."

She looked so hopeful that Rachel wasn't a thief that Jack said, "Maybe." But he didn't believe that. "When Derek disappeared, did Mrs. Meyers say anything about missing jewels?"

"She was as happy as we all were. Billy was an excellent host and champagne flowed. He said, 'Drink up, ladies, the bad man paid for it.' So we drank and ate and laughed hysterically. Barbara is a great mimic, and she did a one-woman show for us, and Mrs. Meyers told us raunchy stories from her long life."

"What about Greer and Reid?"

"Greer wasn't allowed to participate. Too young. Actually, I sent her and Kate upstairs. Reid? He couldn't have been there. A male presence tends to make women tone themselves down. But of course Billy added to the fun."

"And Rachel?"

"Now that I think about it, she wasn't there either. She and Reid were probably doing it in the garage or in the guesthouse or at the cottage or on top of the iguanas. We all laughed at how insatiable they were."

"Even Mrs. Meyers laughed about her granddaughter?"

"The hardest of us all. She often said that she was just like Rachel at that age."

"A scantily clad, promiscuous thief with a bad temper?"

Lea laughed. "You've been around Sara for a long time. That's just what she'd say."

"Thank you. That's a compliment." He took out his phone. "Excuse me," he said as he sent a text to Sara:

Lea saw Rachel with a bag full of jewels. And she was hot and heavy with Reid.

"Don't forget to tell her how Rachel dressed," Lea said. "I think maybe she was Derek's next choice for wife."

The look on Jack's face told what he thought of that. "She wouldn't have fallen for him, would she?"

Lea shrugged. "There's something enticing about older men." She said it with a twinkle because Randal was no kid. Jack tapped on his phone.

Rachel wore little, sulked a lot, and old Oliver may have planned to try to marry her. $$$$

He looked at Lea. "Anything else?"

"That's all I can think of." She looked at her watch. "When's your curfew?"

"I'm to report back at 4:00 p.m."

"Then we better hightail it. We have ten minutes. Want me to drive?"

Jack scoffed, then stood up. "Think you can keep up?"

"Try me."

They ran to the truck, sped out, and arrived at Lachlan House in nine and a half minutes.

Fourteen

LENNY APPEARED TO BE BUSY IN THE KITCHEN, BUT the truth was, he was watching and listening. The caterers were in charge of preparing the food, and Lenny used his scarred face to keep them in line. His fierce looks kept them from bothering him with idiot questions about where what was and did he have whatever. He believed in kids growing up instead of endlessly depending on adults.

This freed Lenny to keep up with what was going on in the house. He felt he owed this as he was eternally grateful to Sara, Kate, and Jack for taking him in. After he was shot, they could have left him alone to take care of himself. He didn't tell anyone, not even the doctor he visited often, but he was plagued with headaches, sometimes blurry vision, and an inability to move quickly.

To repay his saviors, he was determined to watch over them. In spite of their encounters with murders, they still tended to believe the best of people.

Lenny was concerned about the chimney that had nearly landed on Jack. They seemed to dismiss it, but Lenny didn't.

He knew that it had been blown up by someone who knew about explosives. Lenny would have called his old friend Harvey and asked him how it was done, but in '91, he accidently stepped on one of his own wires. To Lenny, it was obvious that Jack—not someone else—had been the target. But why? What did someone gain by taking out Jack? Did it have to do with his father? From what Lenny had heard, Roy was capable of anything. Hitting Derek Oliver over the head? Sure. But sawing his skull open? No. That took a fetishist. Someone deeply disturbed. Someone who would have shown signs of that inclination from a young age.

So far, Lenny had seen nothing like that in any of the people lurking about the big old place.

And *lurking* was the key word. They all seemed to be up to something in secret. He'd seen Lea—the love of Randal's life—rummaging in the Palm Room. She was opening books and shaking them. Looking for what?

The movie star went up and down the back fence like she was searching for fire anthills. If she stepped on one in those little sandals she wore, she'd be sorry. Reid was using a weed whacker to cover the way he was searching the grounds. What were they all looking for? And if it was something so important, why hadn't they come here years ago when the house was empty?

The only person he actually liked was Rachel, and that was because the boy, Quinn, liked her. In Lenny's experience, kids were like dogs. They liked people from their hearts.

But Sara didn't like Rachel, and Lenny couldn't figure out why.

He thought Sara needed to calm down. But then, the two couples, Randal and Lea, Jack and Kate, were so enamored of each other that everything was being dumped onto Sara. As far as Lenny could see, all she wanted to do was to go somewhere quiet and write in her notebook. He'd seen her hurrying from place to place and writing as she rushed. She had too many ideas in her mind to concentrate on just one thing.

This morning as she was rushing through the kitchen, she asked him, "What's a good male name that starts with G?"

"Graham," he said.

"No, can't use it. That's Reid's name. I learned a long time ago not to use the names of people I've met. They like to thank me for using them in my book, then tell me I owe them 50 percent of whatever I was paid. Oh crap!" She was looking at her watch. "I have to go. Keep thinking of names," she called over her shoulder as she ran out of the kitchen.

Through some excellent sleuthing, if he said so himself, he found out that Sara had divided suspects and assigned each person to an interview. Good! Give them a job so they help.

Unfortunately, Sara had taken Rachel. He knew that wouldn't be done fairly. He was sure she'd try to be neutral, but she would take her ill feelings into the interview.

That bothered him, but there was also the fact that all of them were so frantically running from one place to another that they were missing things. They'd even set a time limit on the interviews. *Learn everything there is to know and be back here by four* was their creed. Right. And each suspect was going to be honest and truthful. What a joke.

Sara had asked him about "the boy with the lawn mower." Lenny had no idea who she was talking about. Early in his life, he'd learned to never let anyone know he hadn't a clue about whatever was being asked. His dad had taught him that. "Act responsible and you'll be given responsibility, which leads to knowledge—which contains secrets. Knowing secrets is the to key to it all."

When Sara asked, Lenny acted like he knew all about the kid with a lawn mower. But he was actually shocked. How had he not heard that loud machine? Especially since it would have been going just at dawn? The only person he'd ever met who slept as little as he did was Sara. If she was outside, it was probably barely daylight.

He'd told her he'd take care of it. But who was the kid, and where was he?

Lenny went outside to look for him, but he was distracted when he saw Barbara Adair skulking about. He followed her. Three times he had to hide from the movie star. What was she looking for? She was made up like she was going before a camera and had on some outfit that should have been labeled *Summer in Capri*. Did she have a lover? Jack and Randal were taken so that left young Reid. To be fair, he was probably only a few years younger than Mrs. Adair.

Following her without being seen wasn't easy. Lenny's head injury had affected his entire body. He could no longer "disappear" as he used to. He couldn't slide into doorways, stoop under staircases, or dive through windows as he easily used to do. But Barbara was so intent on whatever she was searching for that she didn't see him. Lenny was tempted to test her concentration by stepping in front of her, but he didn't.

Whatever she was seeking, she didn't find it. Instead, she and Randal went off to lunch. Jack and Kate also went away. Separately. *Can they bear to be apart for two whole hours?* Lenny thought. He'd never come close to being in love and seeing those four obsessed with one another made him glad of it.

When Lenny went back inside, Sara was like a house that was about to explode: agitated and hyperactive. He heard her call the local tearoom and order food to be delivered. What they had in the house wasn't good enough for her?

When she asked Lenny if he'd seen Rachel, he said no—

and he knew he had to *do* something. The way Sara was now, she'd probably have Rachel arrested before she even started to ask questions.

Then an odd thing happened. As Randal and Barbara drove away from the front of the house, in the back appeared a young man Lenny had never seen before. He was impressed and annoyed at the same time. That the boy could hide from him was startling, and it made Lenny feel old and incompetent. He was losing his ability to see all while not being seen.

Lenny lost no time in going after the boy. He was a young man, early twenties, but to Lenny that was a child. "Sara needs you."

He looked blank, like he'd never heard of her.

"Sara? Solving the murder?"

The boy's eyes widened. He was a good-looking kid. Dark blond hair, blue eyes. He looked like he'd been fed nothing but "good for you" food all his life.

"You know anything about VHS machines?"

"Sure. My dad—"

Lenny put his hand up. He didn't have time to listen to a life story. "You're to go with Sara to an old-age home and connect the system. They're researching some guy named Harry Adair. Ever hear of him?"

The kid gave a bit of a smile. "All my life."

Was he some California kid? Knew who directed and produced every movie? "Make the oldies laugh and calm Sara down. Think you can do that?"

His eyes were sparkling. "Sure. I can sing like a forties crooner."

"They're more of a 'Can't Get No Satisfaction' generation."

"Then give me an electric guitar."

Lenny wasn't sure if he greatly disliked the smart-aleck kid or wanted to adopt him. "Just take Sara away and keep her occupied. Don't let her return here until after four. Got it?"

"Yes, sir! I'll do it."

At that Lenny gave a smile—which he tried never to do. The scar on his head wouldn't let one side of his face move. A smile emphasized the imbalance and turned his face into a hideous mask. At the sight, even people who knew him stepped back.

But the kid didn't so much as blink. "Any more orders, sir?"

"Go on," Lenny said gruffly, trying to quit smiling so he looked less scary.

The boy started toward the house, but turned, walking backward. "Is the VHS in the Palm Room? And the great Harry Adair's movies are in there?"

Lenny's smile left as he realized "who" the kid was. He was what Barbara had been searching for. There was a look of her in his eyes. But his walk was pure... Lenny blinked as he tried to place it. He cursed at his brain. It wasn't as agile as it had once been. "The tapes have been moved to the old-age home. You just need to go there and hook the machines up."

"Easy," the kid said, then began running to the house.

Lenny saw a shadow move. He knew from the shape that it was Rachel. He smiled—as much as his face would allow, that is. Since Sara was going to be occupied, maybe he could be the one to find out some things from Rachel.

It wasn't easy, considering the stiffness of his body, but he confronted her. Her look of surprise pleased him. He hadn't lost all of his abilities! "Everyone is gone. Want to have lunch?"

She hesitated.

"Just us. No one else."

That seemed to intrigue her, and he wondered why.

While he'd been outside, the food from Mitford Tea had been delivered and was on the counter.

Rachel looked at the name on the bag. "We'll have tea? In fancy cups? And pink cakes with roses on the top?" Her sneer deepened with every word.

"How about beer and ham sandwiches?"

"Great!"

Lenny put the bag back in the fridge and pulled out bread rolls, lunch meat, lettuce, tomatoes, mayo, and mustard. He popped open the top on a bottle of beer and handed it to her. "You don't act like a Connecticut lady."

"Thanks," she said as she drank. "My husband thought the same thing. He wanted me to live in tennis whites."

"Exposes a lot."

"A country club boy's dream. So what happened to your face?"

"Got shot in the head."

"I bet that hurt," she said.

"A bit." He tried not to smile as he handed her a fat sandwich on a plate. "Here? Outside? Where?"

"Out."

He followed her through the back door and they sat down on the grass in the shade. It wasn't easy for him to fold himself, so he leaned against a tree, his long legs straight out. "So what are you sneaking around looking for?" He took a bite.

"If you saw that, did *they*?"

"No. They're fascinated by some old execution."

"Why?"

He shrugged. "It's Sara. She loves history."

"Execution? You mean beheading? Something like that?"

"Not that far back. So what about you doing the spy imitation?"

She frowned, obviously not liking going back to her. "My

grandmother hid some things here. I wondered if I could find them."

He didn't ask what had been hidden. He figured that if he did, she'd leave. "I heard that Derek Oliver wanted to marry you."

Heard was the key word. *Eavesdropped* was more correct.

She smiled. "He did suck up to me a bit, but I let him know that I found him repulsive."

"Took that well, did he?"

"My experience of men is that if they're hot when they're young, they think they're hot when they're old and wrinkly."

"Then I'm safe," Lenny said, and she laughed.

"You want to know if I had a motive for killing him. No, I didn't. I wasn't even supposed to be here. I ran away from facing my mother."

"I heard you were sent here."

"A lie," she said easily. "I knew I had to deal with my mother, but I postponed it by running here. I was ready to do *anything* to escape the wrath of that woman. I knew my grandmother would be glad to see me." She smiled in fond memory. "You ever have anyone on your side no matter what you did?"

"Not even close," Lenny said honestly. He was piecing things together. Randal had told him the details of the skeleton they found. Rachel was looking for something her grandmother had hidden. The jewels that had been sewn inside a stuffed toy? Did she do that or did Mrs. Meyers? "Have you found what she hid?"

"No."

"You could have returned years ago and searched."

"My life has changed in the last years," she said. "Besides, it never crossed my mind that the house and a lot of the furnishings would still be here. Is that all? Or are there more questions?" When she raised her arm to push her hair back, her short sleeve fell away and showed a tattoo on the inside of her upper arm.

"What's that?" he asked. It was an unusual shape. A symbol, of some sort.

A frown crossed her face, then she quickly covered it. "A moment of sheer stupidity." She stood up. "I have things to do."

Search the guesthouse where you and your grandmother stayed? he thought. He got up too but much less easily than she did. "Gil's at the cottage."

"What?"

He saw the blank look on her face. "There were some pastries left from breakfast. I thought you might want to take some to Gil and Quinn."

"No," she said. "Not now. Maybe later."

"I think Sara wants to see you. Maybe in the nursery?"

Rachel groaned. "More questions. I didn't kill that odious old man. I wouldn't even be here now if it weren't for—" She broke off. "Are we done?"

Lenny gave a nod and she left quickly. She went around the house so he couldn't see where she was headed. It was a ploy he'd used often when he was doing something he wanted no one to see.

As he stood there looking at the place where she'd been, he said aloud, "Forgive me, Sara. I don't like her either."

FIFTEEN

SARA WAS LOOKING AT THE SHELVES IN THE PALM Room. There were many empty spaces and each one had a three-by-five card telling what had been removed. It looked like Lenny was right, that Dora and her team of cleaners could do a good job. Now all she had to do was go to Billy's place and organize it all. What was she supposed to tell them? To look for something, but she didn't know what? And be sure and tell her when they found whatever it was?

On top of that, what was she to do if they found out about Harry Adair's juvenile murder? Say she'd found proof that Barbara Adair had a reason to kill Derek Oliver? They already knew that.

Sara glanced at her notebook lying on an ottoman. It was so pretty. It was light blue leather from Smythson of Bond Street in London. It seemed to beckon to her. Many things had happened since she woke at 2:00 a.m., including a chimney nearly crushing Jack, but nothing had taken the dream she'd had out of her mind. The faces of the people haunted her. The not-pretty girl. The two young men who looked alike but obviously weren't in the same circumstances. Yet they appeared to be friends. It was up to her to create a story for them.

It was a story that she longed to get back to. But she couldn't. There was no way she could say, "You guys work on the skeleton and a psycho murderer who may or may not be here with us. I'm going to plot a piece of fiction. In my pretty blue notebook." Ha ha. Her fantasy.

With a sigh, she picked up one of Dora's cards. *VHS The Way Out, 1951.* "Too early and too late," she mumbled.

"Isn't that redundant?"

She turned to see a young man standing in the doorway. It was the lawn mower boy.

"Hi. I'm Troy."

"Sara," she said.

"The scary-looking guy downstairs sent me up here to help you. I have the great and wondrous talent of being able to hook up VCRs to a screen. I don't mean to brag, but I can also attach them to TVs, computers, and iPads. I can probably connect to other things if needed."

"How about a black-and-white TV that isn't a flat screen?"

"I'm your man."

She was smiling but also looking at him intensely. "You remind me of someone, but I can't figure out who."

"Roy Wyatt? Or Jack? Maybe Cal?"

"What does that mean?"

He went to a shelf and looked at the labels on a row of VHS tapes that had been left behind. "Mom tried to keep me from finding out that she was coming here, but I knew. Unfortunately, she saw me with the lawn mower. Sorry I didn't finish the job on the weeds. I found that old machine in the garage. Dad used one on a movie and he let me play with it so I knew—"

"Mom?" Sara interrupted.

"Barbara Adair. Big deal movie star but just Mom to me."

Sara was blinking at him. "And your father?"

"Harry Adair, the producer."

She frowned. "Then what did you mean by Roy and Jack and Cal?"

"Oh. That. Bio father. That's what Roy is. My real dad liked..." He waved his hand. "You know. So Mom met Roy and made me."

Sara dropped down onto the ottoman. "You're Roy's son and Cal's grandson?" she whispered.

"I am. And Jack's brother. When I saw the chimney coming down, I yelled at him. It's my fault he froze. He called me Evan."

Sara nodded. "He was Jack's half brother. You look like him but with lighter hair and eyes. And you're taller."

"California sunshine and all that healthy food. When I started school—private of course—I'd never even heard of a candy bar. Mom doesn't know it, but I made up for lost time. Why are you looking at movies my dad made?"

Sara was too stunned to think clearly. "Murdered somebody when he was eighteen," she said before she thought.

"What?!"

"Oh! Sorry." She tried to recover herself. She could *not* tell him about his father killing a man and getting away with it. Or that Derek Oliver found out about it and blackmailed him. No, no, no. Or could she?

Troy sat down on the couch across from her. "You have to tell me all of it."

"That's for your mother to say."

"I'm not a minor who has to be protected."

Sara couldn't think what to say, so she was silent.

"I grew up in LA, the sordid city of sin. I know things normal people don't. I know about my father's proclivities. More than once there were, uh, problems. Mom used her influence to keep things out of the tabloids. She's not easily upset, but when she got your invitation to come here, she nearly passed out. I know she was upset about my bio father, but I think it was more than that. I want to know everything."

Sara was still silent, trying to decide what to do.

"Okay, what can I offer in return? I am Harry Adair's biggest fan. If you're looking for something in his movies, I probably know what it is. So what is this about murder?"

"Which one?"

It was Troy's turn to be shocked. "This is getting interesting. If I take you to Joe's Crab Shack for lunch, then go with you to the home and set up the VCRs, will you tell me all of it?"

"I…" Sara hesitated.

"How about entertainment? I heard that my brother can sing. So can I. Think Jack would sing a duet with me?"

When she spoke, it was soft. "I think that meeting you will make Jack cry."

"Me too." He took a breath. "So how many murders are there?"

"Including the execution that may or may not have been of an innocent man?"

Troy's eyebrows went up. "Yes! Every one of them. I'm like my dad and I do love a good murder plot."

Sara knew she should probably keep her mouth shut, but the need to talk to someone about everything was overwhelming her—and this young man seemed like a good bet. He wasn't born when Derek was murdered, so he was innocent of the crime. She had to be cautious about Barbara's side of it all but… "Joe's?" she asked.

"My dad used to say, 'Give a woman fried food and tequila and she's yours.' Of course he meant making them sign contracts that weren't to their advantage, but still…"

Sara laughed. "I'll pass on the drink, but I wouldn't mind a tubful of steamed seafood."

"I have a rental car here, and I know how to get there."

"That's all I can ask of life."

Smiling, they went downstairs.

Thanks to the wide, clean streets of Fort Lauderdale, they were inside the darkened Joe's Crab Shack just minutes later. They were seated and their order was taken.

"Start talking," he said.

She took a moment. "It's like we have pieces of a puzzle but we don't know how they fit together. We don't even know the picture they'll make when we complete the puzzle."

"My dad would have used that line in a movie."

"Thanks," she said.

"Okay. Start with Derek Oliver. I've picked up enough to know you found his body."

Sara hesitated. What should she tell him and not tell him? Certainly nothing about the jewels and the hedgehog. "Basically, the man threw a week-long party and invited people he was blackmailing."

Troy's eyes widened. "And he was threatening my mother about some long-ago murder?"

"Yes, but she didn't know that. Sorry, but your father played a dirty trick on her. He told her he was being blackmailed but for another reason."

"You don't have to tell me for what," he said. "So Mom got here and was told Dad murdered someone when he was very young?"

"That's what we think. Derek Oliver said there was a movie and a script involved. We assume that was his proof."

"No," Troy said. "Maybe there's a script but there's no movie of that."

"How can you be sure?"

"I know all his movies."

"This happened in the forties when Harry was still a teenager," Sara said. "It would have taken him years to get where he could make his own movies. If it's a film you don't know about, maybe it has a forbidden subject. Do you think it might have been two gay men? If so, would it have been shown in the fifties? Sixties? No. The seventies might have done an art house showing. Cocteau's *Beauty and the Beast* was ridiculed then, because we knew the truth about the Beast."

Troy leaned back against the booth. "What do you achieve if you prove that my dad murdered someone then turned the whole thing into a movie? You'd learn my mother had a strong motive for killing the man to shut him up?"

Sara wasn't going to be coy. "We already know that she does. But then, they *all* have motives."

Their food came and for a while they were silent. "Mind if I take on the job of proving that my parents are innocent?"

"I would love that!"

He smiled. "You're on. So tell me about this execution."

"We know next to nothing, but we keep running across it. James Lachlan willed his house and grounds—that used to be worth a lot of money—to his oldest living descendant. The poor man died alone because of the rotten year of 1944. Billy used to light candles and tell it as a ghost story."

"I don't have candles, but I'd like to hear it. Know any available storyteller?"

Sara smiled. "I might be able to tell a bit. It's a very simple story. James's nephew killed a man and was hanged for the crime. James's son was so upset that he ran away and was never seen again. In that same hideous year, James's wife ran her car into a tree and died. Three deaths in one year. I can't imagine. The poor man never remarried, just spent most of the rest of his life in his Palm Room." Sara's head came up. "Although, I just found out that Mr. Lachlan liked Cal a great deal."

"My grandfather."

"He was. Oh, but I wish you'd met him! He was the kindest, smartest, most wonderful man who ever lived."

"You were in love with him?"

"With all my heart," she said.

"So why didn't you marry him?"

"Think I could get a refill of iced tea?"

Troy saw her shut-down look and didn't push further. "That makes three murders. The question is: How are they connected?"

"We have no idea—or even if they are connected. Derek Oliver and Lachlan House. That seems to be where the tie is."

"Why did Oliver want to meet at Lachlan House?" Troy asked.

"He was hitting up Billy's brothers for money, and they sent him to the house to spy on Billy. While he was there, he found out about the murder Harry committed."

"And was never charged with, nor was it spoken about. He got away with it until Oliver found out about it. Somehow. Do I have that right?"

"Yes," Sara said, smiling at his grasp of it all.

"Dates?" he asked.

"Nephew executed 1944, Harry allegedly murdered a young man—a would-be, nobody actor according to your mother—in '45."

"Interesting that the dates are so close together." He took a drink of water. "I don't see a connection, but still, James

Lachlan amassed a roomful of my dad's movies. I guess it's too much to hope he was just a rabid fan."

"As I said, maybe one of those films tells the story of the murder Harry committed. As a writer, I'd never forego telling a good story that I had experienced. I'd just hide the truth in the plot."

He gave a small smile. "Does that mean that in one of your books is the story of why you didn't marry my grandfather?"

"Yes," she said. "It's there, but no one knows which story or what book."

"And no one knows that one of my father's mystery movies is a true story."

"Aren't some of them about rage that drives a person to insanity?"

"'Passion' is what Dad called it. If it was a story about two gay men, as you said, the world then wasn't ready for a movie about it."

"So we need to look for a story that might have different genders."

Troy nodded, but then looked up. "Or we could skip it altogether. We could forget the faraway past and just look at that one week. Oliver was blackmailing them, so we try to find out which one of them killed him to shut him up."

"So who?" she asked. "Which one of these very nice people is going to have his or her life ruined by an evil man like Derek Oliver? Lea? Your mother? Rachel, who wasn't supposed to be there? Reid? He seems mostly to have cut the grass." Sara wasn't going to tell that Reid would own the house until it was made public.

"I get your point. Something really big drove one of them into a killer rage." He paused. "It looks like we need to try to find out anything that is remotely related to this. Maybe there will be clues that lead to a solution."

Sara smiled widely. "I think you might have inherited Cal's brain."

"I'll take that as a compliment. Tell me about my dad."

That caught her off guard. "Oh. Well. Uh." She quit talking.

"How can I tempt you? How about I do what I used to do for Dad? While I take care of all the people at the retirement home, you can stay in a room alone with your notebook for one whole hour."

"Ninety minutes," she shot back.

"You're on. Now tell me about Roy."

"Sugarcoated or the truth?"

"One hundred percent true. I can take it."

"Jack has Roy's motorcycle, and when your mom saw him on it, she fainted."

Troy looked at her in surprise.

When the waitress returned and took their plates, Troy made two orders of three scoops of ice cream. Sara protested. Too many calories.

"I'll eat them if you don't want yours. What kind of motorcycle is it?"

"A huge Harley. Really big. Very noisy."

"More," Troy said.

Sixteen

WHEN THEY GOT TO SHADOW PALMS, SARA WAS happy to feel an atmosphere that was very different from the first visit. Now there was energy in the place. They could hear laughter down the hall. In the communal living room were boxes full of tapes and bound scripts taken from Lachlan House. The residents were rummaging through everything. There were murmurs of "I remember this movie" and "This was one of my favorites." Troy was smiling proudly.

Billy was in his wheelchair and an orderly rolled him to Sara. He was looking at Troy, who was helping them unload the boxes. Billy nodded toward him, his eyes asking questions.

Sara grinned. "Roy's son. Created at your house."

Billy looked at Troy, a beautiful young man, and said, "Then my life has not been in vain."

Sara laughed. "He's here to hook up machines, and to entertain. I'm going to hide away with my notebook."

"Use my lovely new room," Billy said. "Did I tell you thank you?"

"A time or two." She headed down the hall but then stopped. She couldn't resist listening to what Troy had to say. As she would have thought, the son of a famous movie producer, and an even more famous actress, wasn't shy. He was a born performer. He introduced himself as Troy Adair and said the movies were made by his father.

"Wait a minute," a man said. "Wasn't he married to Barbara Adair?"

"Yes." Troy spoke with a perfect blend of humility and pride.

"She's your mother?"

Troy nodded. Modestly.

"Can we—?" about six people said in unison.

Troy raised his hand to cut them off. "Yes. You help with this, and I'll get Mom to come here, sign autographs, take photos, and do the monologue from *Tomorrow is Forever.*"

There was a moment of shocked silence, then a man said, "When do we begin?"

Sara leaned back against the wall and closed her eyes for a moment. She could see Jack in the young man. But it was a Jack who hadn't been subjected to a childhood of abuse and degradation. This young man hadn't had enormous responsibility dumped on him when he was still a teenager.

Sara started to go to Billy's room but then Troy began to explain what was needed. She listened.

"Here's the true story: Two young men got into an argument and one killed the other. The killer walked out and was never found. We believe there was a movie made about this or maybe a script was written. The problem is that the original story seems to have been hidden. Maybe it was changed into being about two women, or a couple. It could be a subplot of a larger story. Or maybe it's just one of multiple murders. The possibilities are endless, but underneath, it's the same story.

We want you to watch the movies and see if it's in there in some form. The same goes for the readers who want to go through the scripts. I can attest that what is written is often different from what goes on screen."

Pleased with what she'd heard, Sara went to Billy's room. It was now much larger and filled with good furniture and linens. She shut the door and gave a sigh of contentment as she sat down in a plush chair.

A funny thing about writing is that it doesn't understand the concept of time. A lot of writers say, "If I don't have the whole day, I don't even begin." That was understandable. The self-hypnosis of writing, where your mind goes to another world with settings and people, hearing them talk, seeing them move, took massive amounts of time. And being interrupted during a scene could make it disappear in a second.

Sara wrote what had been percolating in her mind since her dream. Her first question was whether or not to physically transform the not-pretty young woman. She could make it so someone loved her the way she was, but that brought outside problems. People weren't kind. A handsome husband with a less-than-pretty wife would set off every Mean Girl they met.

Or did Sara sell out and fix the girl's face?

She couldn't come up with a solution, so she began writing background on the young men who looked alike. Were they half brothers? No! First cousins.

Sara delved deeper into that. The mothers were sisters. Twin sisters. It was almost as though she could see them. Pretty girls but with very different personalities. One was a real hot pants. She was in love with a… A what? A criminal of sorts. He—

"Here you are." Kate was standing in the doorway.

It took Sara a few moments to come out of her trance and

realize where she was. She closed her notebook. "Is it time for the meeting?"

Kate sat down on a chair. "You missed it. The boys didn't mind. Dad ran off with Lea, and Jack strapped on a tool belt and went to help Gil. Lenny told me where you went. So who's the kid outside?"

Sara smiled. "Roy's son. Jack's half brother. Cal's grandson."

Kate's eyes widened. "Is that all?"

"Heather's stepson?"

Kate laughed. "Does he have a mother?"

"Barbara."

"I see," Kate said. "And she's been hiding his existence from us. But he escaped his playpen and came here. I take it Jack hasn't seen him." She smiled. "He's the guy Jack thought was Evan."

"You are a clever girl," Sara said proudly. "So how'd your interview with Reid go?"

"Very interesting. Did you see the texts I sent?"

"Of course. Another barroom murder, but this one ended in a hanging. And Greer is a suspect. Randal agrees with that."

Kate held out the brooch Alish had given her. She hadn't had time to study it. Her first impression was that it was old, like belongs-in-a-museum old. It was silver, made in a this-tle design, with a large green stone in the middle. The stone hadn't been cut but looked like it had just been taken from the ground. "Reid's grandmother sent this to you. She called you 'the storyteller.' You're to put it under your pillow at night. She believes she has Second Sight, but Reid says she doesn't. It's your choice of what to do with it."

Sara was looking at it. "I like it." She started to put it in her pants pocket but instead, pinned it inside her shirt, over her heart. "I'll take all the help I can get. Did you learn anything else?"

"I was told a good story but I have no idea how it can possibly be connected to anything. It's about James Lachlan, so maybe it helps somehow."

When Kate said no more, Sara said, "Well?"

"Shouldn't we wait for the others and tell it to everyone?"

"No," Sara said. "Tell me now, then tell them later. On the second round you might remember new details."

"Ha! You're just too impatient to wait. First of all, Mr. Lachlan came from Scotland in a group of eight families. They—"

"Hello." Troy was standing in the open doorway.

"Are they all settled?" Sara asked.

"They're now on their second movie, but no luck so far. Billy had three more tape machines delivered from some place in Miami and—" He broke off as he looked at Kate, who was staring at him.

"I see Jack in you," she said softly.

Troy pulled up a wooden chair and sat down. "Is he with you?" He sounded hopeful.

"He's on a roof."

They were staring at each other without blinking, neither of them saying a word.

"Hey!" Sara said. "This is Troy—this is Kate. Now get on with the story."

Kate hesitated. "Should we...?" She meant "tell it in front of Troy?"

"Yes," Sara said. "Now tell."

Kate had learned a lot about storytelling from years with her aunt, and unlike Reid, she put it in chronological order. She started with the arrival of the eight families in the US. "James Lachlan offered a partnership to one of the men, but he refused and went out on his own. Unfortunately, the man failed at everything he tried—except being elected as a judge. Reid's family stayed with Mr. Lachlan."

"And James succeeded," Sara said. "I guess he took Reid's family upward with him."

"Yes, he did," Kate said. She went on to tell that Alish married James's nephew, son of his wife's sister. Then there was a fight in a bar. She told that James was on a business trip in Russia and the spiteful judge hanged the nephew soon after he was tried and found guilty.

"It was manslaughter," Troy said. "Not a murder."

"True," Sara said, "but that doesn't change what happened." She looked at Kate. "And after that, James's son ran away and his wife died."

"And Alish gave birth to the nephew's son," Kate said. "He was Reid the second. This one is the third Reid."

"And he's still with Lachlan House," Troy said. "I've seen him with the weed whacker. What's he do for a living?"

"Sells insurance," Sara said. "He came back to see if he and Rachel could still be an item."

"And are they?" Kate asked.

"Who knows? Slaps and kisses both. Maybe that's how they interact." When Kate started to ask for an explanation, Sara waved her hand. "It doesn't matter. Did you find out anything else?"

Kate looked at Troy, obviously wondering if it was safe to talk in front of him.

"You can say anything except against my mother," he said. "My job is to prove that she's never killed anyone. Except when a camera was aimed at her."

Kate didn't smile. "Back then, if evidence had shown that your father murdered someone, he could have been tried and sent to jail. Your mother would have wanted to prevent that from happening."

Troy didn't blink. "What did she do with the body? Pick it up and throw it out the window? Drag it somewhere? Dig a hole and bury it?"

Neither Sara or Kate spoke, but they looked at him hard.

"Oh," Troy said. "My bio dad. Think he would have helped Mom?"

Again, the women were silent.

Troy grimaced. "That's a look of, *You don't know everything.* Give me more facts. Where did you find the body? What was left of it, that is? Is there anything that would make you think that Roy did it?"

Acting like he hadn't spoken, Kate turned to her aunt. "I thought you were going to interview Rachel."

Sara jolted upright. "I forgot. I had food ready and everything."

"If it was from Bessie's, it's still in the fridge. Anyway, I saw Lenny and Rachel under a tree. They were drinking beer."

"A sinful lot, for sure," Troy murmured, annoyed that they hadn't answered him.

Kate looked at him. "You might be too much like Jack. This isn't a joke. It's serious."

"You mean I'm like my brother? The love of your life? When he was nearly hit by bricks, I thought you were going to die on the spot."

"Were you snooping?" Kate sounded outraged.

"Yes," he said cheerfully. "I was hiding from Mom, and doing a great job as she still hasn't found me."

Sara ignored their banter. "Lenny was with Rachel?"

"They parted just as I got there, so I don't know if they talked or not," Kate said. "But I think they did because she didn't look happy. I couldn't tell what Lenny was feeling because of…"

"His Quasimodo face," Troy said. "He likes me, so I'll ask him what went on with her."

"I think you should keep out of this," Kate said. "Let us handle it."

He gave a fake smile. "So it's true that big sisters boss you around all the time?"

Before Kate could reply, Sara stood up. "I don't know what Lenny was doing, but I need to talk to Rachel—not that I want to." She looked at Troy. "You stay here. Those old tapes are bound to get tangled, so you can fix them. Kate, find out what Randal was told. We need to put information together."

Kate stood up. "I don't want to say this, but Greer..."

"I know," Sara said. "She was a big, angry girl."

Troy was still seated. "Another woman? *How* did they dispose of the body?"

Sara put up her hand. "Whoever did it left the body on the nursery floor. Billy found it and put it in a closet."

"Then he had to move to the far side of the house because of the, you know." Kate looked at Sara. "We'll stop at Bessie's and get scones. It's late but you and Rachel can have tea."

Sara gave a one-sided smile. "In the nursery. Maybe it'll spark memories."

"Where the body was," Troy said. "So you guys opened a closet and there was a skeleton?"

"Yes," Kate said.

"Was it tied up?" His eyes were wide.

"Hooked by his suspenders," Sara said. "They broke away and the skeleton rolled across the floor. Let's go," she said to Kate.

"Wow," Troy said. "My dad would have loved this."

Kate narrowed her eyes at him. "If you tell your mother any of this—" She didn't finish her threat.

He stood up. "Okay. Got it. I'm to stay here and try to prove that my dad murdered someone and got away with it."

"And your mother may have killed a man and left him lying on the nursery floor," Kate said.

"And if she did, your bio dad must have helped her," Sara said happily.

"You two have a dark sense of humor," he said firmly.

The women laughed as they left.

Seventeen

AS SOON AS THEY WERE OUT OF BILLY'S ROOM, Sara texted Lenny to ask him if he would have tea set up in the nursery. And if you see Rachel, please invite her. I'll be there in thirty minutes. It hadn't been easy to get Lenny to use a phone. He had an obsession with privacy and no one knowing anything about him. "I doubt if Lenny is his real name," Randal had said.

Kate drove Sara's MINI to Bessie's and they went in to pick up two bags of scones. One contained wheat flour pastries, and the other was made with almond flour for Sara's low-carb diet.

"What do you hope to get out of her?" Kate asked when they were back in the car.

"What was she doing with your hedgehog? Did she stuff it full of jewels?"

"Then jam it into Derek's skull?" Kate said. "Maybe the real question is if she sawed his head in half."

"After bashing him, that is. That shows some serious anger—and violence."

"If she and Reid were lovers, maybe they did it together," Kate said.

"That would be ironic," Sara said. "Derek Oliver knew that Reid was the owner of the property. His death kept that from being known. Poor Reid was cheated out of his inheritance."

"So what was the motive?"

Sara shrugged. "The man was a jerk. Maybe he said something that put someone in a rage. Grab something hard and smack him over the head. The end."

"I can believe that. It's the sawing that stumps me. What in the world did the killer do with the brain?"

"Put it in a jar as a trophy?" Sara said. "Slice it up and study it? See what makes a person so vile that everyone who meets him wants to kill him?"

Kate pulled into the driveway of Lachlan House, turned off the engine, and looked at Sara. "Again, what do you hope to get out of Rachel?"

"I'm leaning toward asking about Greer. I'm hearing her name too many times."

Kate tightened her lips. "I liked her."

"You were four. Four-year-olds like anyone who offers them a puppy and candy."

Kate didn't soften. "Promise me that you'll be nice. Don't go in there with your mind made up."

"Okay. I swear it. I'll clear my mind. I'll forget seeing her slap Reid, then kiss him. I'll not remember how she's betrayed our dear Gil. I'll—"

Kate groaned. "I'm going to switch scones, and you'll eat carbs. Lots and lots of carbs!" She got out of the car.

"You're too cruel," Sara said, laughing.

★

Rachel was standing by the door of the nursery when Sara got there. "Hello," she said. "Lenny told me I was invited to tea."

"Yes." Sara didn't like how curt she sounded. She wasn't going to get any information if she started out hostile. She opened the door and went inside. Lenny got someone—probably Dora—to set up a lovely spread. A small round table was covered with a lace cloth and the yellow-trimmed dinnerware gleamed prettily.

"This is lovely," Rachel said. "How very kind of you." She politely waited until Sara was seated before taking the other chair.

Where to begin, Sara thought. *Maybe with a less personal topic than her and Reid. Did you two kill him? No, that wasn't the way to begin.* "Tell me about Greer."

Rachel looked startled. "Is she a suspect?"

"Maybe." Sara buttered a scone as Rachel poured the tea. *She certainly knows her way around a teapot! She even knows how to use the strainer.*

"Greer was nice, quiet, and very young. She worked a lot so we didn't see her much."

"I heard that Oliver was quite nasty to her."

"He treated everyone with disdain, and he seemed to know secrets about them."

"Did he know something about Greer?"

Rachel smiled. "I don't think she'd had enough life experience to have any secrets. She'd lived mostly with her grandmother."

"A forced isolation?"

"Oh no!" Rachel said. "At least not that I heard. Greer and

her grandmother went places and did things and read a lot."
She looked up at Sara. "May I ask you a personal question?"

"Just so long as it isn't 'Where do you get your ideas?'"

"I beg your pardon?"

"Sorry. Writer's joke. Ask me anything."

Rachel's face softened. "Quinn asked me to have dinner
with him and Gil tonight. What do I take? What do I wear?
Maybe I could bake a pie. If Lenny will let me borrow the
kitchen, that is. Or I could buy something. But what?" She
sighed. "Do you have any suggestions?"

Sara wasn't often knocked speechless but Rachel left her
grasping for words. "Gil? Quinn?" she managed to say.

"Yes. Excuse me, but that bookcase behind you is driving
me crazy. Do you mind if I fix it?"

Sara believed in organization. "Sure."

Rachel got up and went to the bookcase and began sort-
ing the children's books. "They were by age and now they're
shoved in anywhere." She halted and looked around. "This
room appears to be the same, but it's not. The little turtle rug
is missing. It was Kate's favorite."

"Turtle?" Sara asked.

"Billy used to say this room was to be untouched. It had
something to do with two little boys. All the furniture and
toys had been custom-made for this room. So where is the
turtle rug?" She nodded to an empty place on the floor.

"I have no idea," Sara said.

Rachel walked to the other side of the room and switched
cushions from a chair to the window seat. "The cottage is
beautiful, isn't it? That big stained glass window is spectacu-
lar. Are you going to renovate it?"

"It's not my place."

"But won't the estate be put up for sale?"

Sara hesitated. "James Lachlan's will leaves it to his eldest descendant."

"And who is that?"

"We're not sure yet."

Nodding in understanding, Rachel stepped back and looked around the room, studying it critically. "That's better." She sat back down at the tea table and filled Sara's cup then her own. "The tea's not quite hot but it's all right. Did you want to ask me things?"

Sara was so surprised by her behavior that she'd almost forgotten her purpose. "What happened to your aunt's jewels?"

Rachel's look could only be described as *blank*.

Sara waited for an answer.

"I don't think they were real."

Sara knew that what they had found inside Derek Oliver's skull was very real. "Is that what she told you?" *To keep you from stealing them?* she wondered.

Rachel looked confused. "I didn't ask. They seemed too big and too gaudy to be genuine." She paused. "What do I do about Gil?"

"You seem to really like him. And Quinn."

Rachel looked at her teacup, then up at Sara. "I've had men in my life. Not many, but some."

"Like your husband?" Sara said.

"I did what I was supposed to do," she said softly.

Sara nodded at that. Like all women, she'd done that.

"But Gil and Quinn are different. How in the world is he single? I don't understand. Are women stupid?"

With that question, Sara softened. She loved Gil. And she'd watched Quinn grow up. Their time with Jack had bonded all of them. "I think so," Sara said. Rachel was waiting for more information, so Sara began doing what she did best in the world: she told a story. She told of Gil's one-night stand that had produced Quinn and all Gil had done since then to keep his son.

Rachel listened in enraptured silence. When Sara finished, she leaned back against her chair. "That poor man." She looked at her watch. "If I'm going to bake anything, I better go." She stood up. "I didn't kill Derek Oliver, and I don't think Greer did either. She didn't like the things he said to her, but she knew it was temporary so she could laugh at them."

"Even when he said she was ugly?"

"She *was* ugly. But that was only on the outside. Ask the others if Greer ever did anything bad to them. You will hear only good."

"What about you and Reid?"

Rachel blinked a few times, seeming to be surprised that Sara knew about that. "It meant nothing."

"Not to Reid."

"We were kids." Rachel looked at her watch again.

Sara was still seated. "What happened to Kate's hedgehog?"

Rachel frowned. "I don't know. She was very attached to it. Her dad said someone she loved gave it to her. When she couldn't find it, Kate got onto Lea's lap and cried and cried. It was heartbreaking." She looked around the room. "I'd like to take this place apart. I figure that little animal fell down a crack somewhere. It wouldn't mean as much now, but I'd still like to know what happened to it." Her head came up. "Did that hideous man steal it? He saw how much Kate loved it so he took it? It's like something he'd do."

"He did," Sara said. "Sort of."

"How do you know that?"

"I can't tell everything I've found out, but Oliver did take the hedgehog, so to speak."

"What a vile man!" She took a step backward.

"Go," Sara said. "Bake a pie for Gil and Quinn." She thought, *And I hope he overlooks that he saw you kissing Reid.*

"Thanks," Rachel said and hurried out the door.

Sara sat where she was. As far as she could tell, she had managed to get no information whatever from Rachel. Instead, she'd been the one to tell all.

But Sara's biggest surprise was that she now liked the woman. That Rachel could see how wonderful Gil and his son were had won her over.

She sighed. Now she had to face the others and tell them she had completely and totally failed in her interview.

Eighteen

SARA WAS TRYING TO FIGURE OUT HOW SHE WAS
going to tell the others that she'd failed when her phone
dinged for a text. Good! Maybe someone in Alaska urgently
needed her and she'd have an excuse to escape her embarrassment.

It was Kate.

> Dad and I are in the library. He's dying to tell us some-
> thing. My guess is that it's about Roy's son. Should we
> act surprised?

Sara replied. We'll act bored. Old news.

Kate sent an emoji laughing to tears.

Sara thought, *Maybe my little brother will distract from my failure.* She went downstairs, but on the second floor she used
the main staircase rather than the narrow one that led down
to the kitchen. The last thing she wanted was to see Rachel
in the kitchen. Little Miss 1950s Homemaker rolling out pie

dough for a man she seemed to like very much didn't fit with what Sara knew. *Why* had she kissed Reid?

You're getting old, Sara thought. Today young people popped in and out of bed with each other for no reason at all. Certainly not love.

When Lenny stepped out of the shadows, Sara gasped in surprise.

"Sorry," he murmured, "but you were right."

Sara's eyes widened. How many times in her life had she heard a man tell her she was right? Three? Four? That was probably too many. "About what?"

"I talked to Rachel. I don't like her either."

Sara refrained from saying that she'd changed her mind. "Tell me specifics."

"She's sneaking around trying to find something her grandmother hid."

"Oh!" Sara said, thinking that maybe it was Mrs. Meyers who sewed the jewels into Kate's toy. "Did she say what was hidden?"

"Of course not. She did say she came here to escape her mother. Not sure if that helps or not."

Maybe she was postponing doing what she was "supposed to do," Sara thought. Meaning marry a man she didn't love. "Anything else?"

"She doesn't seem interested in Gil." There was anger in Lenny's voice.

"But isn't she baking him a pie?" Sara was confused.

"Not in this kitchen."

"Maybe she's using the guesthouse kitchen or the cottage," Sara said. "I have to go. They're waiting for me. My brother is dying to reveal that Barbara and Roy had a son." Sara's smile showed how much she was going to love one-upping her brother.

Lenny smiled as much as his face would allow. "Met the kid. Real smart aleck." There was affection is his voice.

Sara started down the stairs, but Lenny's voice halted her.

"She has a tattoo," he said. "All the kids do now but hers looks old."

Sara nodded and went down two more steps.

"It's a bow, like a ribbon tied," he said.

Sara stopped, opened her ever-present notebook, and drew the tattoo Reid had shown her. "Like this?"

Lenny nodded yes, then gave Sara a look that congratulated her on her sleuthing.

"Thank you," she said. "How's your place over the garage? Need anything?"

"It's all fine, thanks."

They smiled at each other and parted, both pleased at what had been said.

Kate and Randal were in the library, talking about Kate's wedding. If his life had been different, it wouldn't be a stretch to see Randal as a party planner. Whatever he did would be elegant.

Sara felt guilty that they were ignoring Kate's happiness in favor of talk of executions and sawed skulls. She made a vow that she'd get Lachlan House for Kate's wedding even if she had to buy the place.

"There you are," Randal said. "We've been waiting for you."

"Where's Jack?" Sara asked.

"Taking a shower," Kate said. "He and Gil were doing something that made a lot of sawdust. It was all over him."

"Is that what's in your hair?" Sara asked.

With a laugh, Kate ruffled her hair to clean it out. "Dad has some big news to tell us." Her eyes were twinkling.

"Barbara Adair and Roy had a son," Randal announced dramatically.

Sara and Kate looked at him with bored eyes.

Randal, who was quite perceptive about other people, groaned. "How could you already know? Barbara thinks he might even be *here*."

"Really?" Sara said. "Does he—?" She broke off because the door opened and in walked Troy. "You're supposed to be helping with the tapes."

"He looks just like Roy," Randal whispered. He was so overcome with emotion that he stepped back and braced himself against the desk.

Troy was looking at Sara, his eyes alight. "I found a hundred-and-six-year-old man who's old enough to remember how to use a VCR, so he took over." Obviously, he was teasing Sara.

"Hmph!" she said. "And new ways are better? Do you know how to drive a stick shift? Write in cursive?"

"Yes, I do."

"Know how to use a rotary phone?"

"I've seen them in museums. Maybe you could get a job as a guide and demonstrate."

Sara was trying not to laugh. He was good at word jousting. Before she could say more, Jack walked in.

For a moment, he froze, as they all did. As though they were trained for this, the two women went to flank Jack, while Randal stood by Troy.

Jack was staring at the young man. "Who are you?"

Troy seemed too overwhelmed to say anything.

It was Randal who spoke. "This is Troy, your father's son. Barbara is his mother."

Jack and Troy kept staring at each other in silence.

Finally, Jack said, "Chimney?"

"Yeah," Troy said. "That was me. I yelled. I didn't mean to startle you so bad that you nearly got hit."

Again, they lapsed into silence.

Troy took a breath and said, "I can sing. I've had lots of lessons."

"Know any Sinatra?"

"I know some of all kinds of music. Mom made sure of that. Blues to Broadway."

Jack put his hand on the doorknob. "Come on then, we're going to the Brigade." The two men started out, but Jack looked back at Kate and Sara. "You two coming?"

Kate's smile could have lit up a stadium, but Sara didn't move. No, she wasn't going.

"You get hours of peace." Jack looked at Randal. "And you?"

"Dinner with Lea. A friend of mine is making us a special meal. And Reid is going to his grandmother."

Jack looked at Troy. "Your mom?"

Troy grinned in a way that made him look like a clone of his father. "She's with Billy and his minions. I told him that if he pushes her, she'll reenact her every scene in every movie. She loves small, adoring audiences."

"So you've seen her then?" Sara asked.

"Nope."

The way he said it made them laugh.

"Come on, little brother," Jack said. "Let's go eat, drink, and sing."

"And dance with firemen," Kate added.

"My wife-to-be," Jack said to Troy in a fatalistic way.

"I hear you, man," Troy said.

The three of them left together, all of them smiling broadly.

★

Ah quiet, Sara thought when they were gone. She closed her eyes and listened to it. Within minutes, she heard voices, mostly women, who were laughing and excited. Then came children and one or two men's voices. Sara was pretty sure she knew what was happening. Randal probably told Lenny that they were all going out—which meant the dinner the caterers had prepared wouldn't be needed. It sounded like Lenny had invited Dora and her friends. They'd done so much work in getting the house ready for visitors that they certainly deserved a good dinner. Of course they invited others.

Sara knew she should go say hello and tell them to help themselves to wine. She should play the hostess.

Was there a word more hated by introverts than *should*? Add it to *hostess* and it was full-blown terror.

There was no way Sara could escape them. To reach the main staircase, she'd have to go through the living room past where they were gathered. Even if she managed to evade them, the stairs could be seen from the dining room.

Hysteria began to rise in her throat. *Just great!* she thought. *A skeleton falls out of a closet and I don't panic, but a gaggle of giggling women makes me feel like I'm trapped in a burning building.*

As the voices got closer, she looked at the window. Ground floor. Not far above the lawn.

She was small and thanks to many years of gym work she was lithe. She tossed her notebook out, then climbed through the window with the speed of a lemur after a banana. As soon as she was on the ground, she circled around to the kitchen. She knew where she wanted to go: the nursery. That room hadn't brought back the memories she'd hoped for with Rachel, but Sara knew there was something there. Derek Oliver's ghost? She hoped not, but there was definitely an energy in there.

The kitchen was full of people in white uniforms. For once, Sara was glad for her lack of presence. No one ever paid attention to little old ladies. She didn't even have to do her slumped-over, crotchety act to get them to ignore her. They were busy serving dinner to half a dozen women and what appeared to be all of their children and grandchildren. Sara smiled. Good for them.

She opened the narrow door that most people didn't notice and went up the stairs to the top floor. Yet again, she smiled at the lovely silence, then went into the nursery.

As she remembered what Rachel had told her, she looked around. A missing rug. Books out of order. Kate had said the same thing. If Kate saw the disarray, then straightened it, did that mean someone had searched a second time? For the stuffed animal full of jewels? Rachel didn't seem to know what was inside the toy. But she also wanted to tear the room apart looking for it.

The more Sara thought, the more confusing it all was. They had so many pieces of the story, but no connection between them.

As she twisted to look around, she felt a bit of a stab to her chest. The brooch was still pinned inside her shirt. She took it out and looked at it. She couldn't help wondering about the value of the green stone. Was it a raw emerald? She'd written enough books set in the Middle Ages to know it was cut the way jewels used to be. Not faceted so it sparkled. Was it thirteenth century? Or earlier?

Why had Reid's grandmother entrusted something so valuable to a stranger? Was it true that she had Second Sight? Some form of clairvoyance? Did she foresee that Sara would feel, intuit, something from it?

She put her hand to her head. This was too much for her. She'd been going since 2:00 a.m. She'd talked to too many people, heard too much.

The window seat seemed to beckon her. Soft pillows. The fading sunlight of the day. She went to it and stretched out.

She was so very sleepy. *Please let me dream*, she thought as she closed her eyes. *Let me add to the story.*

With the brooch clutched in her hand, Sara closed her eyes and went to sleep.

★

When Sara opened her eyes and realized she was in another dream, she nearly cried with thankfulness. As before, she was floating above, invisible to the people.

She saw a young couple in a beautiful forties car. It was a convertible, black with white sidewall tires. He was driving, and they weren't in Lachlan. In fact, they didn't appear to be in Florida.

The man was beautifully dressed in a lightweight gray suit with a pale blue shirt and a wide tie. From his dress and the vehicle, he must be the young man who was riding a horse in her first dream. When he turned his head, she saw that he looked different. As a person who worked hard to maintain her weight, Sara knew that he'd lost about twenty pounds. His cheekbones were more pronounced, and the weight loss made his shoulders seem broader. He was more handsome than he had been. A 1940s heartthrob.

More important than a physical change was his look of anger, hatred, even. *Something big has happened*, Sara thought.

Beside him, at the end of the wide seat, was the young woman. She looked the same. Teeth, moles, nose. They hadn't changed. It was Alish, Greer's grandmother.

No. That wasn't true. She was twisting a wedding ring on her left hand, twirling it round and round.

Please let there be sound, she thought. *Please, please.*

"It's over," he said angrily. "It's done."

Sara smiled. *Yes! Sound!*

"I know," she said softly. "It's just that Mr. Lachlan—"

"It's his fault." There was rage in the man's voice. "If he'd been here, it wouldn't have happened."

Ah, Sara thought. *The execution of the nephew. Oh no! The nephew was the one Alish loved. It was her husband who was executed. This young man must be James Lachlan's son, Aran.*

His face showed growing anger. "Why was the marriage so important to you?" He gave her a hard look. "You know you won't get any money. I have my own life to live, and it won't be in a backwater town but in a real city. What I've done there will live forever. When it's seen…" He didn't finish his sentence.

"I know."

"You can't tell anyone. You're as guilty as I am."

"I know."

"Stop saying that! If I had any sense, I'd…" When he came to a stoplight, he gave her a look that made Sara's hair stand on end. The woman kept eye contact with him, and Sara could feel her fear. *He's threatening to kill her*, she thought. *Why? What are they talking about? What secret is he threatening her with?*

When he drove forward, his face changed to a smirk, as though he knew something no one else did. "You think you tricked me, but you traded a murder for a marriage. Was it worth it?" He was taunting her.

She hesitated, and the way she put her hand to her stomach made Sara know she was going to have a baby. Whatever had happened, Sara knew it was for the child's sake. She also sensed that the man didn't know about the child.

Sara's writer-mind thought, *Did they play a part in sending the nephew to the gallows? How? And more importantly, why?*

He pulled into the parking lot of a train station, got out, and opened the trunk of the car. With an imperious gesture, he motioned to a porter to come and get his stash of beautiful leather luggage. As it was unloaded, he put his hand to his neck, then adjusted his collar.

When the porter was gone, the young man went back to the front of the car, glaring at her over the closed door. "Remember! You don't know where I am or what happened to me. I no longer exist. If I hear that you've betrayed me, I'll come back for you. Do you know what I will do to you?"

Sara was beginning to understand. James Lachlan's son disappeared and was never heard from again, but Alish knew where he went. She never told anyone.

He looked at her with more anger and hatred than Sara had ever seen before. She knew he was saying that he'd kill her. Sara gasped so loud that the woman flinched. It was as though she heard the sound—and knew she wasn't alone. It seemed to give her courage.

Alish straightened her shoulders. "I know I won't see you again, and I know that someone who loves you is waiting for you. But I also know about my life. I will stay in Lachlan forever. I will have a family and love and security. I will prosper through *you*."

He was obviously startled by what she'd said—and not a little creeped out by it. But then he sneered in derision. "You and your stupid Second Sight. No one believes you. Everyone laughs at you. I will have a hundred women, all of them beautiful." He gave her a look that told of her lack of beauty. "You may think you've won, but you will never get another thing from me." He stepped away from the car. "Remember to keep your mouth shut." He turned his back to her and went toward the train station.

"No women," she whispered. "None at all." She gave a little smile and moved over to get behind the steering wheel. As she drove away, she kept smiling.

Nineteen

WHEN SARA WOKE, SHE HAD CHILLS ALL OVER HER body. They weren't from cold but from what she'd seen and felt in the dream. In the first dream, she'd not liked the man on the horse, but this time she despised him. It was as though she'd seen pure evil.

She didn't know why he'd felt he had to leave town, but the urgency was there. He appeared to have no regret at leaving behind parents who loved him. Sara knew they would never recover from their grief. Even when his mother died, he didn't show himself.

She looked at the brooch that was still in her hand. Reid's grandmother, Alish, had sent it to "the storyteller." Had she also sent Sara the dream? Was it a mystical video of what really happened?

Every second of the dream was vivid. He'd said, *"You think you tricked me, but you traded a murder for a marriage. Was it worth it?"* His tone had been sinister, threatening.

A murder for marriage. What did that mean?

And what about the other thing he said? *"What I've done there will live forever. When it's seen..."* Was he talking about the movie everyone was searching for? James Lachlan's son had already made the movie? When? Before his cousin's trial? Maybe he knew his father would disapprove of such a profession. He left to avoid his father's anger? To escape the possibility of being disowned?

But Sara had met Mr. Lachlan, and Cal thought highly of him. There were times when life at home was too much for Cal, so he would escape to Lachlan House. When Cal was older and bigger, he'd said he was afraid he might kill his father. Might hit him so hard that he'd never get up. Mr. Lachlan's calmness gave Cal a place of safety and peace. But his son ran away from him in fear? It made no sense.

Sara ran her hands through her hair. It was late and she should go downstairs to bed, but she wanted to get away from Lachlan House with all its memories.

She sent a text to Kate.

What does Alish look like?

Good skin, not badly wrinkled.

Sara figured Kate was being nice.

Buck teeth? Big nose? Moles? Like Greer?

Yes.

I'm going back to our house to spend the night. Come for breakfast at eight. With Randal. We'll make plans.

She closed the cover on her phone. She needed the quiet of familiar surroundings to organize what was in her mind.

Their house wasn't far away. She unlocked the door and was glad for the peace of a space with no people. The second "dream" she'd had played through her mind on an endless loop. Going round and round. The brooch was in her pocket. She felt it was her connection to what she'd seen. *Seen* was the right word. Not made up, not created from conversations and her own imagination, but it was something real that she'd watched while it happened in the past.

She put her handbag on the hall table, then began to walk through the house. When she'd bought the place, it had been in bad shape. The house was the reason she'd returned to her hometown after a lifetime away. To her historian's mind, Lachlan was like a medieval village, and the owner, prob- ably a duke, lived in a castle and presided over all. When the house had come up for sale, it had been a trophy to Sara. She'd come from nothing, had been looked down on by all, but in the end, she owned the "castle," the biggest house in Lachlan.

Jack, so very young then, had remodeled it for her. The best thing about the house was bonding with him.

Sara went outside to the pool, the water glistening in the house lights, then to the patio with its big grill. How many hundreds of meals had they shared there? First it was Jack and her, then Kate came, then Randal.

Inside, Sara went through the formal living room, the fam- ily room with the big TV, then to Kate's apartment. She liked to check that there were no leaks and no malfunctioning plumbing. The apartment opened to a small private patio that had a fountain with a statue of a girl dancing in the rain. Sara knew that Jack and Kate used to spend time there together. They'd always been friends.

She stood outside, looking up at the night sky and the stars.

Everything was going to change. She was happy that Kate and Jack had at last admitted they were in love, but what next? Would they buy some cute little house somewhere? Of course Jack would tear out the kitchen and put in a new one. Would he build a playhouse in the backyard? She had an idea that they wouldn't wait long for children.

Randal lived in the little guesthouse beside the big house. For the last few years, he'd spent most of his time inside the big house with them. They'd become such a good foursome that they could spend hours together in silence. Jack and Kate often exchanged computers as they helped each other with their businesses. Randal studied physiology online so he could help his clients with their physical problems. Would he and Lea live together? In their own house?

"It's all going to change," Sara said aloud.

She went through the far door to Jack's big room. It opened to the garage so he could come and go without being seen. Not that he spent much time in there. From the beginning, he and Kate had been almost inseparable. Wherever she was, he was nearby.

But then, Jack had gone away for months, and when he returned, he was almost a different person. Or maybe it was that he'd at last figured out what he wanted in life.

She straightened Jack's coverlet, checked that the windows were locked, since he liked to open them, then went down the hall. She walked back through the house to her bedroom suite on the far side. With its private garden and big bathroom, it had always been her sanctuary. Now she imagined the huge house being empty, with just her there. She'd have to send Kate a text asking if she could stop by to see the baby. There'd be no toddler wandering about the place, sitting on Aunt Sara's lap while she read a story—one that Sara had written.

Between the evil of the dream and her thoughts about her
life, she felt herself going downward into what could be a full-
blown depression. She took a hot shower and put on one of
her huge T-shirts. This one said, Don't Blame the Butter for
What the Bread Did.

She felt better but still, between the dream-vision and
thinking of the coming change, she didn't feel good. She
opened a cabinet, pulled out a bottle and a little crystal glass,
then poured herself some Mandarin Napoleon. It was her favorite liqueur. It wasn't easy to find, but Randal had a source
and made sure his sister always had some. It didn't go with her
low-carb, no-sugar diet, but tonight she needed it.

She sat up in her bed—Dora had put on crisp, clean sheets—
and began to write about what she'd seen. She added every
detail she could, from the car to the clothes, to the facial expressions of people.

She wrote the reasons she'd been told of why Aran left. He
was upset over his cousin being hanged, but maybe thinking
that it was his father's fault was too much for him.

But Sara was seeing something else. In the dream, Alish
had been deeply afraid of the man. Something had gone on
between them, but Sara had no idea what. It almost sounded
as though they had conspired in some crime.

He was threatening her, but at the end, Alish had stood
up to him. "I will prosper through you," she'd said. What
did that mean?

At the end, when his back was to her, Alish had smiled.
"No women. None at all."

"Ah!" Sara said. *Was he gay? Is that why he'd left his home?
He wanted to escape the stigma associated with that? In the 1940s,
he would have been an outcast.*

Sara looked at the clock. It was nearly ten thirty. For a
morning person like her, that was very late. She turned off

the light and snuggled under the down coverlet. As she was dozing off, she thought, *When it is seen… A movie? Gay man? Harry Adair? A murder of passion? The script? Were they all tied together?*

Everything whirled about in her mind. *Tomorrow I must see Alish. Must ask her questions*, she thought before she fell into a deep, dream-filled sleep.

Twenty

THE BRIGADE WAS QUIET, BUT ONE OF THE BAND
members was setting up to go onstage. Everyone knew they
were making an unscheduled appearance because Jack was
there. Within an hour everyone in Lachlan under the age of
thirty would have heard what was going to happen at the
Brigade. Live music and Jack Wyatt singing. It was going to
be a profitable night.

Halfway down the narrow bar, Jack, Kate, and Troy were
in a booth. The table was full of food and beer. It was Mexi-
can with a Florida touch: seafood and chili. Divine.

Kate was on one side, Jack and Troy across from her. The
brothers were absorbed in each other. If Kate were a different
person, she might have been angry at being ignored, but she
was like her aunt. Sara said the jealousy gene had skipped her.
Kate was deeply glad that Jack and Troy had found each other.

The men were sitting close together and quietly asking each
other about every detail of their lives. Troy told of having a
celebrity mother, and Jack talked of spending time with Sara

in New York. The only thing Jack sugarcoated was about their father. Roy Wyatt had been brutal to Jack. Kate knew that if Sara hadn't come along, Jack would probably be in prison. His juvenile record wasn't something to be proud of.

As Kate sipped her drink, she noted how much they looked alike. Troy wasn't as dark as Jack, and he didn't have the cautious look that Jack always wore, but they both favored their father. She could see Barbara's softer jawline in Troy, but the eyes were like the photos she'd seen of Roy.

Whatever else you did, Roy Wyatt, Kate thought, *that you created these two makes up for it.*

As she looked at them, so happy to be together, she thought how sad Jack was going to be when Troy went back to California. "What do you do?" she blurted out to Troy. She hadn't meant to interrupt them, but it just came out.

They turned to her and Troy smiled. "I have a rich, famous mother. I don't do anything."

He said it with so much good humor that Kate laughed.

"I invited him to work with Gil and me." Jack wasn't smiling and Kate knew he was upset at the idea of Troy leaving.

"Get on a roof in a Florida summer?" Troy said. "I can't see that. Maybe—" He broke off as the door opened and in came a long line of firefighters. One by one, they went past the booth, each smiling at Kate and her smiling back.

They were a truly beautiful group of men, all in perfect physical shape, their uniforms pristine.

"No suspenders?" Kate asked.

The captain said, "When they heard you were here, I had to force them to wear shirts."

"Spoilsport!" Kate called after him.

When the parade ended, Jack groaned.

"They like *you*," Troy said to Kate.

"It's mutual," Jack said. The jealousy gene had *not* bypassed him.

"Maybe I'll become a firefighter," Troy said.

"There's a lot of training," Kate said. "Hauling equipment up ladders, carrying women and children out of burning buildings, driving that big, long, heavy truck. It takes muscles and brains."

Troy looked at Jack, who was giving Kate looks to cut it out, and grinned. "Guess I hit a sore spot."

Jack grimaced. "I sing—she dances."

Kate smiled. "With every one of them."

She sounded so happy that even Jack laughed.

He looked around the booth toward the stage. The band was almost set up, and the lead guitarist nodded to Jack. When he sat back, he turned to Troy. "Sure you can do this? We've had no rehearsals, nothing. Sometimes I'm slower on songs, sometimes faster."

"You lead and I'll follow."

Kate loudly groaned. "Don't tell him that! Next thing you know, he'll be expecting *me* to do that."

"I gave up on that long ago," Jack said, eyes sparkling.

"Let's go before you two do it on the table," Troy said.

"What do you know about such things?" Jack shot back.

"Well, Dad, I'm not a virgin."

Laughing, Jack got up. "Okay, kid, see if you can follow along."

Kate leaned back against the booth and watched as the two of them walked toward the stage together. From the back, they looked so much alike—and that thought made her frown. It seemed to bring back a memory, but she couldn't quite grasp it.

When Jack and Troy got on the stage, there was applause of anticipation. The bar was beginning to fill up. "This is my little brother," Jack said into the mic. "He says he can sing but I haven't heard him, so let's see what he can do." Jack spoke to the head of the band, then he handed the mic to his brother and stepped away.

They played "The Way You Look Tonight." Sinatra, long and slow.

Many of the people there had never heard the song before. Some slow danced, but most just listened. Troy had a beautiful voice and, like Jack, he seemed to have an excellent memory for lyrics.

As he sang the old song, Kate's head seemed to spin. A memory was coming to her, but it wasn't the one she'd briefly glimpsed when she saw Jack and Troy walking away together. This one was different. That song had been playing that night. It was one of Mr. Billy's favorites.

She closed her eyes. It was Lachlan House, she was with Greer, and they were doing something they shouldn't. *Spying*, she thought. The grownups were having a party, and she and Greer were hiding behind the door, peeping around it, and watching. Greer was nearly grownup, but they treated her like she was as young as Kate. Mr. Oliver had used a word Kate had never heard before: *retarded*.

It must be the night Derek Oliver wasn't there, Kate thought as the memory became more clear. *And some of them knew he was dead*.

Billy came into the vision, a big green bottle of champagne in his hand. "Drink up, my dear friends," he said over the loud music. "Tonight we party as though it is our last."

And he knew it would be, Kate thought. He'd found the body and put it in the closet. He knew there would be no more parties. He wouldn't even be able to occupy the whole house. It was his last night of joy.

Lea saw them peeping around the corner. "You're too

young to be here," she said, frowning as she escorted them into the hall. In the next minute, she smiled and handed them a grocery bag. "I put in sparkling apple juice and pastries. Now take it upstairs and let no one see you."

Grinning, Kate and Greer ran through the kitchen and up the steep stairs to the nursery. It was their favorite place.

They quickly unloaded the bag of treasures. Cream puffs, chocolate truffles, two big slices of pie, little cakes, and two bottles of what they liked to pretend was champagne. There were even a couple of pretty glasses.

"Do you like cake or pie better?" Kate asked as she picked up a little cake with lavender icing with a pink rosebud on top.

Greer was looking around and frowning. "Someone has been here."

"The woman who cleans?" Kate asked. "I like her. Sometimes she lets me help. I got inside Mr. Oliver's tub and scrubbed away the gray ring. He's a dirty man."

"Look at that closet. There's a white line around it. That's glue. And your dog's string is caught under it."

"Oh no!" Kate started to get up but Greer stopped her.

"That door is sealed. Leave it alone. And the turtle rug is gone. Who did this?"

Kate saw that she was right. "You should get your grandmother. You said she was magic and can see things that are going to happen. Maybe someone told Mr. Oliver something bad, and he went away and took things with him."

"I don't think he left," Greer said. "Reid drove his car away." She took a deep breath. "And I think my grandmother was here."

"When?" Kate's eyes were wide. She'd heard a lot about the magical grandmother.

"Today. I don't know why she came here, but I know she

has secrets. She's why I never went to a real school. Reid said that if I stayed home, Grans would behave herself."

"Did she do something bad?"

"I guess so."

"Did she do something to Mr. Oliver?"

"I don't know. I know that man was saying bad things to Reid, and that made Grans angry. She gets real mad. I went to school at first, but a boy was mean to me. I told Grans and she picked him up and threw him across the playground. He flew very far."

Kate's eyebrows were almost up to her hairline. "Did the boy stop being mean?"

Greer looked sad. "All the children stopped speaking to me. No one got near me, not even the teachers."

★

Kate came out of her memory-trance with a jolt. *And the next morning, everyone left*, she thought. It was as though they all knew that something bad had happened. When Kate went downstairs, her father was packing clothes, and the house had that eerie feeling of being empty. The first thing she looked for was her hedgehog. Her dad said they didn't have time to look, that they had to leave for home immediately. Kate knew that meant leaving Greer and Lea and all the fun and laughter. "Home" was her sad, complaining mother. It was Lea who held Kate while she cried. Not long after that, Lea also left—and Kate didn't see her again for twenty-five years.

She looked up to see Garth standing at the end of the table. He was a firefighter, married with kids, and he was a fabulous dancer. He didn't say anything, just held out his hand. She took it, and they went to the dance floor.

Jack and Troy started a duet, and as she'd hoped, they were

perfectly in sync. She'd never seen Jack look so happy. When he saw her gyrating with Garth, his scowl lasted only seconds.

It was nearly two hours later that Kate left the dance floor. As she'd promised, she'd danced with each firefighter, all while laughing and teasing. When she needed a break, she went back to their booth and downed a mug of beer in one drink. When she put the mug down, Sheriff Daryl Flynn was sitting beside her. That he hadn't taken the seat across from her meant he had something private to tell her. They'd always been friends.

The sheriff helped himself to salsa and chips and the waitress brought him a beer. "So how's the investigation going?" His head was close to hers so they could hear each other.

"Great." Kate held out her left hand to show her ring. "Jack and I are engaged."

"That's a shock. I never thought you two would become a couple."

She ignored his sarcasm. "Aunt Sara says we can have the wedding at Lachlan House."

"Wasn't there a murder there? I'm not sure, since I've heard next to nothing about it."

Kate groaned. "You're not going to let me have even one night off, are you?"

Daryl looked at Jack and Troy on the stage, singing about old-time rock and roll. "They look like father and son."

"Jack is just twelve years older than Troy."

"I could believe that," the sheriff said.

Kate laughed. He was implying that at twelve, Jack was sexually active. Considering that, at the time, he'd been in love with a high school girl who... She didn't want to think about what happened then. "Do you have something to tell me?"

"Yeah. Years ago I kept a kid out of jail. His dad said if I ever needed a favor to call him."

"Hmmm," Kate said. "Just one kid? One favor?"

He'd finished the whole basket of chips and another one was put on the table. "So maybe I have a boxful of what I call Favor Cards."

She smiled at him. "Which one was this?"

"Big deal investment guy. Knows everyone in that world." He paused to chew. "It's been bothering me about Billy. Why didn't he report finding the dead body?"

"Because of his brothers," Kate said.

"Right. Those brothers. We've been told they're monsters, yet Sara got them to pay for everything. Doesn't sound all that monstrous to me."

"I see. There are always two sides to everything. So you asked someone who might be able to find out the other side."

"You're a smart girl. I called in the favor and got some answers. Did you know that when Billy was in his twenties he was a tennis superstar?"

Her face showed her surprise. "I can hardly imagine him outdoors."

"We all have that impression, don't we? I saw what you guys did to where he lives now. Movie machines, popcorn, all of it. You've turned that sad old place upside down."

"It's all from Aunt Sara," Kate said. "What about Billy and tennis? And not reporting a dead body?"

"Billy won every competition match—until one day he didn't. He got so mad about losing that he beat the winner to a pulp. Put the kid in a coma. He woke up, but he was never the same. The brothers kept Billy out of prison by paying the family millions not to identify their little brother as the assailant. After they got the case settled, the brothers told him it was time for him to go to work."

"They put him in the accounting department," Kate said.

"Yes, they did. And I can tell that you know how that went."

"He helped himself to the money that came in. So then they made Billy spend a year in construction."

"Yes," the sheriff said. "They showed him what his life would be like if he didn't behave. After that, they sent him to Lachlan House and told him that if he ever got into any trouble again, they'd throw him on the street. By the time Billy found the body, he was already hiding the fact that he was illegally selling the furniture."

"So the brothers didn't do that," Kate said. "If Billy reported finding a dead body, the brothers were sure to classify that as 'trouble.'" Her head came up. "Was Oliver blackmailing Billy too? Was he was going to tell the brothers what Billy was doing?"

"I don't know."

"What about the skull being sawed open? Did Billy do that? And the brain...?" She grimaced. "You know, removing it."

"I don't know for sure, but my source said the brothers hinted that Billy had some serious psychological problems as a kid."

Kate swallowed. "Small animals harmed? That sort of thing?" Her stomach clenched.

"Possibly."

She leaned back against the booth. "Alish and now Billy."

"Who's that?"

"A magic grandmother who was very strong. And had a serious anger problem."

For a moment, the sheriff was quiet as he watched the singers. "Roy would be proud of his sons."

"Who told you about Troy's parentage?" She held up her hand. "Of course it was Dad. Did you tell him about Billy?"

"No. Just you. So when are you going to solve this thing?

And how is Sara? Randal said she's been wandering around kind of mindless."

"She has a book idea and it's obsessing her."

"A book about what?"

Kate was surprised at the question. "I don't know."

He crunched a hot tortilla chip loaded with salsa. "My wife has read all her books. She says Sara writes about her life. When Jack was remodeling that big house, Sara wrote four books about restoring old houses."

"She did." Kate's voice was rising. "Do you think that she's filling her notebook about the murder? But she hasn't told us?"

He shrugged. "What do I know? It's just that you guys are taking a lot of time to figure out nothing at all."

Kate felt defensive. "Jack and I have been busy. And Dad and Lea have found each other. So maybe we have been a wee bit neglectful, but..." She trailed off.

"Sure. Love comes first. Beats the heck out of working on the murder of a man everybody hated."

Onstage, Jack said, "My brother and I are going to take a break."

"I'm outta here," the sheriff said. "I don't need two Roys interrogating me."

"Ah, come on, Troy is nice."

Her insinuation that the man she was going to marry wasn't "nice" made him laugh. In the next second he'd left the building.

Jack and Troy took their seats, cold beers were put in front of them, they drained them, then more were served. The Brigade took care of their free entertainment guests.

"Had enough dancing?" Jack asked.

"Not nearly enough."

"Was that the sheriff?" Troy asked.

"Yes." Kate gave a look to Jack to let him know that Sheriff Flynn had told her something important.

"Now there's a job I might like," Troy said.

Kate and Jack looked at him with interest.

"He's retiring," Kate said quietly. "He needs a replacement."

"Does he?" Troy reached for more chips and salsa. "Does he really?"

Twenty-One

AS USUAL, SARA WOKE UP EARLY. IT WAS NICE TO be in her own bed. Her mind was so full of her dreams that she needed to occupy herself to clear it, so she got up and dressed. When they'd gone to Lachlan House, they'd left the fridge full. It was hard to believe that was just a few days ago. Sara began cooking, and when everyone arrived, she had enough for a dozen people.

"Something on your mind?" Jack was teasing. He knew she often did physical things to calm her thoughts. "My bathroom could use a good scrub."

Ignoring him, she looked at her brother. "Still think Barbara did it?"

He was setting the big dining table. This much food deserved the Coalport china. "Her mind was on worrying how her gay husband would take it that she was pregnant."

"She wasn't concerned about Harry killing a man?" Sara asked. "Or did she pay Derek Oliver off so that aspect of the murder just disappeared? Vanished?"

Randal was unperturbed by his sister's snappiness. "Her baby was more important to her than an ancient murder that had little chance of prosecution. Even now there appears to be no proof."

Sara grimaced. "The person blackmailing her disappeared and no one asked why?"

As they sat down to eat, Jack gave Kate a look of *What's wrong with her?*

Kate shrugged. She had no idea. "How about Lea?" she asked Jack.

"As she told us, she thought Oliver would eventually show up. She was dreading the divorce."

"Lea never searched for him?" Sara asked.

"No. However, I did find out that Derek's next choice of wife was Rachel. And..." He paused to pull the ring out of his pocket and put it on the table.

That effectively made everyone grow quiet, then they looked at Randal. He took the ring and examined it. "Garnets. Not worth much. I never saw it before."

"Sure?" Sara asked.

He raised an eyebrow. "Are you asking me if I know my gems? Like I know that the green stone in the necklace you often wear is an emerald while the sparkly white stone is fake?"

Sara picked up the ring. "This just seems to back up that Rachel had her grandmother's jewels."

Kate nodded. "We just don't know if she was stealing them or hiding them."

"I think hiding," Randal said. "Derek Oliver would have wanted the big emerald the most."

"He got it," Jack said, and they thought of it rolling out of the man's skull. He looked at Sara. "Lea asked me why you didn't marry Cal."

They turned to stare at Sara, but she pressed her lips together and said nothing.

Kate broke the silence. "What else?"

"This is off the subject of murder," Jack said, "but Lea told me what great friends Cal and James Lachlan were. I didn't realize it was so strong. He was a real father to him." He looked at Sara and Randal. "Did you know that Granddad's mother cooked for James Lachlan?"

Sara's face showed her surprise. "Renata? I'm surprised that man she was married to allowed that." She didn't want to say the name. She turned to her brother. "Did you know that?"

"I had no idea. I stayed away from Cal's father. He was a horrible man."

"He was!" Sara looked at Kate. "Did you find out anything interesting from Reid?"

"Personally interesting, yes, but I can't see what it has to do with the murder. Although, it makes me glad that Reid is to inherit the property."

"Did you tell him?" Sara asked.

"No, of course not. We'll have to do that with champagne."

"And a lawyer," Randal added under his breath. He was always leery of the legal system.

They looked back to Kate, eager to hear her story.

For the second time, she told of the eight families coming to America, of the jealous judge, and the quick trial and hanging.

"But Alish married the poor man first," Sara said softly. "Before the execution." They turned to her, waiting for her to explain, but she didn't. "Anything else?"

"Her house was odd," Kate said. "There was nothing personal in it. No photos, nothing. I didn't realize it, but I was hoping for some pictures of Greer. Maybe even of Greer and me." She sighed. "But she did have the brooch."

Sara removed the old brooch from her shirt pocket and put it on the table.

Randal picked it up and immediately his eyebrows raised.

"Real?" Jack asked. They knew he was asking about the old stone in the middle.

"Very." Randal put it down as though it was blazing hot—or that he didn't trust himself with it.

"Reid said his grandmother recently decided she has Second Sight." Kate didn't smile, but the two men did. She may as well have said fairies had flitted about the room.

"She's always had it," Sara said. "Her entire life."

"And how do you know this?" Randal asked.

Sara opened her mouth to speak but closed it. She was a writer. Someone who made up stories. In the past, she'd written of her dreams. If she told that she believed her last two dreams were real, that she was channeling someone else's memories, she feared she'd see patronizing looks on their faces. She loved all the people around this table and it was reciprocated, but she balked at telling them what she'd "seen."

"Okay," Jack said when she didn't answer, "what about you and Rachel?"

"Wait!" Kate said. "I'm not finished. Some interesting things happened last night."

"You mean the way you were throwing yourself at the entire Lachlan Fire Department?" The looks the others gave Jack said he was being ridiculous. He gave a small smile. "Or do you mean what you and Flynn talked about?"

"Right," Kate said. "Sheriff Flynn told me something, plus, I had another memory." She told both stories clearly and concisely.

When she finished, they looked at each other. Her stories seemed to add two new suspects, Billy and Alish. But murder was one thing while what was done to the victim's head was another. They began to speculate about who could have done such a hideous thing.

"Anyone," Randal said. "Any person can be driven to the point of insanity." From his experiences in life, he knew more about being taken to the brink than they did.

"Alish," Sara said. "She comes up in everything. If Oliver was harassing Greer and calling her names, maybe Alish protected her."

"By bashing in a head, yes," Randal said, "but sawing open the skull? It seems far-fetched due to her circumstances."

Sara glared at her brother. "You mean because of her age? Why does everyone believe that growing old cleanses people's souls? Mentally sick young people don't become sweet little old dears just because of the passage of time. And don't forget that the murder happened twenty-five years ago! We were all younger—and stronger—then."

For a moment, they stared at Sara. She was getting angry.

"What have you been writing?" Kate asked.

"What?"

"You heard me. You write about your life, so what are you putting in your notebook? A love story about Jack and me?"

"No!" Jack said.

The two women were staring at each other, oblivious of the men.

Sara's face was turning red. "Nothing important," she muttered. "Just some thoughts on the 1944 murder."

"The one Harry Adair committed?" Randal asked.

Sara nodded. "And the execution. I think everything is connected."

"None of the people at Billy's place have found anything," Jack said. "Troy keeps in contact with them. They've seen every movie three times and read all the scripts, but they haven't found anything like what we told them."

"Maybe Adair didn't write about it," Randal said.

In unison, the others turned to look at him. Their faces said, *"A writer has a story and doesn't tell it?! Impossible!"*

Randal put his hands up in protection. "Okay, just a thought. But Troy doesn't know of any movie that fits the bill, and he's seen everything."

Sara looked at her brother. "If you'd killed someone and made a movie about it, would you let Kate see it?"

Randal grimaced. "She read that damned book about *me*. If I could have stopped that, I would have." He looked at Sara in understanding. "Maybe Harry hid his story. Have you figured out anything? Something you aren't telling us?"

"A marriage for murder," she said, then held up her hand. "Don't ask me what that means. I don't know."

"But you're the one who made it up," Jack said.

Kate was staring hard at her aunt. "If Alish does have Second Sight, I wonder what the depth of it is." She nodded to the brooch on the table. "I've read of people being able to transmit thoughts through objects. Especially *old* artifacts."

Sara wasn't ready to tell of the clarity of her dreams. But she was rather good at spinning the facts. She could say lots and tell nothing. "All this has made me think of a possible book. What happened to James Lachlan's son? Why did he run away after his cousin's execution? Did *anyone* know where he went? We keep hearing about a movie but it doesn't seem to exist— or does it?" She took a breath. "We don't know why Derek Oliver was murdered, but my mind keeps going to the past, and yes, I've been writing it all down. Any more questions?"

They could tell that Sara had been pushed as far as they dared.

"You haven't told us about your time with Rachel," Randal said. "Did you learn anything new?"

"No. I failed completely. She said what we already knew,

that someone had yet again ransacked the nursery. She was quite upset about it, and while we were there, she started putting things back in order—just as Kate did. Since that area was closed off for twenty-five years, it could have been rearranged a long time ago. Maybe by a cleaning crew."

"No," Kate said. "I was in there during the renovation. The room was in the correct order. I'm sure that one of our guests went through it. It's just a gut feeling, but I believe that person was looking for my hedgehog."

"Then it was probably Rachel, since she was seen with it," Randal said.

"But she was bellyaching about things being out of place," Jack said. "If she made the mess, complaining about it makes no sense."

"Maybe she was lying and covering up what she'd done," Kate said. "I wish Greer were here. She'd know."

They were silent as they thought of the death of the poor, sad young woman. She'd not had much of a life.

"We may not solve this one and I'm not sure I care," Sara said. "Everyone is better off that the man was gone. And it appears to be a one-off. A crime of passion."

"Except for the chimney nearly killing me," Jack said.

"That could have been an accident," Sara said.

Jack's eyes blazed. "I did *not* leave a chimney in such a bad state that it fell. And what about the text sent from Kate's phone? And her business card on the ground? How do you explain those things?"

They were silent, as they had no answer.

Jack was frowning. "I'm going to get some clean shirts." He went down the hall to his room.

"I need fresh clothes too." Kate went to her apartment.

When Sara and Randal were alone, he said, "You don't really believe that Jack left a chimney like that, do you?"

"Of course not. But I want to believe it. Otherwise I'd have to think someone was after Jack."

"But why?" Randal said. "Money? To stop the investigation? Killing *you* would be more likely to achieve those things."

"True." She was unperturbed at his observation. "We need to—" She cut off because Jack came down the hall and from the look of him, it was something bad. "What happened?" she asked. "Tell me you didn't get a call from your mother."

"Rachel," Jack said quietly.

"Injured? Went home? What?" Randal asked. "And who told you?"

"No one." Jack sat down on a dining chair.

Kate came out of her apartment carrying a tote bag. "What's going on?"

"Something's happened to Rachel," Sara said, "but Jack hasn't told us what."

"I'll go to the house," Randal said. "Whatever's happened, everyone will be a mess. Should the sheriff be called?"

He was halfway to the door when Jack said loudly, "No!"

Randal went back to them, and they waited for him to explain.

"She's not there," Jack said. "She's here. In my bedroom."

They looked at each other for moment, then went down the hall to Jack's bedroom. There, lying peacefully on the bed, looking like she was sleeping, was Rachel.

"You checked that she's dead?" Randal asked Jack.

"Of course I did!" He snapped, because one time he'd assumed a person was deceased but he wasn't. Jack wasn't going to make that mistake again.

They stared in silence at the woman. She looked as though she might sit up at any moment.

Jack turned to Sara. "Who besides you doesn't like her?"

"I changed my mind," Sara said. "We had a good time yesterday. Sort of. If it weren't for a murder investigation we might have become friends."

"We have to call someone," Randal said.

All four of them groaned. Whichever law enforcement agent they talked to was going to bawl them out.

"I'll text," Sara said. She was an expert at getting out of making telephone calls.

"What are you going to tell whomever you text?" Randal asked.

She had her phone in her hand. "Daryl. Dead body found in Jack's bedroom. What do we do?"

Randal looked at it. "Concise and horrible. It's perfect."

While the others stared in silence, Sara ran to get her camera and the shortest, fastest lens she had. She even slid the flash onto the top. In Jack's room, she moved all around the bed as she took a lot of photos. It was while she was leaning over the bed that she saw the tattoo. As Lenny had said, it was the double R—just like Reid's.

"How do you think she was...you know? Killed?" Kate asked. "I don't see any marks."

"Maybe she was killed elsewhere and put here," Randal said. "If we could turn the body over, we might see an injury."

But no one dared touch her.

"Poison," Sara said as she made sure her aperture was wide-open. "Her vodka was laced and she was dropped off here. She staggered inside and..." Her eyes widened as she looked at Jack. "Sometimes you leave your windows open, so I checked this room last night. Everything is locked."

He knew what she meant. While Sara had been sleeping just a few feet away, Rachel had died on his bed. Of her own accord or with help, they didn't know. "Who knew you were spending the night here?"

"Lenny, you, and Kate."

"You told no one else?"

"No," Sara said. "But I could have been followed. I didn't think to look."

"Maybe no one realized you were in the house," Jack said. "Oh no! Yesterday I said I had to go home to get some clean clothes. Several people were there."

"If one heard, they all did." Randal was looking at Jack. "I think this is a warning to *you*."

"Why me?" he asked.

Sara's phone pinged. It was a text from Daryl.

Touch nothing. I'm in Boca. be there soon.

She showed them. "So I guess we wait. Let's go into the—"

"Hey!" Gil was standing in the doorway. "I pounded on the door but nobody answered. What are you guys up to?"

Jack tried to block his friend from seeing what was on the bed, but he didn't succeed.

When Gil saw Rachel, he tried to go to her. He was a large man, and it took both Randal and Jack to hold him back. It wasn't easy to get him down the hall, into the living room, and seated on a couch.

"She's...?" Gil asked.

"Yes. I'm really sorry," Sara said.

"She can't be gone," Gil said. "We just found each other. She was with us at home and it was like we'd always been a team. She and Quinn watched a movie together. He *talks* to her. She's the best woman I've ever met. Smart and funny and—"

Kate sat down by him and took his hand, while Jack sat on the other side of him. Sara and Randal went to the dining room and began clearing away the breakfast dishes.

"This is not good," Randal said when they were alone. "Someone has more in mind than some old murder. There's something contemporary going on."

"Why?!" Sara said. "What did Rachel know?"

"She didn't have the jewels since they were inside the skull."

"But maybe the murderer didn't know that. He or she wanted to know where the jewels were and when Rachel didn't know, she was removed."

"What's ironic is that if she told the killer she'd sewn them into a hedgehog, the murderer would know they were in an unreachable place."

"And that would make Rachel unneeded," Sara said. "Since she knew who the killer was, she had to go."

"Of course. So why is this person also after Jack? The chimney and now his bedroom. It's like Jack is the real target." Neither of them had answers.

Sara left Randal to fill the dishwasher and went back to the living room to Gil. He looked awful, and he was still talking.

"You know what I went through with Quinn's mother and I've dated some women, but Quinn hated them all. I always found out that he was right. He and I—"

Sara interrupted. "Where is Quinn?"

For a moment Gil's face was blank, then he showed his shock. "I told him to wait for me in the truck."

At that moment, Quinn entered the room from the hallway leading to Jack's bedroom. "You forgot about me," he said to his father, sounding hurt. "Who's the woman on Jack's bed?"

"Trauma," Sara said, and went to the boy to hug him.

He stepped away from her, frowning. "What's going on?"

Gil got up and went to his son. "I'm sorry. Rachel wouldn't want you to be sad. We have to think of her as she was."

Quinn pushed away from his father. "Are all of you crazy? That's not Rachel. Is that woman dead?"

Gil reached out for Quinn, but he moved away.

"That is *not* Rachel!" Quinn shouted.

Each of them had had experience with grief. Denial was the first step of it.

They formed a half circle around Quinn, with no one knowing how to comfort him.

Jack stepped forward, his hand extended. In the months they'd spent together in Colorado, he and the boy had become close.

Quinn was about to take Jack's hand when a woman spoke.

"I don't meant to interrupt, but Lenny said all of you were here, and the door was open. I made muffins."

Slowly, they turned to look at her, then froze in silence.

It was Quinn who reacted. He plowed through the circle, nearly knocking Kate down, as he went to the woman. He threw his arms around her, lifting her from the ground.

Randal caught the basket of muffins before they hit the floor.

"I told them!" Quinn said in triumph. "I told them you weren't her."

The others stood still and stared.

Laughing, the woman broke away from Quinn before he crushed her, and looked at him. "I'm glad to see you too. Have you had breakfast?"

Jack was the first to recover from shock—and he didn't look happy. Without a word, he stepped behind the woman, put his hands on her shoulders, and guided her down the hall to his bedroom.

There on the bed lay the woman who looked like the one in front of Jack. Rachel was dead on the bed and Rachel was being held in Jack's strong grip.

"Is she...?" Alive Rachel asked.

"She's dead." Jack's voice wasn't kind.

"I guess you want an explanation."

Jack raised an eyebrow but said nothing as they went back down the hall. The others were sitting in the living room, with a space open on a couch for Jack, and for the Rachel who was alive.

Kate, Sara, and Randal were frowning, their faces serious to the point of anger. They didn't like being played for fools.

On the opposite couch were Gil and Quinn. They were enjoying the freshly baked muffins, a platter of fruit, and big mugs of cold milk. They were very happy. Quinn was wearing a smug I-told-you-so look. Having outsmarted so many adults was a highlight of his life.

Jack and the woman sat down on the couch, waiting in silence for her to explain.

She took a couple of breaths, let them out, but said nothing. She looked at Kate. "Do you still like the coconut pieces the best?"

Kate's mouth dropped open. "Greer?"

"Yes."

Kate was blinking. "That's it! Last night I saw Jack and Troy walk away, and they looked so much alike from the back. It reminded me of something but I couldn't remember what. From the back, you looked like Rachel. Lea said that."

"Only from the neck up." She was smiling, showing her perfect teeth. "You grew up to be so pretty and now you're to be married. It makes me feel old." She looked at Randal. "I'm sorry for what happened to you, but I'm glad Lea waited for you, and—"

Sara cut her off. "Your grandmother sent you away so she wouldn't be blamed for the disappearance of Derek Oliver. But she knew he hadn't disappeared. He was dead."

Greer nodded. "Yes. She can 'see' things but her abilities are limited. She can't predict world disasters. It's centered on

our family. What's important is that she knew that if I stayed
in Lachlan I would be accused of murder."

"Does Reid know you're alive?" Randal asked.

"No!" Greer said quickly. "My brother is upright and law
abiding. Grans didn't tell him anything because he probably
would have felt a duty to tell the sheriff. The one before this
one, that is."

"The man who set my brother up," Sara said under her
breath. She was studying Greer intently. "I feel stupid that I
didn't see that you were two people. But then, I think maybe
Rachel kept herself hidden, but I believe I saw her from a
distance. With your brother. And there were little clues. You
called Mrs. Meyers 'Grans.' Yesterday there was a lift at the
end of your sentence. Pure British. Have you been living in
England? Tell us everything and please start at the beginning."

Greer smiled. "Good sleuthing. Yes, I live in London. I
work for a law firm of three very old lawyers. I keep their
files in order and remind them of where they're supposed to
be when." She paused. "I guess I should start on the night
that dreadful man disappeared..." She looked at Kate. "After
we had our picnic upstairs, and after we went to bed, Grans
woke me up in the wee hours. She'd had one of her visions."

"Was it in the form of a dream?" Sara asked.

"I think they are," Greer said. "She never talked about
them, so I'm not sure. Have you had dreams?"

Sara didn't answer the question. "What did Alish do?"

"She said I had to go with her and to do it quietly." Greer
frowned. "She had everything prepared for me to leave."

"She must have had a premonition that it was going to be
needed," Sara said.

"I guess so. All I know is that she had a packed suitcase
and my passport. When she drove me to the airport, she told
me about her vision. She said that the man was dead and that

someday the body would be found. When it was, *I* would be accused of the murder. Worse, she said that she'd foreseen that I would be found guilty. She said that years ago she'd arranged for me to go to relatives in Scotland, and..." Greer's voice gave a little hiccup. "She said that from then on, I was to have no contact with her or my brother or anyone in the US."

"That was hard." Randal spoke from experience.

"Yes, it was. I stayed with my uncle and his family for years. They were very good to me, and I got rather good at carding sheep's wool." Only Kate smiled at that. "During that time I obeyed and I had no contact with anyone in the US. My Scottish relatives were lovely, but I missed Grans and Reid very much. When I turned twenty-one, I decided I'd had enough of mud and sheep, so I went to London."

"And got a job with your lawyers," Sara said.

"Yes, I did." Greer smiled. "For once my looks worked in my favor. My lawyers didn't want some young girl who'd have lots of boyfriends around, or after a year she'd quit to get married. I guess I should have been insulted, but it was nice to be wanted. We were a perfect match."

Sara circled her face with her hand. "Your transformation didn't happen quickly. You had to have started preparing for this long ago. Healing takes time."

Greer nodded. "During all those years, I heard nothing from my family, but I had an alert on my computer for anything about Lachlan." She looked at Sara. "Notices were rare, but I saw your name a few times. Anyway, on my twenty-fourth birthday, Grans sent me money through my uncle. It was a nice six figures, and she told me I was to change my looks. I didn't know if something awful had happened or what, but I liked the idea of changing. I immediately made an appointment with a Harley Street plastic surgeon. He asked who I wanted to look like."

Kate smiled. "You showed him that photo of you and Rachel, didn't you? I remember it. You two were side by side. Barbara said that with makeup, Rachel could be made to look like you."

"But not the other way around," Greer said. "And you're right. I showed the doctor that photo. Rachel and I were the same height, same coloring, but that was all. It took years, but I had teeth, skin, and nose done. And I had a personal trainer who nearly killed me in the gym. I lost the weight and reshaped myself." She smiled in memory. "My dear lawyers were so polite. They never asked about my bandages or what the English call the railroad tracks on my teeth."

Sara nodded to Greer's arm. "You didn't duplicate everything about her."

"That odd tattoo? She wouldn't tell me what it meant."

"Rachel and Reid," Sara said.

"Oh," Greer said as she thought about that. "I wish I'd pushed to know. Then maybe..." She sighed. "Anyway, I want to make it clear that it was never an intentional impersonation. Certainly not planned. After I was...transformed, I guess you'd say, my life didn't change much. But then I was fairly happy. I was never one for going to clubs or joining anything. For a while, I had a boyfriend, but it didn't work out. I assumed my life was as it was going to be. But then, abruptly, everything changed."

"Your alert told you what was going on here," Sara said.

"Exactly." Greer looked at Kate. "I owe everything to a woman in your office. She posted online that Lachlan House was being put up for sale."

"Melissa," Kate said. "She shouldn't have done that. The house wasn't under contract. It still isn't."

"I'm glad she did. When I saw that the house was going to be sold, I guessed that the body would at last be found and everyone would be questioned. Maybe I shouldn't have done it, but I wanted to know more. I called Melissa and she talked a lot."

"Of course she did," Kate said. "She's incapable of keeping a secret."

"She told me that I couldn't buy the house now because the listing agent—you—were throwing a party, and you were inviting a movie star. I wasn't sure but I thought maybe it was Barbara. If so, maybe you were recreating *that* party. After I hung up, I thought that if I wanted information, Rachel was the one I should talk to."

"The snoop," Kate said.

"Right. I asked my lawyers to please get Rachel's number and I called her. She told me of the party that was being given to celebrate Billy's life, and that she had no intention of going. She seemed to think the party really was for Billy. But I didn't think so. I had an idea that it was for a different reason, especially since you people were involved. If the body had been found, maybe if I helped solve the murder and prove that I didn't do it, I could reappear. As myself. I could see my family again. Maybe I could even have a real life." She looked at Gil and Quinn with love, and they smiled back at her. "I didn't let myself think about it, I just told her that I'd like to go in her place. As her."

No one said a word until Jack spoke up. "How hard did she laugh at that?"

Greer's eyes sparkled. "Long and loud—and quite nastily. Rachel was never what one would call a nice person."

"She used to say terrible things to you," Kate said.

"Oh yes, she did. She said I was the ugliest person she'd ever seen."

"You're certainly not ugly now," Jack said.

"Thank you," Greer replied.

"I would have loved to have seen her face when she saw you!" Kate said, and they smiled at each other.

"It was grand, and worth all the pain to see her look of shock when she first saw me," Greer said. "We had a few weeks to work on hair and makeup and her teaching me to speak with that flat Connecticut accent." Greer made an eye roll. "Rachel was not a patient teacher."

Gil had been silently listening to the story, then he and Quinn stood up. "I need to go to work." He held out his hand, Greer took it, and the three of them went out the front door. There was silence for a few minutes and they all knew Gil and Greer were kissing goodbye.

When Greer returned, she took her place on the couch. "I guess you have some questions for me."

Randal spoke first. "Didn't your grandmother foresee that the body wouldn't be found for twenty-five years?"

"I guess her visions didn't tell her that. She did say the body was hidden somewhere, not buried, and it would be found relatively intact, but she didn't know when. She just said that when it was found, people would look for me. And it's true. Everyone seems to have spoken of my anger and the abuse I endured from Mr. Oliver. All of it. Even dead, I'm a suspect."

"And you faked your own death," Jack said.

"My uncle did that. He even sent a coffin here. I have a lovely headstone. It has an angel on it." She paused. "Considering what's happened, I think it was all good, but the waiting has been horrible."

"Rachel didn't tell you everything," Sara said. "She had her own plan."

"You heard my call," Greer said. "I thought you might have. And you're right. Rachel told me very little of the truth of what went on with her during that week. And she didn't tell me that she was going to come here. She didn't even hint that she and my brother had been lovers."

"You're the one who slapped him," Sara said. "And Rachel kissed him." She let out a sigh. "Mystery solved."

"That first night after dinner, I was trying to sound like I knew anything." Greer looked at Kate. "I had to use bits that you and I had seen to try to fill it in."

"Aunt Sara and I got into the big cabinet and I remembered several things you and I had seen. Rachel had my hedgehog."

"*What* is the interest in that toy?" Greer asked, her eyes wide.

No one answered her.

"I get it." Greer sounded sad. "I'm not on the inside. Secrets are to be kept from me."

"You certainly kept them from us," Sara shot back at her.

"I did. Sorry. I should have trusted you."

"Did you find out anything from the other guests?" Randal asked.

"Other than that Rachel and my brother were hot and heavy? No. But back then, he seemed to believe they were going to get married." She gave a sound of disbelief. "Rachel told me that she was handed over to some New England hedge fund guy and told to marry him. She said she never had a choice about where her life was going."

Kate gave snort of laughter. "Poor Rachel. Forced to live in a multimillion-dollar mansion instead of a two-bed flat with your brother."

Greer smiled. "That's just what I thought."

"Too bad they weren't told that Reid—" Kate didn't finish, but only Greer didn't know the end of that. Too bad Derek Oliver didn't live long enough to tell Reid he owned the Lachlan Estate. Reid should have taken over ownership long ago. Maybe with good management, it could have become a big citrus industry.

"Did you learn about anything besides her and your brother?" Randal asked. They all knew he was asking about Lea. Was there any hint of her guilt?

"I tried to get information from them." Greer paused. "It's so different being around them now. I'm treated as an equal, not as a nuisance." Her head came up. "I think people are searching for things, but I'm not sure what they're trying to find."

"In the nursery," Kate said.

"Yes. There are missing items and rearranged things. I've tried to remember it all by going over this trip hour by hour. I got here early. That's when I met Quinn and Gil and we watched an old movie. Then we—"

"What movie?" Sara asked quickly.

"Nothing important. The tape had a worn cover so I thought maybe it might be interesting. *Only* something was the title. It was good. Strange but it held your interest. Some gorgeous young man made love to women, then killed them. I think it has a cult following."

"Never heard of it," Jack said. "Can't be too big of a cult."

"I've never seen *Rocky Horror Picture Show*," Sara said, "but people still pay to see it. I bet the tape was taken to Billy's place. What happens in the movie?"

"I don't know," Greer said. "I fell asleep before the end."

"We've been looking for a movie," Randal said. "From the 1940s. I'm not sure it means anything to this case, but my sister believes—"

"This is getting nowhere," Jack said. "We need to decide how to handle the fact that Greer is alive."

"Should we gather everyone, then she shows up and we see who passes out from the shock that she's not dead?" Sara asked.

"Then she gets killed a third time?" Randal said. "I really don't like that. Someone sneaked into my sister's house while she was sleeping."

Sara smiled at her brother in gratitude.

"The murderer will see that we know Rachel is dead," Kate said.

"The reactions will tell all," Sara said. "If we can read them. But can we risk it?"

Jack was looking at Kate and Sara. "I don't like taking such big risks."

"Nor do I," Randal said. "We have to—"

He stopped talking when the front door opened and in came Sheriff Flynn. The look of disgust on his face said everything: *Yet another death. Probably the fault of the Meddling Medlars.*

Without a word, Jack stood up and led the way to his bedroom. Minutes later, the two men returned, then the sheriff went outside to make some calls. The others silently waited for him.

Sheriff Flynn came back in and sat down on one of the couches. "Are those muffins?"

Sara and Kate jumped up to get fruit, butter, and orange juice for him.

During this, no one said a word. They were waiting for the pronouncement of their fate. Would this second murder cause Broward law to take over the case? Tell the Medlar-Wyatt group to go away? They stole glances at Greer. They didn't want to say it, but it was quite possible that she would be accused of the old murder—or for both of them. She had motive and opportunity. And the way she ran away and faked her own death might reinforce her guilt. Add her impersonation of the dead woman and there was a strong case.

They stayed silent while the sheriff ate a muffin and a bowlful of berries.

Finally, he turned to Greer. "You look like the dead woman."

Greer nodded.

"So who are you?"

"Reid's sister."

"What was he being blackmailed for?" the sheriff asked.

Greer's eyes widened. "I don't know. He and Rachel were a couple, but that doesn't seem like blackmail material."

"Did he ever have a big fat emerald ring?"

"Not that I know of," Greer said. "Was it stolen?" She looked at Kate. "Rachel may have done it. She—"

There was a loud knock on the door, the kind that said that if no one answered immediately, the door would be knocked down.

Jack got there first and opened it. Randal and the sheriff were behind him. Men with a stretcher were outside. "Let's go around the side." Jack led and the others followed.

When the women were alone, Sara looked at Greer. "I want to go to Alish, but I don't want your brother there. He's too protective of her. It's the 'old people are fragile' syndrome."

At the mention of her grandmother, tears came to Greer's eyes. "I want to go with you," she whispered.

Sara was seeing this as a writer, playing it forward in her mind. "That won't work. You're dead."

"Twice," Kate said. "You're dead as Rachel and dead as Greer. You don't exist in any form."

Greer grimaced. "This isn't what I thought would happen. I thought the murderer would be revealed, then Rachel and I would stand together. We'd astonish everyone. It would be a good laugh."

"In this fantasy of yours, who was the murderer?" Sara asked.

"Barbara. She would put on the most wonderful performance as she was taken away in handcuffs. Flashes would be going off."

"Billy could do that," Kate said.

"They'd go together." Greer stood up. "Remember how the two of them used to do scenes from movies? My favorite was the one where Barbara wore pants and pulled her hair back to be a man. Then she killed Billy. 'You have stabbed me in my heart,' he said. 'But I go to Valhalla and I will wait for you there.'" Greer put the back of her hand to her forehead, and fell onto the couch.

Sara and Kate were staring at her.

"I don't remember seeing that," Kate said.

"You were probably in bed." Greer was looking at their expressions. "What did I say?"

"Why Valhalla?" Sara asked.

"I don't know. Back then, I thought he was saying vanilla. Years later I saw a Viking movie, heard the term, and realized that's what Billy had been saying. He was dying and going to Valhalla heaven. You two are looking at me very oddly."

"It's just that we've been trying to find an old movie about a murder and we haven't found it yet," Sara said.

"I assume Billy would know," Greer said.

Sara looked at Kate. "But he hasn't told us. How interesting. Mr. Tennis Champion with a violent temper when someone crosses him didn't tell us about playacting a movie death scene."

"Especially a scene that sounds just like what we asked him to find," Kate said.

Sara gave a little smile. "I think we should ask Billy about what he hasn't told us."

"I agree," Kate said.

They heard voices coming from down the hall. It looked like the men had finished their task of removal. There'd been no sirens so maybe the death was to be kept a secret—for a while anyway. Kate and Sara braced themselves for what they knew was coming. They were going to be bawled out by the sheriff. He was fed up with murders in his town.

Suddenly, Sara had a thought, and turned to Greer. "Head-stones of angels cost a lot. Is your grandmother rich?"

"I don't think so, but she and I never discussed money. I think maybe she had some sort of inheritance."

"'I will prosper through you,'" Sara whispered. Kate and Greer looked at her. "It's something I heard someone say. Only prosperous people can afford stone angels. They—" She topped talking because the three men appeared. "How long do we have to solve this?" she asked.

"To solve this murder?" Sheriff Flynn asked. "Or to wait for the next person to be killed?" He was staring at Greer. "What are we going to do with you? You show up and the murderer will realize he got the wrong one."

"I don't think he did," Sara said. "I think he wanted Ra-chel—" The sheriff's look made her stop talking.

"It doesn't matter who, what, or why. The murderer will know he screwed up." He frowned at Greer. "You, young lady, will be as good as dead."

"Oh," was all Greer could say.

"How about if Gil and Quinn take her to Colorado?" Jack said. "We'll get her out of here."

Sheriff Flynn turned to him. "She impersonated a woman who was probably a thief and maybe a murderer, but she's to-tally innocent? You think that'll hold up in court?"

"He's right," Greer said.

Jack didn't say a word as he sat down by Kate, with Ran-dal on her other side.

The sheriff looked at Greer. "You're to stay with Gil, but

you don't leave this town. I'm going to deputize Gil so he'll keep watch over you."

Greer blinked a couple of times. "Will he wear a uniform? And a gun?"

Her meaning was so clear that Sara, Jack, Kate, and Randal had to swallow to keep from laughing.

The sheriff glared at them. He was not amused. "I can see that all of you are overcome with grief at the death of that poor woman. What about her family? Does she have children? People who love her?"

They lowered their heads. He was right. They'd been much too frivolous about this.

"Rachel has a daughter," Greer said. "She lives in Texas. They're estranged. Her ex-husband remarried. I can find out about the rest of her family."

"You do that," Daryl said. "But don't tell them that someone took her life away from her. I want—" He stopped when his phone buzzed and he read the text. "That was Bea." She coordinated his office and kept up with everything. "The woman has been taken to the hospital."

"Not the coroner?" Sara asked.

"Not her!" the sheriff snapped. "The old woman. She fell down the stairs." He looked at Greer. "She's with you."

Sara was the first one to understand who he meant. "Alish? Is she all right?"

Daryl looked at her with interest. "You have some connection with her?"

Before Sara could speak, Greer said, "They share dreams."

Daryl threw up his hands in surrender. "A dead body falls out of a closet, a head dumps out jewels, a dead woman shows up in Jack's bed, but *you* are playing with your dreams. Are you gonna get a book out of it? Are you—?" Again, his phone buzzed. This time he turned pale. "It's Cotilla." He glared at them, then went to the front door. "Yes, sir?" he said, then left, firmly closing the door behind him.

Sara gave a loud sigh of relief. "That bawling out wasn't as bad as I thought it would be."

"About a seven," Kate said. "We've had tens. Or maybe we've grown tougher. At least nobody cried."

Jack was looking at Greer. She seemed to be thinking hard.

"Jewels? In someone's head?" Greer asked. "I guess that was Mr. Oliver. But how did they get there? How was he killed? Did someone—?"

Sara spoke loudly. "Alish is in the hospital!"

Immediately, Greer let go of her thoughts about Derek Oliver. "Yes! I was distracted. I must go see her." She stood up. "Where is she? Could I use your loo before we go?"

Sara pointed the way to her bathroom. As soon as she was gone, Sara said, "Of course Greer can't go anywhere in public. People think she's dead and someone knows Rachel is dead. *I* am going to go see Alish."

"They won't let you in," Randal said. "You're not a relative."

"We could lie." Kate obviously assumed that they'd all go.

"No." Sara looked at them. "You three are people who get attention. Jack, the nurses will recognize you from the Brigade, and Randal, wherever you go, people notice you. Kate, those overworked doctors would probably propose to you."

They didn't reply because they knew she was right.

"I'll take a cane," Sara said. "No one will even look at me." She turned to her brother. "Can you find out where she is? Her room number? I hope she's not in the ICU."

"*Fell* down the stairs?" Jack said. "We're supposed to believe that's just a coincidence, what with all that's going on?"

Sara looked at Kate. "We need to coordinate this. You keep Reid busy while I go to the hospital."

"Like hell she will!" Jack said. "She—"

Randal ignored Jack's outburst. "Reid, Alish, Greer. The whole family comes up often. Didn't I hear that Ivy is on a job in St. Petersburg?"

"That has nothing to do with anything," Jack snapped. "Kate isn't going to go—"

Kate looked at her father. "Of course! Reid lives and works in St. Pete." She turned to Jack. "Stop bossing me around and text your sister. Ivy needs to do some spying. On second thought, I'll text her. You'll tell her three words."

"And you'll write a book," Jack said.

Sara and Randal said in unison, "It's a perfect match." They smiled at each other. Sara was going to miss her brother when he moved in with Lea—if she hadn't killed anyone, that is.

When Greer came out of Sara's bedroom, everyone went silent. "Did I give you enough time to figure things out?"

No one replied.

Greer looked at Sara. "I'm going to the hospital to see my grandmother. I can show my passport to prove that I'm related to her. If I do that, I figure it'll take about four minutes for the killer to hear that I am actually alive. I wasn't run over by a train, and I wasn't left dead on Jack's bed. That should stir things up quickly."

They were staring at her in shock.

"Unless you figure out another way to get me in to see my grandmother, that is," Greer said. "Do that, and I'll play nice. Whatever, I *am* going to see her!" She looked at their silent faces. "Anyone have any idea how to do it?"

"Carol Burnett," Sara said.

Randal smiled in understanding but the young ones looked blank. "That might work," Randal said.

Twenty-Two

THE DISGUISE SARA HAD PLANNED FOR GREER WAS to go as a gray-haired cleaning person. Randal made a call, then told them that Alish wasn't in the ICU, but she had a *no visitors* status. Not even relatives were allowed in to see her.

Sara said, "I guess that's off, then."

Randal gave a snort. "Oh ye of little faith." He said they'd need ID badges and that was no problem. It was easy to someone with Randal's criminal past. A quick trip to an office supply store and Randal had what he needed. By the time Kate had applied makeup to Greer and Sara, and had chosen outfits for them, Randal had an ID for Greer and a visitor pass for his sister.

After Kate got through with her aunt, Sara stared at herself in the mirror. She looked twenty years older. "If this is what you wanted, all I had to do was wash my face," she muttered.

There was a lot of suppressed laughter.

Minutes later, Sara and Greer were ready to go.

"You'll go see Billy?" Sara asked Kate.

"Yes, I told you," Kate said. "I'll grill him hard. Jack will threaten to punch him if he doesn't tell us everything. Tennis, movies, all of it."

"Turn off his oxygen tube and that should do it," Greer said. She too looked older in her wiry gray wig. Kate had padded her slim body, then rummaged in the back of Sara's closet for her "fat clothes," meaning what Sara had worn when she was much heavier.

"I keep some as a reminder," Sara had said.

The clothes were too short on Greer but that added to her camouflage as a stereotype of a cleaner.

Sara turned to her brother. "If Lea is looking for something, find out what it is."

Randal grimaced. "I got it. You don't have to tell me again." His eyes twinkled. "You want me to help you to the door? Or should I get you a walker?" He held out a cane to her. It was an antique with a silver fox at its head. She did not ask where he got it.

"Help yourself!" she snapped as she took the cane. "Do your job and I'll do mine."

"I'm here to help if you need it," he said sympathetically. Randal stepped away before his sister could smack him with one of her boxing punches.

Sara practiced her hesitant walk as she went to the front door. She turned to look at them. "All of you know what to do?"

"We do," Kate said, "but Jack is going to wait for you outside the hospital. No, don't give me any backtalk. If you get caught, he'll know how to bail you out of jail. He's done it many times."

"On that happy note..." Jack said as he opened the door and they went outside.

When they got to the hospital, Sara knew she was going to

have to congratulate her brother for a job well done. A man who had lots of scars and tattoos greeted Sara and Greer at a side door. He looked at Sara, bent over and leaning heavily on the cane. He seemed to fear that she might die at any moment.

Sara stood up straight, stuck the cane out like a sword, then made a few hard jabs.

The man grinned. "So you're Randal's sister?"

Sara bit her tongue on a snarky comeback. This man was probably one of her brother's companions in some crime. It was better to stay on his good side. "I am," she said.

The man gave Greer a cleaning cart to push, then went upstairs in the elevator with them. At the fourth floor, he held the door open, but he didn't get out. "You got the room number?"

Sara nodded.

"Good luck." Obviously, he wasn't going with them. He probably couldn't risk being caught.

She and Greer separated as the elevator door closed and, as Sara had predicted, no one looked at an old woman toddling about on a cane. She stepped back to let a patient on a gurney be rolled past.

Finally, she reached Alish's room and Sara went in. Against Greer's protests, they had agreed that Sara would have a few minutes alone with Alish.

It was a private room, an expensive one, and as Kate had noted, there was nothing personal in it. No flowers or cards, no photos. No funny stuffed animals to cheer up the sick person.

The woman was asleep. Sara set the cane on a chair, then went to the bedside and looked at her. Yes, this was an older version of the young woman she'd seen in her dreams. She was what Greer had once looked like.

Sara's first thought was that she was one of those rare

women who looked better as she aged. That often happened with men, but not with women. Age had softened the harsh features she'd had in her youth.

Alish opened her eyes. She didn't seem in the least surprised to see an unknown woman standing there.

Sara didn't bother with preliminaries. "Did someone hurt you?"

Alish said nothing.

But Sara could see that she understood. "You and I have a connection."

Alish nodded.

"We're trying to find out—" Before Sara could complete her sentence, the door opened and in came Greer with her cart. It was too early!

Greer went to the opposite side of her grandmother's bed and stared at her, seeming to drink her in.

Sara doubted that Alish would recognize her. After all, Greer had had extensive surgery, and she was now done up like a caricature of a cleaning person. Sara started to explain who she was, but Alish raised her hand and her eyes filled with tears.

Greer was also crying as she took her grandmother's hand in both of hers and kissed it.

"You are here. You are beautiful," Alish said, her voice quite strong.

"I came to see you."

Sara glanced up at the camera in the corner of the room. There were machines all around. Alish had an IV in her arm, an oxygen tube at her nose, and a pulse clip on her finger. They had little time before they'd be run out of the room. "We're trying to find out who killed Derek Oliver."

Alish didn't take her eyes off her granddaughter. "I did it.

I sawed his head open and removed the brain. I rolled it up in a rug."

If Greer was shocked by this, she didn't show it. "In the turtle rug."

"Yes." Alish smiled, showing protruding teeth that had not changed since she was a girl. "He was hurting you and Reid. I couldn't allow that. I had to stop him."

"And you put the jewels in his skull," Sara said.

Alish looked at her. "What jewels?"

Maybe it was the connection they had or maybe it was Greer's blasé attitude at hearing a confession of murder, but Sara was sure she was lying. "Who are you covering for? Reid?"

Instantly, Greer got angry. "You think my brother is a murderer?"

Alish reached out and took Sara's hand. "You must send her away. Protect her."

When Sara looked at the hand grasping hers, she saw a tattoo on her forearm. It was so old she could hardly make out the numbers. *4-12-44.* "What is that date?"

"My wedding."

"For the husband whose grave you won't leave?" Sara asked.

Alish made no answer.

Sara felt like screaming in frustration at the lack of answers. She glanced up at the camera, then back down. "Are the dreams true? Do they come from you?"

"Yes."

Sara spoke quickly. "There were two men. Then later, one drove you to a train station. He was the nasty one. The one on the horse."

"Aran," Alish said and her grip on Sara's hand tightened.

"That's James's son," Sara said. "He ran away, but you knew where he was. Did he make a movie?"

"Yes, he did. No, he didn't."

"What does that mean?" Sara's voice showed her exasperation.

Again, Alish didn't answer.

Feeling frustrated, Sara blurted out, "Why does someone want to hurt Jack?"

For the first time, Alish's eyes showed shock, maybe even fear. "No, not him." When her eyes widened, a machine began to frantically, loudly beep. "The mark," Alish said. "The mark. This must stop." She clutched Sara's hand so hard it hurt. She was a very strong woman!

Seconds later, the room filled with doctors and nurses. Sara and Greer were pushed away. One nurse glared at Sara. "Whatever you said to her is about to kill her. Get out!"

Greer led the way through the crowd to the door, Sara behind her.

"All right," a nurse said to Alish, then turned to Sara. "She keeps saying, 'Tell her of the mark.'" The nurse glared at Sara and Greer. "I've never seen you two before. Let me see your badges."

"Send me the truth!" Sara shouted loud enough for Alish to hear.

When Alish's machine began beeping louder and faster, Sara and Greer scurried out the door, ran to the stairs and down them before the nurse could find them. When they got outside, Jack was standing by Kate's car. He saw that they were out of breath, opened the door, and the two women slid into the back seat.

Jack didn't have to be told to drive away quickly.

As soon as they were on the highway, Jack passed a big canister of wet wipes to them. "Kate thought you two might like to remove the makeup."

"I love my niece," Sara said as she began wiping the thick,

ugly foundation and the brown contouring lines off her face. Her handbag was on the floor and in it was a case of her daily makeup. She applied it.

As for Greer, she wiped away the grime, then left her skin bare.

"Ah, youth," Sara said.

Jack drove them to the Cracker Barrel in Pembroke Pines, where Randal and Kate were waiting for them.

They wanted to talk to each other but with Greer there, they said nothing but what a nice day it was.

Jack, a native Floridian, said, "It's Florida. The weather is always nice."

"Except for hurricanes," Kate said.

"Better than snow," Jack shot back.

"Skiing is nice," Kate said. "You can—"

The waitress interrupted to take their orders, and after that, they were silent.

Greer stood up. "I'm going to the restroom."

The second she was gone, Kate said to her aunt, "Tell us every word."

"Gladly." Sara spoke fast. "Alish wouldn't say if her fall was an accident or not, but she did say she killed Derek Oliver. She knew his head had been sawed open and the brain removed. But she did *not* know jewels had been stuffed inside."

The others were leaning forward, listening to every word.

"And yes, the dreams I've had are real."

"*True* dreams?" Jack said loudly.

Sara put up her hand in dismissal. She didn't have time to deal with his doubt. "It was a dream of Alish with two men, one nice and one a jerk. Later, the bad guy drove her to the train station. Alish said that was Aran."

"The missing son," Kate said. "So she knew where he went. Sorry. Go on."

"I assumed he was going to LA so I asked if he'd made a movie. Alish said, 'Yes, he did. No, he didn't.'"

"Cryptic," Randal said.

"Very," Sara answered, then leaned farther forward and lowered her voice. "Alish was calm through all of this, but when I asked if someone wants to hurt Jack, she flipped out. The machines started beeping and Greer and I were ordered to get out. We—"

"Greer is coming," Kate said, and they sat up straighter.

"Murders only happen when she is here," Randal said quietly.

"Anything else?" Jack asked Sara quickly.

"I told her to send me the truth."

"Through email?" Jack asked.

"In a dream." Randal was looking at his sister in curiosity. "With the brooch."

"Yes," Sara said as Greer took her seat.

"What did I miss?" Greer asked.

"I just told them of our visit with your grandmother," Sara said. "What were your impressions?"

"I don't believe she killed anyone. I think she foresaw what was going to happen and got me out of the country."

"But she knew details," Sara said.

"Obviously, she did see the body," Greer said. "That it was so violently mutilated reinforced her need to get me out quickly."

"Why you and not Reid?" Kate asked.

"I don't think he was there. Now that I know a bit more, I think he was probably with Rachel. That gave him an alibi, but I had none. Could someone please tell me what's going on with these jewels?"

No one said a word.

After a long silence, Sara looked at Kate. "So what did Billy have to say?"

Greer gave an eye roll but she didn't ask any more questions.

Their orders came and after the waitress left, Kate said, "Oh, but Billy is a good actor! His tone was 'I didn't tell you about when I played tennis? How remiss of me. I was frightfully good at it.'"

"He got the frightening part right," Sara said.

"But of course you persisted." Randal gave his daughter a look of pride.

"Yes, I did. Billy finally admitted to denuding the house of furniture, and yes, Derek Oliver was blackmailing him about that. Billy said he didn't tell us because he didn't think it was important."

"What about the movie bit he and Barbara did?" Greer asked.

"He seemed genuinely surprised at that, and I had to listen to several minutes of his telling me that those little sketches were part of why he was such an interesting host. But he didn't remember one that was specifically about Valhalla. However, he did say that maybe he wrote it, so it was an original piece."

Jack was typing out a text on his phone and they looked at him. "Just asking how my little brother is doing."

Randal gave a sigh. "So, not much new information from Billy. But I didn't expect much."

"Sorry," Kate said. "But now we know Billy isn't to be trusted."

Sara looked at her brother. "What did you find out from Lea?"

"She's been searching for a safe."

That got everyone's attention.

"She said that she'd never found her husband's will, and

after we discovered his papers, she remembered hearing about a safe. She was looking for it."

"So why didn't she tell *you* what she was up to?" Sara asked.

"You are an advocate of independent women but this woman is supposed to ask a man's permission to *look* for something?"

They turned to Sara for her response.

Sara gave a small smile. "I stand corrected. Did she find one?"

"No," Randal said. "She figured it would be in the nursery or the Palm Room but she's found nothing."

"We are running out of time," Kate said softly. "Everyone is a suspect. Lots of motive and opportunity, but nothing for sure."

Jack's phone buzzed and his face lit up. "I asked my brother if he knew of any connection to Valhalla and Vikings. He sent me a photo." He passed his phone to them. It was a picture of a gorgeous young man, shoulder-length blond hair, in the costume of a Viking, complete with horned headdress.

Troy had written **This is my dad. He was an actor before he began directing and producing.**

Kate was the first to speak. "Maybe we need to look for movies Harry Adair was in, not ones he directed."

Sara said, "My guess is that he'd be uncredited, as one of the chorus, so to speak. Like in *Ben Hur* with a cast of thousands."

Jack's phone buzzed again and his eyes widened, but he put his phone away and didn't speak, nor did anyone ask what the message was.

Greer understood. It was private, not for her. She stood up. "I think I'll go to Gil's house."

"Take my car." Randal handed her the keys. "I'll go back with them." It was obvious that he didn't want to leave the group.

Greer thanked him, then left.

When she was gone, Jack showed the text he'd received from Sheriff Flynn.

Prelim. Poison. Looks like suicide.

"Rachel killed herself?" Kate asked.

Jack frowned. "How'd she break into the house? How'd she know where we live? *Why* did she kill herself?"

No one had an answer.

TWENTY-THREE

THEY WERE AN UNHAPPY LOT AS THEY DROVE BACK to Lachlan House. They were feeling that they'd made no progress in finding the killer. And as Kate had said, they were running out of time.

"I want to be one of those TV detectives," Sara said. "In the last five minutes, they put together every word everyone has said and *voilà!* they know who the murderer is."

"I don't think Rachel killed herself," Kate said.

"I agree," Randal said. "I think she thought she'd find the jewels, sell them, and give herself a new life."

No one replied, because it was what Randal had thought he would do with his own life.

Maybe because they were feeling like losers, Jack pulled the car as far to the back of Lachlan House as possible. They went in through the kitchen.

When they were inside, Lenny looked at Sara and nodded toward the back window. Reid was outside trimming the grass. Lenny said, "It's as though he knows he owns the place."

Sara didn't ask how Lenny knew about Reid's inheritance, but then she was a bit afraid to hear his answer.

Lenny nodded toward the hallway. "They found something and they're waiting for you."

Sara's heart gave a little leap of hope, and she followed the others into the living room.

Barbara, Troy, and Lea jumped up from the couches. Their faces were alight with excitement.

"We couldn't find Rachel," Lea said, "but maybe that was a good thing. Or not. We aren't sure until we see it." She looked at Barbara. "You explain."

"Billy called me and he was very upset." Barbara paused to be sure she had everyone's attention. "He said he expects to be hauled off to prison at any moment and it is all my fault. Such drama! I finally got it out of him that he couldn't remember where he and I got one of the stories we reenacted. It was about a Viking and a man being stabbed in the heart."

Barbara could hold her own when it came to drama. Again, she paused and waited for everyone's attention. "I remembered where I'd heard the story."

"From a script?" Troy asked. His hint was that was the only thing she ever read.

The others hadn't seen mother and son together, and now they saw the deep affection between them.

"No, darling, it was a program from TV. *Unsolved Mysteries*. I remember how Billy and I were drooling over the host, Robert Stack. We were laying bets on which of us could make him smile. I said—" She cut off at Troy's look. "Anyway, I thought of trying to find the episode online, but that would take ages since I didn't remember the name of anyone involved. I knew Billy and I had found it on a VHS tape in the Palm Room. But I checked and it wasn't there, nor was it in the stash you'd taken to Billy. So where was that tape?"

She waited for an answer, but no one spoke. "I'll have to apologize to Rachel when I see her, but the room she's in now is the one I had when I stayed here the first time. I knew it had been beautifully redone but maybe there was some little cranny that had been missed, so I ransacked it." Barbara's eyes sparkled. "I had to climb on a chair but I found the old tape stuck at the back of a top shelf of the closet. It's almost as though someone had hidden it there." She gave them time to think about that.

With a flourish, Barbara withdrew a VHS tape from her bag. "Taaa–daaa. It's an episode of *Unsolved Mysteries* with that delicious Robert Stack hosting. I met him once. He was—"

"Mother!" Troy said.

Barbara smiled. "I haven't had time to see it, but I do vaguely remember Billy and I drinking too much wine while we watched it. Perhaps it's just my intuition, but I believe the story you've been looking for came from this show."

There was a hesitation of about three seconds, then the seven of them nearly stampeded up the stairs to the Palm Room. Troy, their resident electronics man, put the tape in the machine. They found seats on chair, couch, and floor, then settled back to watch.

Robert Stack, 1950s heartthrob, came on.

"See what I mean?" Barbara said about the handsome man.

"I do indeed," Sara answered with enthusiasm.

When the first segment came on, the room was silent as they watched. There were some video reenactments that went on behind the announcer telling the story.

This is the unsolved murder of a young man who has become a cult idol, Taylor Caswell.

It was 1944, and young, handsome Taylor Caswell had made only one movie, prophetically called Only Once. *While he was waiting for his movie to premier, Taylor lived in a cheap apartment in a two-story complex in Los Angeles. It was said that he kept to himself and befriended none of the other tenants.*

When his movie was just a couple of months away from being released, a young woman who said she was his wife arrived. She told the landlord she hadn't heard from her husband in over a week and would he please unlock the door. The landlord said the woman was so unattractive that he didn't believe she was the wife of such a good-looking man as Taylor Caswell. Only after she showed him a wedding photo of the two of them did he agree to unlock the door.

To the man's horror, they found the young actor lying on the floor in a pool of blood. He'd been stabbed in the heart.

The landlord immediately called the police. Later, he said that the wife did not seem surprised to find her husband dead, and while he was on the phone, she went into the bedroom. When she came out, he saw her putting what looked to be letters in her handbag.

All of it upset the landlord so much that he ran downstairs to his own apartment and downed a shot of whiskey. When he returned, the wife was gone. The landlord realized he didn't know the woman's name. In Los Angeles, the movie capital of the world, many people had made-up names. The wife probably had Taylor Caswell's real name. Even though they searched, no one, not even the police, could find her.

For weeks, the police questioned people about the murder victim. The tenants said the only person they'd ever seen visiting the actor was a tall fair-skinned man. One tenant said, "He was like a blond Viking." Another tenant said, "He seemed to like the Viking man more than any woman." As befitted the time, this statement was ignored.

It wasn't until later that the police found out that the week before Taylor Caswell's movie came out, the wife had gone to her husband's agent and presented documentation of a trust fund that she'd had set up. All profits from the movie were to be sent to the trust fund. People said that it was almost as though she foresaw that he was going to die since the papers had been drawn up months earlier. The agency's lawyers laughed at her. The movie was barely D-list and it wasn't expected to do well— which is why Taylor Caswell's contract had given him generous rights to whatever profits there were. Those rights were given in lieu of the higher salary he should have received.

In the first year after the movie debuted, they were right. Few people saw it. But then critics began naming it as one of the hundred best films ever made. After that, the movie began to be discovered by the public. It became a cult hit. Today, it's said that millions have been sent to that trust fund. Whoever that wife was, even though she was deemed "unattractive" by everyone, she ended up with very fat bank account.

As for Taylor Caswell, his murderer was never found.

★

Troy put the tape on Pause and they sat in silence. There was a publicity photo of the young, handsome Taylor Caswell frozen on the screen.

Sara gave Kate a look to tell her that they needed to talk. Sara wasn't about to tell the others—the suspects—that Caswell was the man she'd seen in her dreams. He was Aran Lachlan, the son who'd run away from home and sent his parents into a deep depression. He went to Hollywood, changed his name, made a movie, then was murdered.

"That's the man we saw in the movie."

They turned to look toward the door and were startled to see young Quinn standing there.

He and Sara exchanged smiles. Kids and older people were

alike in that they were not seen. "Is he from the movie you saw the first night?"

Quinn nodded.

"Where is that tape?" Jack asked.

Yet again, Quinn gave a look of being triumphant over the adults. He turned to Troy. "You took it out of the machine."

Even though most of the old tapes had been sent to Billy, lying on the shelf was one with a worn label. *Only Once*. It had been in the machine since the first night. Troy hadn't looked at the label when he removed it to put in the tape his mother had found.

Sara repressed laughter as Troy put the movie in the player. She got up from the ottoman and followed Quinn out of the room. They high-fived. "Well done!" she told the boy. "So where is everyone?"

He knew she meant Greer. He lowered his voice as they walked to the bedroom where Rachel/Greer had been staying. "She's been telling Dad and me all about her life. She had her nose cut open and she said we could go to Scotland to see her family. Dad said I can wear a kilt."

"I'll research your family and find your tartan—except that's an English idea. I'll buy you the finest sporran, one that's worthy of Lieutenant Colonel Johnny Thompson."

He smiled. "I'm supposed to get Greer's clothes and her passport."

Sara gave him a sharp look.

"I know. I can't say her name. It's all a secret." His face showed fear. "No one is going to kill her, are they?"

"No!" Sara said. "Let's pack while they're watching the movie. We can throw stuff out the window and Lenny can help you take it to my car."

Quinn grinned at that. "Gr... Rachel said she hid her passport. There's a loose board in the closet. It's—" He stopped because Sara had frozen in place, eyes wide. "What is it?"

"I know where there's a good hiding place. Lea has been looking for a wall safe, but there's somewhere else something could be hidden. I need to go. I'll send Lenny up to help you. Is that okay?"

"Oh yeah," Quinn said. "He's cool. We have a bully at school. I wish I could take Lenny there to have a talk with him." He was smiling at the thought.

"I think Lenny would love that. I need to go." When Sara got to the door she wasn't surprised to nearly run into Lenny. She assumed he'd heard it all so she just waved her hand and he nodded.

"I hate bullies," he said as he went into the bedroom to help Quinn.

Kate was standing in the hall.

"Why aren't you watching the movie?" Sara asked.

"Because whatever you are up to is always more exciting than any movie—and a whole lot more dangerous. There's an active murderer on the loose. Where are we going?"

"To the cottage. I need to search a hiding place in there."

"Tell me where it is and I can go look."

"No," Sara said. "It's time for me to face the past."

After they told Lenny where they were going, the two women left the house together.

★

As soon as Kate unlocked the cottage door, Sara began shaking in fear. *This is absurd*, she told herself. *It all happened long ago. It's over. Done with.*

But for all her thoughts of encouragement, the second she stepped inside the pretty room, it was as though she'd never left it. She could almost feel Cal there. Her memories were vivid, crystal clear.

In front of her was the beautiful stained glass window. "Mr. Lachlan bought this window at an auction and had it installed here. It doesn't really fit, but..." Sara could feel her current self fading away. Writing, traveling, people she'd met over the years, seemed to leave her. "I lost my virginity in this room."

Kate said nothing but quietly waited for whatever her aunt wanted to tell her.

"Cal cut the grass here. He always seemed older than he was. He was doing garden work when he was twelve. He doubled his workload after his mother, Renata, died. His father remarried the same year she passed."

"Was his new wife nice?" Kate asked.

"No," Sara said. "She looked on Cal as a nuisance. She used to say that when she had kids, she'd send Cal away. But she never had any."

"How'd she like you?"

"Exactly as much as I liked her." Sara sighed. "It especially hurt since Renata adored Cal. If it hadn't been for him, I'm sure she would have left. Back then, the father was always given custody. He just had to say his wife had screwed someone else, and *zap!* he got it all and the wife was cast out. Renata couldn't bear losing Cal."

"How did she die?" Kate asked.

"We never knew. She just died. No long disease, just... gone."

"Not...?"

"Suicide?" Sara asked. "No, she wouldn't do that to her precious son."

Kate took a breath. *Did she dare ask about the Great Secret?* "Cal stayed in Lachlan and you left."

Sara took her time before answering. "Our plan was to

leave town the week after we graduated from high school. Cal had a college football scholarship and I had student loans. But the day after the graduation ceremony, there was an accident. His father was under a car, working on it, and the jack fell. It crushed his legs and he was paralyzed. In one second the support of them all was dumped on Cal's very young shoulders."

"But you left town anyway," Kate said.

"Yes, but not because of that."

"Then why?"

Sara went to the big window and put her hand on the glass. "On that same day, the man my best friend, Tayla, was planning to marry, Walter Kirkwood, raped me. Violently raped me."

"No," Kate whispered.

"Someone had told Walter that I was trying to force Tayla not to marry him. He was in a rage. He found me alone and..." Sara waved her hand. "The horrible details don't matter. It was a very long time ago. Afterward, I was trying to walk home. I was bruised and bloody and my clothes were ripped, and I saw Tayla. I told her what Walter had done to me." Sara paused. "She didn't believe me. She said I was a liar, and she left me there, bleeding and torn." It took Sara a few moments to calm herself. "When I got home, I cleaned up as best I could. I had a lot of bruises and deep scratches, and I..."

"Did you tell your mother?"

"Of course not!" Sara said. "I think Randal saw me when I came in, but I'm not sure. I went next door to Cal. I'd never seen him like he was on that day. He was glassy-eyed, traumatized, bent over, his head in his hands. Walter had said he was going to tell Cal that I'd wanted it, that I'd been eager for it. You see, back then, rape was *always* the girl's fault. If she'd worn a low-cut top four years before, then it was said that a man couldn't be blamed for his actions." Sara paused.

"I assumed that's what Cal had been told. He began saying that his life was over, that he could never leave town. In my stupidity, in my *vanity*, I thought *I* was the cause of it."

"Because of the...the purity thing?"

"Yes. Girls didn't bed-hop then. *Reputation* was the number one word in my generation of women. Keeping our reputation clean was the most important thing in our lives. I assumed Cal no longer wanted me. I was soiled. Unclean. It was exactly how I felt. Dirty." Sara stopped, her chest heaving.

"What did you do?"

"I had some money hidden so packed a suitcase and left Lachlan. I had no idea where I was going. I just got on a bus and went. It was the lowest point in my life."

"Cal was too upset to hear you, wasn't he?"

"Yes. I didn't know it, but he'd just come back from the hospital. He'd been told that his father would forever be in a wheelchair, and Cal knew his life was over. He wasn't the kind of person to run away to play sports and leave behind a crippled father and a stepmother without financial support. Cal knew he'd have to turn down his scholarship and stay in town to run his father's auto shop."

"When Cal realized you were gone, he had no way to contact you, did he?"

"None at all. I was impressively clever in disappearing without a trace. I had good grades so it was easy to get into another university in another state. I got a job and—" She waved her hand. "It was over a year before I heard what happened. By then, Cal had impregnated Donna, and of course he'd done the honorable thing and married her."

"But you did see him again," Kate said. "I've pieced that much together. So why didn't you *stay* with him?"

"About three years after I left, I sent my parents my contact information. I knew they'd give it to Cal. He called and we met. Not here but upstate, and we talked."

"Did you tell him what Walter did to you?"

"No! I still thought of that with shame. Besides, my mother had told Cal I left town because I'd heard that his father had been hurt. Since Cal wouldn't leave town, she said I'd dumped him. I went with that story. I said I had to get out of Lachlan and see the world."

"Did he believe you?"

Sara gave a small smile. "No, but he didn't say so. What he did say was that he'd get a divorce and we could live together anywhere in the world that I wanted." She looked at Kate. "But that would have meant leaving his son or taking the child away from his mother."

When Sara paused, Kate silently waited. She felt her aunt had more to tell.

"You see, there was something else. Something I've told no one until now." She took a long breath. "After what Walter did to me, I knew I was injured, but I didn't go to a doctor. I had too much guilt. Did I ask for it? Had I caused it? It wasn't until about two years later that I went for a pap smear. The doctor sat down on his little stool, and said, 'Who did this to you?'"

Sara paused for a moment. "I had to have some repair surgery, but in spite of that, I was told that I'd never have children."

Kate's voice was soft. "You would never take the child from his mother and you knew you couldn't give Cal any children."

"Right. And I knew Cal would hate himself if he left them all—his father, stepmother, wife, and son. I couldn't do that to him."

Both women were silent, thinking about all that had been said.

Kate spoke first. "What an extraordinary, truly fantastic…"

"Story?" Sara's voice held the deep sadness she'd held inside for so many years.

"No. Coincidence," Kate said firmly. "You and Cal graduated from high school, which I know that back then meant marriage age, and immediately, everything happened."

"Are you again saying that it's good I didn't marry Cal so you and Jack aren't related?"

"Not at all. I'm just looking at the facts. A car fell on Cal's dad and crushed his legs. It didn't kill him, just injured him enough that Cal had to stay home to run the business and support everyone. Then *on that same day*, Walter Kirkwood was in a rage because he believed *you* had poisoned his girlfriend—your bestie—against him."

"I didn't do that. It wasn't my business. Tayla knew I didn't like Walter, but then, she thought Cal was a bore. We used to say that we were equal." She looked at Kate. "What are you saying?"

"You've taught me this—if you want to know what happened, look at the result."

Sara's face was blank.

"What are the odds of this? In *one day*, you lost everything, but who got it all?"

Sara's eyes widened. "Donna. Cal ended up having to marry her. She'd always wanted him. In school, she made a fool of herself over him. She *hated* me. She—" Sara sat down on the window ledge. "She couldn't have done that. Crushing a man? Setting up a rape? She wouldn't."

"Ha!" Kate said. "Haven't you read Jane Austen? A woman will do *anything* to get the man she wants. Donna didn't have money or beauty or even brains. But she married the cream of the crop. All she had to do was kick over a car jack, tell a few lies to Walter, and wiggle up to a healthy young man who had been abandoned by the love of his life. Then Donna stood back and waited. She must have been joyous when she came up pregnant."

Sara's voice was low. "Cal said he didn't remember sleeping with her. He woke up and there she was beside him in bed. He was embarrassed and apologized to her."

"He had a foggy memory?" Kate said. "Didn't your generation invent recreational drugs? Sounds like something was given to him. Slipped into a drink?"

Sara's voice was a whisper. "Cal never loved her."

"Neither does Jack. She wasn't a grandmother to him."

"Donna only loved her son, Roy, and she ruined him."

"In the long run, you won. You kept Cal's love. Always."

"He and I met many times over the years. Somewhere in the world. We had our own life. It wasn't conventional, but it was good."

"I know you did. I listen. And now you have Jack and me. Who does Donna have?"

"No one." Sara put her shoulders back. "I don't know if any of this is true, but suddenly, I feel...different." She looked around the beautiful cottage. "I'm not afraid of this place anymore. It's almost as though Cal is here, but in a good way." She paused. "I can feel... I don't know what it is, but I'm lighter. Mind and body—and the past." Her head came up. "I think I'm going to try to solve a murder. I'd like to ask Reid some questions. *Did* he know he was to inherit this place? We assume he didn't know, but we aren't sure. And has Alish really been able to keep Greer's nondeath a secret from him? And oh yeah, did he happen to know that his grandmother says she killed a man then cut his skull open? Wonder what she did with the turtle rug. I'll see you later." Sara hurried out of the cottage.

★

Sara may have felt better, but Kate felt like the wind had been knocked out of her. She'd felt her aunt's pain as she told of the brutal rape. And later, Sara'd had no one she could tell because she knew she'd be blamed.

And there was Cal with his crippled father. Kate had never heard anyone say a good word about the man. Cal's son, Roy, had grown up with a heart full of anger. He'd taken a lot of it out on his son Jack.

Kate sat down hard on the low window ledge. She had no doubt that all that pain had been caused by some girl who lusted after the captain of the high school football team. She wanted him no matter what it cost other people.

Kate had her phone in her pocket and she texted Heather, Jack's mother.

What happened to Roy's mother?

Heather answered right away.

She's in the hospital. Dying. Cancer.

Does she have lots of visitors? With tears being shed?

Heather sent a line of laughing emojis.

Kate closed her phone. There seemed to be a moral in this, but she didn't know what it was. When you want something, don't go after it at the cost of other people? Was that it?

When this gets done, Kate thought, *I'm going to visit the woman. I want to see her before the devil rises up to take her down to where she deserves to be.*

It was when Kate stood up, ready to leave, that she remembered why they'd come to the cottage. Sara knew a hiding place that was in the cottage. Did it hold something? Where was it?

TWENTY-FOUR

WHEN SARA LEFT THE COTTAGE, SHE WAS MOVING fast. It felt good to have told Kate what happened to her. It made her see that a big part of the pain she'd buried inside her for so many years was because of the mindset of the times. Rape was always a woman's fault, and men suffered no repercussions.

She shook her head to clear it. She needed to think about now, not the past. She saw Reid on the far side of what was left of the large estate. He was shoveling mulch around some trees. Lenny had said, "It's as though he knows he owns the place." *He sure does seem to believe that*, Sara thought.

Since she'd been around Jack and Kate, she'd learned to keep her phone with her. She backed up against a palm tree, with Reid in sight, and sent a text to her brother. He would know how to handle what she needed to tell. She gave a brief description of where there was a hidden compartment in the cottage. It was behind a wooden panel and it was insulated as a drinks cooler. Mr. Lachlan used to put a couple of cold beers in there for Cal. "If you're old enough to do a man's job, you're old enough to have a beer," he'd said.

When that was done, she went to Reid. "Hi," she said.

Turning, he smiled at her, but he kept shoveling.

Sara didn't want to waste time. "Who do you think should inherit this place?" She kept her eyes on him as he paused to look toward the back of the house.

"I have no idea. James Lachlan died years ago. Wouldn't the new owner have taken over by now?"

She didn't answer his question. "Did your grandmother ever talk about this place?"

Reid stopped work, used a bandanna to wipe the sweat from his face, and leaned back against a tree. His eyes took on a dreamy look. "Other kids were read fairy tales, but all I wanted to hear about was this house and what went on in it. Grans used to tell me of the lavish parties. My grandfather was a handsome man, so he was allowed to attend and dance with the ladies. No matter how old they were, he led them onto the dance floor. Their diamonds sparkled like a thousand candles."

Sara was blinking at the deep emotion in his voice. "And Alish?" she asked softly.

"She was never invited, but my grandfather used to sneak her a plate of food. He made sure she got the best of all that was served. She'd sit outside and watch through the ballroom windows." He seemed far away, living in that long-ago time.

At last, he gave a sigh and came back to the present. "I've decided I should show you something." He held out a piece of old fabric. It was torn on the edges, and about four inches square. There were giraffes printed on it.

Sara took the fabric and looked at him in question.

"On the night Derek Oliver disappeared, I found it stuck in the doorframe of the nursery. I didn't think anything about it at the time. I was like everyone else and happy the man was gone."

She held up the fabric. "Who does it belong to?"

"My sister. Ask Kate. She liked Greer's giraffe shirt." He paused for a moment. "The night Oliver disappeared, Grans came here. She got my sister, took her to the airport, and sent her to Scotland."

"Why?" Sara asked, feigning ignorance.

"I don't know—and I can assure you that I asked. I loved my sister, but suddenly she was gone. I never saw her again. Years later, we had a funeral but it was a closed coffin. I didn't even see her then!" He nodded toward the fabric. "I stuck that in a box in my bedroom at Grans's house and forgot about it, but being told a body was found has made me remember things." He stared at Sara. "You don't think my sister did anything, do you? She always had, uh, problems, so Grans kept her isolated. She wasn't allowed near other people, especially children. Grans even told *me* to stay away from her. Sometimes I got the idea that my sister was...dangerous."

Sara started to put the fabric in her pocket and he nodded okay. "I don't know the answer to any of that. For all that it seems that we solve murders, we have to report everything to the sheriff. I'll certainly tell him about this." *And I'll tell Gil everything,* she thought. "Where is Rachel?" She watched him closely, and his expression showed surprise, but something else that she couldn't identify. Anger?

He grimaced. "Don't ask me. I got dumped."

The way he said it made her smile.

"Not enough money, I guess."

"Did you tell her about your successful company and that you are just pretending to be the lowly gardener?"

When he grinned, Sara had a flash that there was something familiar looking about him. "I'm old-fashioned. I wanted her to love me, not my bank account. Have you ever felt that you live in the past?"

"All the time," Sara said.

"Did you know that Rachel was friends with the young man of the family who used to own your house? He was rich, so he was one of the candidates for her to marry. What was his name? Alexander?"

"Alistair Stewart."

"That's right. I know she liked him a lot."

"He could be charming." *Is this why Rachel went to my house? Old times' sake?*

"I'm curious about Aran Lachlan," Sara said. "What was he like?"

Reid shrugged. "Grans rarely mentioned him, but I got the idea that she may have hated him. He seemed to think the earth belonged to him. Today we'd call him a narcissist."

"Have you—?" She broke off because she saw Jack walking toward them. "Uh-oh. Looks like I'm wanted."

"How many suspects do you have?" Reid asked.

"None. All of you are very nice people. If I were writing this, I'd call it *A Murder of Kindness*."

Reid gave a snort. "Whoever did it should be praised. Derek Oliver was hated by all who met him. I got the idea that Billy's brothers sent Oliver here as a punishment."

When Sara looked at him, she saw a flash of hatred so strong that all the hair on her body stood on end. *What horrible thing did Derek Oliver do to you?* she thought.

Jack had reached them. "There you are. We need you."

"It's always good to be needed." Sara forced a smile. She was still chilled by Reid's look.

As soon as they were out of earshot of Reid, Jack said, "Did you have a good vacation? You and Kate have tea and sandwiches in the cottage?"

Sara was glad Kate hadn't told him the awful story. Not yet, anyway. "Cucumber with buttered bread and clotted cream scones. It was divine."

Jack gave a snort at her joke.

"Well?" Sara demanded. "Tell me everything. Or did you and my brother settle down with the girls and watch that movie?"

"Randal found the cubbyhole in the cottage and..." Jack paused. "And he found a safe in the wall of the Palm Room. He's in there now opening it. We thought you'd like to see what's in it. Or maybe you want more tea."

They had reached the back door of the house, but Sara grabbed his sleeve and pulled him into the shade. If there is one thing Floridians know about, it's shade. "Tell me everything!" she said.

Jack leaned against the wall and put his hands in his pockets. "Guess what was hidden in your beloved cottage?"

"Old beer bottles?"

"DNA."

"What?"

He grinned. "Hair samples and vials of liquid were in envelopes. There were twenty-three of them. All of them were labeled with the names and dates of the birth of people. They seem to be mostly from Lachlan."

"But why?"

Jack shrugged. "I don't know. All any of us know is that James Lachlan loved the newly discovered DNA. That's why his will put a forty-year hold on this place."

"Right," Sara said. "Maybe he was hoping his son left behind a kid." She didn't mention her dream where she saw that Aran was probably gay.

"Bea came and took all of it," Jack said. "She sent everything to Broward to be analyzed. She has a friend over there so they'll be taken care of ASAP."

When Jack didn't move, Sara knew he had more to say. "What about the movie?"

"Randal and I didn't stay to see it, but it seems to be some horror flick with a guy killing women after he screws them. I don't get why it became popular. Anyway, the important thing is that Barbara's late husband, the famous producer and director…"

"Who was being blackmailed for murder by Derek Oliver."

"That's the one. He was in that movie."

"As what?" Sara asked.

"Lea said that Harry Adair played a waiter to the star, that guy, Taylor Caswell. It was too small a role to be credited, but Lea said it was a fiery moment."

"Eyes locked, lightning flashing back and forth, curtains turning to flame? That sort of thing?"

"So says the romance writer. And yes, that's pretty much how Lea described it, but not with your flair."

"I bet Barbara recognized the look from her life with him, but what about Troy?"

Jack sighed. "Lea said he was quiet, but it was easy to see that he'd seen that look on his father's face. Probably used to embarrass the kid. As for Barbara, she said, and I quote, 'That bastard! To do that in front of the cameras!'"

Sara laughed. "That's the Hollywood version of 'Don't do it in the streets and frighten the horses.' So now we know that Harry knew the actor, Taylor Caswell."

"Who was found stabbed in the heart."

"I guess Derek Oliver saw the film, recognized the look, did a little research, and figured out who might have killed Mr. Caswell."

"Don't forget the letters the wife may or may not have stolen and that the wife is still alive. That would be evidence. If they exist, how did Oliver get them?"

Sara gave a look of shock—as though she'd just remembered something.

"What is in that overactive mind of yours?"

"Aran. Alish didn't marry Aran." Sara put her hands to the side of her head. "She married Reid. But Aran went to Hollywood. I'm confused."

"*You* are confused?" Jack said. "I have no idea what you're talking about. You plan to share any of this with us?"

"I wish I knew enough to be able to share. I need to get to Alish. She knows everything."

"Great. You'll set off alarms again. Maybe this time you *will* give her a heart attack."

"Ha! That woman is strong enough to outlive us all. What else have you learned?"

"Nope," he said. "It's your turn to spill. What did you find out from Reid?"

She handed him the piece of fabric. "He found this in the doorframe of the nursery the night Oliver was killed. It's from Greer's blouse. That night Alish put her on a plane and sent her to Scotland."

"Because Greer had just killed a man? But how did Alish know?" He raised his hand. "Don't tell me. That Second Sight you and Kate love so much. So Greer killed him and sawed his head open because...?"

"Because it's in her nature? I don't know. Remember that Greer admitted she'd been kept isolated her whole life. Reid said Alish kept her away from other people, especially kids."

Jack looked like this new information was too much to handle. "Great. She might be a psychopathic killer and she's with Quinn."

"I wonder what the full story is of why Greer was taken out of school and educated at home. Not just the cute one of Alish tossing some kid like a Frisbee."

Jack had his phone in his hand and was tapping out a message.

"Are you warning Gil?"

"Yes." He pressed Send, then flicked through his messages. "Before we send Greer to the guillotine, look at what Ivy sent. She did some investigating of your dear friend Reid and came up with some interesting stuff when she had lunch with one of the executives of the company." He handed her his phone, open to Ivy's text.

Halfway through the second bottle of wine, she told me that the founder of the company had a gambling problem. He ran the business into so much debt that it had to be sold. Reid bought it, but the son of the gambler still runs it. She said that Reid doesn't seem to believe in work, just paychecks. The son thinks someone bought the company for him.

What does the company do? Jack had texted back.

Something to do with computers. Creating software programs, maybe? I'm not sure. By then, she'd had too much wine to be coherent. BTW, they all despise Reid and laugh at him. But not to his face. They don't dare. He's said to have no sense of humor. Certainly doesn't go to drinks with the peons after work.

Sara gave the phone back to Jack, her eyes wide. "Wow. Not insurance but computers."

"Bet he'd know how to send messages from Kate's phone to mine."

"He told us a flat-out lie." Sara's head came up. "But why would he be after *you*? Did you wink at Rachel, his great love? The woman he returned here for?"

"The woman he doesn't seem to realize is missing? That one?"

"He said she dumped him."

"And he took it well?" Jack asked. "No anger? No declarations that he'd waited for her for years so she owed him?"

"Maybe——" Sara began, but the door to the house opened and Lenny stepped outside.

He looked at Sara. "You need to come in here."

Sara nodded. "So who is going off the rails this time? Barbara at her late husband for forgetting that the camera was on? Or is it Gil? He's probably angry and ready to fight to defend his new girlfriend. Or maybe Lea finally confessed to murdering her husband."

Lenny may have rolled his eyes but the state of his scarred face made that expression undetectable. "Your brother can't open the safe."

Sara gasped. "This *is* an emergency." She took off running, with Jack behind her.

When they got upstairs, they saw that only Randal was in the Palm Room. He had removed the painting by the Brazilian artist to expose a small safe set in the wall. He was diligently working at the combination lock. Sara had seen that look of concentration many times. When Randal was a child, it meant he'd taken something that wasn't his.

"So how'd you find it?" she asked. "By sniffing it out or did you use telepathic connections?"

He was unperturbed by her snide remark. "People in glass houses…" He glanced at his sister. "I think you should tell us about your dreams. Not the short, comic book version, but the complete story, especially the parts you're hiding."

"I thought you didn't believe in my dreams."

"With you, my darling sister, I'd believe anything."

With a sigh of frustration, Randal stepped back from the locked safe.

"Can't do it?" Sara asked.

"It's not the same as opening a door lock. There are thousands of possible combinations. I need some specialized tools."

Sara had a flash of memory. She seemed to see Alish's forearm. "Try 4 12 44," she said softly.

Randal gave his sister a look, then deftly twisted the dial. The safe opened.

"What the hell?!" Jack said. "You need to explain where you got that number."

"It's a date," Randal said, "and my sister knows much more than she's told us." He reached inside the safe, pulled out a VHS tape, and handed it to Jack.

"*A Wrongful Death*," Jack read off the label.

Instantly, Sara did an internet search of the movie title and scan-read it aloud. "Uh... 'Back then it was called porn and couldn't be shown to the public. Mild by today's standards. Two men were in love with each other. Movie doesn't show sex, but hints at it.' Here's the important part. The plot. 'The victim confided a crime he committed and the lover wrote it as a screenplay, meaning that the world would be told what he'd done.' Hmmm," Sara said. "Wonder what crime it was. Anyway, there was a fight and the actor was stabbed with a kitchen knife." She looked back at the article. "'Because of what was, at the time, an illegal relationship, there wasn't much publicity about the case, and only a rudimentary investigation.'" She looked up at them. "The killer was never caught."

"Credits?" Jack asked.

Sara smiled. "Harry Adair. Director, producer, writer, and he acted in the role of the landlord. It looks like we have a movie showing the motive for the murder. A fight over a crime being revealed. But then, how could Harry resist writing a good story? He should probably have done a book first, then a script. That would get double royalties. He—"

Jack spoke up. "I wonder if Barbara is *sure* her husband

wasn't here at Lachlan House back then. Maybe he sneaked in, killed ol' Oliver, then sneaked back out."

"And took the brain and his saw rolled up in the turtle rug when he left?" Sara asked. "I like it."

Randal gave a snort. "That night this house was full of people sneaking around. But no one saw anything or anyone unusual?" He had pulled out an envelope full of old newspaper clippings and was flipping through them. He turned to his sister. "Where did you get that date for the combination?"

"It's Alish's wedding date."

"Is it?" He handed one of the clippings to her.

It told about Reid Graham being hanged for killing a man in a barroom brawl. It also told that his uncle, James Lachlan, was out of the country when it happened. There was nothing in it that they didn't know.

"Look at the date," Randal said.

It was the date Alish had tattooed on her arm—the day of the execution. "I guess they married on the day it happened."

Randal handed her another clipping. It was short, telling that the condemned man, Reid Graham, had been allowed to marry his sweetheart, Alish Sullivan, three days before he was to be executed. Even Death Cannot Keep the Lovers Apart, the headline declared.

"She had the execution date of another man tattooed on her arm?" Randal asked. "Not the date of her marriage but the day of the hanging? Isn't that just a bit odd?"

"Especially since she hated Aran Lachlan," Sara murmured.

They were silent for a moment, each of them trying to piece it all together.

"I guess we better watch this movie." Jack sounded like he'd rather walk across nails.

Sara waved her hand. "Tell Lenny to make a pitcher of margaritas and some nachos and the women will love watching it. You can go repair something."

Jack's face brightened and he looked at Randal. "Movie or yard work?"

"I get to run the weed whacker," Randal said.

"If there's anything left that Reid hasn't cut down," Sara said. "He's as good at yard work as he is at lying."

When Randal raised his eyebrows, Jack said, "Give that tape to my little brother and we'll go outside and I'll tell you everything I know."

Randal looked at his sister. "I'd rather know what you do." But Sara had her lips tightly closed. It was obvious that she wasn't going to tell him what she was keeping to herself. "You're on," he said to Jack and they left.

When Sara was alone in the Palm Room, she looked at the Brazilian painting. *How does it all fit together?* she wondered. *What was James Lachlan up to? It was as though he was trying to tell them something from the grave.* He encumbered the house for forty years. He saved DNA samples. Why was that date tattooed on Alish's arm? Greer. Rachel. Barbara. Harry Adair. The actor, Taylor Caswell. How did everything come together?

Sara heard voices in the hall. The women were coming to watch the second movie. Quickly, she grabbed the envelope of newspaper clippings and left the room. She'd go upstairs and read them. Poor James Lachlan—he'd returned from a business trip and found that his wife's sister's son had been hanged. And soon after, James's son had disappeared.

But Alish knew where Aran had gone, Sara thought.

She reached the blissful silence of the playroom, shut the door, and leaned against it. In her pocket was Alish's brooch. She took it out and held it tightly. "Tell me," she whispered. "Tell me what happened."

She went to the window seat and stretched out on it. To

her utter delight, she felt sleepy. To an insomniac like Sara, this was unusual. She rubbed her thumbs on the brooch. "I want to know," she said. "All of it. The truth."

She closed her eyes and was asleep instantly—and a dream began. As before, Sara was watching it.

Two big, burly men were dragging a young man between them. One of the men was older, the other one younger—nearly as young as the man they were pulling along the barren, concrete-walled hallway.

"Coward." The younger man sneered at the man he was clutching.

"I've known him all his life and he's always been a coward," the older man said. "He's sneaky and conniving, and he bullies little kids. He always thought he was better than us."

The man between them fell onto one knee and the two jerked him upright. They didn't speak to him.

"At least he did right by that girl."

"Humph!" the older man grunted. "He should have. She's carryin'."

"What?"

"She's expecting," the older man said. "A baby. I've got five of 'em so I know what a woman looks like then."

The young man shook his head. "Won't do her any good now."

"You don't know James Lachlan. When he gets back, he'll tear that judge apart. And he'll take care of the wife and the baby. You'll see. He'll—" He cut off as a heavy door swung open. There wasn't much light coming from it.

They again pulled the young man upright.

"For once in your life," the older man sneered into the prisoner's ear, "do something honorable."

The man in the middle didn't respond. He muttered something that sounded like, "Not me," but the guards ignored him. They went forward and the heavy door loudly closed behind them.

The scene faded to black and Sara, her spirit hovering above them, thought, *No. I can't wake now. I still don't understand.*

The scene began to grow lighter and she watched intently.

A man was gathering up a load of clothes to put into a laundry cart. He looked at a shirt collar and frowned. It appeared to have blood on it. But when he looked closer, he grimaced. "Ink," he muttered. "Where did he get that?" He knew that anything unusual was to be reported to the warden. But then, he looked around. No one was about. He wadded the shirt into a ball and went through two rooms. The windows were barred and there were a couple of armed guards in the background. They barely glanced at the man with the laundry. When he got to a room that was piled high with coal, he opened the heavy iron door of the incinerator that gave the place its hot water. The man threw the shirt into the fire.

He smiled as he watched it burn. He knew there was something wrong about the shirt, but he didn't know what it was. What he did know was that it was better to destroy it than report it. Every report agitated the warden and caused problems for everybody.

Still smiling, the man turned away and went back to the laundry cart.

Again, everything went black and this time, Sara knew the dream was over.

When she woke, she understood. *Ink,* she thought. Ink was the clue she'd needed to understand it all. But she wanted verification. Who should she ask? Barbara came to her mind.

In writing novels, it took Sara thirty thousand words to introduce characters and set the scene. But Barbara was used to scripts. Four lines were considered a soliloquy. She sent a text to Barbara.

In the movie, what was the crime committed by the victim?

A pancake flip of Tale of Two Cities.

Sara knew exactly what she meant and it fit with what she'd pieced together from her three dreams—and from what she'd deduced. **Any ink involved?**

Made a neck as red as a 1940s lipstick.

Sara smiled. *Show-off!* she thought. They were both showing themselves as creative people.

Still smiling, happy to have figured out some things, she got off the seat and looked out the window. Jack was to the far left, hitting big weeds with his whacker. Randal was nowhere to be seen. Was he with Lea? But then Sara looked to the right and halted in place. She leaned so far forward that her head touched the glass.

Plodding across the grass, heading toward the cottage, was Greer. It had to be her as Rachel was, well, *unalived*, as they called it online. *She shouldn't be here!* Sara thought.

But worse was that she was helping her grandmother walk. Alish! Who was supposed to be in the hospital! Greer was taking her—dragging her?—to the cottage. Why? Was it voluntary? From what they'd heard recently, Greer could be a real psycho.

Sara grabbed her phone. Who to tell? Lenny had no phone. Jack was closest. Sara sent a text to him.

Greer & Alish are in the cottage. I'm going to them. Come now.

She looked out the window to Jack. Of course he didn't hear his phone over the noise of that machine. Sara got off the seat and began running. She went down the old stairs to the kitchen but it was empty. Not even Lenny was there. She didn't have time to stop and search for someone.

She flat-out ran to the cottage, flung the door open, and there was Greer, leaning over Alish as she reclined on the little couch.

The smile Alish gave her had such warmth that Sara's frantic feeling left her.

"You heard me," Alish said. "Not many people can. You saw. You heard."

"I did," Sara said. She could feel herself relax. This woman was a kindred soul. A person who listened and watched. Someone who saw more than she told. Sara pulled up a seat and sat down while Greer handed her grandmother a glass of water, then sat down.

"She was leaving the hospital, sneaking out." Greer's voice was full of fear, her eyes beginning to tear. "I know I wasn't supposed to show myself but I couldn't help it. I needed—"

Alish reached up and took her granddaughter's hand. "I felt you. I wanted to see you."

"Will you tell me?" Sara asked. "What really happened? The ink." She looked at Greer. "You had the birthmark removed from your neck, didn't you?"

"Yes," Greer said. "Kate said it looked like an elephant. She liked it but I didn't. Reid had one too but it's gone. I guess he had it lasered off."

Alish nodded. "He did. He hated it, and I knew why."

"Please tell," Sara whispered, and Alish nodded.

Twenty-Five

"I THINK YOU SHOULD GO BACK TO THE HOSPITAL," Greer said. "You shouldn't have left."

Alish looked at her granddaughter's hand, then held it up for Sara to see.

Sara understood. It was about youth. Greer's hand was unlined, no wrinkles or spots, but pure, clean, young flesh. Young people wanted to hold on to life. Greer wanted her grandmother to return to tubes and needles and endless doctors. All to stay alive, even if only for a few more days.

But Sara knew that there came a time when a person accepted death. The concern was *how* it would happen. With or without pain? Long or slow? Or the best, quick and unexpected?

It was easy to see that Alish was ready to leave the earth. She didn't fear going. She just wanted to enjoy what she could, especially to be with her granddaughter who she obviously loved.

And there was more. From Alish's eyes, weak and watery,

and oh so very tired, Sara could see that the woman wanted to tell. To confess. To leave behind the truth.

But first, Sara wanted to know the answer to the question of "who?" She looked at Greer, then to Alish with her eyebrows raised.

"No," Alish said. "I sent Reid away to his company in St. Petersburg. I got one of the nurses to send Sheriff Flynn a text saying Reid pushed me down the stairs. He said he will have men meet Reid there. When they return, I will tell what he did to that blackmailing man. The sheriff will—"

Greer pulled her hand away and sat up straight. "Are you saying that Reid is the one who killed Mr. Oliver?"

"And Rachel," Sara said calmly, then looked at Alish. "She knew too much?"

Alish nodded.

"I don't understand," Greer said. "You sent me away for my whole life. But back then, did you know that Reid did that?"

Sara looked at Greer, her face stern. "She protected you. She kept you safe. She couldn't betray her grandson, no matter what. You can't ask anyone to make a choice like that."

Alish was swallowing hard, glad that Sara understood. "It was my fault. I did it all."

Sara put her hand to the side of her neck and said, "Ink."

Alish let out a sigh that seemed to be relief at the truth being known.

"You're saying that my brother is a murderer?" Greer's voice was rising in anger. "I don't believe you." She started to get up.

Sara turned fiery eyes on her. "You can sit and listen to what your grandmother has to say or you can get on your platform of superiority and condemn everyone. It's your choice!"

Greer sat back down.

"Scotland," Alish said. "It's all from there. Two sisters. They were identical twins."

Sara nodded. "I guessed as much. Mary and her sister."

"Like your books." Alish smiled. "I've read them. Very entertaining. You have twins. One good and one bad."

"Too boring," Sara said. "My twins are always different, not good and bad."

"Mary was sweet and kind and very quiet. Her sister—I cannot bear to say her name—loved parties and people and being the center of everyone's attention. Every male for fifty miles wanted her."

"Except for one man," Sara said. "James Lachlan."

"James was as poor as the rest of us, but there was something inside of him. A light that people could feel. He was different from us."

"And the sister wanted him," Sara said.

"She did. This was before I was born, but my mother told me of it. The sister wore red and let her hair hang down. She exposed bits of her body—shameful things then."

"And Mary?"

"She did the washing on Mondays, the baking on Fridays. She hardly ever left the little stone cottage of her parents. There was no man courting her. The sister made sure of that. If a man came near Mary, the sister stepped in. She was so bright and vibrant that the men turned away from Mary."

"But not James," Sara said. "A true hero. He could see beyond the flashing eyes and the exposed skin."

"Mother said no one was more surprised at the proposal than Mary was. James walked to the cottage, went to her father, and asked for Mary's hand. Of course the man agreed. James had an aura about him that a person could feel. After Mary's father approved, James asked Mary if she'd marry him. She was hanging clothes out to dry. She was so astonished all she did was nod. Mother said Mary was so shy that she never spoke to James until the morning after the wedding night."

Sara laughed. "I love that! Wish I'd used it in a book. Sex before words. Perfect." She paused. "But what did the sister do?"

"My mother told of the rage of the girl in the weeks before the wedding. Mary had somehow won the man every female wanted. The man everyone knew was going to achieve success. There were lots of little 'accidents.' Mary was burned, things fell on her, her wedding dress was torn. On and on."

"I've written about jealous sisters." Sara paused. "She was the mother of the first Reid. Who did she marry?"

"No one," Alish said. "The sister found a man who looked like James. He was tall and handsome. He wasn't from our village but from the city. He was also a thief, a liar, and some said he was a murderer."

Greer had been silent through this, but she spoke up. "Your husband's father. My great grandfather."

"He was," Alish said. "I was told that the sister cried to Mary that she'd been raped and was to bear the man's child. But my mother had seen her with the man. She knew it was a lie."

"Is this why the families left Scotland?"

"Yes. Had they stayed, the sister's life wouldn't have been worth much."

Sara grit her teeth. "I know about women being blamed for whatever happens to them from a man. So the sisters gave birth to boys who looked alike but one had a birthmark."

Alish nodded. "Reid had a big red mark on his neck. It was said that his robber father also had that mark, but no one knew for sure. When they got to America, the sister wanted to live with James and Mary, but he said no. Mother said

James knew the true nature of the sister and didn't trust her not to kill Mary."

"In an accident, of course," Sara said.

"With no question. James found a good husband for her, but she treated him badly. When her son looked like Mary's boy, the sister hinted that James was the father. It hurt Mary, but she never confronted her sister. Mary was generous and kind to both of the boys."

"Was Reid always bad?" Sara asked.

"Yes," Alish said. "But not to me. I have never been..." She broke off, her eyes sad.

"A man magnet?" Sara said cheerfully. "*Femme fatale?* One of the buxom beauties on the covers of my novels?"

Alish smiled. "Exactly so. I wasn't asked to dances by other boys, but Reid did. He was so handsome! I ignored the stories of what he did to others. He—"

Greer interrupted. "But didn't you *see* what he was? With your powers?"

Alish closed her eyes for a moment, then opened them. "I did. But I was so young and so in awe of this beautiful man that I paid attention only to the parts I wanted to see. My future was linked to him. That's the *only* thing I wanted to see."

"He hated Aran," Sara said softly.

"Passionately. Even more than the sister hated Mary. Aran had the money, the house, the father everyone admired. Reid's mother was scorned, his father laughed at. Reid's hatred of Aran was all-consuming. It ate at him."

"But I saw them together on the horse," Sara said. "They looked like friends."

"How did you see that?" Greer asked.

"A dream I sent her," Alish said, then looked back at Sara. "Reid covered his hatred. Only I knew of it. He said he'd been acting all his life and that's what led to him to leave Florida."

"To make a movie," Sara said. *"Only Once."*

Greer's eyes widened. "The movie I saw with Quinn and Gil. The actor who killed the women was my grandfather?"

"Yes," Alish said.

"He was gorgeous," Greer said.

"And as deadly in real life as the man in the movie," Sara said. "After the movie was done, he returned here to Lachlan, didn't he?"

Alish's heart was beating so hard a vein in her neck was throbbing. "Yes," she said quietly. "I think he wanted to rub Aran's nose in it, but it didn't happen. On his first night back, he killed Tom Skellit in a barroom brawl. He was an awful man and was drunkenly saying that Reid was nothing and never would be. One punch and he fell. He was dead."

"Manslaughter at best," Sara said. "Maybe even self-defense, but the judge…"

"Came over with James and was a failure at everything. Out of spite, he sentenced Reid to hang."

"But he wasn't executed," Sara said.

Greer frowned. "Yes he was. We all know that."

Sara put her hand to her neck. *"Reid* didn't hang."

Tears began to slide down Alish's face. "I knew I was going to have a baby and I was desperate. It's no excuse, but back then I felt it was. And Reid had spent years making me hate Aran."

When Alish was silent, Greer said, "I don't understand. What happened?"

Alish looked at Sara for her to finish.

"Alish visited Reid in prison and he talked her into getting Aran to visit with her. The plan was to switch identities. Clothes. And the birthmark." She glanced at Alish. "She agreed but only if Reid married her before they did it."

"A marriage for murder," Alish whispered. "It's what I traded for."

"The judge agreed and three days before Reid was to be hanged, your grandparents were married. Then…" Sara paused, looking at Alish.

"Early on the morning it was to happen, Aran and I visited Reid to say a final goodbye. I'd had to beg and cry to get him to go with me. I paid the guard to leave us alone. He thought we wanted to do something unholy—and we did, but not what he thought." She turned to Sara.

"You and Reid drugged Aran, changed clothes, and inked his neck," Sara said. "The birthmark was how the men could be told apart." She took a breath. "I saw Aran being dragged to the gallows. He was hardly awake." She looked at Alish. "The date of the execution is the tattoo on your arm. This Reid said you wouldn't leave Lachlan because you wanted to stay with your husband, but it was Aran who you wouldn't leave."

Alish nodded. "I didn't want him to be alone."

"Mary!" Sara said.

"She died in the car crash. No one believed it was an accident. She couldn't bear losing her son."

"Who she thought had run away," Sara said. "I can't imagine her grief. Did James know the truth of what happened to his son?"

"Not for years, but he did figure it out. He didn't tell me directly, but he hinted at it. By then, Reid, known as Taylor Caswell, had been killed in LA. He never saw his movie. Never knew of his success."

"Maybe it was karma," Sara said. "Did James know of your part in it all?"

"I don't know. I never wanted to know. He was always kind to me and to Reid's son. James insisted he be named Reid II so maybe he did know."

"My father," Greer said, "was a good man."

"Very good. But the third Reid—your brother—was like the first one, and like Mary's sister's thief lover."

"When did you know about your grandson?" Sara asked.

"By the time he was two, but then, I was watching for signs of what he could have inherited. When Greer was born, I saw the hatred in his eyes. I *felt* it."

"He never hated me!" Greer was defensive.

"That scar on your leg?"

"Mother said I fell on some rocks."

"He pushed you. The scars on your feet from stepping on glass? Reid did that. You had vomiting attacks often. I don't know what he fed you."

Greer's face seemed to fall. "Our parents?"

Alish took a breath. "The mechanic said the brakes had been cut, but the police could find no motive for anyone to do such a thing. You see, I was the one with the money, so Reid wanted to live with me."

"The money from the movie royalties," Sara said.

"Yes. It's what I'd foreseen. If I got Reid to marry me, our child and I would have money to support us forever. I didn't know how it would work, but I knew it would."

Greer seemed to have lost all color in her face. "This is why I wasn't allowed to go to school."

"I needed you close to me, and I managed to keep Reid under control. When he grew up, I bought him a company to play with, to make him feel powerful. He knows that if I die of any so-called accident, my money goes to charity." She looked at Greer. "Nothing was ever willed to you as that would jeopardize your life."

"But then he killed Derek Oliver," Sara said. "Why? Reid was to inherit this place."

"I don't know," Alish said. "I didn't ask. He came to me that night, after it was done." She hesitated. "He wore a look I'd seen on my husband. When Reid changed clothes with Aran, there was a gleam in Reid's eyes. It was a look that was a mixture of pleasure and excitement. The night Derek Oliver was killed, I saw that same look. Reid handed me a rolled-up rug and told me to burn it. I didn't ask about the contents. All I knew was that I had to get Greer out of the country. I'd seen what that look could lead to."

"And you faked her death," Sara said.

"A few years later, Reid began asking about her. I think he'd found something of hers."

"He had a piece of fabric from her blouse that was caught in the doorway."

"Maybe he thought she'd seen something."

"I didn't see anything," Greer said. "I tore my blouse that morning. I was looking for Kate's hedgehog."

"What about Jack?" Sara asked. "We think someone has been trying to hurt him."

"I don't know about that either," Alish said. "All I'm sure of is that I can no longer control my grandson. Years ago, he was very angry when the rich young woman, Rachel, wouldn't marry him."

"Now Reid appears to be a success, but Rachel still said no." Sara looked at Alish. "He lost control of himself. This time, it was a murder for marriage but it still didn't work."

Alish reached out to squeeze Greer's hand. "At least I have one success of my marriage for murder." She looked at Sara. "You must save her."

Sara looked at Greer. "Until I hear that your brother is in

custody, I want you out of here." She took her phone out of her pocket and sent a text to Gil.

Come and get her. Take her to Colorado.

Yes, was Gil's immediate reply.
Sara's phone buzzed. It was a text from Sheriff Flynn.

Reid isn't in St Pete. Where is he?

There was a text from Kate. **I can't find Jack.**
Sara look at Alish. "Reid isn't where you sent him." She saw the look of fear that came into the woman's eyes.

"He wants this house." Alish's voice was hardly above a whisper.

"It's his!" Sara said loudly. "If he'd let Derek Oliver live, Reid would know that."

"He would have claimed the house if he could have," Alish said. "It represents everything to him, what he should have been given but wasn't. It's the life he should have been born into."

"Like his grandfather." Sara stood up. "Jack. There's something about Jack. Where is Reid?"

"Maybe in the mausoleum. He always liked that place."

Sara left the cottage and ran across the property to the other end, where the stone mausoleum of James and Mary Lachlan lay, their son entombed beside them. Sara hadn't seen the place since she and Cal had been there. It had given her cold chills. He'd teased her, saying she usually liked graveyards.

Sara said, "I like history. You find out a lot from reading headstones." She'd frowned at the big mausoleum. "But this place is different."

"Haunted by the dead?" he'd asked, still teasing.

"Far from it. It's still alive."

Cal had halted, the big shears in his hands as he cut away Florida's rampant growth. "Okay, that's it. Tell me your story of dead people who are still alive."

She'd sat down as far as she could get from the stone structure and made up a story for him, as she often did. She didn't tell him that her story had nothing to do with the Lachlan tomb. That was real, not made up.

Now she saw that door was open a couple of inches. She hesitated before pushing it fully open. She should wait for others to come. She should...

When she saw a flicker of light, a candle, then heard a sound that seemed to come from Kate, she pushed the door open.

Against the back wall, Kate was tied to a chair, her mouth bound with a gag. It was the sweaty bandanna Reid had used earlier. Her eyes were wild with fear, and she moved her head to the right, directing Sara to look.

Stretched out on the tall stone coffin of James Lachlan was Jack, his arms crossed over his chest. The pose of death.

Sara took a step toward him and put her hand on his heart. He was alive. She gave a nod to Kate.

Through all of this, Sara had not looked behind her, but she knew what was there. Reid was in the darkest corner, a gun pointed at her.

Sara willed her heart to slow down so she could think. She knew about narcissistic personalities, people who believed they were entitled to have whatever they wanted. She also knew how they liked to talk about themselves. It may all be flamboyant, self-loving lies, but they loved the sound of their own voices.

"This should all be yours," she said quietly. "Why isn't it?" She was trying to sound caring, even concerned.

"You," he said.

Sara suppressed the urge to defend herself. "My writing? The searching for the story of your family?"

"That man! He was a boy. That's all he was. Then *him*!" Reid nodded toward Jack.

Sara didn't understand, but she needed to stall. "Did you know that the handsome man in the movie, *Only Once*, was your grandfather?"

That startled him so much that for a moment his hand wavered and the gun went down a bit. "My grandfather was hanged for murder. I was told that by my rich, greedy grandmother. She gave me little."

Sara bit her tongue to keep from replying. All narcissists thought that there was never enough given to them. "She should have told you the truth."

"About a movie star relative? Yeah, she should have, but that wouldn't have helped. He kept it all secret."

Sara wasn't sure who "he" was. James Lachlan, maybe? "But Derek Oliver found out the truth?"

Reid gave her an appraising look. "Are you trying to put me into one of your stories?"

"I want to know what Jack has to do with anything," she said truthfully. To her left she saw a flicker of movement. Kate was trying to work free of her bonds. Sara stepped forward so Reid's eyes looked at her, away from Kate. "What does Jack have to do with any of this?"

Reid gave a snort of derision. "You think you're so clever but you didn't figure it out?"

"No," Sara said honestly. "I didn't."

"The Palm Room filled with Brazilian art? Oliver knew! He searched and snooped and dug into everything. Lachlan had it all in that room."

"Brazil," Sara whispered. "Renata. Cal's mother. She cooked for him."

"You stupid woman! They were lovers. Callum Wyatt was James Lachlan's son."

For a moment, Sara was so shocked, she forgot the circumstances they were in. With her many years of plotting novels, she could follow that bit of information from the past to the present. "If Cal was the son, then..." Turning, she looked at Jack. "By James Lachlan's will, that would make Jack the owner of this property."

She looked back at Reid. They needed to get back to Derek Oliver. "He said that *you* owned the place, then he took it away from you."

When Reid gave a curt nod, Sara looked at him with genuine sympathy. She knew about wanting something with all your heart, then losing it. "That night when he told you, you lost sight of the world," she said softly. "Your soul left your body. There were no thoughts, no conscience. You floated above yourself and watched what someone else did." She took a tiny step forward.

"Yes," he said.

"You hit him but it wasn't enough. He'd taken everything from you. Your toolbox was there and he was lying on that silly rug with the turtles on it. It's where your sister played." Sara took another step. "She got so much, didn't she? Your grandmother loved her very much. You took from the man who'd stolen from you, but you knew you'd be the one blamed. Misjudged as your grandfather was."

"And Kate." His upper lip went into a sneer as he looked at her tied to the chair.

Sara blocked his view with what seemed to be a natural movement. Not fast, not abrupt. "Kate's hedgehog. It filled the gap. Pesky little animal. Too much attention was given to a mere child. What had she done to earn it?"

Reid gave a curt nod.

"I bet you were tired by then. It wasn't as though *you* had done something bad. So you rolled up the rug and took the… the debris away. To your grandmother. She'd fix it. She's always taken care of things, hasn't she? Greer's accidents. What happened to her at school. Grans fixed it all."

"For her," Reid said. "Never for me."

Sara stepped an inch closer. "And she did. You gave her the rug and Derek Oliver disappeared. It never happened, did it? And Greer was sent away. You had your grandmother to yourself."

Reid was looking at the floor, then suddenly, he stood upright. "But I got nothing. This house belongs to *him*." He pointed the gun at Jack, who was unmoving on the stone coffin.

Sara, now only a foot from Reid, put her head down and rammed him in the stomach. Years of boxing and weight training had made her strong.

Knocked off-balance, Reid fell back against the wall, the gun went off, with the bullet hitting the ceiling. He brought the grip of the gun down onto Sara's head and she collapsed to the floor.

In the next second, Gil threw the door of the mausoleum open. Lenny and Sheriff Flynn were behind him.

Sara said, "Jack," then passed out.

EPILOGUE

EVERYTHING CHANGED.

Both Jack and Sara spent some time at the excellent Broward Health while they recovered. They were quiet patients as they thought about their futures and what they wanted to happen.

Jack had trouble getting over his anger. He had accepted what appeared to be a sealed bottle of water from Reid. It was laced with something that made Jack pass out. When he woke up, Sara was strapped to a gurney and Kate... He didn't like hearing what had been done to her.

Reid had been taken away in handcuffs. He was saying he was innocent.

By the time Jack and Sara were released from the hospital, they knew what they were going to do.

Jack didn't feel right inheriting Lachlan House by himself so he paid his half sister, Ivy, and his half brother, Troy, each a third share of the appraised value of the house.

Jack and Kate asked Sara to move in with them. It seemed

right as they'd always lived together. She thanked them, but said no. She added that she'd love to rent the cottage from them. She said she had an idea for a time travel fantasy featuring a young librarian, and Sara wanted to write it.

Lea had no desire to go back to a state with brutal winters. She and Randal moved into the guesthouse.

They received word from Arthur and Everett that they liked the dry heat of Arizona and wanted to stay there. Kate happily sold the big Southwest Ranches house, and Lenny and Dora—who had become a couple—moved into the apartment over the garage at Lachlan House.

Gil, Greer, and Quinn spent a glorious summer in Scotland meeting all of Greer's relatives. Quinn wore a kilt the whole time they were there. When they returned to the US, Gil bought one of the places near Lachlan House. He and Greer had their wedding reception in the ballroom. By then, she was six months pregnant and they wanted to be near what had become their family.

Troy and Sheriff Flynn hit it off well. When Troy told his mother he wasn't returning to California, she protested. But Troy stayed firm. So Kate did the deal of selling Sara's house, fully furnished, to Barbara Adair. She kept Kate's apartment for when she visited her son—which was often.

Alish didn't live very long after Reid was arrested. To her last day, she said that nothing was his fault, that he'd inherited the evil that was inside him. She said that one man had been executed because of her and she couldn't bear for it to be repeated. She'd even given up her beloved granddaughter to protect him.

Before Alish died, she made arrangements with Sara.

Aran was removed from a grave that bore the name of the first Reid, and was laid to rest beside his parents in the mausoleum.

Alish was put in the Lachlan cemetery. Barbara used her connections to find the coffin of the actor named Taylor Caswell and move it to lie beside his wife.

Barbara refused Sara's suggestion of telling the story of who murdered the young actor. "Killed because of a script?" Barbara said. "I don't think so!" Troy told Sara she should write the screenplay and give Barbara a fabulous part. "It might work." Sara and Troy laughed together.

It was after Alish's death, when her barren house was being cleared, that the turtle rug was found deep inside a chest freezer in the garage. The contents, with its abundant DNA, would ensure that Reid wouldn't be freed for lack of evidence. No one said out loud that by keeping the contents of the rug, Alish had again condemned someone.

As for poor Rachel, the only thing Reid said was, "She laughed at me." It was all the confession they got out of him.

It was Kate who went alone to the hospice to visit Cal's wife, Donna.

The woman looked very bad, but her eyes glittered in what appeared to be amusement. "So she figured it out." Donna's tone was triumphant, as though she'd won a war she'd been fighting all her life.

Kate didn't sit down, just looked at the frail old woman in the bed. She had many wires and tubes attached to her.

A thousand thoughts came to Kate but she knew most of the answers. She just wanted to make sure. "The car?" she asked.

"One little kick." Donna gave a bit of a smile and her pulse rate went up.

"Walter?"

"He loved to hate anybody." Donna's smile grew wider.

Kate's mind twirled about with her thoughts of all the pain this woman had caused people. She started to leave, but turned back. "Was it worth it?" She glanced around the empty room. No flowers, no cards, no photos.

When Donna stopped smiling, Kate grinned broadly. "Sara, Jack, and Roy's other son, and I are a family. A very, very *happy* family."

Kate left the hospital with her shoulders back and her head high. She needed to stop at the florist. She had a wedding to plan. Her own wedding.

But that was another story.

★ ★ ★ ★ ★